# 1635
# THE WEAVER'S CODE

## THE RING OF FIRE SERIES

*1632* by Eric Flint
*1633* by Eric Flint & David Weber
*1634: The Baltic War* by Eric Flint & David Weber
*1634: The Galileo Affair* by Eric Flint & Andrew Dennis
*1634: The Bavarian Crisis* by Eric Flint & Virginia DeMarce
*1634: The Ram Rebellion* by Eric Flint & Virginia DeMarce et al.
*1635: The Cannon Law* by Eric Flint & Andrew Dennis
*1635: The Dreeson Incident* by Eric Flint & Virginia DeMarce
*1635: The Eastern Front* by Eric Flint
*1635: The Papal Stakes* by Eric Flint & Charles E. Gannon
*1636: The Saxon Uprising* by Eric Flint
*1636: The Kremlin Games* by Eric Flint, Gorg Huff & Paula Goodlett
*1636: The Devil's Opera* by Eric Flint & David Carrico
*1636: Commander Cantrell in the West Indies* by
Eric Flint & Charles E. Gannon
*1636: The Viennese Waltz* by Eric Flint, Gorg Huff & Paula Goodlett
*1636: The Cardinal Virtues* by Eric Flint & Walter Hunt
*1635: A Parcel of Rogues* by Eric Flint & Andrew Dennis
*1636: The Ottoman Onslaught* by Eric Flint
*1636: Mission to the Mughals* by Eric Flint & Griffin Barber
*1636: The Vatican Sanction* by Eric Flint & Charles E. Gannon
*1637: The Volga Rules* by Eric Flint, Gorg Huff & Paula Goodlett
*1637: The Polish Maelstrom* by Eric Flint
*1636: The China Venture* by Eric Flint & Iver P. Cooper
*1636: The Atlantic Encounter* by Eric Flint & Walter H. Hunt
*1637: No Peace Beyond the Line* by Eric Flint & Charles E. Gannon
*1637: The Peacock Throne* by Eric Flint & Griffin Barber
*1637: The Coast of Chaos* edited by Eric Flint & Bjorn Hasseler
*1637: The Transylvanian Decision* by Eric Flint & Robert E. Waters
*1638: The Sovereign States* by Eric Flint, Gorg Huff & Paula Goodlett
*1635: The Weaver's Code* by Eric Flint & Jody Lynn Nye

*1635: The Tangled Web* by Virginia DeMarce
*1635: The Wars for the Rhine* by Anette Pedersen
*1636: Seas of Fortune* by Iver P. Cooper
*1636: The Chronicles of Dr. Gribbleflotz* by
Kerryn Offord & Rick Boatright
*1636: Flight of the Nightingale* by David Carrico
*1636: Calabar's War* by Charles E. Gannon & Robert E. Waters
*1637: Dr. Gribbleflotz and the Soul of Stoner* by
Kerryn Offord & Rick Boatright

*Time Spike* by Eric Flint & Marilyn Kosmatka
*The Alexander Inheritance* by Eric Flint, Gorg Huff & Paula Goodlett
*The Macedonian Hazard* by Eric Flint, Gorg Huff & Paula Goodlett
*The Crossing* by Kevin Ikenberry

**To purchase any of these titles in e-book form, please go to www.baen.com.**

# 1635
# THE WEAVER'S CODE

ERIC FLINT
JODY LYNN NYE

1635: The Weaver's Code



A Baen Books Original

Baen Publishing Enterprises
P.O. Box 1403
Riverdale, NY 10471
www.baen.com

ISBN: 978-1-9821-9366-9

Cover art by Tom Kidd

First printing, October 2024

Distributed by Simon & Schuster
1230 Avenue of the Americas
New York, NY 10020

Library of Congress Cataloging-in-Publication Data

Names: Flint, Eric, author. | Nye, Jody Lynn, 1957- author.
Title: 1635: the weaver's code / Eric Flint, Jody Lynn Nye.
Description: Riverdale, NY : Baen Publishing Enterprises, 2024. | Series: Ring of Fire ; 37
Identifiers: LCCN 2024026486 (print) | LCCN 2024026487 (ebook) | ISBN 9781982193669 (hardcover) | ISBN 9781625799845 (ebook)
Subjects: LCSH: Time travel--Fiction. | LCGFT: Fantasy fiction | Novels.
Classification: LCC PS3556.L548 A6186668 2024 (print) | LCC PS3556.L548 (ebook) | DDC 813/.54--dc23/eng/20240624
LC record available at https://lccn.loc.gov/2024026486
LC ebook record available at https://lccn.loc.gov/2024026487

Printed in the United States of America
10 9 8 7 6 5 4 3 2 1

*To Lucille Robbins (Flint)*

Many thanks to Bjorn Hasseler for
helping me keep the canon straight.

# Chapter 1

Margaret de Beauchamp, eldest surviving child of Baronet Sir Timothy de Beauchamp, baronet of Churnet and Trent, waited patiently on a bench in the outer court of the Palace of Whitehall, nervous to see the king or the Earl of Cork. Such exalted personages were so far above her station that she trembled inwardly, but recalled the import of why she had come all the way to London from Staffordshire. She kept her back straight, not that her stiff, tight-waisted bodice would allow her to slouch, and arranged her voluminous woolen skirts so they didn't weigh too heavily on her knees. Courtiers and court ladies in their gorgeous silken clothes and shining, coiled hair passed in and out of the enormous double doors, careful not to cause the portals to make a sound as pleas were being heard within.

She studied each of them as they passed. Not a single familiar face, alas. She hoped to find at least one friend in London who would give her more of a grounding in the ins and outs of pleasing His Majesty with her family's desperate plight. If not, she would have to rely upon what she had been told by the de Beauchamps' neighbor, dowager Lady Pierce, who had been a lady-in-waiting to His Majesty's late mother, and on the gossip shared by the other passengers in the coach and the various inns she had passed on the way down from Staffordshire. *Be honest, be flattering, and be brief,* one man had warned her. Truth to tell, she must indeed be brief, or her breath would fail her and she would swoon before His Majesty. Not a posture that would impress him. She had to find calm within her. Margaret began again to murmur the Lord's Prayer under her breath, hoping the divine would give her courage.

Her mother would have done better before exalted personages than Margaret could. Delfine, Lady de Beauchamp had been at court until de Beauchamp made his suit, and retired to the cold north to wear wool instead of silk. Poor Mother. How dismayed she was to see how their household had deteriorated in the last two years, but like the lady she was, she kept her counsel to herself. Her six children—five, after the untimely death of Margaret's elder brother—could read her concerns.

Margaret determined not to let her worries overwhelm her, otherwise she would not be able to make a coherent plea once she reached the foot of the throne. She had rehearsed her words many times, even penciling a few notes on a scrap of paper which she kept hidden in the pocket tied on her hip along with the few coins to pay bribes. Two of those coins had already been dispensed: a copper to the guard who had directed her through the busy corridors to this anteroom, and a small but bright silver three-penny bit to the secretary, a good bribe indeed, to make certain that she would not be forgotten when supplicants were admitted to the court chamber. His Majesty had not yet appeared, so the rumors had it, but the Earl of Cork was hearing smaller suits and cases. He must listen to her. He must!

No question but it was going to be a long wait. She had been lucky to secure a spot on one of the plain wooden benches against the deep brown linenfold wall. Others milled around.

Lovely clothing the men and ladies of the court wore. The men's clothes were as bright and showy as peacocks, in blossoming tunics with slashed sleeves, knee-length trousers and hose made of Ottoman silk and Venetian velvets. The ladies looked no less brilliant, with touches of embroidery and lace enlivening their oversized, starched white collars, perhaps in defiance of the enemy French making an edict against lace trim on one's clothing only this year. Hair was scraped severely back from the face except for a few curls allowed to dance impishly upon the forehead, and fastened at the back with many pins. The side locks were curled in sausages close to the cheeks, not unlike the cylindrical hair-stalls of three centuries past. She envied those whose station and wealth allowed them to wear silk and eastern fabrics, then chided herself.

Why should she be ashamed of who she was? *Her* station was nothing of which she ought to be ashamed. The eldest daughter of a landed baronet—and a fine estate it was, too!—had as much place here as any of those with loftier titles. She had been taught to walk in the fashionable French mode by Lady Pierce with her back straight and her hips thrust forward. Still, to be able to gleam like reflected fire, as the enveloping russet gown on the chestnut-haired lady just going by, would have suited her so well and lit up her plain brown hair and ruddy cheeks, making her seem more than a country girl.

She had to settle for the best and finest worsted cloth that the Staffordshire guilds could devise, dyed a deep, rare blue, every panel subtly different. Would any of the passersby know the difference? Even her maid, Hettie, who waited on a bench outwith the anteroom, wore goods of outstanding quality. And even the brightest of silk no doubt concealed wool petticoats to keep out the chill of the palace. Finery was only the surface. It was the spirit underneath that gave one character.

*Vanity*! she thought, with a shake of her head. Her confessor, the reverend Mr. Olney, would chide her when she next attended services at the family chapel.

She smiled wryly at herself. No need to go to the confessor when she could hear his lectures in her own mind.

The tall young woman sitting next to her on the backless bench touched the fabric of her skirt.

"Tha's a beauty," she said, in a burring accent Margaret couldn't place. "What's it made out o'?"

"Wool," Margaret said, with a kindly smile. She hadn't paid much attention to the others waiting for their turn beyond the doors including her neighbors. This lady, for lady she must be, wore black velvet shot with silver thread, and her thick, ruddy hair was wound into fashionable sausage curls.

"So fine," the woman said wonderingly. "It doesn'a feel itchy at all. Wool's usually itchy, nae matter how long it's fulled or treaded. I ought to know. It's plentiful enow in our demesne, but warm as it is, it's a trial to wear without ye use thick linens beneath."

"Ours is not. My father's flocks are famous for their long-staple wool. The longer the staple, the fewer the cut ends in the cloth, and the less irritating it is to the skin." Margaret sighed. That was exactly why she was there.

"What ails ye?" the woman said, with almost a motherly look. Margaret realized that they were close to an age, around nineteen years. At their age, though, the other could indeed have had a child already.

"Flocks," Margaret said, with a rueful expression, "are expensive to maintain. One would think that all one needs is clean, open grassland and shepherds to keep away the wolves, but there's so much more."

"Tell me all abou't," her companion said, raising her hands and letting them drop to her lap. "I've naught in the world but time." "World" seemed to have ten or twelve R's the way the redheaded woman pronounced it.

"I hope...I hope to see the Earl of Cork," Margaret said.

"And I, as well," the young woman said, forthrightly. "But forbye what else would we be doing here? We've all been waiting these many days for the wee man to grant us an audience. It seems the king himself, in all his grievin', is no' hearing petitions, leaving it all in the Earl of Cork's lap. How d'ye call yersel'? I am Ann de Sutherland. My father is Earl Sutherland."

Margaret rose and curtseyed. "It's my honor to meet you, Lady Ann."

Ann grinned, showing a bit of mischief behind her smooth cameo of a face. "Sit down, won't ye? Ye'll lose your place on the bench. There's no' enow spots to perch."

Margaret followed her gaze. Indeed, a couple of the languid personages standing nearby had begun to sidle toward them. She plopped herself down on the hard wood. The others stopped and pivoted on well-shod heels, pretending to be interested in something across the room from her. She smiled, too.

"Thank you for the warning. I'd not noticed the crowd has grown."

"Ye mentioned the wolves, but there's more kinds than the one that chase your sheep. Then what's yer name, fine lass? We shall be friends."

"Margaret de Beauchamp," she said, extending a hand tentatively. Ann took it in both of her own and pressed it warmly. "My father Sir Timothy runs our flocks on our estate in Staffordshire. But you've come much farther!"

"Well, my honorable Margaret, that may be true, yet it's to the same dead end that we've come," Ann said, with a graceful upturned palm. "Me mam sent me to become one of the queen's ladies-in-waitin'. I've letters of introduction from past dames of my acquaintance who have served Her Majesty, but a'er th' tragedy o' Her Majesty's passing, I must sit here until the Earl of Cork gives me leave to depart, or brings me into service in court. I've proof enow I'm the best there is at waiting!" The girls laughed. "But what ails your sheep that you must ask the king for a favor?"

Margaret lowered her voice so their neighbor on Ann's other side couldn't hear.

"Tax," she said. "Wool attracts so much duty on every step of the way from the sheep's back to the finished cloth, it's scarcely worth the trouble to shear the poor mites. When we only take a pound and a half of good fleece from a single beast, only a few shillings are left from a finished bolt of cloth after we pay the spinners, dyers, fullers, sayers, and weavers. Every piece of good woolen is inspected to see if it fits the standard, and that's another cost. We can't raise prices far enough, or those bringing in cheaper cloth from the Low Countries and farther away will steal all our business. We make every economy possible, but Father will fall short this year in what he owes to the Crown. I am here to ask for mercy. Even a small respite would hearten Father. We'll do what we can to pay the full share the next year."

"No' the next quarter?"

Margaret shook her head. "Impossible. We had a hard winter, lost a mort of lambs in the heavy snow. So, you see, it's a large favor I must ask. Hundreds, I'm afraid."

"I'll pray to the Good Lord for him to open his heart to you," Lady Ann said, kindly. "I've heard he is a sensible man." She studied Margaret's face, and shook her head. "Let's no' dwell upon it, or we'll both be weeping. Have ye any good gossip from home?"

"Nothing much happens in Barlaston," Margaret said, with a rueful smile. "How is it in Sutherland?"

Ann chuckled. "Much the same, I fear. But so much is afoot here in London! Hae ye heard of the Americans?"

"Only a bit, and half of that is rumor," Margaret admitted. "They appeared like magic in the midst of the Germanies, and stopped an army with but a few men. My brother is a ship's captain." She paused, waiting for Ann's disapproval, and was grateful when it didn't come. Her mother found it to be a terrible disgrace that the gentry would even think of resorting to a *trade.* How she felt about Margaret stepping in to the estate's wool trade had been the subject of many a heated argument, even though others of their class had been ennobled for becoming successful merchants. "His ship stopped to deliver cargo in the Netherlands when Grantville . . . arrived? He has not seen the Displaced Lands himself, but he heard many wild tales. Beyond that, I have heard little than they speak a crude form of English. But how can that be?"

Ann looked pleased. "Well, I would say ye can ask them yersel', for there are some who are here as *guests* of His Majesty." The word "guests" bore a cynical emphasis. "They came on a diplomatic visit from the President of this Grantville, and since then have inhabited rooms in the Tower, never meeting the king at all. I had just come to London then, and saw a peep o' them before they were swept up and shown His Majesty's hospitality. They looked ordinary enough, though I have heard they wield wonders, the likes of which no one has ever seen, and tidings of things yet to come for centuries. They say they come from the future. Hundreds of years on!"

"Never!" Margaret said, fascinated. She crossed herself with an absent gesture. "If it's so, such a miracle must have been vouchsafed by God for a good reason."

"I'm sure it has that," Ann agreed, "though poor mortals such as we can only guess at it." She shook her head, and her curls danced.

Margaret's curiosity began to get the better of her. Such amazing creatures were only steps away. "But the Tower is under heavy guard!"

Ann smiled. "A few shillings make a good key to that lock. A few of the gentlemen here have gone to have a gawk. I must admit I'm dyin' to do it mysel', but I dare not. A queen's lady must not show unseemly curiosity. But we dinna hae to turn away and stop up our ears if someone we know and trust *happens to tell us all about it.*" Her carroty eyebrows rose with clear meaning.

Margaret sat back on the bench. What a marvel! If indeed people had come from the future, the world was even more wondrous than she could conceive. Her mind spun with all the things she could ask them. What would the world become? Whom would she marry? (The very question made her blush.) What were they doing here in their past, and what did they think about it? Surely centuries in the future people would be living among the clouds like angels, not on the muddy Earth, and wearing clothes made of sunbeams that never got cold, no matter what the weather.

Or, would they? Mayhap they would still make use of the natural resources that the folks now employed. Like wool, perhaps?

"Tell me, how were their clothes?" she asked.

"Oh, nothin' out o' the ordinary," Ann said. Her eyes twinkled. "Yer bound to do it, aren't ye?"

Margaret blushed again. "I shouldn't."

"Why not? Who 'ailse will tell me what they're like?"

The big doors opened. Everyone in the anteroom fell silent. A couple of men-at-law in their long black gowns gathered up their satchels with an expectant air. A narrow-faced man with fair skin in modest though good black wool breeches and tunic emerged.

"My lords and ladies, his lordship will hear no more cases today," the man said. His eyes told Margaret he hated to be the bearer of disappointment, but his set jaw showed he had no choice. "Pray return at eleven of the clock tomorrow."

"I require to speak to the Earl of Cork about my son's inheritance!" This came from a plump, older woman whose fashionable salt-and-pepper ringlets had clearly been augmented with bought-in tresses. "My thieving in-laws will have stripped the house bare by the time I return! He is only fourteen. He cannot stop them without the force of law!"

The man bowed to her. "I am sorry, Lady Brakespur. His lordship has many commissions from the king and must see to those first. Tomorrow, if you please." He gestured with the back of his hand toward the door.

With a collective sigh, the assembled rose and made for the exit.

"Now's your chance," Ann whispered, gathering her full silk skirts in both hands. "I must return to my auntie in our rooms. I'll hold a place for ye on the morrow. Go now!"

Margaret needed no further spur. "Tomorrow," she promised.

# Chapter 2

Her maidservant cast worried eyes on the deep stone archway under which they passed from the boat that had brought them along the Thames to the Tower. It had to be nine or ten ells thick. Margaret thought the Tower's walls must be able to withstand musket and cannon fire for weeks' worth of bombardment, and the mighty keep that rose foursquare above them was also powerfully constructed. Those within were safe as a chick in the egg, though so many of them had no choice in the matter.

"Madam, is this right?" Hettie whispered, as they followed the stout man in the scarlet livery and flat black hat, the Yeoman Warder who had taken Margaret's small offering with a sideways glance to make sure no one had observed them. "Should we be in tha' castle? Will they let us out again? Should we ha' brought Percy with us?"

Margaret eyed their guide. It was not lost on her that under the ornate red-and-black tunic, the Warder was fully armored and carried a fearsome halberd with the air of one who knew how to use it. Her only defense beside her wits was a short but sharp knife concealed in a scabbard in her garter. She'd scarcely be able to fight her way out with that. Neither would the man who had acted as their escort from Barlaston. Percy was the son of the head grounds keeper, he was supposed to be an apprentice weaver, but since his master had been crippled a few years ago he spent more time assisting his father. He was big and strong, to be sure, but no fighter. They'd left him at a pub just outwith the walls with a coin or two.

"We will be able to go away again," she said. "We've done no wrong. And our guide here would not keep you, at all, since it is by my order that you accompany me."

Hettie clutched Margaret's cloak. "I would not leave you, madam! I would stay, no matter what foul dungeon they plunged us into!"

Margaret patted the young woman's arm.

"All will be well."

She didn't feel as calm as she looked. Such a practice of going to see those who lived in the Tower, for one reason or another, was common enough, or so she was told, but the place, once a royal palace, was still a fortress. Executions had been done here, including taking the sacred lives of two queens. Her knees quivered. If she was trapped here, how would she fare?

Her misgivings gave way to calm as they passed through the Thomas Gate and into the greensward at the heart of the keep. Other curiosity-seekers, almost all of them men in fashionable dress with tall walking sticks, strolled about, looking up at the forbidding stone walls at the small glass windows of the residences.

"It don't look like a prison," Hettie said in a low voice. "Not as such."

"Your destination is here, my lady," the Yeoman Warder said, stopping beside a low doorway with a pointed stone arch. He had a kind face, and the humor in his eyes told Margaret he had heard everything that she and Hettie had said. His voice was thick with a Lancastrian accent, not many miles from where the two of them had come. "I shall inquire if the guests within wish to receive you." His free hand, the one not holding the halberd, turned up slightly to reveal the palm. Margaret took his meaning at once and reached for her purse. The Warder glanced away as she put a coin into his hand. He ducked under the archway and mounted the narrow stone stairs beyond.

Margaret waited with stretched nerves until he returned.

"They cry your pardon for a few minutes' grace, until they can make themselves presentable to such distinguished visitors," the Warder said. He spread his feet to shoulder's width and put the butt of the halberd on the ground, and stared across the green like a statue, until they heard a short but incomprehensible call from above. Margaret and Hettie looked up.

"All right, then," the Warder said. He tilted his head toward the stone stairs. Margaret grasped Hettie's hand and pulled her forward.

They mounted to the first floor, where the Warder stood to one side next to a heavy wooden door bounded by iron straps.

"I'll be searching your reticules and pockets on the way out again," he said, solemn-faced. "In case you want to smuggle one of them out."

Hettie looked horrified, but Margaret stifled a giggle. The man was kind and had a sense of humor. She liked him despite his fearsome appearance.

"Well, come in already!" A tall, narrow-faced woman opened the door. She had a strangely nasal voice, albeit not unpleasant.

"Lady Mailey, this is the Honorable Miss Margaret de Beauchamp," the Warder announced in formal tones.

Lady Mailey took Margaret by the hand and pumped it warmly. "Very nice to meet you. Thank you, Andrew."

The uniformed man touched the brim of his black hat. "My lady." He stumped down the narrow spiral staircase, leaving Margaret standing shyly on the threshold.

Lady Mailey gave her a sharp look.

"Well, don't stand there letting the flies in. Come in! You, too," she said, when Hettie held back. "Where are you from?"

"We come from Barlaston, near Stoke-on-Trent," Margaret said, following her hostess into a small sitting room, rendered even smaller by the large number of cases and boxes that crowded the furniture. A woman dressed in blue, who appeared just a few years older than Margaret, rose and smiled when she entered. She was of a surprising height, and her teeth were marvelously white and straight, like an angel's. Through a door to the right, a big man crouched over a table, his hands busy. She couldn't really see what he was doing, but as soon as he noticed her scrutiny, he rose and closed the door between them. Before it shut, Margaret thought she saw two or three other people in the room. "My father's estate lies to the south of town."

The young woman smiled and extended her hand to both Margaret and Hettie. She had a firm, friendly grip.

"It must have taken you days to get here!" she said.

"Only four," Margaret said, proudly. "We came by fast coach most of the way, to the eternal detriment of my spine, until we could come to a barge that brought us the rest of the way east along the Thames. The tolls cost more than the road journey, alas. Four pounds! But our coaches made good time. The roads were not too wet. I thought that we might come afoul a few times when we struck some deep ruts, but good folk nearby helped us out."

"I noticed that the English roads are pretty poor anywhere but the city here," the young woman said. "We've been used to better in Grantville. Oh, I'm Rita Stearns Simpson. My brother Mike is president of the United States of Europe. I'm the ambassador from the USE to England."

"Your Excellency!" Margaret hastily dropped into a curtsey, spreading her skirts out with both hands. Hettie followed suit, crouching deeper than her mistress.

"Oh, stop it!" Rita said with a laugh, taking Margaret by the arm again and escorting her to one of the settees. She gestured Hettie to a stool beside the small table. The servant perched herself on the seat with her back as straight as a rail. "I'm not noble at all. I'm just a girl from a small town in West Virginia. It's Melissa who's the important one here."

"*You* stop it," Lady Mailey said, with a look that shut both Rita's and Margaret's lips at once. "Don't scare the poor girl into running away. We get few enough visitors as it is. What brings you here, Margaret?"

The visitors' expressions were so friendly that Margaret felt she could be frank.

"Curiosity, madam," she admitted. "I had heard you were from... from the future. I wanted... I expected... ?"

"That we'd have two heads apiece and speak in tongues?" Lady Mailey retorted, but her eyes were full of humor.

"Perhaps that you would look different than we do," Margaret said.

"And do we?"

Margaret studied the two women. "You look... healthier than most. I believe that you might be of an age with my mother, Lady Mailey, but time's been kinder to you."

"Superior nutrition," Lady Mailey said at once, ignoring Rita's broad grin. "Hygiene, childhood vaccinations, and nutrition. We've been trying to educate people to improve conditions in Thuringia, where our town landed, during what more sensationalistic people have named the Ring of Fire. It's appalling the way people in this era feed and care for themselves. Even the wealthy waste their resources, as scanty as they are. I believe that we are already making a difference in the lives of ordinary people."

"In education, too," Rita added. "Melissa has been spearheading that. People are hungry to learn."

Margaret found herself delighted by the energy and intelligence of her new acquaintances. Such a difference from the plodding folk who minded the estate's sheep and produced the wares from their backs. While she and all her siblings had been tutored by Dr. Angelus, an Oxford University graduate, only her younger brother Nat had gone on to university, at New College. In time, he was meant to succeed their old dean in the church. For the rest of them, a higher education was deemed unnecessary. Angelus introduced them to Greek and Latin, poetry and art, but complicated essays and analyses were less important than reading, writing and figuring. Margaret prided herself on being able to sweep her eyes down a list of numbers and adding them rapidly in her head, but always wanted to know more.

"What subjects do you teach them? I have a hunger to learn."

"Oh, now you have opened the floodgates!" Rita said, with a grin.

Lady Mailey smiled. "I'd have to do an assessment of what you already know, child. I want to fill in the blanks. Generally speaking, we start with basic literacy and health matters, and expand outward, depending on aptitude and attitude. Literature, art, philosophy, history—although the history as we knew it is being altered every day—practical skills, medicine, chemistry, physics, and biology, to name a few." She tilted her head and eyed Margaret. "You liked school, didn't you?"

"I had a tutor, but I wished that I could have attended university," Margaret said. Before she knew it, she had burst out with her history and that of her siblings. How, now that her first brother had passed away and the brother a year younger than she had become a merchant, she had been groomed to take over the wool production from her father, carrying on a tradition that had been in her family for centuries. Margaret's father's lands were part of a parcel detached from the Duchy of Lancaster by its duke in the fifteenth century, as a gift for having been of "significant service to his lordship in matters of advice and finance," thus raising a family of merchants to producers, when the situation was usually reversed. It was a great responsibility for which she wasn't at all sure she was equal, yet she vowed to undertake it with good will.

Her two hostesses listened attentively. She realized after she paused to take a deep breath that she had been filling their ears for a solid quarter of an hour without stopping. "I apologize, truly. I've been talking about myself when I want to know all about you! Is it true that a thousand of you have arrived from the future by magic, bringing astonishing philosophical devices with you?"

Rita laughed. "That's true," she said. "We don't have much in the way of those with us here, but over in Grantville you'd see things that you've never seen before. We're trying to better the lives of the people around us. It's something that we can offer other countries. I'm here to establish friendly relations with the king of England." Her expression turned rueful. "He doesn't seem in a big hurry to meet us."

"He is no doubt in mourning for Her Majesty," Margaret said, sadly. "I regret having to make the journey during this tragic time, but I had no choice."

"Well, it must be a good reason, if you had to make an eight-day round trip."

"Our fortunes are tied up in the wool trade," Margaret said. "Father keeps large flocks, and our estates spin and weave the fleeces into cloth for sale within England and overseas. His Majesty makes ever heavier demands upon every stage of the process. My father needs respite from all of the taxes due this year, or we may have to sell assets that have been in our families for centuries. Fields, manors, flocks, the wherewithal of the shearers, spinners, weavers, and dyers, all are required. If one must be sacrificed, the whole may collapse with its lack. I..." Margaret fell quiet. She didn't want to criticize the rapaciousness of the Crown, taking all it could from those who were not in a position to argue because their chief customer was also their liege lord. Every sack of wool had a levy placed on it, as had been custom for the last three hundred years. It supported Their Majesties and their various overseas wars, not to mention the heavy costs of maintaining castles and court. She raised her hands and noticed they were shaking. She put them down again in her lap. "...I hope his lordship will hear my appeal and be generous."

Lady Mailey patted her shoulder.

"I haven't had the pleasure of the man's acquaintance, but a few friends of ours have had some run-ins with him. Since what you do benefits the crown directly and doesn't challenge his authority, I hope he'll be better to you than he was to them."

"I'm impressed that she came all this way alone to talk to the king," Rita said. "Your dad trusts you to negotiate on his behalf? He didn't send one of your brothers instead?"

Margaret dropped her eyes. "My elder brother Julian was meant to be the heir to the business, but he died of the fever two years ago. His loss struck our family so hard. I stepped in to support my father in his place. I have done my best to learn all I can."

Rita put a gentle hand on Margaret's knee. "I'm so sorry. But I admire your dad for considering you to take over. You both sound pretty extraordinary. It can't be easy, being a woman in authority in this day and age. I'm a nurse, and just getting men to listen to me is tough. Even though they need what I have to tell them."

"That is so true," Margaret said with a laugh. "I have to use half the words and twice the tact of any man." Rita's eyes twinkled. "I'd back you in a deal in a minute. I bet you can bring success to your dad's business."

Margaret felt oddly cheered by her kind words. She liked these Americans a great deal, and regretted that their acquaintance would be so brief. In time, she felt she and Rita would become close friends. Lady Ann would like them, too.

"I should feel hope. My brother James's success as a merchant at trade has turned the tide for us in the last few years, but our debts are becoming more than can be encompassed. He has had his profits much curtailed by the barricades to the Germanies and Holland. He has had respectful dealings with the East India Trading Company, but the manufacturers in the European provinces are beginning to steal our customers altogether. I don't know what we will do if it continues. We could be left with bolt upon bolt of fine cloth, and nowhere to sell it."

"Yours won't be the first industry to be overwhelmed in that way," Lady Mailey said, thoughtfully. "I haven't had much time to read up on the wool trade in detail, though I believe there is at least one fine text on it in the Grantville library..."

"I would love to read that book," Margaret said, enchanted. To think that the future history of her family's trade existed!

And not so far away as three and a half centuries hence, but only at a physical distance, in the Germanies. Although, at that moment, that seemed as distant as the moon herself. If only the trade embargoes and wars would cease enough to let her through to it as a mere traveler! She sighed.

Lady Mailey smiled. "I hope that you will get the chance, my dear."

"Thank you, madam," Margaret said. "I . . . suppose that you shall be departing as soon as you may once you have your audience with His Majesty?"

"We're prisoners, actually," Rita said. At Margaret's horrified look, the girl waved a casual hand. "Detained at His Majesty's pleasure. It almost sounds nice when they say it like that. And you know, they have been mighty nice to us. The rooms are kind of small here in the Tower, but they're pretty comfortable. And warm. I live in the mountains—or I did—but our houses are a lot better insulated than yours. Castles are cold!"

"You will hear no argument from my quarter," Margaret said fervently. "Our manor house is as cold and creaky as a dotard, with leaks and squeaks, letting in every gust that passes."

The girl laughed with delight. "And they said Shakespeare's dead! You're a poet."

Margaret felt her cheeks burn.

"Nay. Just the mistress of shepherds, weavers and potters, hoping the king's ear and heart are open." She glanced down at the girl's dress. The weft was dark blue, the same as the sky's reflection in a peat pool, but with white or particolored threads twisted in the warp. "What an unusual weave."

"I don't know anything about weaving, really," Rita said. "It's kind of ordinary where I come from. It's called denim. A couple of the ladies back home sewed it together for me out of a lot of old blue jeans. Tough wearing, but fashionable."

"Those two terms are not often combined in my world," Margaret said. "Hard wearing is for work, and fashion is too delicate to last." She examined it closely, with an eye trained by guildsmen who had been at pains since her childhood to make certain that she understood the excellence of their work. With the young woman's permission, she rubbed the cloth between thumb and forefinger. It draped into handsome, heavy folds that would have been the delight of the great artists, yet it felt as strong as tweed, but soft, not catching on her skin at all. "Most interesting. The fineness of the fabric is like unto the silk makers here in London! This must be the work of master weavers who have spent their lives improving their craft!"

"Probably some kid in China running a power loom," the young woman said, with a wry expression.

Margaret didn't know what to make of such a comment. She had heard that the people of the United States had strange, casual ways about them, and had seen marvels that not even Good Queen Elizabeth's Magister John Dee could have imagined. Questions knocked at her lips, but she had already stretched the boundaries of good behavior.

"Forgive me, but we have taken too much of your time. We had better go." She rose.

Hettie, who had listened in silence with wide eyes all that time, cleared her throat meaningfully. Margaret shot her a look of reproach.

Her hosts noticed the maidservant's expression.

"What do you need, child?" Lady Mailey asked. At Hettie's hesitation, she turned the half-stern look upon her. "Speak up! We're not going to eat your entrails."

Instead of replying to her directly, Hettie turned to her employer. "They're well-spoken enough, madam, but they could be anybody!"

Margaret felt her cheeks burn even more fiercely. Over the course of their brief acquaintance, she had come to believe wholeheartedly in the Americans, but Hettie was right: they were wonderful spinners of tales, but hadn't produced anything that would prove their claims to have come from the future. Fortunately, Rita Simpson understood.

"We haven't *vouchsafed you a miracle*, is that it?" she asked. She rummaged around in a nearby chest and came up with a tiny, rectangular black box with what looked like a shining sequin on the end. "Here, take this. Don't use it too often, because the battery will wear out, and we don't have replacements. Yet. And don't show it to anyone you don't absolutely trust, because we're not the most popular people in these parts."

She held out the device and pressed on it with her thumb.

A beam of light shot out of the sequin, like a bolt of sunlight from heaven in the dim room, and drew a perfect circle of white on the far wall. Hettie let out a little scream and covered her eyes. Margaret just stared in growing delight.

"It's an LED flashlight," Rita said. "I think I got it as a gift from our insurance agent."

"It must be worth a fortune!" Margaret exclaimed.

"Nope, it was free. He wanted our business." She dangled it from a sinuous metal tether and dropped it into Margaret's palm.

"Thank you, my lady!" Margaret said, clutching the prize in both hands.

"Tuck it away," Lady Mailey said, as shuffling and clanking erupted from beyond the door. "I think I hear the warder coming up the stairs. He always makes plenty of noise so we can greet him without embarrassing ourselves." Margaret obeyed, putting the small square in her reticule. She couldn't wait to get back to the privacy of their rooms and experiment with the *flashlight.*

"Come along, Hettie," she said, and offered a curtsey to her hosts. "Lady Mailey, Lady Rita, it has been a true pleasure to make your acquaintance. Thank you for the gift. I promise I will keep it a secret."

"Come again soon," Rita said. "We're not going anywhere. For a while."

Margaret beamed as the warder appeared on the threshold. "It would be my honor."

"The pleasure is all ours," Lady Mailey said, with a smile.

"Harry, come in," Tom Simpson said, leaning over the microphone of the small radio set. "Dammit, Harry, where are you?" Gayle Mason tweaked the dials a little, and the static lessened.

Rita held the antenna dish in the open window, shading it from view from below with a fold of her cloak. When she noticed anyone looking up at her from the river walk, she smiled down at them. Most of the time, the passersby looked bemused and dropped their gaze. A few stared openly. Rita shook her head. *Just a lady getting a breath of air on a cold spring night*, she thought.

On the table, the speaker crackled.

"That's Agent X-13 to you," Harry Lefferts' voice brayed from the round black disk. "Besides, you were supposed to say 'Open Channel D.' Didn't you write that down?"

"I haven't got that much paper in here," Tom said. Melissa, sitting beside him on a wooden stool, rolled her eyes, and Rita grinned. "And I'm not going to waste it on keeping track of your spy-guy aliases. One of these days Cork is going to order a search in here, and I don't want anything written down that he can use against us. How are you doing at getting us out of here?"

"Operation Spring-Time?" Harry asked. "I'm working on it. We're making progress."

Tom glanced up to Rita. She scanned the river. In the growing gloom of the evening, she saw dark figures of people passing along the opposite bank of the Thames. On the water itself, sturdy boatmen ferried customers up and down in small boats each illuminated by the globe of light from a single lantern. It was so quiet that she could hear the conversation of the passengers. She shook her head. No one was close enough to overhear anything.

"Do we have a timetable? Things are getting worse here. Wentworth took being locked up like a man, but Cork can hardly leave him or Cromwell alive for long. He's read the history. I don't hold out a lot of hope for our safety, either."

"You can count on me," Harry said, with his usual brash confidence. "You know it. If I have to go charging in there by myself, guns blazing, I'll get you out. But that's pretty ordinary. I'm working on something spectacular, and spectacular takes time."

"Can we pull back to something merely stupendous that makes use of a shorter timetable?" Melissa asked. "I'd like to get home sooner rather than later."

An appreciable pause filled with static made Rita wonder if the radio had stopped working on Harry's end. "I'm working on it. I don't have the connections here that we've got in Germany. Juliet and George are trying to fill in two gaps. I can get you *out*, but *away* is taking more time. I need the right people and the right equipment."

"What kind of people?"

"People with tight lips. And boats. And at least two wagons. We'll get there. Sherrilyn just got back. I need to see if she found what we're looking for. Tomorrow, same time?"

"Tomorrow."

"Got it. X-13 out."

# Chapter 3

"It's all a marvel, to be sairtain," Lady Ann whispered, her blue eyes filled with delight. "To talk w' people who come from the future! Did they tell your fortune?"

She and Margaret huddled together in the anteroom on the extreme end of a wooden bench the day after the visit to the Tower. Margaret had been able to relate her experience of meeting the Americans without worry of being overheard, as long as she didn't mention the flashlight. This she had demonstrated to her friend very privately in the garderobe with Hettie guarding the door. The small device now reposed in her innermost pocket slid around on an internal tie like her money purse so it could not be reached between plackets.

"Nothing like that. They are very kind," Margaret repeated, pitching her whisper so it could be heard by others in the anteroom who were frankly eavesdropping. They could all have done the same, and visited the Americans, if they had chosen. "They invited me to call again."

"And shall ye do it?" Lady Ann asked. She squeezed Margaret's hands. "O' course ye will! And ye shall take me w' ye. I've a passion to go and see them for mesel'."

The gentleman in apple-green silk only a step away looked as though he was going to ask to be a third in the party, but looked hastily away when Margaret glanced over at him. Lady Ann chuckled.

"Mistress Margaret de Beauchamp?" A courtier with long,

curled hair and a very handsomely embroidered lace collar bedecking the shoulders of his blue silk suit emerged from the linenfold doors. Margaret rose from her place on the bench, her back straight as a poker. "This way, if you please, madame."

Having Hettie with her would have given her confidence, but the man gave her no time to call for her servant. Margaret squared her shoulders and minced forward, careful to keep her posture in the fashionable manner. She had rehearsed and rehearsed again that morning what to say and what not to say to the great man once she was in his presence. Lady Mailey had put it so succinctly: her family's industry was of great use to the crown. To squeeze it dry would profit neither them nor His Majesty. If only she did not faint dead away before she could utter a word!

To her great relief, the Earl of Cork was not unaware of the way he struck visitors. When the gentleman announced her, the small man in black rose from the ornately-carved chair at his desk and smiled at her gently.

"Mistress de Beauchamp," he said. "A great privilege to make your acquaintance."

"I am honored that you have seen fit to hear me, my lord," Margaret said, curtseying deeply.

"Aye, and I am proud to be of service to eenyone who serves His Majesty so well." He gestured to a small chair before his desk. "Pray be seated, Miss de Beauchamp. How may I assist ye this day?"

Margaret liked the burr in his voice. It reminded her of the people from Manchester and Liverpool she had met who came to Staffordshire to take the woolsacks and finished fabric to the ships.

"My lord, my father, Sir Timothy, is only the latest in our family to give such service to the crown. We have provided the finest of woolens to His Majesty's court and troops. My father even has a kindly note written to his father from the late king proclaiming his gratitude and noting the excellence of our goods. We have striven to be good and loyal subjects, giving only the best of our produce to His Majesty and his royal ancestors for centuries now. As I don't doubt you know, the past two winters have been fierce in the Midlands, causing a decline in the number of sheep running in our fields, and hence the number of fleeces that may be shorn from them. Still, we have willingly paid all the tariffs and taxes asked of us. My lord..." She noticed that the genial expression on his face had frozen. No doubt he was aware of what she was about to say. She swallowed hard. There was no way to sweeten the truth, nor would delay improve its flavor. ". . . My lord, we are aware of our obligations, and wish dearly to fulfill them, but the income from our trade is to fall short this quarter. And"—she caught her breath—"possibly the quarter to follow. We hope that my brother's voyages abroad will make up the lack in the summer, but for now, my father begs—I beg—His Majesty's forbearance for now. We will do our best to make up the remainder in the last quarter."

The noble's brows drew down over the bridge of his sharp nose. "Well, now, Mistress de Beauchamp. Taxes are the responsibility of every subject of His Majesty."

"And well aware of it we are, my lord!" Margaret wrung her hands. "We would not ask at all if we could avoid it. I apologize sincerely for the necessity." She felt tears sting at her eyes. *I will not cry and shame my father*, she insisted to herself. *I will not!* "If His Majesty would show mercy to faithful subjects, it would only endear him further in our hearts."

"Love does not fill pocketbooks, my dear," the Earl of Cork said. His face softened slightly. "Ah, but it's been a hard season for us all, so it has. Let me think on it a bit, and enquire of the king as to his will. Come back again on the Friday, and I'll have an answer for ye then." He stood up. Margaret sprang to her feet. the Earl rang the small bell on his desk. The audience was at an end. She curtseyed even deeper than she had upon entering.

"I thank you, my lord," she said, her dignity restored. The flunky arrived and she followed him into the anteroom. Lady Ann looked a question. All Margaret could find the strength to do was raise her shoulders in a shrug. Waiting was agony indeed, but wait she must.

To her dismay, Friday brought doubly bad news. In her turn, Lady Ann had disappeared through the linenfold door at the summons of the blue-suited flunky. She returned with an uncharacteristic frown on her lovely face.

"Och, it's only to be expaycted!" she said, shaking her head and making the long, carroty curls dance. "With nae queen, His Majesty has nae need f'r ladies in waiting. And finally, he's sent word to let me go. His lordship gave me all the courtesy in the world, but bid me godspeed and fair weather on ma return to the Highlands! At least it's the spring, and the seas ought to be ca'm enough. If I'm not to be a queen's maid, me da'll no doubt see about getting me married off. I don't mind. There are some likely lordlings there about who'll make me a good match."

"You're going home?" Margaret cried, feeling her heart sink.

"Aye." Lady Ann took Margaret's hands and squeezed them. "Wish ye could come alongside me. I feel as if we've made close friends."

"Oh, I feel that way, too!" The young women embraced, to the amusement of the others in the anteroom.

A gentle "hem!" close to her shoulder made Margaret sit back. The man in blue silk lowered a lugubrious mien to her.

"Mistress de Beauchamp?" As Margaret made to rise, he held up a hand. "No, mistress, no need to rise. The Earl of Cork regrets that he has no time to see you today."

"Shall I return on the morrow, then?"

He shook his head with a practiced little smile that wore sorrow on its corners, and lowered his voice to a murmur. "I am afraid not, mistress. He sends his deepest apologies, but His Majesty requires all taxes and tariffs to be paid this year without fail. He salutes your father's adherence to the crown, and is grateful for centuries of service, but requires the sums due. The crown's expenses must be paid. He will give you a month's grace past the coming quarter-day to pay your yearly tariff, but that is all."

"Oh, but if I may make a personal appeal to His Majesty?" Margaret pleaded, shocked to her core. Her father would be devastated! She had watched her brother bargaining enough times to hope that his tactics would work here. "Please, I have come such a long way. Perhaps if I may ask him myself? We would be pleased to offer bolts of fine cloth as a gift in thanks to him . . . and *anyone* else who aids us. Our woolens are renowned, as you might already know."

The official's expression didn't change, and Margaret's heart sank. The bribe wasn't good enough. "I am very sorry, mistress. The king is receiving no visitors. His lordship wishes you a safe journey home, and looks forward to receiving the statutory funds."

"So, all Father's investment in me as his agent were for naught," Margaret said, wringing her handkerchief in her hands.

It was already wet through with tears, but she had no other. Hettie clucked over her like a hen, rubbing her shoulder. The Americans sat beside her on the settee with sympathetic looks. "I have failed his trust in me. We will probably have to sell some of the smaller estates. Baronet Macy to the east has always been interested in the pastures in the curve of the river. It's some of our best grazing land, but he's willing to buy. Father will be beside himself with woe. He counts on every asset."

"I'm so sorry," Rita said, patting her knee. "I know that's hard news to take."

Margaret shook her head. "All that wool that we've been sending to the warehouses in Liverpool and here in London, waiting for the merchants to take abroad is not enough to make up the shortfall. I've been to see our storesmaster, Robert Bywell. The hauliers have had less to do than we like, and the boatmen have been taking jobs from other companies on the side to make ends meet. The markets have been as tight as a cork in a bottle. It feels like casting what pennies we have into the bottom of a deep sea, and no mermaids bringing us pearls in exchange. We need three hundred pounds now, and as much by the end of the year. It's hopeless."

The Americans had been more than cordial to receive Margaret once again. They had welcomed Lady Ann with alacrity. Lady Mailey had immediately taken to her, as Margaret knew she would. They were two wise souls, who immediately found common ground on which to converse. Margaret wished that that intelligent perspective would rub off on her, and give her some wisdom to bring back to her father.

"I wish I had a fortune to give to ye," Lady Ann said, lifting her hands. "I've no' that much of gold in my purse that I could lend to thee, and I've my journey home to pay for. I'd give ye what I could, but accidents happen, and I may need every coin at hand." She slapped her knee. "I'll have ma father send ye the sum when I return home. He'd do it readily for a true friend of mine. Ye can pay it back over years, I promise. There'll be no hurry in th' world."

Though she was touched deeply. Margaret shook her head. "It might take you a month or more to get home, and the tariffs need to be paid sooner than that. Besides that, my father would rather die of the pox than incur more indebtedness. I mean no offense. He could countenance asking the king for mercy, or sell assets to our neighbors, but he would prefer to have the fewest possible know of our need. And with the shortfall likely to amass further in days to come—well, there's no end to it that I can see. But I thank you for your kind offer with all my heart."

Rita raised her eyebrows to Lady Mailey and the other women in the room, and seemed to gather some consensus. "What if we could lay our hands on the money here in London?" she asked.

"I can't ask you, either," Margaret said. "As with Lady Ann, you'll likely need all the funds at your disposal because of..." She stopped, realizing she almost committed a terrible error of tact.

But, dismayingly, Lady Mailey picked up at once on her thought.

"Because of our unjust incarceration?" she asked, with that acerbic tone. "Don't worry about us. On the other hand, your father might be worried about knowing that the funds came from the strangers the king has clapped in the Tower."

"That shouldn't be a problem," the big man, Rita's husband Tom, said.

"But it is," Lady Mailey said, turning to her compatriots, stern-faced. "Sir Timothy doesn't need the stigma of being aided by potential enemies of the Crown."

"I didn't think of that," Tom said. The big man frowned. "We're not enemies, but I suppose the king is afraid of what our history books have told him."

"It works out the same," the former schoolteacher said. "Any association with us could backfire upon Sir Timothy later on." Margaret didn't understand the pointed expressions that the Americans exchanged, but she comprehended the sentiment of the words. It was true: her father would be wise not to attract negative attention.

"What about a straight purchase?" Rita asked. "I could, er, send a message to my brother. I'm sure he'd be happy to buy quality woolen cloth for uniforms for the new navy."

Margaret gave her a small smile. She was so grateful for her new friend's kindness. "I'm afraid what bolts we have left after the shipments that went to the continent with my brother that we could satisfy such an order." She knew too well that a wet winter and illness among the weavers had cut well back on the expected output. The guild master had been scathing, as if he expected Sir Timothy to change the weather.

"Well, we could advance you the money for future goods," Rita said. "I'm sure you're good for it. Let me . . . let me send a message to him and ask."

"That could take weeks," Margaret said. "We have too little time. Best for me to make preparations to return home. Bad news will not improve with keeping."

So, selling the assets it would have to be. Hundreds of years they had managed the gift from the Duchy of Lancaster and it would all be lost in one generation. She rose and signed to Hettie to gather their outer garments.

"Thank you all for giving thought to aiding my family," she said. "It comforts me greatly to have made such warm friends. Allow us to take our leave. I must prepare to return home, too. I must speak to our boatmen about taking us upstream to meet the northern coaches."

"Don't lose hope," Rita said, giving her a warm hug.

"Hope we have in plenty," Margaret said, as Andrew Short arrived on the doorstep to escort her and Lady Ann to the gate. "I thank you all."

"Did you hear that?" Tom said, as the door closed behind the visitors. He had to force himself to keep his voice low. "She knows boatmen. And *hauliers* has to be the same as teamsters. Harry is looking for a large boat and wagons. She could hire them for us!"

"No!" Melissa declared, flatly. "We don't want her involved. This is going to be a massive and dangerous operation, and one that will be considered treason. Everyone who is helping us already risks torture or hanging. The least that Cork will do would be to confiscate her father's estates. Those are already at stake because of the tax burden. The king's a terrible money manager. It's in our history books. I don't want that poor girl thrown in prison. It won't be as comfortable as we've had it. Don't ask her!"

"You're right, Tom," Rita said, cutting off Melissa's protest. "Have her make the connection to the right people, and Harry will do the rest." She smiled brightly. "I think that's worth three hundred pounds, don't you?"

"Harry won't like shelling out that kind of money," Tom said.

"He made plenty on his illicit art sale," Melissa said, with some asperity. "He can spare a share for a good cause."

# Chapter 4

On her last day in London before traveling home to Scotland, Lady Ann asked Margaret to dine with her. She had ordered food brought to her rooms in the sumptuous residence in which she resided, a far cry from the modest lodgings that Margaret occupied. Her servants, a white-haired older couple in neat white linen and plaid woolens, Thomas and Annabelle, fussed over both of them like children. Ann affectionately called them "Auntie" and "Uncle," and invited Margaret to do the same. The table was laid with monogrammed cloths, all of the finest quality. Crystal glowed in the light of a silver candelabrum heavy with an enameled coat of arms. Margaret felt honored to sit at such a table.

"At the least, we can empty a bottle of wine togaither," her friend insisted, as Thomas poured a sweet-smelling red into a cup for Margaret. "Ye've been in the dumps for a day or more. No' that I can blame ye for it, but ye've done all ye can. I've faith in your father to make as well as he can out of the situation. He sounds a sensible sort."

"And so he is," Margaret said, taking a sip. The wine was excellent and warmed her to her core. "I only wish I had better news to give him. I sent word to Master Bywell to make arrangements for me and Hettie to take ship upstream. He said with the spring rains easing, we could travel as far as Oxford."

"Better on your backside," Lady Ann said, with a laugh. "My journey will be mostly by sea. I doubt not I'll be well sprinkled with the spring rains by the time I see home again."

"Tell me about your home and your family," Margaret said. "I feel as though I've known you all my life, but we've had only a few days together."

"I hope ye'll see it one day," Lady Ann said, lifting her glass to her friend. "Tis the truth, but I'll be happy to set eeyn on it again. Weel na, it's an old pile of stones in the farthest north of the farthest north. . . ."

Late that evening, they made warm farewells, with promises of letters every month, or as often as possible. With the warmth of the wine and the company raising her spirits more than a little, Margaret, with Hettie and Percy, set out again for their rooms. Lady Ann insisted on calling a sedan chair for them, "to spare ye the mud," as the spring rains had indeed begun, and insisted on paying for it. The enclosed conveyance, borne between two horses fore and aft, with lanterns swinging like the lights on a ship, was painted with a coat of arms that she didn't recognize. Master Bywell had told her of many a noble house that allowed the servants to make a few coins in the hours that they were not needed by the family. London was so expensive that Margaret understood the need to eke out one's wages. She would be grateful to be going home, even if it was as the bearer of bad news. Exciting as it had been to come to the city, it had been hard on her pocketbook, and harder still on her hopes. And yet, she had made good friends, shining stars in the sorrowful sky.

Lady Ann's footman, a tall man clad in neat dark blue livery, helped her and the maid through the door and offered them blankets against the cold of the night. Though Lady Ann had paid, this was yet another call for a coin or so to exchange hands. Margaret was ready with a tip. It seemed to please the footman, for he tucked the cloth around her feet with some care and only slightly less for her maid who sat opposite. With a half-salute to her, Percy swung up onto the back of the horse at the rear. The door closed and she heard the man cluck to his horses. The carriage lurched slightly as they set off.

"It shouldn't be more than half an hour's ride," Margaret said.

The chair was well-kept and clean, smelling of sandalwood and beeswax. The inside had been lined with tapestries showing riders and hounds on the hunt. There were leathern windows to lower for air, but she found herself staring at the closed shades instead and let her body move with the rocking of the carriage. So much had happened in their visit to London, only the news from the Earl of Cork had been bad. Otherwise, she had much reason to be grateful.

"Are you all right, mistress?" Hettie asked, after a long silence.

"Oh, yes, I'm fine," Margaret assured her. "I'll miss Lady Ann, and Rita and Lady Mailey. I hope it's as all of them said, 'au revoir,' not 'farewell forever.'"

"Goodbyes are hard," Hettie said, sympathetically. "What's ahead won't be so easy, neither."

Margaret shook her head. Her heart felt heavy. She had been so excited to come to London and to speak to the king as her father's representative. How terribly she had failed him. "Best not to borrow trouble until we must. Father is resourceful. We will all put our heads together and come up with some manner of saving our estates."

"God will provide," Hettie said, and crossed herself. Margaret followed the gesture absently.

"Here, now, this is no' the way to me lady's lodgings!" Percy protested. "Ye should'a turned at that corner there! Wheel around, man!"

"No, lad, we're goin' that way," the footman said. "Sit tight, lad. I know a better way."

Margaret lowered the blind. A wave of stench redolent with urine and rotten fish washed in over them. The buildings around them, ill-lit by yellow flames coming from filthy lanterns, were not of even the modest quality of the street near the castle. They were heading east, well away from Whitehall.

"Hold on!" she called to the footman. "This isn't the way we are supposed to go! You must have been given the wrong directions. Take us to Great George Street, sir!"

The man frowned down at her.

"Sorry for the ruse, your highness, but there's someone who has to talk with you. Won't take but a moment."

Margaret was shocked.

"Am I being kidnapped?" she demanded. "Let me tell you, sir, I have very little money, and my father is heavily indebted. I will be worth nothing to you as a hostage. Or..." Her resolve wavered. Worse things could happen to a couple of lone women in the alleys of London, or so she had heard. She drew the knife from her garter and held it before her. "We'll sell our honor dear, sir. That I assure you!"

The man grinned. "You have spirit, no doubt about it. Your virtue is safe, your highness. Bide a moment, and all will be revealed."

Percy jumped down from his mount and pulled open the door of the sedan chair.

"Get out, me lady," the boy said, holding a rough hand in to her. "I'll take ye to yon inn until I can make arrangements for yer safety."

Margaret and Hettie cast aside their blankets.

"Ah, no, you don't," the footman said, swinging down from his saddle. He walked toward them, his hands up to show that they were empty. "There's people who want a word with your mistress. It'll only be a short time."

Percy turned to confront him, drawing his own knife.

"Run, me lady!" he shouted, leaping at the blue-clad man. "I swore blind to yer sire I'd bring ye back safe! Get in the hostelry! Th' innkeeper will mind you!"

"Ah, you young fool," the tall man said, shaking his head. He elbowed the door of the sedan chair closed. Percy jumped for him, but the man caught his arm as he lunged. With a downward chop of his free hand, he knocked the knife out of the boy's grasp. It bounced noisily away over the cobblestones. Percy grappled with the man, seeking to twist his arm up behind his back. The footman shook his head, as if in disbelief that the boy would challenge him. He countered every move, and grabbed Percy by the nape of the neck. He had the skills of a practiced soldier.

Terrified, Margaret fought with the door. The footman had somehow secured it so she couldn't open the latch.

"Go out the winder, my lady," Hettie said. "I'll boost you. Go on!"

"I can't leave you!"

"What will your father say if I let harm come to you?"

"We will both be safe," Margaret said. She leaned out the window and pricked the rump of the forward horse with the tip of her knife.

The horse let out a loud whinny of surprise and galloped down the street. The rear horse had no choice but to follow.

She looked back. The man gawked for a moment.

"Runaway horse!" he shouted, dashing after them. Percy followed, keeping almost abreast of his opponent. "Save my lady!"

*Curse his quick wits*, Margaret thought.

People scuttled off the busy street, away from the panicking horses. A couple of men clad in stained aprons stepped out and attempted to catch the forward mount's harness. The confusion did succeed in slowing down their progress a little. A wagon full of barrels lumbered out in front of them, blocking their passage. The lead horse neighed and rose to its rear hooves, pawing the air. Margaret and Hettie held onto the sedan chair's frame. A slender man with sleek black hair took the moment to jump up and catch the lead horse's bridle.

"There ye'are, me darlings," he said. "Safe and sound." Margaret plunged her hand into her pocket and handed him whatever coin came first to her fingers.

"Thank you, my good sir," she said. At last, the door yielded to her efforts and sprang ajar. "Come on, Hettie."

The man gawked astonished at the gold in his palm. Margaret dragged Hettie out of the chair and into the nearest doorway.

The shop, a draper's, was closed for the night, but the deep recess before the closed portal gave them a moment's shelter.

"We'll have to find a carriage," Margaret said. She pulled her hood over her head and crept out from the doorway. The dark-haired man was holding onto the halter of the now calm horse. The footman had caught up with him, and was casting about to find Margaret.

Percy, bless him for the innocent that he was, spotted them turning out into the street, and headed toward them with a glad cry.

"Why, tha' she is! Mistress de Beauchamp, come with me now!"

Margaret groaned inwardly, as the footman opened his long legs and outpaced her escort. Before she could escape, he clamped her firmly by the arm. His expression was a combination of concern and innocence.

"My lady, I regret the bad behavior of the horses! Let me see you safely into this hostelry, where you may have refreshment while I make all ready for your conveyance homeward. How his grace will chide me for my inattention to the steeds!"

A crowd had gathered from the shops and inns nearby. Margaret opened her mouth to scream that he was not her servant, and that she was being abducted.

"Do not make another sound," the tall man said in a low and menacing voice that belied his bland expression. "I've got a dagger in my hand, and I'll do more than prick you in the rump with it. Make this easy, and I'll get you back to your rooms before you know it."

Margaret nodded without speaking. She shot a warning look to Hettie and Percy, who followed her, wide-eyed with fear. She glanced back toward the sedan chair, but it had disappeared.

"Nay, I don't trust you enough to stay within it," the footman said. "We stay on foot."

Her best shoes were coming to ruins over the soiled cobblestones of East London. She had to jump to avoid splashes of filth being flung out of upper story windows to drain into the open sewers at the center of the road. More than one woman with an indecently low-cut bodice eyed her, wondering if she had come to ruin and was competing for their customers. Margaret felt her cheeks burn with shame. Her escort, curse him, seemed to read her mind, and was amused by what he perused there.

"Quality doesn't come to these parts often, except to attend the theater," he said. "You're far afield for that. Never mind. The inn ahead is respectable enough."

He led them over the busy bridge toward Southwark. Indeed, she could see the golden shell of the Globe Theater rising almost on the water's edge. Its upper edge seemed ablaze with lanterns. Pennants fluttered in between them, welcoming theatergoers. She found herself gawking at it over the shoulders of other pedestrians who were abroad at this late hour.

"Show's ended for the night," the man said. He identified himself as Tony, but gave no more information. "Not as fine as in Master Shakespeare's day, but well enow. I saw him once, when I was a lad, in his last play, eighteen years gone."

"I've never been," Margaret said, intrigued despite her situation. The night winds whistled down the black expanse of the Thames and made her shiver. She held her cloak close around her shoulders and thanked divine Providence for her warm clothing. "My neighbor, Lady Pierce, went frequently as an attendant of Her Sainted Majesty Queen Elizabeth. She told me many tales."

"Go sometime. I know many who would give all their teeth and one hand to attend. Don't miss the chance. As much as it has diminished, there's still none finer."

Hettie looked nervous the whole time, though she admitted that the market where she shopped for Margaret's meals was not far from their path. Margaret absorbed the information in a trance, soothing her maid with pats on the arm. She no longer felt in danger, but it was more as if she was drawn into one of those storied plays herself. Could she be the heroine, like Rosalind, to confront a foe who might come to be a friend? Still, she kept her dagger near to hand.

Disconcertingly, Tony, as he insisted she call him, spotted it.

"You can keep the sewing-needle if you wish," he said. "I can take it away from you anytime I want. And no one will mind your cries. I promise no ill will come to you, and possibly much good. Keep walking. We're nearly there."

Harry Lefferts sat at a table in the rear of the inn, his long legs stretched out and crossed nonchalantly at the ankle, his sword at easy reach. The innkeeper had kept the pitchers of beer coming to the four men. The barmaid, an attractive, plump girl with thick blonde hair and pink cheeks, hovered close, sending him longing glances. She was worth a good leer, so Harry obliged her, but kept his hand on his mug. Gerd Fuhrmann did take a grab at the girl's buttocks. She danced away with a coy, "Oh, sir!" Juliet would have scored her a seven out of ten for delivery. Felix Kasza grinned and flipped the girl a small coin, which she ostentatiously put down between a pair of sumptuous breasts. Harry had no doubt that action had indicated a willingness for either a quick fondle or a more extended session in one of the rooms at the top of the dark stairs in exchange for more coins. George Sutherland had said this place was just on the low edge of respectability, but suited to their needs of the moment.

He glanced surreptitiously at his watch, which he kept hidden most of the time under his ruffled cuff. Getting two of his men to keep an eye on Lady Ann's quarters hadn't been difficult. George Sutherland also knew a couple of grooms who would lend him a carriage or another light vehicle, and Tony Leebrick looked like a trustworthy senior servant. The lady's elderly servant had confided to the guy delivering a cooked roast to the apartment that Lady Ann was leaving in the morning, so he knew Melissa's prospect wouldn't be staying late. What was taking so long?

At last, Tony's face appeared over the heads of the other

patrons in the smoky room. After a quick scan, his eyes met Harry's and he pushed forward, a small group in tow. As they got closer, Harry eyed the three people. The tall, lanky boy he dismissed immediately as the necessary male escort for women traveling alone. The girl in plain clothes and a good but not fashionable green cloak was obviously the maid. He started to study the brown-haired woman in blue whose arm Tony held fast to but his eyes were caught by a pair of intelligent hazel eyes. They were sizing him up as much as he was appraising their owner. He grinned.

"Mistress de Beauchamp? I'm Harry Lefferts. Have a seat and let's talk. I think we can do each other some good."

"No, thank you. I prefer to stand. I will not be staying long." She shook George's hand off her. "I do not wish to deal with strangers who abduct me."

"I'm not a stranger," Harry said, with his most winning smile. "I'm a friend of a friend. Rita Simpson. Have a drink, Miss de Beauchamp. The beer's not too bad."

The girl tossed her head. "Anyone can know a name. I am going. Come, Hettie. Percy!" She turned and took a couple of steps toward the innkeeper, probably to ask him to supply her with an escort.

Harry smiled. She had all the guts Melissa had told him about. "Show me your flashlight, Miss de Beauchamp." In spite of herself, she glanced back at him, her mouth agape. "How would I know about that unless I knew her?"

"But she's imprisoned in the Tower," Margaret said, lowering her voice to a whisper. "How could she tell you?"

"How did *you* get to meet her?" Lefferts countered. "It's not sealed up like a drum. A lot of people come and go every day. The right price greases a lot of palms. Maybe I swept in like the wind and out again. Anyhow, prove *you're* the right person."

The hazel eyes narrowed with annoyance.

"I'm not the one who has a favor to ask!"

"Don't you? I hear you came to town to get help from the crown and got the bum's rush. That's what my old grampaw used to say. I'd say we have the grounds for bargaining." He beckoned with one long hand. "Come on, let's see it."

"God's blood, sir!" came an exclamation, followed by a loud crash.

Margaret and everyone in the tavern turned their heads to see.

The buxom server had dropped her tray and turned to confront one the customers. "You keep your bloody hands to yourself, or I'll haul ye to the gutter!"

The loud clatter distracted and silenced everyone, which emphasized the woman's loud and profane reaction. It was a few minutes before Margaret could react. She was not unaware of how carefully the man was studying her reaction. If he was truly a friend of Rita's, the device in her pocket was a token of good faith. If not...

Margaret was uncertain. She knew that what she did next would perhaps change her life, hopefully, but not necessarily for the better. Harry Lefferts beckoned again. His accent did sound like the peculiar English that Rita and Lady Mailey spoke. Unnerved, Margaret felt for the bench. The big man clad in black shifted over to give her room. Hettie helped her to sit.

Feeling as if she was even more out of control of the situation than she had been in the Earl of Cork's company, she reached into the pocket around her waist and brought out the little black square. Harry clapped a hand on top of it before it could be seen by anyone nearby and drew it to him across the tabletop. He cradled it in his palm and glanced at it as though reading a playing card. He smiled, and Margaret suddenly realized he was a very attractive man, very certainly used to getting his own way by force or by charm. Well, she had plenty of charming men in her family, and didn't let them get away with liberties. She extended her palm to get her treasure back, but Harry put it into his own belt pouch.

"Trade you," he said. "I have to prove to Rita I saw you. Here's mine in exchange."

Instead of a black box, he offered her a small golden cylinder the length of her forefinger with a button on one end and the same kind of glass sequin on the other. Words were printed upon it, but she didn't take the time to read them. Flashlights must come in many shapes and sizes in this marvelous, faraway United States of America. She didn't dare try it out in the common room of the inn, or ask him all the questions knocking at her lips, but tucked it away.

"So, you're an—" Margaret stopped when Harry put his finger to his lips. "So, you come from there, too. But what do you want from me? If you spoke to . . . to her, you must know all. I have nothing that I can offer . . . people like you."

"You have connections," Harry said, leaning over the tabletop and staring deeply into her eyes. "We need help."

"What kind of connections?" Margaret asked, bewildered. "My father owns sheep and employs shepherds, weavers, and dyers."

"Men who can keep their lips zipped," Harry said, his voice very low.

"I . . ." Margaret stared at him. "I don't know what that means."

The muscular man with the scarred face at Harry's right let out a guffaw. "The Mädchen is right to tell you to speak plainly! Tell her your needs, and no more of your movie-gangster talk."

Harry seemed abashed.

"All right! Miss de Beauchamp, I need a wagon and horses, maybe two wagons. Not flashy, just sturdy. I need two river boats that can carry a lot of weight, and I need them pretty soon. I mean really soon. Like tomorrow. I'll pay good money, more than fair prices for them. But more important is that I need people who will take the money and not talk about it before or afterwards. Do you know anyone you can trust around here?"

Margaret stared at him. "Is that all? A barge and a couple of wagons? I can easily find you a captain who will take your goods from Tilmouth. What kind of cargo will you be carrying?" Now Harry hesitated. Margaret peered at him, summing up his expression with a practiced eye. He wasn't lying to her, but he was afraid to say too much. The confidence he wore like armor concealed genuine fear. That puzzled her. "Rita sent you to me for a reason. You're trusting *me* now with these questions. Why the need for secrecy?"

"The less you know about it, the better," the tall man said, his expression serious.

"No," she said firmly. "If it's contraband, you had better let me go now. I swear I will say nothing, but I can't be involved in anything illegal. I have nothing of my own, but my father's lands could be confiscated if I am accused of abetting a crime. But I will help you to a noble goal."

"It's noble, all right," Harry assured her. "The noblest. Rita and Melissa'll be very grateful. I will, too. I really can't say anymore here. Lives are at stake. Will you help us?"

Margaret made up her mind and nodded once. She could ponder over her regrets later.

"You're one of a kind with Rita and Melissa," Harry said. "And Rebecca Stearns. You don't know what kind of a compliment that is."

"I understand other people's secrets," Margaret assured him. She hesitated, knowing what shape such negotiations might take. "I may have to offer coin in advance to those I approach. And . . ."

Harry needs must have been on the sharp end of a bargain or three himself, for he smiled.

"You'll be taken care of," he promised. "You're giving me a shortcut I don't have the means to take myself. And here's an advance for your connections." He leaned forward and pushed the hammered pewter pitcher toward her. Almost like a magician's trick, a small cloth bag appeared alongside it. Margaret accepted the pitcher and urged the bag over the table until it fell into her lap. "When's the soonest you can you talk to your people?"

"Is dawn soon enough?" Margaret asked. Keeping her hand low, she guided the purse into her pocket. It felt heavy. Even if it was full of coppers, it would do as a goodly bribe. "You said the matter is urgent, but I believe that I would cause a stir if I went to the docks at this hour. They'll be up and working at the crest of the sun."

Harry sat back, clearly relieved. "Dawn's soon enough, for sure."

"One more thing," Margaret said. She nodded toward her lap. "I will use this well to smooth the way, but I am taking a tremendous risk on your behalf, becoming involved with . . . you." Harry nodded, and she knew he understood. "I believe that my services should also be rewarded."

For a moment, she wondered if Harry thought her too bold, but he grinned. "Sounds fair. How much do you want, Mistress de Beauchamp?"

At least she would be able to bring some largesse back to her father. She raised her chin in defiance. "Fifty pounds." It was a princely sum, and she expected him to negotiate, but he didn't even blink.

"Okay, it's a deal. I don't want anyone else seeing us together, so I'm sending a guy tomorrow. He'll be waiting outside your lodgings. I'll vouch for him. You make sure your connections are worth trusting. Tony will drive you home now. Thanks for listening, Mistress de Beauchamp."

"I am glad to have done so, sir, though I may regret my impulsiveness later." Margaret extended her hand. He clasped it.

"Soft but strong," Harry said, running a thumb over her fingertips. Margaret felt a frisson run up her body. Such an intense, intimate touch. She wanted to pull her hand back, but at the same time, she didn't. "Calluses on your fingers and palm. You do work back there in Staffordshire, don't you? Not snooty at all. You probably won't see me again, Mistress de Beauchamp. And don't go back to the Tower, got it?"

Margaret was glad to understand her first American slang. "I . . . got it, sir. Tell them it was my pleasure to make their acquaintance. And yours."

Harry grinned at her. "Likewise."

# Chapter 5

Instead of one of Harry's "guys" waiting for her on the morrow, there were two: a big, tousle-haired man and a woman nearly as large, with a tightly laced russet-colored bodice constraining a mighty bosom. The man sidled up to her and spoke in a low undertone, unlikely to be heard by the bakers' boys and sweepers already moving through the streets.

"Mistress de Beauchamp? Harry sent us. I'm George Sutherland, m'lady. This is my wife, Juliet."

"An honor, mistress," Juliet said, grasping the sides of her skirt and dipping her head and shoulders in a grand curtsey. She had a theatrical look about her, with somewhat exaggerated movements. Hettie eyed her with displeasure, but Margaret gave her maidservant a severe glance to quell any discourtesy. They were English, thank divine Providence. She would have to make no excuses for strange accents or customs. And they were Sutherlands! Margaret felt that to be an omen, that they had the same surname as her friend, minus the nobility, of course. Harry Lefferts could not have chosen better.

"I am pleased to make your acquaintance," Margaret said. "My servants are Hettie and Percy."

George Sutherland gave them a sharp nod. "They're staying behind. My wife will mind your needs. I'll swear to her safety."

"This hussy will not have a care for my mistress!" Hettie protested. Juliet looked amused rather than offended.

"No, it will be all right," Margaret said. "Go back to our

quarters and wait for me." She glanced at the Sutherlands. "We won't be long."

Hettie snorted in indignation, but obeyed. She grabbed the goggling Percy by the arm and dragged him back toward the hotel. Sutherland grinned.

"Thanks, m'lady. You're right to trust us, I swear it. Harry would have my balls if I let anything happen to you. We've a boat waiting to take us downstream to the Docklands. This way, if you please."

Margaret stood in the stern of the small vessel as the pock-marked young boatman plied the dawn-dark waters with expertise. He handed her gently up onto the quay to which she directed him, and smiled at the coin she pressed into his palm.

Internally, Margaret was quaking with nerves. Part of it was the excitement of being involved in A Conspiracy. The rest, well, wasn't it natural to fear the unknown? She trusted Harry Lefferts, though she couldn't say why. He must have a genuine connection to Rita, or how else would he have known about the treasure in her pocket? His pocket, now, and she had the new one. She felt the lump of the golden cylinder's outline through the heavy woolen fabric of her cloak and the skirt beneath. Normally, she would lend no credence to talismans, but that was what she considered the flashlight to be.

She found her father's agent counting bales in his warehouse and shouting at men in shirtsleeves who were piling them up or casting them down for conveyance to the ships on the quayside. The place smelled familiarly of lanolin, sweat, raw wood, leather, and candle-smoke.

"Master Bywell!" Margaret pitched her voice to carry above the hubbub.

Robert Bywell had known her since she was a babe. He turned, showing tobacco-stained teeth, swept off his wide-brimmed hat, and offered a big, work-roughened hand to her.

"Well, Mistress de Beauchamp! I hadn't thought to see you again this journey. How be ye?"

"Well enough," Margaret said. She took in his glance at her companions. "And you? How is Mistress Christine?"

"The babe's a boy," he said, proudly. "My sixth. And my eldest daughter's nearly old enough to marry."

"Congratulations," Margaret said, warmly. She felt in her

newly fattened purse for one of Harry Lefferts' silver coins. She held out a crown. "For Christine."

"She'll be glad to have the gift and your good wishes," Master Bywell said. He tucked it away. "Now, how may I serve you? Ye're not often here on the docks at this hour of the day. Is all well?" He gave a pointed glance toward the big man at her elbow. Margaret knew that one word from her, and no one would ever see the Sutherlands again.

"It is," Margaret said. She deliberately jingled the pouch so the coins inside it rang. "My friends here have need of your services."

"Ah, it's like that, is it?" Bywell asked, with a knowing nod. "Well, then, come to my room, and we'll discuss the needful."

They gathered around his table, as full as the Earl of Cork's of important paperwork. Bywell swept the piles to one side so he could see the faces of his visitors.

"So, what is it I may do for the friends of my old employer's daughter?" he asked.

"Have a pipe on me," Juliet said, with a beguiling grin. She offered her pouch of tobacco, and the three of them filled their pipes. George laid out the details that Margaret had heard from Harry Lefferts the night before.

Wreathed in sweet-smelling tobacco smoke, Master Bywell mused over the newcomers' request. Margaret kept quiet. Such private dealings were common. The only detail that needed to be kept secret was any connection to the Americans in the Tower.

"Ah, well, I know that Master Loggia has a cart he doesn't mind hiring out," Bywell said. "He's as close-lipped as a clam. But I know that it's in poor condition. It looks as though it needs to be put out of its misery."

"As long as it can roll along even a mile it'll do," George Sutherland said. "And the second?"

"I've one I will lend, though I want it returned in good order," Bywell said. "Matters are slow at the moment, but the Good Lord willing, prosperity will return soon."

"Sir, I would be glad to make assurances, but the Fates may dictate otherwise. If it should happen that the wagon may not be so easily restored to you," George said, "I'd be obliged if you would name a price for it as though you will need to replace it. Within reason, of course."

Master Bywell was amused. "Of course. While it may be

inconvenient to purchase a new one, I'll be fair as to the cost. As for a pair of barges, hmmm." He peered out the clearest of the slagged-glass panels of the window beside him. Margaret tried to see what he was looking at. "You say you only need them for a day or two? And no questions asked?"

"Aye," George said, his eyes watchful. "To the benefit of the owners, no questions either way."

"But a barge—you can't just take a man's livelihood and not expect him to be concerned for its well-being. And horses—they take a lot of fodder and care, as well you know."

"Well that I know," George said. "We've brought along enough for them to be *well cared for.*"

"How much will it take?" Margaret asked Bywell. The merchant looked thoughtful.

"Well, my lady, not so much as I'd charge him as a stranger, and not so little as I'd charge you if it was you on your own. After all, I'd not be speaking with these fine folk at all if you had not vouched for them. Is that fair?"

"It is," Margaret said, with a glance at the Sutherlands to make certain that it was agreeable to them as well. "Make your details, then. I will sit quietly here and oversee your negotiations."

"Yes, my lady." Bywell sent his clerk running. In a short time, the lad returned with a couple of rough-looking men in woolen tunics and long sea boots. Then, the real bargaining began.

The boatman wanted information regarding the well-being of their barges. Sutherland assured them that no harm would come to the craft. He explained that he needed them at a time and a place that would be revealed later on. "Without a word to anyone else, mind you. That's vital, or we finish right here."

Margaret expected that they would cavil at the mystery, but they simply nodded. Her presence acted as a surety that nothing foul was afoot. The greater the secrecy, the greater the payment to come. Such an arrangement would benefit all of them. Sutherland was a fair negotiator. He kept his expression neutral, as did the other men. Bywell sat back, smoking Juliet's tobacco, nodding occasionally. Margaret was pleased, seeing that they were almost coming to terms. All seemed to be well. She was doing right by Rita and her other new friends.

And, with the spring sun's rising through the crude window, she realized what the American must have sent her to negotiate for. What could be more noble than Rita's freedom? The words almost burst free from her lips. With difficulty, she kept herself quiet, with hands now clenched in her lap. But how?

Juliet eyed her, pipe still between her lips, and gave a short, sharp shake of her head. Margaret understood. She sat back on her tailbone to think.

Two boats were surely more than was needed to carry away the five or so people she saw in the Tower apartment. And two wagons? She remembered the calculating expression on Harry Lefferts' face. He was a man who *dared*. He had a plan. In her mind, she could see the escape unfolding, with one boat leading the authorities astray, and the second one carrying Rita and the others to safety disguised, possibly, as bales of wool or sacks of grain. Yes, that was it! That was why he needed two of each. What a clever man he was!

But a problem knocked at her mind. The Tower had been a stronghold for centuries. How was Harry to whisk five people out of its interior? Perhaps it was just as he had said the night before: he would sweep in and out like the wind, carrying his countrymen with him. She prayed with all her heart to divine Providence that he would succeed. She stared at the two boatmen, willing them to agree with George Sutherland.

The big man held out his hand. "So, it's a bargain, then?"

"Near enough," the first boatman, an older man missing four front teeth among the remaining yellow stubs, sputtered out. "But we'll want payment in advance."

Sutherland's brows went down.

"Half was what we said."

"What you said, no' what we did," said the second one, a burly man with greasy hair and pockmarked skin. "Ye'll make off with our boats and leave us with naught."

"Now, now," Bywell said, holding up his hands. "Let's have no talk of thieving. He's offering a generous price."

"But to get them back in sound shape is what we want," said the first boatman. He crossed his arms, ignoring George's hand. Sutherland's face didn't change, but Margaret sensed that he was going to say something he would regret. She jumped in.

"But won't you be on board to sail them for this gentleman?" she asked. "It's not as though he knows the perils of negotiating this river as you do."

The four men relaxed.

"Aye, that's true," George said. "I'll say that my employer would agree to that. Sail steady and swiftly, and remain silent as the grave afterwards."

"How far afield are we going, then? Shall I tell my wife to stay the evening meal?" the toothless man asked.

Margaret could tell that George was reluctant to let out any details he didn't have to, but it was a fair question. He and Juliet exchanged glances, as if they could read one another's minds.

"At Romford our business will be finished," he said. "The carts must meet us there."

Bywell nodded. "I'll send them out two days before. Ye've only to give the word."

The first boatman held out a hand. "Done, then." His colleague extended his as well. With a look of relief, Sutherland grasped them. "We'll no' give any word to our crew. They'll mind what we captains tell them."

After that, the negotiations finished swiftly, followed by a tot of rum all around. Margaret only touched her lips to hers. It was agreed that on arrival the final installment of the payment would be made to each barge's master, who would take over the tiller again. Up until that point, the English crew had what Sutherland called, with careful emphasis on the words, *plausible deniability*, a phrase Margaret made a point of memorizing so she could ask him about it on the way back to her lodgings. Bywell brought out cups and a bottle of Spanish jerez.

"Never too early for good fortified wine," the merchant said. He poured for all and lifted his cup. "To everyone's good health."

The two captains departed, money in their purses and a warm glow in their bellies. Margaret felt satisfied that she had done her friends a good deed.

"One more thing," Sutherland said, as soon as the boatmen were out of hearing. "Speaking of plausible deniability. The man with the cart—he wouldn't happen to have a friend nearby who knows his way around a lathe? It's my employer's request."

Bywell grinned widely, his pipe clenched in his teeth.

"Happen he does. And as silent as the grave as well. A good fellow, with a number of children, all of whom need new shoes, you understand." George understood. A slight clinking as silver changed hands. Bywell smiled broadly.

"Good business this morning," he said. "I believe that it bodes well for us all."

"Aye, from your mouth to Heaven's ear," Sutherland said.

"You did well, my lady," Juliet said, as they plied the waters back to the small hotel. "Your da raised you as a born merchant. Not too much said, but not too little, either. Your part's done. I hope you'll never know what you've done today, but you've our gratitude. Ours and Harry's."

Margaret held her tongue until the boatman helped them out onto the slimy stone steps, accepted his coin with a tug of his lanky hair, and pushed away from the bank.

"Farewell, m'lady," George said. "You won't see us again, I hope."

"Take good care of them!" Margaret burst out. "They showed me such kindness."

The Sutherlands looked at one another. Margaret bit her tongue, wishing that she could take back her words. She backed away from the two, fearful that they would throw her into the river. In her good clothes, she'd likely swamp and drown before anyone was close enough to save her.

Juliet laughed.

"Ye've a brain, and guts to boot. Harry chose better than he knew."

They escorted her to the door of her lodgings. The midmorning crowd was growing. Animals and carts as well as passersby jostled them in the narrow street.

"Go about your business, my lady," George Sutherland said. "Don't go back to the Tower, and don't think twice about anything you hear after this."

Margaret nodded. "I . . . understand."

He handed her a leather bag. It was heavy with coin, even more so than the purse Harry had given her the night before. She had forgotten about her own reward of fifty pounds. Generous for one morning's work, indeed.

"Sorry it's not more," Juliet said. "God be with you, dear. And thanks." She gave Margaret a kiss on the cheek. She and George linked arms, and they disappeared into the bustle of London. As Margaret lost sight of them, Hettie came out of the door and bustled her inside, clucking all the while. She took Margaret's cloak and beat it as though it was an untrustworthy groom.

"Taking you away like that! It's not respectable! I trust you're safe and well, mistress?"

Margaret realized she had the bag clutched in both hands. When they were safely in her rented apartment, she undid the leather ties and looked inside.

The small coins weren't silver. They were *gold*. With a wordless noise, she spilled it out on the wooden table. That... that couldn't be just fifty pounds. "Help me count, Hettie! Quickly!"

As Percy stared open-mouthed, the two women counted and stacked the clinking disks. Margaret's heart pounded. She had to be dreaming! How could Sutherland have handed this over so casually? He'd had it on his person the whole time! Hettie stood back, her hands clasped together as if in prayer.

"Twenty, thirty, forty... three hundred pounds! Oh, mistress! I've ne'er seen so much coin together in my life!"

Margaret had wondered what her worth was to Harry Lefferts. Now she knew. It was the value of her family's estate and business for the entire year.

The sum was enough to save her father. For now.

She looked sternly at her servants.

"Not a word, mind," she said. "You've never seen this. It must get home safely to Barlaston. Do you understand?"

They nodded. Margaret pushed the gleaming yellow mass back into the leather bag and tied the drawstring tightly around its neck. From the other pouch, she found five-shilling crowns and pushed them into Hettie's and Percy's palms. It wasn't three hundred pounds, but they looked well satisfied, as was she.

Bless the Americans! Bless them all. She wished them safely out of the Tower and out of England. No word from her would ever endanger them.

"Your trunks are packed, mistress," Hettie said, coming into her small bedchamber a week later. "Your cloak is brushed and looks as new as new. The weather is fine. I'll be glad to say goodbye to London. Pray the ruts in the road north aren't too bad."

"I'm ready," Margaret said. She took a few steps. The weighty purse containing the coins was tied to a girdle and well-muffled underneath her skirt between her knees. She was aware of it every moment, though with her fashionable posture and walk, no one would be able to tell it was there. No doubt she would feel its discomfort keenly over the coming journey, but it would be worth the pain to see her father's face light when she poured the tiny golden angels out onto his counting-table. And, oh! To be at home, to sleep in her own bed, and hear the familiar noises of sheep and the rattle of the looms. She was glad to have ventured forth, but would be grateful to return safely to her own place.

Though she had listened to the gossip in the inns and eating-houses in the evenings, she hadn't heard anything to suggest that Harry Lefferts had put his plan into action. Master Bywell had sent one of his clerks with a note from his wife thanking her for the gift of money and a prayer for her safety returning home. No other word from any quarter.

Margaret smiled to herself. Her great adventure was at an end. In a way, she regretted it, but it had happened! She had met travelers from the future, and she had not only a fortune to give her father, but a treasure of her own the likes of which would never be seen for another three hundred years. Through the good wool of her cloak, she touched the golden cylinder, Harry's flashlight. A small miracle, reflective of the other marvels that had befallen her. She sent up a short prayer for the success of their enterprise.

"The wagon is here, mistress," Percy said, all but falling in the door in his excitement.

The weather was indeed fine. May had come in like a bouquet of flowers. Despite the miasma of London, Margaret still smelled the scent of spring flowers on the air.

The cart conveyed them to the coaching inn, where she paid passage for herself and her two servants. Her modest trunks were loaded onto the rear of the handsomely varnished vehicle. Four healthy-looking bay horses shifted from hoof to hoof in the creaking traces. Percy clambered on top of the coach. beside the porter above the boxes. One of her fellow passengers, a prosperous-looking man of her father's age with thinning black hair, aided her on the swaying iron steps. The added weight of her concealed purse made the first step up a trifle difficult, but her benefactor kept her steady. He also handed Hettie up, who clucked in abashment at the courtesy.

"There, my dear," he said to Margaret. "Why don't you and your maid take the forward-facing seat? I am sure none of us mind traveling backwards." He collected nods of agreement from the two other men who boarded after him.

"Thank you for your courtesy, sir and gentlemen," Margaret said. The man smiled and settled his own belongings opposite her. The interior was clean and smelled of lavender. The cushions on the seats had been freshly stuffed with wool. The little comforts boded well for the journey.

She made herself comfortable in the near-side corner, watching out of the window. A faint pealing of bells in the distance began, and Margaret absently counted the strokes of the clock. The driver, a lean man in a leather cape and in no hurry, emerged from the door of the inn and sauntered toward them.

"Eight o' the clock, mistress," Hettie confirmed.

The driver leaned in the window and beamed at them with a genial smile.

"Welcome, then! All ye bound f'r Stoke?" They nodded to him. "Well, then! We'll be off." He swung up and out of sight. Margaret felt his weight slightly settle the springs of the coach.

The horses wheeled on the stones of the courtyard, and the coach lurched into motion. An old man sitting on a bench at the inn door swiped a hand in the air as if to bid them farewell.

"Wait!"

A dignified-looking man in black coat and breeches hurtled toward them, his face reddened like a beetroot. He batted at his shoulders and arms, dislodging pale dust from his clothes. Margaret's heart stopped beating. Hettie clutched for her mistress' hand. Something must have happened! Her part in making negotiations had been found out. He was coming for them! She and Hettie would be taken to the Tower and tried for treason!

"Halt, driver! I say, halt!"

The coach bobbed as the driver reined in his team.

Margaret trembled. What could she do? She couldn't run with a bag of gold between her knees. And the coins would only serve to prove her involvement in the conspiracy. She was doomed.

The man flung open the door and threw himself inside. The coach curtseyed and swayed.

"Praise God, I nearly missed it!" On his knees on the floor, the man gave the passengers an embarrassed smile. He was still covered with gray dust. "Master Peter Woodsmith, attorney-at-law, ladies and gentlemen. By the Lord, my employer would have my head if I was another day's delayed!"

Margaret smiled at him weakly. The men on the facing bench

shifted to make room for him. Luckily, Master Woodsmith wasn't a big fellow.

"Did you fall into trouble?" the older man asked, in a voice that clearly meant *why couldn't you have been here early like the rest of us?*

"Not I!" Woodsmith said, his face losing its choleric coloring. "But something's afoot! Have ye heard the news about the Americans?"

Margaret found her voice, though her heart was barely pulsing again. "Nay, sir. What has befallen them?"

"By the Lord, the Tower of London is attacked! The Earl of Cork's men are all dead. Blown up! And all the American embassy escaped! The stones of the walls are falling like leaves. I just barely escaped having one fall on my head! Praise God, I was spared, but it put me behind time, I can tell you that."

The others murmured in amazement. Hettie's eyes had widened so round Margaret thought they might fall out.

"Tell us more," Margaret begged him. With all the artifice in her command, she leaned toward him, a rapt expression on her face. "I have heard something of these Americans, but I would like to know more. Tell us all!"

"Well, mistress," Woodsmith said, clearly pleased to have such an attentive audience, "I know not much of *how* it befell, but I can tell you what I saw, and an adventure it was, too!"

Margaret patted her maid's hand and settled in to hear the yarn, pleased that she knew much more than the men around her would ever know. Rita and the others were free! Please God let them remain ever so. And none would ever know her part in it. She trusted Harry Lefferts to keep her name from being revealed as was part of their bargain. All she had to do now was convey the gold in her care safely to her father.

Still, she hoped that someday she could tell her children of the way she had been woven into the fabric of an adventure—in a purely respectable way, that was.

# Chapter 6

### *June 1634*

Charles, by right of God, king, sovereign and lord of the Empire of Great Britain and its possessions, first of his name, paced angrily like a caged animal in the royal menagerie. His entire assembly of ministers and senior staff did their best to blend against the many life-sized oil portraits of His Majesty's ancestors. Only his chancellor, Richard Boyle, the Earl of Cork, stood in the center of the room, the focus of His Majesty's anger, because the perpetrators were not there.

"And you have done nothing in an entire month? Nothing at all to secure the safety of my realm and my people? My person? My children?" Charles's long hair was tangled like a wild horse's. Though he was fuming inwardly, Boyle stood without moving, his expression bland, for, in his experience, to react to the king was to make the outburst worse and more long-lasting.

"Your children, sire, have been under heavy guard since the incident," the Earl of Cork said. "And a full company is here within the corridors of Whitehall and outside the windows, so that no one could possibly approach to threaten you. Your safety is paramount."

"But the explosion destroyed an entire wall of the Tower of London. A wall! And more detonations beside. Who knows if there are more charges planted. I want to leave London. I am not safe here."

The Earl of Cork delved deep within himself for patience. It wasn't easy. He was as furious as the king. "Your Majesty, every room has been inspected again and again. We have no reason to believe that any of the perpetrators remain in the city. It is unlikely that they are even still within the country."

"Why have you not brought them to justice?"

It was a question that Boyle had asked himself every day since May when the escape had occurred. He had no answers.

"We are searching for them everywhere, sire. We have been seeking anyone who may have been involved in the enormity. The investigation is questioning those who might have even the smallest connection to the disaster. We have found nothing yet. I promise you that you shall be informed of any developments."

The king stopped to glare directly at him. Boyle could see that the king's eyes were bloodshot, and his skin looked saggy. He had not been sleeping, which meant that the court physician had been unable to dispense a sedative or even a calming draught.

"You have allowed my greatest enemies to become enlarged upon the nation, my Lord of Cork," Charles snapped out, enunciating every syllable. "And why has the outer wall of the Tower not yet been rebuilt?"

"It is under way, sire," Boyle said. He could have launched into a full explanation of the difficulties and expenses involved with the restoration of the palace, but Charles wasn't interested.

He would never forget the moment when it happened. The BOOM echoed the two and a half miles down the Thames and broke windows in countless buildings. Rowers and runners had taken more than a half hour to arrive at Whitehall with the report of the explosion. They'd had to wait for pieces of two-hundred-year-old granite blocks to stop raining down from the sky before it was safe to move. And the devastating blows came one after another from that moment onward. Discovering that he had lost some of his best men. Learning that his high-profile prisoners had vanished into thin air. Seeing the ruin of the Globe Theater, which he thought of as a parting slap from the Americans. So much had occurred during the chaos. He hated chaos.

The king, still mired in his own misery, blamed Cork for the mess, and insisted on an immediate solution to repairing it. Because half the wall was blown out, prisoners who remained behind in locked quarters were having to be shifted to other places. And the river side, the most obvious side of the fortress, was a ruin. Any visitor to the capital city would see it and laugh.

Charles felt humiliated. If Boyle could have laid hands on Strafford, Cromwell, or any of the missing Tower guards, he would have run them through with his own sword.

What did amaze him was that literally no one was killed in the blast. To him, that meant that there was a widespread conspiracy with nearly everyone informed as to what parts of the palace grounds to avoid and when. As large as the Tower was, the catastrophe was big enough to have injured or killed at least a few innocent souls, but no one seemed to have been in the way when it fell. Organizing funds for the repairs was only part of his duty. He had to find and punish the guilty, and in a public manner that would satisfy the king's—and his—thirst for revenge.

At last, the king released his ministers to leave, to go back to their job of governing the nation, since Charles scarcely showed an inclination to do so. Boyle concealed a sigh of relief as he and the others bowed and backed out of the room. Sharing a look of sympathy with the Lord High Admiral, he turned toward the corridor in the direction of his office. Courtiers bowed to him as he passed. He regarded them with a cool inclination of his head, and kept moving.

Though the king was paying no attention to the many responsibilities he had, that did not mean at all that suits and petitions ceased to come in from all quarters. That, on top of all the other tasks Boyle needed to shoulder, was just one more grievance he could not and never would air. Uppermost in his mind remained the investigation into the explosion and who may have been involved.

So many people had come to and gone from London during that time that it was virtually impossible to trace all of them, but he tried. Boyle felt in his bones that there must be a connection between Whitehall and the Tower. His investigation covered anyone who had visited or been seen in the Tower during the weeks before the escape. He even sent a man northward to Sutherland to interview the Scottish noblewoman who was dismissed from court shortly before the disaster. But she had taken no one north with her but an elderly couple. His agent returned with no satisfactory information. She had no reason to take vengeance upon the king, nor did she have any connection that he could determine to Strafford or Cromwell. She had visited the Americans at least once, according to one of the cooks who served the residences in the Tower, but so had dozens of others who had business in Whitehall. It was as much a form of entertainment to the denizens of court as seeing the wild animals or an execution on Tyburn Hill.

The Scotswoman had also been spotted speaking to a merchant's daughter in the anteroom to the court in Whitehall, another petitioner. Cork had cudgeled his brain to recall whether he had interacted with the girl, and flipped through his files of correspondence. Yes, impoverished gentry, no one of moment. She had asked for help with taxes on behalf of her father. Not much to go on there. He had also checked the tax rolls. Sir Timothy de Beauchamp, baronet of Churnet and Trent had paid up within the month's grace he had been given. Probably sold off some assets to make that quarter-day payment. Boyle vowed to keep an eye on the de Beauchamps; if perhaps there was a chance to seize the estates when they failed to make the following year's tax payments, he would swoop down at once. For the crown, of course.

"My lord?" His secretary, Phillip Haymill, knocked on the open door.

"Yes, Haymill?" Boyle looked up at him. The pale-faced man had worked in the palace for years in other capacities than serving the chancellor. Boyle had been inclined when he took office to make a clean sweep of anyone who might have had any doings with or sympathy for Strafford. If there had been grumbles about the changeover, he had not heard any of them. Haymill had been a minor functionary in acquiring supplies for several ministries, and was known to be good at organization.

"Mr. Logan is here, sir. And there are," Haymill consulted a folded note, "thirty-two petitioners in the anteroom awaiting your pleasure."

"Send Logan in." Boyle said. Briefly, he consulted the correspondence on his desk. Nothing that demanded his immediate attention. In a moment, a man with thinning brown hair under an old-fashioned hood arrived. Boyle waved him to the seat on the other side of the desk.

Logan leaned across the leather-topped table. "No joy in the East End," he said, without preamble. "Those carts we found out in the marshes of which I told ye, none will claim them. They're about clapped out. The markin's on 'em, one I found the owner's name and went to him, a seller of wines and spirits, Hawkins. He says he sold the cart on, three, four weeks back. Knows nowt o' where it's been since. The other's like an old tart. Everyone's 'ad her, and nobody knows who 'ad her last. But the barges," here Logan's eyes gleamed, "cut adrift downstream. 'Ad to claim them back from the salvagers. Cost ye five pounds in all, sir. I've got witnesses to say that they were the crafts that went downstream loaded with men and women on the morning of the explosion. One in good condition, markin's says it goes back to a Master Bywell in the warehouses. Agent for a number o' merchants. Gave me lip, 'e did, fought back furious when I pressed 'im about aught to do with the Tower catastrophe. Didn't like bein' accused of anything."

Boyle knew what Logan meant by "pressed." It didn't amount to torture, but came just short of leaving visible bruises. If he was an ordinary man, Bywell would hold no secrets back only to make the discomfort stop before it ascended to pain.

"I would not have trusted his word. Did you search his premises?"

"'Course I searched! Warehouses, outbuildings, even his house. Me and my men couldn't find a trace of gunpowder or nothin' to connect him, and we looked everywhere. Not a thing. Dead end. And 'e wants 'is barge back, if you please, claimin' I has 'no right to retain his property.'"

"Give it to him," Boyle said. "And charge him the five pounds for its safe return." He made a note of Bywell's name. "Keep an eye on this merchants' agent. He may know more than he says." Something about Logan's account of the man's smug regard irritated Boyle. His instinct told him not to simply turn his back. The boat had, after all, been involved. If only the cursed thing could talk! "That will be all, Logan."

"Yes, my lord." The man bowed and removed himself from the office. Haymill would pay him what was agreed.

Boyle stared into space. Every avenue that he had explored thus far had not yielded any useful information. He would not back down, nor would he stop looking for co-conspirators. One day, he vowed, he would lay hands on those who had blown up the Tower and turned faithful guards into traitors.

In the meanwhile, he needed to mollify the nobility and gentry on the king's behalf. Across the country, more every day were agitating to have Charles recall Parliament. But, owing to the king's reading of future histories, he was absolutely unwilling to do so. Even polite pressure from overseas allies was proving no match for Charles' obduracy. He feared the headsman's sword, as well he should. Cork himself was afraid of what would happen to both the king and to himself if there was an uprising. It had happened, or would have happened. The twisting of history was such a conundrum that the Laocoön himself would find it too convoluted. But the dramatis personae were there still. And the greatest agitator and future tyrant and regicide, Oliver Cromwell, was now at large. He could summon up supporters, wherever he had gone. Too many people knew the contents of the Americans' books.

It was better to keep agitation down, by whatever means he had at his disposal. Some of them disliked having their voices muted, citing Magna Carta. They were all talk, and he could ignore them. Some refused to pay their taxes. The de Beauchamp wench that spoke to him the previous April, wanted to pay, but claimed they couldn't. That might or might not be true. She wasn't alone in that claim. Perhaps it was time to start confiscating the lands or chattels of those who had fallen behind on their remittance to the crown and were loudest in their protests over being disenfranchised. A few examples would no doubt make the others fall in line. He had a whole company of mercenaries still in his employ. Some he had sent abroad, but the others here could earn their keep by applying a listening ear to find out which ones were truly loyal, and which ones might cause trouble and pay heed to Cromwell, should he approach any of them. Boyle often found that sending a few bully boys into trouble spots kept larger problems from arising. But that took money, so shaking down the northern lords and gentlemen for the cash to pay the mercenaries for keeping them under His Majesty's thumb seemed almost poetic.

He called for Haymill to summon his captains.

# Chapter 7

### *April 1635*

"Dear Mother..." Margaret de Beauchamp chewed on the end of her pen, a wooden stick with a metal nib that just barely held the ink in its pin-hole reservoir. She tapped it on a waste paper, then scratched out a few more words on the dainty, pale blue pages that had been a travel gift from their neighbor in Barlaston, Lady Pierce. "I'm safe and well. This letter will not reach you until after the *Meadowlark* returns to Liverpool, but I am keeping my word to write every day to you. Our journey southward was unremarkable. Thank you for the anise sweets. Hettie hid them from me as a surprise until we were aboard and settled. I'm not certain how long the voyage will take, but the weather is fine. The captain hopes the sunshine will continue at least a few days."

What more was there to say? She had written almost the same for the last few days, and the stack of paper grew apace. It would be quite a journal by the time she reached her destination, albeit a sadly repetitive one. She couldn't voice her inward concerns about what lay ahead of her, as well as what lay behind her.

After her visit to London the previous spring, she had told only her father about the bargain she had struck with Harry Lefferts. At first, he had been delighted with the sum of three hundred pounds, which had satisfied the tax burden on the manor and the woolens produced by their flocks and weavers, then the two of them realized that Margaret had struck a devil's bargain. Between them, they had concocted a fairy tale of a windfall from a noble benefactor. When friends pushed for more details, they offered apologetic shrugs to explain their silence. Such a boon was not unknown, and their friends didn't want the de Beauchamps to suffer repercussions should the secret benefactor become known.

Margaret assured him that no connection could be made between the disappearance of His Majesty's "guests" from the Tower and Margaret's visit to an East End tavern. Master Bywell and his friends had been well paid for their silence. They did not talk to strangers about a pair of carts and two days' use of a pair of barges. She prayed that none of them would even countenance reporting a rumor that the employer of their employer had played a role in treason against the crown, even nearly a year after the event. Margaret's stomach turned at the terrible stories she had heard about torture and execution for such perpetrators. She knew that humble men would not be accorded comfortable quarters in the Tower, but strung up on Tyburn Hill for the amusement of the mob. She and her father, however, would not escape humiliation as well as bankruptcy before being dispatched. The sight of the headman's block in the yard at the center of the Tower played a prominent role in her nightmares.

The hearty cries of the sailors going about their tasks distracted her into looking out of the window of irregular, wavy glass set into the door of the captain's cabin where she had taken refuge. Her quarters, such as they were, were in a small chamber belowdecks that she shared with her servant Hettie and a massive chest containing pistols, balls, wadding, and shot for the two swivel guns mounted aboard the merchant ship bearing her towards the Germanies. They hadn't a window there, but they could have pulled open the port for air. Should the *Meadowlark* have been threatened by pirates, she and Hettie would have been evacuated even farther below decks, into the noisome and cramped crew quarters and guarded there, among the hanging hammocks and cargo, until danger passed. She never went down there at other times. The smell was worse than a barnyard: dung from the animals mixed with the sweat of unwashed sailors' bodies, pitch, lamp oil, rotting fish, and a hundred other odors. Margaret's eyes watered every time she went past a ship's ladder. She shook her head and stared off into space to compose the next line in her letter.

Her brother James, his face ridiculously distorted by the glass, appeared at the door and waved. She waved back, but not before he disappeared again. Margaret laughed. James was ship's lieutenant on the *Meadowlark*, but primary negotiator to find buyers for their goods when the ship made harbor. Young he might be to take the position of a ship's lieutenant at eighteen, but he was his father's son and his sister's brother. The *Meadowlark* was forty percent owned by the de Beauchamps, and someday would be his own to captain. If. If all went well, and the family suffered no more downturns. Her journey was intended to help prevent the current threat.

James' light brown hair, a twin to hers, was scraped back in a queue bound with leather ties and pitch, as most of the sailors wore theirs. He had told his family, with great glee, how the boiled pine tar helped keep down vermin.

"The ticks just fall off and die when they touch it," he had explained over dinner, his hands imitating the insects going belly-up. Their mother had insisted that she was going to faint at the mention of vermin, but that was her response to anything that made her even the least bit queasy.

Thinking of that, Margaret was glad in that she took after her father's side of the family. The de Beauchamps had first come to England in the train of William the Conqueror. Her first ancestor in this country was Guillaume, Sieur de Beauchamp, who captained a ship of soldiers and engineers, and had been given a small manor in the Sussex after the war ended. The family stories claimed Guillaume could stand at the bow of a storm-tossed ship and never feel the bucking waves.

Lucky for her that both she and Hettie proved immune to sea-sickness. The other passengers for Hamburg, a Dutch merchant and his wife, had spent the entire journey so far in the junior officers' cabin, heaving up even the least bites of food or sips of water. Hettie had kindly helped to nurse them, as their manservant seemed worse than useless without cookshops to procure viands or apothecaries to mix soothing draughts. Margaret spared a moment's thought for her mother, for whom she was the apothecary to hand when such was needed. Poor Mother!

The rest of the ship's complement consisted of sailors, deck hands, and the three officers: James, the lieutenant; First Mate Owen Latimer, James' superior officer; and Master Adam Forest, captain of the *Meadowlark* and a minor partner in a consortium of merchants, including Margaret's father, Sir Timothy, which owned the ship and a few small concerns both on the continent and in

Great Britain. There was a second lieutenant, but he had remained behind in Liverpool to recover from a fever. The *Meadowlark* also played host to twenty-two Irish mercenaries who were on their way to offer their services to the United States of Europe. They were friendly fellows, who had paid for part of their passage by helping out on the ship. They "dossed down," as James put it, with the ordinary crew, but spent their free time in the evenings playing music on deck, drinking, and gossiping like a flock of goodwives. They had very much adopted Hettie as their muse, and sang songs that made the girl blush. Margaret, they treated like a precious votive statue. She rather envied her maidservant the easy interaction with the bluff (and some very handsome) soldiers with their lilting voices and easy attitude.

The noise outside settled down to the usual buzz of conversation among the sailors and the thump-swish of the mop or paintbrush on the endless maintenance of a ship. Ships were like horses. They ate their heads off whether they were needed for a task or not. Margaret sighed. She wondered whether her family would have to sell their interest in it after this journey or whether they could keep it. All depended upon the kindness of no longer strangers, but friends. She had a tremendous favor to ask. Again.

Almost a year had passed since her memorable visit to London. None but Hettie and Percy, who had remained behind at home, knew all the details of her connection to the daring and much storied escape from the Tower by the Americans and most of the yeoman guards, not to mention other prisoners like the dastardly Oliver Cromwell and the disgraced Thomas Wentworth.

She still felt a tingle of excitement when she thought of Harry Lefferts, the dashing and handsome agent who had enlisted her aid, and put into her hands the means to rescue her family's estates from being seized for taxes. Not that she would have welcomed him as husband or lover, but he was so unlike any other man she had ever known. She had described him to her mother, who sighed deeply as though she was watching a romantic play. Harry had the confidence and daring of the Devil, Mother had said, but with a shake of her head and a rueful smile. And the generosity of an angel, Margaret thought but didn't say. She knew that her friend Rita Simpson had told him exactly what sum the de Beauchamps needed, and he'd had it handed over without ceremony.

In June of 1634, on a chance that Rita had returned safely to Magdeburg, Margaret had written to her in care of Government House. To her delight, Rita wrote back, her news couched in terms that Margaret understood, but would be incomprehensible gossip to anyone who intercepted it. She was not in Magdeburg, which she abbreviated as M., but in Ingolstadt with her husband, Tom, who had been stationed there, a city that held at least a few merchants from every trading nation in Europe. She gave a new address to which letters could be sent without problem.

The two of them had carried on a warm correspondence since then. Americans were still not welcomed in England, so Rita had offered Margaret an open invitation to visit Magdeburg, promising to introduce her to many more "friends" (in other words, Americans) and show her wonders beyond a flashlight. Margaret still kept that hidden away in an embroidered pocket held by tapes underneath her skirts.

With her father's blessing, she had written, in obscured language, profuse thanks for the gold. What she had done in exchange amounted to so little. Rita assured her that the favors were more than equivalent—in fact, she held that Margaret's contribution far outweighed Harry's. Margaret was often frustrated by having to communicate in ciphers, but letters could be and often were intercepted and read, maybe even copied, long before they could reach the recipient. As the child of a merchant, she knew that spies were everywhere, in every field of endeavor. Information had as much currency as any coin or item.

But much of their letters were friendly missives full of family gossip and notes about everyday life. Margaret sent anecdotes and funny stories of personalities of the people of the manor, and how they celebrated holidays and feast days. Rita began to teach her basic phrases in Amideutsch, the combination language that the Americans and native Germans used to communicate. Margaret treasured her letters. She told her family that Rita was merely someone she had met in London, like Lady Ann. Once she invoked the name of her noble friend from the north, her mother and sisters assumed Rita was a wealthy Englishwoman who was married to a landsknecht or a higher rank in the Germanies and traveled hither and yon, and had a brother of high rank in government service. Only her father, and now James, knew the truth.

She sighed and blew on the ink of her letter. One of the adages that Rita had quoted in a letter had become Margaret's newest motto: no good deed goes unpunished. Having been gifted the sum to rescue the family estates for one quarter, Sir Timothy had thrown himself with the best of goodwill into managing the wool trade to make certain they would never again have to rely on the kindness of others. They sold everything that the weavers could make, and shipped fleeces overseas for slightly more than it cost to ship them. Net profit was better than no profit. But he, and Margaret, could see another shortfall in the not-too-distant future.

The winter had been a wet one, and they lost many lambs. Numerous sheep had also fallen ill with the foot-fell, an infection that damaged their hooves. Sheep were distressingly delicate with regard to their health, and the shepherds were frantic trying to keep their charges alive. Their efforts were on the largest part successful, but the recovering sheep's pelts reflected their wintertime illness. The shearing had produced thinner fleeces than usual, hence the income from the flocks was smaller than expected. The Weavers' Guild began to talk about taking action against the de Beauchamps, and even moving to other districts to ply their trade if their wages were not paid in full.

Sir Timothy had pleaded with them to be patient. He did the best he could to make do, yet it seemed no matter how many leaks he plugged in the family accounts, another one sprang into being. He began to entertain offers for some of their land, until both Margaret and James pointed out that it would be like scooping away his underfooting until none was left, and the family would have no income whatsoever. Another appeal to the crown had no way of succeeding, since the Earl of Cork was still firmly ensconced in Whitehall, and the king showed no interest in ruling.

Again, they found themselves in the position of promising funds that they had not yet earned with no hope of ever catching up again. Something needed to be done.

A recently received letter from Rita Simpson put an idea into Margaret's head. She remembered Rita's kindly offer to have her visit, as well as the possibility of introducing her brother to the Prime Minister of the USE purchasing cloth for uniforms, and sent a subtly worded missive in reply suggesting she would like to see Magdeburg and ask the advice of the *up-timers*, a word she had only learned since encountering Rita in the Tower.. She didn't want to sound as though she was begging, though her heart was in her boots when she handed off the letter to a merchant who was taking ship from Liverpool for London two weeks from then, and onward to the continent.

To her relief and delight, Rita was thrilled to be able to host her young friend. From her return letter, Margaret saw that the American understood her plight all too clearly, and was again willing to help in whatever way she could. Lady Mailey was abroad, but promised on her next journey home to set aside the books for Margaret to read, and perhaps even to borrow. Rita was still in Ingolstadt, but if Margaret could tell her when she wanted to visit, Rita would be happy to make a trip home to meet her, and—Margaret could hardly believe such an honor—host her in the Presidential Palace.

She had brought the notion to her father. Sir Timothy was red-faced with shame at having to rely upon the kindness of strangers. Margaret did not want to hurt his pride further than it already had been damaged, but both knew it was the most likely avenue to keep the manor intact. Hundreds of years had the de Beauchamps brought quality woolen cloth to market. Both of them hated to think that his would be the final stewardship.

Her father argued that the journey would be perilous. Margaret argued that Rita had promised her safety from Hamburg onward and back again. She had so many opportunities awaiting her in the USE. The promised books on weaving would be at her disposal. She had paper in plenty sealed into an oilcloth package so she could copy details down for the use of the guild. Some of the master weavers were enthusiastic about seeing into the future, while others condemned anything to do with Grantville and the Americans as coming straight from the Devil. Margaret suspected that once the details were put before their faces, the weavers would forget their misgivings. Anything that gave the Barlaston guild a leg up over their competitors in other towns was not to be scorned. Sir Timothy still refused. But when James promised that he would escort Margaret safely, Sir Timothy finally gave his consent.

Her mother was less easily persuaded, but Margaret had dropped the lofty titles of her new friends copiously into conversation, reminding her that Rita and her brother were people of note. Mother was worried about her safety, and whether Margaret was sufficiently well trained not to embarrass the family among nobility. Lady Pierce had taken umbrage at that thought, as she herself had trained Margaret to appear in the court of St. James. At last, her mother gave permission, and Margaret had made arrangements to go.

She signed the letter of the day to her mother, noting with dismay how brief it was, and folded it up to seal with one round of wax and the carnelian ring that her father's mother had bequeathed to her. The carved bezel had the image of a sheep with a bell around its neck. Tucking the letter into her box with the others, she brought out a book bound in black calfskin and embossed with the dullest possible title imaginable to her: *Mathematical Proofs of Geometry and Trigonometry.* All of the ship's officers had seen her perusing it, and teased her a bit about becoming a scholar. She was, indeed, attempting scholarship, but it was Rita's letters on the Magdeburg language she was studying, not the means of calculating angles. Each phrase had been written out in both the Amideutsch and transliterated syllable by syllable into Rita's American English. "*Danke,*" she whispered, careful that no one else was near enough to hear her. "*Danke schoen.*"

She hoped fervently she could make herself understood in the newest part of the Old World. Not long ago, she had met a Frenchman at one of Lady Pierce's dinner parties. She tried out the language as imparted by her teacher, and was embarrassed to discover that her tutor had no ear for the accent, and her pronunciations caused the well-dressed foreign gentleman to purse his lips together to stop from laughing. Rita would be kind, she knew, but who could speak for the others she might meet? Best to grow a thick hide and prepare as best she could. Her pride was going to suffer enough as it was. James could speak the German tongue as well as a number of others with whom the *Meadowlark* traded, and had a few words of Amideutsch, but she couldn't steal his time away from his duties except during meals.

Her last instructions from Rita were as strange as the words in the new language. "Take the steam tug," the American had written. "There will be a ticket waiting for you."

Hettie came into the cabin bearing a pitcher and a plate. Margaret had to jump up to hold the door open so her maidservant could enter. Hettie found an empty spot on the table to place her burden down. Her face was flushed red.

"Are you well?" Margaret asked her.

"Ah, it's those Irishmen," Hettie said, looking righteously indignant. "They're incorrigible."

"They appreciate a pretty girl," Margaret said, and watched Hettie's cheeks dimple. But she kept her stern demeanor.

"Well, they daren't flirt with you, and Frau de Kuiper has been ill this entire time, so they're not overburdened with choices."

"Do not denigrate yourself," Margaret said. "Isn't Oliver Mason still calling upon you?"

Now Hettie blushed in truth. That tall young man had definitely been appearing regularly at the kitchen door of the manor house on the maid's days off. Margaret favored her with an indulgent smile. She enjoyed a good love story. And it helped to pass the time to have appreciative gentlemen paying attention to oneself.

# Chapter 8

Margaret sat on a half-barrel against the side of the stern cabin with an open book in her lap. The west coast of Wales was passing by at five knots, according to James' calculations. They were making good time. She couldn't help but admire the distant green mountains, and the smoke-wreathed towns and cities on the coastline. Hettie perched on a box beside her, mending a stocking with deft stitches around a wooden egg.

For lack of other occupation, the mercenaries had formed up and were doing drills together, with canvas wound around their swords to keep from cutting one another. Perhaps two in three had seen some real action, and the rest were youngsters from the country who were escaping from a hard life behind a plow.

"Yer all eedjits!" Ian Callaghan shouted at the group. A good-looking fellow with long, fair hair from just west of Dublin, he had taken on the role of commander. No doubt he would be a fine officer with some training. "Discipline! You'll all be kilt first time ye get jumped by a Dane! Hold up yer guard, ye fools! Now, try again."

The muffled clatter of sword on sword formed a rhythm in Margaret's ears. She turned another page in her book, and read halfway down, until she heard her First Mate Owen Latimer's voice.

"Sir!"

Curiously, she peered around the side of the cabin. Latimer rushed to Master Adam Forest, and pointed out over the starboard side of the ship. The captain hurried to the rail. Margaret stood up to see what he was looking at.

In the distance, another ship was approaching. It was smaller than the *Meadowlark*, but carried more sail. They'd seen all sorts of craft plying the Irish Sea; it was a busy waterway, serving all the ports from Penzance up to Fort William in Scotland. This one was moving much faster than they were, perhaps seven or eight knots, and looked as if it intended to intersect with them.

Forest looked alarmed. "Look at those sails. Almost sure to be pirates!"

Margaret peered at the approaching ship. She had not noticed before, but the newcomer's sails seemed as if they had been patched together time and again. The *Meadowlark* sported a patch or two, but these looked ragged. Pirates! Hettie had heard the word, too, and clutched her mending to her chest.

"Shall I have the men take up arms, sir?" Latimer asked. "We'll be outnumbered."

Though it was still far away, Margaret could now pick out the shapes on the deck, and her heart sank. The small ship was crowded to the gunwales with men!

Forest looked as though he was about to speak. By then, the Irishmen had stopped their sparring to see what was going on. The captain looked them up and down, and a broad smile broke out on his face.

"We'll not be, but they won't know that. You lot!" he called to the mercenaries. "In approximately half of the hour, we will be encountering hostile forces. Arm yourselves, but don't show yourselves right away. We have the opportunity for the element of surprise!"

They stared at him, not moving an inch. Margaret tried to will them to spring into action. Why were they not moving?

A small knot of the soldiers formed around Ian Callaghan, talking and waving their arms. In a moment, he patted the air to quiet them, then stepped forward to meet the captain.

"Mr. Forest, it's a fine situation in which you find yourselves, but we are soldiers for pay. What will you give us to defend you?"

Hettie looked shocked. She had clearly expected them to stand forth like gentlemen, but Margaret knew they were businessmen first and foremost. She put her hand on Hettie's arm to keep her from making an outburst. The captain never lost his smile. He was a businessman, too. He understood that the mercenaries were negotiating because they could. They were passengers, not crew under Forest's command. They had a right to ask for wages befitting their worth. If it was not such a serious situation, she would have enjoyed watching the bargaining.

"Pay, is it?" the captain asked, rolling back on the heels of his sea boots. He consulted the air, then met Callaghan's eyes. "Well, how about an extra measure of gin in exchange for your service? Or whiskey. We've got that, too. Your choice."

"One?" Ian asked, weighing the offer. "Each?"

"Of course, bloody each," Forest said. "What good's a sip do a man, eh?"

The knot formed again, then Ian emerged from it.

"Two measures each, and you have yourself a bargain."

"Two. Done and done." The captain put out his hand, and Ian shook it. He smiled.

"Now, what's the plan?"

The captain outlined his idea. Margaret listened with open admiration. This was not an unknown experience for the crew, she realized. She trembled for her brother's sake, knowing that he had faced pirates before, but not with the same advantage as on that day.

The Irishmen unwrapped the canvas from their swords and went below for their pistols. All but a few were to stay below until summoned. The captain called for the rest of his crew, James and the five able seamen.

Latimer emerged from the officers' quarters with a heavy box and distributed pistols to the crew, along with powder and balls. James brought forth cutlasses and made sure each man had one.

He noticed his sister and her maidservant watching, and his eyes widened in alarm. He waved sharply at them.

"Get below!" he ordered them. "Don't get in the way."

Margaret and Hettie gathered up their goods and moved into the doorway of the captain's cabin. Two of the crew ran to the swivel guns, one mounted on the rail on either side of the ship, and loaded them. The *Meadowlark* didn't have any cannon. At the captain's order, they took their caps and coats from the cabin below and held them up on their swords. Those flapped in the wind like scarecrows which, Margaret mused, they were no doubt supposed to be. But would they fool the pirates? The sloop was fast approaching, scooping the wind in its surprisingly large sails.

"We should close the door, mistress," Hettie said, trying to pull her inside to safety.

"No, I want to see what happens," Margaret insisted. "We'll close it when we must. One door won't save us if anything goes amiss."

"Leave the sails up," Forest shouted. "You lot," he called to the Irishmen still on deck, "lie down until I give the word! Crew to the starboard rail, now! Make yourselves look like an army!"

The crew obeyed, carrying their mock companions with them. The captain stood in the middle of the poop deck, holding his coat and hat aloft.

As the sloop came closer, the crowd of pirates began to shout and wave their own cutlasses, attempting to intimidate the merchant crew. Margaret was surprised by how calm the sailors were. They exchanged grim smiles.

There was movement on the other ship. She couldn't tell what they were about until she saw the black O of a gun's barrel turned toward them. She ducked inside just in time, and heard the ROAR! as it discharged. She heard cries of pain from the crew, and hoped no one was killed. Clattering arose as the shot peppered the hull and side of the cabin with metal. Margaret and Hettie clutched each other. She dared to peer out the crack in the door.

The captain's coat had a hole in its back, and his elegant hat had been knocked off onto the deck. The first mate's coat now lacked a sleeve. Two of the crew near the deck had red running down the arms of their white linen shirts, but they were not down. They shouted defiance at the pirates. The sails flapped loudly overhead. Some of the debris had punched holes in them, slowing down the merchant ship.

But the attackers had launched another onslaught as well. When the gun fired, the ships had come into contact, one hull slamming into the other. Margaret and Hettie were thrown off their feet by the impact.

Huge metal hooks came flying over the rail of the ship. Just as swiftly, they bit into the wood, and went taut. They had grappled onto the *Meadowlark*! Margaret handed herself up, hanging onto the knob of the door.

"Fire!" Forest shouted.

The swivel guns reported, with a noise between a pop and a roar. Clouds of black smoke rose and retreated astern with the wind, but not before the acrid smell made Margaret's eyes water. On the pirate ship, a handful of men went down. The others paid them no mind. Half a dozen leaped up onto their own rail, preparing to board. The pirate deck guns fired one more rally.

"Close the door, mistress!" Hettie shrieked.

The pirates leaped over the rail and onto the deck of the merchant ship. They wore ragged, dirty clothes, their hair clubbed back like James' but greasy. Nearly all of them were barefoot. Margaret thought most of them looked English or Irish, but a few had the darker complexion of Spaniards, even a couple of Africans. They chopped at the crewmen near the rail. More of their number swarmed up, preparing to board.

"Now!" Captain Forest shouted, freeing his cutlass.

Like spring traps, the crewmen and the mercenaries who had been lying on the deck leaped to their feet and fired their muskets at the invaders. Four of the pirates fell immediately, and their fellows leaped on their bodies onto the deck.

They regretted their action, for the rest of the Irish soldiers swarmed up out from belowdecks, firing their muskets as they came. They and the crew unlimbered their swords, and charged the pirates. They were met by raised cutlasses and knives, and it turned into a bloody clash.

Margaret felt grim pleasure at the astonished look on the faces of the invaders. They had expected only the crew to be on board, that was to be sure. One look at the superior force facing them, and as many pirates as were still on their feet leaped back over the rail. They began hacking at the ropes holding the grappling hooks in place.

"Fire!" Captain Forest called out again. The swivel guns spoke, peppering the pirate ship with small but deadly shot. More of the invaders fell. Margaret heard screams of pain.

The mercenaries rushed toward the other ship. A couple of them leaped up on the rail, swords raised.

"Come back!" Forest shouted. "We don't need the ship!"

Ian Callaghan raised his arm, then swept it down. The mercenaries pulled back, swords still raised.

"Let the cowards cut and run!" he shouted. "To me, men of Dublin!"

The pirate vessel, now holed in its sails and the side of the hull facing the *Meadowlark*, turned its rudder and fled on the wind to the southwest, putting as much distance between the two ships as quickly as it could. Ian and his men jeered after them. The pirate's deck was no longer as crowded as it had been. Margaret estimated that they had lost a third or a half of their number.

On board the *Meadowlark*, Captain Forest ordered his crew to throw the dead pirates overboard. No survivors remained.

"Hell's bells, but you'll have to mend those, James," Forest said, peering up at the ragged tears in the sails. He picked up his coat and hat from the deck. "And my coat! Look at that ruin of a fine garment."

"I'll mend it for you," Margaret said. The captain glanced at her.

"I ordered you below deck, my lady. But I'll take the kindness as your penance."

"Yes, Captain," she said, meekly. She was nearly breathless from the excitement of the moment. In retrospect, she was grateful that things had not gone amiss.

"Who needs physicking?" Forest shouted out. A few of the mercenaries and two of the crew made their way forward. Ian Callaghan stepped up, clutching the sleeve of his coat.

"I was wounded in your service, captain!" he said, his voice a pathetic wail.

Forest moved his hand and looked at the slash in the two layers of fabric and the flesh underneath. "Pah. Nothing that a bandage and a tot of gin wouldn't cure."

Hettie came forward with a roll of clean linen already in her hand. Ian looked down at her with a smile.

"At least someone takes my pain seriously."

Hettie blushed. She and Margaret helped to bind up the wounds of the few who had been injured by the pirates' cutlasses, and sew up torn shirts for the others. None of the wounds were serious. She and her maid were full of praise for the men's heroism. Though the captain still chided them for not locking themselves away safely, even he was pleased to receive the flattery for saving the ship so cleverly. Margaret thought she even saw Ian Callaghan steal a kiss from Hettie after she mended his shirt and coat.

The crew had to pry pieces of metal from the walls of the cabins and the side of the hull. Margaret almost laughed at the strange assortment of iron scrap that had been used as cannon fodder. The two gunners cleaned their weapons and stowed away the extra ammunition in the chest in her cabin. In little time, the *Meadowlark* was trim and fit again.

"Ah, that's the way of it!" Forest said, shrugging into his mended coat. Margaret had pieced the embroidery back together again with deft stitches. "I'm proud of the lot of you! Gentlemen!" he addressed the Irish soldiers. "Thank you for your service in saving my ship! Extra gin for all!"

The crew cheered.

# Chapter 9

The *Meadowlark* docked at last in Hamburg, after the rest of the journey had been uneventful. The seas had relaxed somewhat as the weather warmed, though never attained the ease of silk that her brother had promised her. At least, the spring day was bright and sunny, with only a few billowy clouds decorating the sky. The ailing Netherlanders were helped ashore by a group of barefoot deckhands. These kindly kept any comments to themselves, and wished the pair a good journey home. The man, much thinner than he had been at the outset of the voyage, offered small coins to each of them. He and his wife had never emerged during the pirate attack, and had queried why the ship had felt as though it had bumped into something while plying the Irish Sea. The captain was very glad to see them go.

James himself led other hands in helping Margaret and Hettie to debark with all their luggage. He reached into his own pouch to distribute tips to his fellow crew. Margaret thanked them all warmly. Hettie said fond farewells to a few, including Ian and a couple of the other Irish soldiers. Margaret was amused to watch them swarm her. Her maid may have been considered plain of face, but her charm brought her numerous admirers and friends, more than Margaret had, if truth be told. She loved Hettie dearly, and was pleased to see others appreciate her.

"This way!" James said. "Your bags will follow us when the carter is free." He had put on shoes to come ashore, and his clubbed hair was freshly washed in seawater. Margaret couldn't wait to reach her hostelry and have a bath.

The quay teemed with men and a very few women, all in workaday woolens and linens, mostly dyed in shades of brown, dark green, ecru, and black. Here and there, Margaret spotted some clothes in surprisingly vivid colors, almost always on the backs of folk who walked with an air of inner confidence that she had come to associate with the Americans. She even spotted three who wore the blue denim of Rita's enviable skirt. Margaret assessed the locals as she passed. They couldn't all have been folk from the future, as Rita and her family each seemed to have brilliantly intact smiles, and most of the people here brandished teeth in shades from yellow to black, often with large gaps in between. She made a note to ask what the connection might be between the two groups when she had a chance to sit down with her friends.

Little fashionable clothing was to be seen in the busy streets immediately adjacent to the port, nor inland a street or so to where the inn was located. These domiciles housed people of the working class. The gentry must have been farther inland and uphill. Margaret stuck close behind her brother, keeping her cloak from brushing the narrow stone walls, daubed as they were with grime and lichen. A donkey-drawn cart that looked far too wide for the passage came barreling toward them with a stout, red-faced man on the seat. James pulled both of them up a stone stoop and into a doorway to make way. The gray-feathered geese in the woven cages on the wagon hissed at them as he passed.

"It's as bad as the Shambles!" Margaret exclaimed. The legendary maze of streets in York had been one of her first trips out of Stoke with their father.

"Smells nicer, though," James said. "You'll learn soon enough that England falls behind the continent in cleanliness. Here we are."

Washington's Crossing was the name of the inn, and the image on the large painted hanging sign was one that Margaret had seen reproduced in a penny paper: a man in a tricornered hat and wrapped in a fluttering cloak standing in the bow of a rowboat. Although histories that had come from the future identified the man as the first president of the United States, she didn't truly see how Mike Stearns connected to George Washington. Again, more questions. She hoped she could remember to ask about everything she wanted to know. Lady Mailey would be put to the test, in sooth. Apart from that, it was nothing fancy at all. Inside, a host of men, some in naval uniforms but most of them in the same kind of garments as James, sat at long, rough-planked tables, drinking from tall ceramic cups that had hinged lids, and pulling bread and meat from platters to eat in hearty mouthfuls.

"Herr de Beauchamp!" A round-cheeked woman with blonde braids wound over her ears beamed at James and set her tray down on the nearest table. That was the last of the words that Margaret could understand as the lady swooped down on James and enveloped him in a powerful hug. James emitted a few phrases in German too rapid to follow. The lady let him go and wrapped her arms around Margaret in a rib-cracking embrace. Hettie stayed a pace behind, as was proper, but the lady hugged her, too.

"*Wilkommen!*" the blonde woman boomed, setting them back on their feet.

"I didn't know this was a custom in the Germanies," Margaret gasped, getting her breath back.

James laughed. "Frau Engelmann is an old friend! On my first voyage here, she took pity on a poor, confused English sailor boy who got lost in these streets, gave me a square meal and my first words in Deutsch. Her cooking's well known in these parts. It's plain but very good."

They took seats at a table that was under the open window. Though a brisk and cool breeze came in from the direction of the sea, Margaret was glad to sit on something that wasn't moving. The sturdy wooden bench underneath her had been worn smooth from use, and the tabletop bore the results of countless bored patrons with knives. "*Ich lieve Freya,*" which even Margaret could tell was misspelled, lay at the edge closest to her right hand.

Frau Engelmann arrived and set down a tray with a thump. She dealt out three of the massive earthenware cups and placed a platter between them laden with food.

"Wurst, sauerkraut, bread of course, and roasted potatoes," James explained. He took his knife from his belt and speared a mighty grilled sausage on the tip. He bit into it with every expression of pleasure. "Have some!" he added, through a mouthful. Margaret didn't bother to chide him for poor table manners.

"When in Rome, do as the Romans do," had been quoted to her time and again by Lady Pierce. Though it originated from a Papist saint, it seemed very sound advice.

She and Hettie had their own utensils they carried wrapped in a cloth in Hettie's reticule. With careful knife and fork, Margaret sawed a piece from one of the sausages and sampled it. The spices were unfamiliar but very savory.

"It is delicious," she declared, urging Hettie to help herself. The maid reluctantly took a small piece of meat. Her eyes widened as the flavor touched her tongue. Hettie needed no further urging, and though she waited for her mistress to take food first, she dined heartily. Even the sauerkraut, spiced with caraway seeds, was met with wordless sounds of approval.

"Their bread is heavy, but it is as good as anything Mistress Barden makes in Barlaston!"

Hettie's words emerged in a sudden lull in the conversation. Many people glanced her way. Almost all of them went back to their private talk.

A couple of rough-looking men had come in about that moment, and took seats near the door. One had longish black hair, framing a hawklike face, and the other was rounder with fair hair. The two kept glancing at the Englishwomen. Margaret felt alarm. She remembered how vulnerable she and Hettie were, alone in a strange country. James could defend against one or two assailants, but he wasn't going to accompany her on her onward journey. She hoped that Rita's promise of safety wasn't an empty one.

Margaret swallowed her fear along with a draught of the innkeeper's ale. Her father's daughter was not going to be put in dread by a couple of strangers, who were no doubt minding their own business. She trusted that, with normal precautions, she and Hettie would find the Germanies to be as civilized as Rita promised, and that they would arrive in Grantville safely.

She lowered her voice and leaned close to James. By now, the two men had looked away, but something about them troubled her. She made a mental note of their faces.

"Do you know them?" she asked.

James essayed a casual glance toward the door.

"No one I've ever seen before. I'll ask Frau Englemann." He sauntered to the bar with a coin held between his fingers. The innkeeper met him with a smile, and exchanged a few words with him. He came back, looking relieved.

"She said they're regular customers," James explained. "They've been in for a meal the last four or five days. They give no trouble."

"That's a relief," Margaret said, and dismissed them from her mind. "Where do we find the steam tug that Mistress Rita mentioned?"

James tilted his head toward the door of the inn. "It's half a street's length downhill from here. Sooner or later, you'll hear the screeches of the ship's whistle, sounds like tortured souls. It's the great beast coming in to dock. It's one of the wonders of the world, a boat driven not by oars or wind, but by steam! It can cover ground faster than a horse can gallop and carry fifty men for miles without stopping."

Considering the tiny flashlight that she carried in her hidden pocket Margaret didn't doubt for a moment that her brother was right. She knew the Americans were capable of miracles.

The next day, after a refreshing bath and a change of clothes, James led Margaret back to the waterfront to meet the merchants with whom the *Meadowlark* traded and receive the shipment that they had brought from England. One of them, Herr Christiansen, a small, fussy man with a bulbous nose and a florid pink complexion, was dismissive of the sister of a mere ship's mate, but Herr Schwartz, long-faced and dressed all in somber black, offered her a friendly smile, and even praised her attempts to speak German and Amideutsch. Schwartz showed them around the warehouse. It had a surprisingly narrow front, but the building extended a very long way back, much like the townhouses in London. Margaret guessed that the businesses were taxed on their frontage. No limit seemed to be placed on height, though, as the ceiling swooped up at least thirty feet. The smooth wooden floors had been freshly swept, and the inventory on hand sorted with neat placards written in black ink in the difficult but beautiful German hand.

"Hey-up!" A worker looked up from assisting a customer and gestured toward the double doors.

"The delivery is here from the *Meadowlark*!" James declared. He ran to help the merchants' boys open the doors wide. A couple of oxen ambled slowly inside, drawing a heavy goods wagon laden with muslin-wrapped bales. The potent smell of lanolin rising from the fresh cloth reminded Margaret of home. Jacky, one of the deck hands, grinned at Margaret from the board and pulled the brake. The oxen, dull-eyed, came to a stolid halt.

James clambered nimbly up to the top of the pile and cut the ropes holding the bales in place with his belt knife. Together, he and the ship's hands tossed them to the ground. Each of the bales represented a legal weight of cloth as marked by the import officials, and Margaret was proud of the contents. Her family's weavers were among the best in England.

Herr Schwartz nodded to one of the employees, and the young man undid the burlap wrappings on one of the bales. Lengths of smooth ecru cloth slithered out. Schwartz and Christiansen walked around the contents, picking up one or another piece to examine it.

"You will see that this is very fine fabric," James said, holding out one length and displaying the tight weave. "Suitable for fine ladies' wear, soft even for babes. We've managed to make it as light as eiderdown."

To Margaret's dismay, the merchants seemed unimpressed, even dismissive of five months' work of forty weavers.

"It is . . . good enough," Schwartz admitted at last, although his face said otherwise.

"What would please you more, *mein herr*?" Margaret asked with concern. "I can inform my father to make whatever changes you would wish to see in future shipments."

Schwartz turned to her with a kindly expression. "Fräulein de Beauchamp, no offense is meant. It is as good as anything the local weavers make can. But the shipping from England to us to the price adds muchly—much." He smiled, wrinkling his nose as if ashamed of his imperfect grasp of English. "From Holland same, similar cloth comes, over the land. Useful and plain it is. But more cost we welcome it not."

Margaret nodded. "I understand, sir. But we offer the experience of centuries and the fleece of the finest sheep in Europe."

"Yes, yes," Schwartz said, with an impatient wave. "But our customers with their purses speak. They not the sheep nor the weavers see, only the value. Expenses and obligations we have."

By then, the bales had been offloaded. Margaret felt defeated as Herr Schwartz and Herr Christiansen turned away to the wooden desk next to the door. James joined them and began to speak in a low voice. From the drawer, Christiansen brought out a leather bag. He spilled coins into a tray and began to tell them over with careful fingers. James looked hopeful, then dismayed, even a little angry. He didn't raise his voice, but his pronunciation became more clipped. Margaret couldn't follow the rapid spate of German, but it seemed as though the merchants were trying to shortchange the sum that had previously been agreed. The discussion became heated, though no louder. It went on for a good, long time, then James glanced over his shoulder toward his sister. To Margaret's surprise, she heard the word "Americans" emerge from the unfamiliar language. The merchants' gaze followed his, and their eyebrows went up. Schwartz murmured something to his partner and gave him a fierce glance. Margaret was horrified that he would invoke her friends. He must have a good reason, or so she hoped.

With an evident show of reluctance, Christiansen pushed more coins toward James. Her brother kept his eye on the pile until it was of a size that satisfied him, if not completely. He swept the money up and tied it into a leather bag that he stowed in his belt pouch. He bowed to the two merchants and came to offer his arm to Margaret.

"What was that about?" she whispered. Keeping a smile plastered on her face, she curtsied to the two men as James drew her out to the street. "Why did you mention the Americans?"

James grinned. "I told them you are a friend to them, that you are here to visit Frau Simpson. They aren't a secret or a foe here, only at home in England. They have done a great deal of good to the people in Europe, especially in the Germanies. They're not merely a curiosity; they're neighbors, and a small merchant house like this cannot afford to make enemies of them. You have the ear of one of the most powerful of them, and that impressed Schwartz, who was able to persuade Herr Christiansen to keep his word. It might even work again next time, though I'm going to persuade Father to find another brokerage with whom to trade."

Margaret opened and closed her mouth with a snap. She had kept the story of her experiences in London so far away from her lips except among immediate family that to have them discussed openly, feared, maybe even loved, unlike at home, that it pulled her from one set of thoughts into another, newly formed one. She fell so deeply into it that James poked her in the side with a forefinger just in time for her to wake up and avoid treading into a puddle.

"What happened when you were in London is long forgotten," James said. "No one recalls the why or the wherefore, only that the Americans performed more of their magic and vanished like the myths that some still insist they are. As far as I or you know, they did it all with their mechanical wonders. Isn't that right?"

His eyes insisted, and Margaret wanted to agree. And James was right: no one needed to know how she came to become acquainted with them, only that she had. Secrets were not limited to the strangers from the future. Everyone had some things that were never discussed, yet continued to have an influence on things far from them like...like gravity. Sir Isaac Newton was yet to be born, if the future history books were accurate, but things fell to earth even without his intervention. Or hers. She hoped fervently that no one would question her connection too closely, or make assumptions that would put her and her family in peril.

"Come!" James said, taking her hand. "We will go up and buy you tickets for the boat."

Margaret doubled her pace to equal his, and Hettie hurried along behind.

She heard it long before she saw it. A plume of white steam rose over the red-tiled roofs of the buildings, and the screech of a terrified and lost soul evinced a like moan from her. She and Hettie halted, to the great annoyance of the people behind them.

"It's just the ship coming in," James said, pulling them close to the side of the walkway. The acrid smell of a tanner's shop made Margaret's eyes tear, even as she admired the colorful leathers that hung from lines looped across the doorway. "How I wish we had marvels like this in Staffordshire. Never again to be troubled by becalmed winds, or concern that the currents are not with us."

Another shriek interrupted him, and Margaret clapped her hands to her ears. This part of the future she did not like.

Her discomfort was forgotten as soon as they threaded their way down the street through the crowd to another part of the quay, where the Elbe River met the waters of the bay. This structure resembled a longhouse in the moorlands, except that it was constructed of sound red brick, similar to the warehouses that stood a little farther back from the waterside. One long door stood open to receive passengers. The other opened out upon a narrow dock. In the river adjacent sat a monster of a machine. The noise that they had heard came from an open metal mouth at the top of a tall pole at the stern of the vessel. Below it, instead of an ordinary rudder, the ship had a wheel, one half submerged in the water. It had mighty metal arms attached to it, and those led to a huge cylindrical tank.

"That's full of water," James explained, indicating the tank. "There's a furnace underneath it that is fed by coals. It produces steam that drives those arms, which propel the ship through the water."

Now that the vessel was docked, it seemed as though the crew, strong young men in dark blue coveralls, were dampening down the fire to clean out the burning chamber. A tall, bulbous chimney perched above all, belching black smoke that left smuts of soot on everything close by. On the prow was the vessel's name, *Metahelios.*

Apart from the soot, the steam tug was cleaner than her weavers' workroom. The shallow-draft vessel had a large cabin behind the wheelhouse. Margaret guessed that that was where they would stay during their journey upriver. Men in neat, dark blue wool uniforms with red flashing on the shoulders busied themselves about the ship, assisting a few important-looking passengers ashore, offloading bundles and crates, and bringing supplies, including a hefty load of coal, onboard. Their black boots were polished to a gleam, and they wore round blue caps with black bills above their eyes.

"Are they soldiers?" Hettie asked.

"Sailors," James said. "They are part of the USE navy. It's a good job for men without many skills, as long as they're willing to work hard and learn manners."

He led the way to a glass-fronted booth labeled "Information" and "Auskunft."

*"Guten tag, fräulein,"* he said to the young, brown-haired woman seated behind the glass. He held up two fingers and indicated his sister and her maidservant. *"Zwei billete for Fraulein de Beauchamp, bitte."*

The woman smiled politely at him, then glanced at Margaret. Her eyebrows went up. *"Ist du Fraulein Beechmann der Englischer?"*

"De Beauchamp," Margaret corrected her. "Yes, I am English."

"*Ja, ja.*" The ticket seller opened a wooden box on the desk to her left and flipped through the papers inside. With a triumphant flourish, she produced an envelope. "*Zwei billete, Mit freundlicher Genehmigung von Frau Simpson.* Vith compliments," she added, pronouncing the words carefully. She pushed the white card through the semi-circular hole at the bottom of the pane of glass. "*Am morgen, acht ur, Bahngleis Zwei.*"

"Eight o'clock of the morning," James said, passing the envelope to his sister. "But you should arrive earlier, of course."

Margaret opened the envelope to reveal gleaming white pasteboards that had been beautifully impressed so that the print could be felt on the reverse, like the finest invitations to great houses. In English and German, they read, "One (1) Passenger, One Way, Hamburg to Magdeburg."

James' eyebrows went up. "Looks like Mrs. Simpson is treating you to a fine journey," he said. "Travel aboard these launches is not inexpensive."

Margaret could hardly find words. Once again, the Americans were showering her in generosity.

"Will we have to procure provisions for the journey?" Hettie asked. "How many days will the train take?"

"Less than two," James said, his eyes twinkling. He pointed to a framed notice printed in black with gold and red capitals. "There's the timetable. About forty hours. You will arrive on the second day by the dinner hour. You will dine with the officers and the other important passengers."

"It's a wonder!" Margaret exclaimed.

"You'll find that the United States of Europe is full of wonders," James said. "You've barely seen a glimpse."

# Chapter 10

James escorted them to the front of a hotel where a horse and carriage were waiting. The blond, bearded driver tipped him a salute with the end of his whip.

"I'd best be getting back," James said, leaning down to kiss Margaret on the cheek. "The captain wants me to oversee the rest of the unloading, and we've more bargains to make among the merchants. This is our first journey abroad of the spring, so he wants to bring goods back to sell in London and Liverpool. Wilhelm will take you into the heart of the city and drop you before a hotel where you can dine. Hamburg is a fine place, safe enough for women to walk around on their own. Enjoy the sights!"

He handed them up into the open vehicle, and smacked the horse on the rump. Wilhelm chuckled at him as the carriage lurched forward.

Margaret stared like a child as the warehouses and modest business premises gave way to humble cottages, then rows of houses, and finally grand town houses, all of red brick with tiled roofs. The farther in they rode, the finer the garments of the people walking on the streets. Here and there, she saw women attired as she was, with sausage curls bouncing on the shoulders of dagged sleeves and tight bodices. But most of Hamburg fashion was different. The clothing seemed softer and more relaxed. At first, she thought it wasn't as flattering to the figure, but the silhouettes were becoming in a different way. Collars, too, were not starched or tight to the neck, although lace was still present on most people. Even men's fashion had changed. Breeches fit more slimly. She realized that hardly anyone had padding in their clothing, allowing the true lines of the body to be more revealed. Was it unseemly? She broke off when she found herself staring at a very fashionable man in black silk breeches and hose with a doublet of many colors that didn't seem to have been woven but was perhaps knitted? He caught her eye and raised his brows at her. She blushed and turned away as the carriage drove her past him.

"I wish I could turn around," she said. "How do you think that coat was made?"

Hettie glimpsed back over her shoulder. "I couldn't say, mistress. It's . . . different."

The center of Hamburg bustled just as much as London. If it was not for the shapes of the buildings, which indeed were quite different, and the clothing, one city could have passed for the other. Wilhelm brought the carriage to a halt before the doors of a large town house.

"The Town Hall," he said, in clipped English. He pointed to the left to a building that looked as though it had been enameled with blue paint. "The great houses." This was accompanied by a gesture to the right. "I return of the clock four." He swept his hand up so they could see the soaring clock tower of a church that stood in the next street. *"Guten tag, meine frauen."*

He helped them down from his vehicle. Margaret put a coin into his hand, which he received with a salute. He leaped lightly back into the driver's seat, and clicked his tongue to urge the horse away.

A porter near the door of the hotel bowed slightly and made as if to open the portal. Margaret shook her head, and he resumed his stance.

"Let us take a walk first," Margaret told Hettie. "I'm not hungry yet. James advised us to see the city. I'm eager to take that opportunity."

The town hall bustled with black-coated clerks and serious-looking gentlemen carrying reams of paper. Instead, Margaret turned toward the "great houses."

Margaret kept her eyes open for thieves or people watching them too closely. She had left most of her money in the care of Frau Engelmann, but she could ill afford to lose the sum she carried on her person. Hettie stubbornly insisted on securing her own few coins in the lining of her hat. They were careful to walk in sunlight, keeping away from darkened doorways or narrow alleyways. She caught a glimpse of two men walking several yards behind them and glanced back to look. No one was there. She told Hettie of her uneasiness. Regardless of James' insistence that they were relatively safe, they were in a strange city, where they knew no one.

With caution in mind, the two women strolled cautiously, avoiding boys delivering parcels to the lower doors of the domiciles and servants shaking out rugs or dumping cans into the gutter. The houses were indeed lovely, with soaring, painted facades that reminded Margaret of Christmas gingerbread. Men and women took the soft spring air walked up and down the clean-swept pavements, nodding to one another. A young man walking a brace of handsome, slim brown sight-hounds tipped his hat to them. Margaret returned his salute with a courteous nod of her head. She and Hettie wound their way through the passersby, none of whom seemed the least bit interested in them. The strangest of buildings was a free-standing shop that had ornamental arches of brilliant yellow to either side. It seemed to be very busy, mostly with people her own age coming and going. Margaret smelled cooking meat and onions as they went past.

They followed the winding thoroughfares, past small shops, coming onto open-air markets only a street or two past the grand houses. Chickens squawked from wicker cages, and baskets of early peas and bunched carrots and radishes exuded their fresh, earthy smell from trestle tabletops. Daffodils stood in tin tubs up to their leafy knees in water. The sellers offered bouquets of the bright yellow blossoms to Margaret. She waved them away with a smile.

"They're still yet to bloom at home," Hettie said.

"I fancy they'll be full on fields of sunshine when we return," Margaret said. "Oh, look!"

As they passed the produce market, hanging banners of fabric fluttered in the morning breeze. Much of it was ordinary linsey-woolsey cloth in browns, ochres, and greens. In between the displays lay tables of stacked bolts in brighter colors, and a red-cheeked woman wielding a pair of shears stood ready to measure and cut for her customers. Margaret made her way through the crowd to take a look at the offerings. *Professional curiosity*, she thought.

She rubbed the fabric between her hands, examined the weave and the dye. The cloth had been fulled smooth, and would be suitable for ladies' garments. The colors were more intense than the ones her family's dyers used. She wondered how they had achieved the brilliant purple, or that acid green shade. And that blue! But how nice the woolen fabric felt. She smiled, admiring the cloth's drape.

"You know!" the woman said, coming to her side. She emitted a spate of German. Out of it, Margaret could only pick up a word or two.

"Yes, my family sells cloth like this."

The woman shook her head. *"Nein Englische, bitte."* She held up the end of a hank of cloth and brought a length of a finer weave over to compare. *"Gut. Besser. Ja?"* One was good, and the other clearly better.

*"Ja,"* Margaret agreed. "Fine weaving. I mean, *Fein webart.* How many . . . *gewinde* per *zoll*?"

"Ach!" the woman exclaimed, pleased at Margaret's clumsy German. *"Zwei hundert."*

"Two hundred threads per cale," Margaret translated for Hettie. "Very fine, indeed. This is as nice as anything we sell." The thought struck her suddenly, and she felt a pang of regret, if not shame. That was precisely what Herr Schwartz had been trying to inform her. And the price was indeed smaller than what the de Beauchamp fabrics would sell for. *"Danke. Guten tag, lieb frau."* That didn't sound quite right, but the woman seemed to understand her.

Margaret was thoughtful as they came away from the market stalls. Hettie tried to cheer her up.

"Look there, mistress," she said. Near the end of the street stood another cloth merchant, but within a storefront, no goods displayed outside. The name over the door, Hans Oberdorn, had been painted in gold in the fantastic, ornate script that the Germans used.

Even through the glass, Margaret could see the shimmer of the fabric. "Silks," she breathed.

If woolens and linens were the workhorses of her trade, silk was the nobility. Not quite feeling her feet on the pavement, she went to stare in the window.

The shop had two broad storefronts, taking up the breadth of a fairly good-sized building. Behind the paned glass of the first one, glimmering bolts in jewel colors were set upright upon wooden stands. They framed what could only be a court dress of brilliant red, with gold and bronze insets in the skirt and sleeves, and round jewels set into nests of embroidery. Margaret admired not only the handsome cut of the gown, but the astonishing beauty of the fabric of which it was made. If the fine purple, blue, and green of the merchant in the market were flowers, this display was a rainbow garden, more vivid than mere wool could hope to achieve. She shook her head in wonder.

"Look at that," Hettie said, pointing to the ruby skirts of the gown, framed by a split overskirt of gold-spangled velvet. "It's like they were able to paint a picture in the cloth."

Margaret leaned closer to see the repeated pattern, like a fairy's dance set in tiny, gleaming threads. "Brocade silks," she said. "It's an intricate weave that is only made by master craftsmen. Father took me to see a silk weaver in London once. The threads are so fine that a breath might take them away. Lady Pierce has one rather precious apparel of brocade that a London trader brought from the Far East. She wore it on her best court gown's bodice when she went to formal dinners in the palace. That is . . . so lovely."

She studied the beautiful expanse of red fabric, wishing that she could take it in her fingers and examine it. Lady Pierce's silk piece was softer than a baby's skin. She looked at the other fabrics on display. Some of them were plain satins, but a few were intricately patterned. She couldn't imagine how costly an ell of those were.

Margaret became aware of a familiar sound, that of looms in motion. It was coming from the other storefront. She drew Hettie with her to look.

Indeed, behind the glass, a weaver was hard at work at a broad wooden loom. Margaret scarcely made note of his slim figure or swiftly moving hands, only that the heddles of the loom were tiny by comparison to even the finest in her father's parlors. Under the master weaver's hands, the shuttles went this way and that at a rate of speed that was hard to follow. Three young people, apprentices by their humble shirts and tunics, turned the warp wheel and made adjustments to the machine. The device stopped for a moment, while one of the apprentices came forward with a shuttle filled with brilliant, shiny blue thread to replace a depleted one on the loom.

"I wonder if they will let me take a closer look at their work," Margaret said. She looked around for a bell-pull, but to her surprise, there was not even a door. The broad glass front admitted no access at all.

"Here, mistress," Hettie said, guiding her back to the other window. Margaret had not even noticed the handsome carved door beside it. On the wall, she spotted a flower made of bronze with a knob worn shiny with use in the center. "Try that."

Margaret tugged the knob. From within, a musical cascade of bells sounded. She peered through the window and saw movement. A pale-haired man came into the display room, then disappeared behind a partial wall. She heard latches lifting, and the door swung open. Margaret almost expected to smell the familiar odor of lanolin, but was met by a dry, spicy waft of air.

*"Ja, fräulein?"* He seemed to be a broader-built copy of the man in the next room, with the same silver-gilt hair. She realized from the drape and subtle shimmer that his clothing had been woven from silk as well, but as a broadcloth. How wonderful to be able to use such precious fabrics in one's day-to-day wardrobe! She cleared her throat.

*"Er, bitte, Ich bin Margaret de Beauchamp. Meine vater ist weber in England..."* The man pursed his lips in amusement as she tried to explain in her poor German and Amideutsch who she was and what she represented.

*"Ich spreche Englische,"* he said, graciously. "Fräulein Beauchamp, *wilkommen.* I am Franz Oberdorn. My many grandfather founder of this shop was. I have not heard of your business, as I not know many in England. Do you also the silks make?"

"No, but we weave fine woolens," Margaret said. "Churnet House."

Herr Oberdorn emitted a dismissive sniff. She saw immediately that her standing fell several levels in his eyes.

"He's high and mighty because he thinks you only make cloth for everyday wear," Hettie said.

"Hettie!" Margaret exclaimed, with a look that meant, "we will discuss this later." Hettie looked abashed, though unrepentant. She made as if to withdraw from the doorway. "I beg your pardon, Herr Oberdorn. We will not trouble you further."

*"Nein, nein,"* came a voice from within. A woman with the same silver-gilt hair came in. Margaret estimated her to be the same age as her mother. The corners of the lady's flower-blue eyes were creased with merriment. "We welcome all from the trade.

I am Madchen Oberdorn. Forgive my brother. He does not deal with the English speakers so often. Don't let him get you down, as my *Amerikaner Freund*, Herr Stone, would say. How may we help fellows of the loom? To purchase, are you here?"

"Curiosity only, I'm afraid," Margaret admitted. "I was watching the gentleman next door plying the loom. I wondered . . . if it was not an imposition, whether you would allow me to see him work more closely?"

*"Nein!"* Hans protested, just as Madchen said, "Yes! Of course."

Her brother glared at her, and reeled off a spate of angry German. Although, to be fair, most German language sounded harsh and judgmental to Margaret. Madchen laughed at him and shooed him away.

"We must learn from one another to advance in our craft," she said, taking Margaret by the hand. "I learned the weave when I was very small, but to join the guild I was not permitted. Yet, when our father ascended to *der Himmel*, it was I he chose to steer the horse? Is that the term?"

"To take the reins?" Margaret ventured. Madchen smiled.

"Yes, that is it, what Herr Stone says." She gestured toward the back of the shop. "Come with me, *bitte*? We will see what our *Bruder* Walter is making."

She brought them up a flight of steep, narrow stairs to a landing. At the top, she gestured to a bench with a basket of cloth items beside it. In a niche beside the bench, a basin and pitcher with a linen towel awaited.

"Over your shoes will you wear these?" she asked. "To avoid dirt on the silk, you understand? And to wash your hands before touching?"

Margaret sat down and slipped the muslin bags over her shoes. Each had a drawstring to fasten it around her ankles. Hettie knelt to see to her mistress' shoes, then covered her own. Both of them washed their hands thoroughly. The cleansing made Margaret feel as though she was going into a sacred place, like a church.

Madchen waited patiently, then guided them through a solid wooden door to another set of steps, just as steep, that led downward. Another door at the bottom opened up into the workroom. Beside the loom in the window, three smaller looms stood against the walls deeper into the room. A trio of men, younger than the siblings yet older than the apprentices, concentrated on their work. Margaret guessed them to be journeymen studying under Walter, getting ready for their examinations in mastery and to perhaps open up their own businesses one day. The nearest of them was working on a piece of brilliant gold. She realized that the weft ran over several warp threads at a time, creating satin, a skill she had never dreamed of seeing.

At their arrival, Walter only glanced up for a moment from his work, never breaking his rhythm. He clipped out a command to a brown-haired boy standing beside the loom to advance the warp, cranking the finished cloth onto the beam. Walter's foot moved from treadle to treadle, causing the shed to change as the shuttles ran back and forth. Unlike the satin, the brocade was made with multiple weft threads over the warp. Margaret moved as close as she dared, her eyes fixed on the moving threads. The making of it was as beautiful as the finished product. The cloth shimmered blue like the heavens. In between, the raised patterns floated like islands on a lake. The intricate designs delighted her, but the loom advanced very slowly, making only a fraction of an inch at a time. No wonder it was a luxury fabric. So many hours were devoted to its production.

"That thread's as fine as a fairy's eyelashes," Hettie said. She had whispered, but her voice was loud enough to carry in the workroom. The nearest apprentice smiled, but kept his eyes on his task.

"It is an ancient art," Madchen said. "Comes to us as many hundreds of years, the patterning of the silk."

As familiar as Margaret was with the skill of weaving, having set her hand to it often over her life, she was able to follow only imperfectly how Walter Oberdorn plied his loom. He had a marvelous hand at keeping the tension exactly right. The wefts were not too loose, not too tight, so each pass lay smoothly between the selvedges. It looked as though it would need neither fulling nor pressing before it was sold. Any lady or gentleman would be proud to have such beautiful fabric on her or his back. While she was proud of her family's business, she felt envy for the Oberdorns.

She glanced up at the sound of heavy footsteps. Hans stumped down the steps with a varnished wooden tray in his hands. He looked a little ashamed, but presented the tray with a smile. It bore a bottle and four glasses. Madchen took it from him and placed it on a table well away from the loom. She beckoned the two women to join her, and served them small glasses of rich red wine. Hans lifted his glass to Margaret.

"Wil—welcome," he said. "I did not mean disrespect when you arrived."

"None taken," Margaret said, graciously, offering a return toast to Hans and Madchen. "Thank you so much for allowing us to see your shop. I hope that you will allow us to become friends with you. I see we have much to learn."

"Of course!" Madchen said. "We would be delighted to exchange correspondence with you."

"Would you like to see finished goods we have made?" Hans asked, when they had drained their glasses. "Many fine bolts we have."

Margaret happily followed them into the shop itself. Madchen invited her to sit down on chairs that had been upholstered in brocade. Hans, now enthusiastic about their visitor, brought one piece after another to lay in her lap.

"For the Elector of Saxony!" he exclaimed, spreading out a pure white piece with gold thread depicting a hunting scene. "Many months to weave this took!"

Margaret looked at all of them, turning over each piece to inspect the other side. Even the floating threads underlying the raised designs looked beautiful. She couldn't keep her eyes off one piece in particular. It was blood red and woven with a pattern of roses and leaves. The fabric flowed over her hands like water, as if it couldn't keep its shape.

"So beautiful it is, yes?" Madchen asked, with a smile.

"How . . . how much does it cost?"

"Enough for a dress for your size . . ." Madchen named the price per bolt, which caused Hettie to gasp aloud. Margaret almost emitted a similar noise, but swallowed it. Such a sum would feed a flock of sheep for a week in winter.

"I'm afraid I cannot," she said. "We are on a buying trip for goods to return home, my brother and I." Hans' lips pursed again. He was dismissing her again. Margaret's pride was stung. "May I purchase a small piece? I would like to bring a gift to my mother."

"Of course! And, as you are fellow weavers, you must have the discount of courtesy." Madchen clapped her hands, and a young woman in a pale blue dress with a white head wrap and broad white apron appeared. She gathered up the scarlet fabric and carried it to a smooth beechwood table. She placed a measuring rod on the fabric and brandished a pair of gleaming shears.

Margaret came over to survey the piece. She didn't want to look poor, but she didn't want to use up all of her money on one extravagance. There was no way to guess her expenses in Magdeburg. With trepidation and regret, she pointed to the marker for one foot on the measuring rod.

The girl smiled, showing no disapproval for her modest purchase. With an expert's skill, she swept the shears down the width of the red silk and folded it up, embossed side in. She brought a sheet of white foolscap out from underneath the table and wrapped the fabric into a neat envelope, tucking in the edges of the paper so it stayed closed. With both hands, she extended it to Margaret.

"To your good health, madame," she said.

"I shouldn't have bought that," Margaret said, as they walked away from the market. The sun was beginning to sink past the high roofs on the west side of the street, taking Margaret's spirits with it.

"Yes, you should have, mistress," Hettie said.

"Think what I could have bought with the money! It's half of what a horse costs!"

"Well, you don't need half a horse, mistress," Hettie said. "Think of how pleased your mother will be with the gift. What shall you make with it?

"A small purse?" Margaret mused, mollified for the moment. She began to picture ideas in her mind, and hoped her skill would pay tribute to the fabulous material. "A cover for her Bible? A cap for formal occasions? But it's so pretty, I know she will want to look at it, not wear it on the back of her head. And a locket or a pomander for Lady Pierce. She has been so generous to me."

"There, you see? Two gifts out of it. Money well spent."

Despite her shame at buying the expensive fabric on a whim, Margaret couldn't stop thinking about it. She couldn't believe she actually owned a piece of silk brocade.

They returned to the hotel and took a late luncheon at a table with a white linen cloth near a front window. A man in a greasy apron brought out two platters and left them before the women with hardly a glance back. Margaret sawed through the grayish rondel of meat and picked at the mound of strange little bits of dough covered in sauce beside it.

"Truth to tell, madam," Hettie whispered, "Mistress Engelmann's food is better."

Margaret gave her a sly smile and a nod.

# Chapter 11

The next morning before half past seven, Wilhelm was waiting outside Washington's Crossing for Margaret and Hettie. He helped them into the carriage and loaded up their baggage. Showing their tickets to one of the uniformed porters, they were allowed through the sturdy metal gate to walk out onto the dock beside the hissing ship alongside other travelers.

A gentleman in dark blue uniform with more decorations on his sleeves, shoulders, and cap greeted them and the other travelers at the gangplank.

"Welcome aboard, ladies and gentlemen," he said, in English and German. "I am Herr Captain Schroeder. We are very pleased to have you as guests on our voyage to Magdeburg."

Margaret, Hettie, and the couple of women curtseyed to the captain. The men, four dignified-looking gentlemen in the fashionable Hamburg style and half a dozen in various military uniforms offered their own courtesies. The captain gestured to his sailors to assist them in boarding.

All of their baggage but a basket of travel provisions Hettie insisted upon bringing was taken in charge by a pair of the uniformed sailors. A third man helped them up the narrow ladder and showed them to their cabin.

Behind a handsomely carved door of varnished wood, their small private chamber had a tabletop that pulled down from a bracket on the wall, a padded leather chair, and a single bed that was wide enough for both of them, woven wool curtains over a single glass window, lights that glowed like the flashlight in her pocket, and a hatch concealing a wash basin with a capped pitcher. The attendant, who spoke excellent though accented English, advised them to keep the window closed when the ship was moving to avoid having the smoke come inside. The two women set about exploring their new quarters with all the curiosity of a pair of kittens, until they were alerted by a discreet cough.

"Ahem!" The sailor stood by the door, his open palm turned upward beside his hip. He carefully did not look down toward it. Trying not to laugh, Margaret placed a small silver coin on his palm. James had advised her on the size of tips to offer that were neither too large nor too stingy. The man must have been able to identify coins by feel or weight, for he gave a satisfied nod. He left them alone and slid the door closed.

The room was surprisingly warm in the cool spring weather. Margaret undid her cloak and Hettie bustled to hang it up on the metal peg beside the door.

"Everything is so . . . so clean, mistress!" the servant girl declared, looking about. "No carriage that we have ever ridden has been so clear of dust or dirt. And Hamburg seemed so tidy as well."

"James was right about the many wonders," Margaret said. "England feels so far behind in standards compared with what we have seen here on the continent. We must save up all our impressions to take home. Not that we can make changes all of a sudden, as we have had no Ring of Fire to cause them."

"I'll keep my eyes open, my lady," Hettie promised.

"Bless my soul," Margaret said, settling on the leather seat with an unladylike thump. It was very comfortable, like her father's favorite armchair. "My letter home to Mother today will be interesting, at least!"

A sharp whistle and a shout from a deep male voice heralded the departure of the ship. Margaret and Hettie went to the window to watch. They felt a strong thrumming underneath their feet as the steam began to drive the stern wheel. Within minutes, the landscape started to whisk by outside the window. Margaret quickly understood why the sailor had advised them against opening the glass, as wisps of sooty smoke from the engine curled around the craft.

Outside, fields of crops, the bright green of spring, interspersed with herds of cattle and sheep, whisked by. It became a game as Margaret tried to identify the breeds of sheep before they dropped out of sight. Travel by steam tug was faster than she had ever dreamed, much faster than a cargo ship, or even on horseback! The rumble coming from beneath the floor was both alarming and soothing at the same time.

"I wonder how quickly we are traveling," Margaret whispered.

"As fast as birds fly," Hettie said, looking out astonished.

Once the women had their footing, they left their compartment and explored the rest of the ship. The men rose and smiled at Margaret as she came out on deck. One of them rushed to hold the portal open for her. She almost retreated back to their compartment, but Hettie poked her in the ribs from behind, urging her forward. Margaret straightened her spine and nodded politely to them.

Though there was a good-sized crew, the ship didn't feel crowded. The other two women occupied the cabin behind theirs, closer to the steam engine. The two cabins on the other side of the long, narrow senior officers' cabin had been assigned to the somberly-dressed gentlemen, but the soldiers had been sent belowdecks to stay among the crew. A peek below showed how cramped they would be for their journey, but it was only for two nights. James had warned her that the craft had a very shallow draft, making it possible to traverse the river at speed.

The other two women sat on stools on deck, handiwork in their laps. They had brought half a dozen children with them, who hurtled around the deck like a roomful of excited cats, all but bounding off the walls.

Behind the ship was tethered an unmanned barge. It carried the passengers' baggage as well as crates, boxes, and bags of cargo labeled with mysterious codes in colored paint. That made sense to Margaret, not to waste the opportunity to bring goods and mail up and back between the cities. And at such impressive speed! Less than two days to traverse the distance, but as smoothly as gliding in a punt. This would be a lovely experience to write in a letter to her mother. Lovely, that was, except for the coal smoke. She coughed as a stray breeze pushed a cloud of it down from the smokestack past their faces.

Children on the riverbank, seeing the *Metahelios* approaching, jumped up and down, waving. Margaret smiled and waved back to them until they disappeared behind trees around a bend.

An officer with a small quantity of gold braid on his shoulders came up to them.

"Ladies, the captain's compliments, and would you be pleased to join him for luncheon?" He spoke English, but with an American accent.

"Yes, thank you very much," Margaret replied. He took her arm with a smile. Margaret was struck again by the perfectly straight, white teeth he had. Self-consciously, she closed her lips to return the smile. Her own teeth were yellow by comparison, and one of the first molars on the right bottom was missing due to a childhood misadventure. If she could ask Rita without embarrassment, she would find out how to bring home that matter of dental hygiene to England. The list of what she wanted to know grew line upon line with every passing hour.

"Thank you, good sir," she said, hoping she had not been staring. "Come, Hettie."

"Yes, mistress," Hettie said.

Though the trip was to last until well after sunset the next day, Margaret felt no weariness in staring out the window at the passing landscape until the light disappeared. The ship docked now and again to take on coal and water for the boiler. She and Hettie watched as men in all-in-one garments brushed ash out into a metal cart and trundled load after load of black lumps on board to pile into the bin beside the firebox. The clatter of tumbling coal was deafening. It was one of the few detriments to travel by steam tug.

The food was of surprisingly high quality despite having come from a small mess kitchen. Captain Schroeder offered polite small talk, and encouraged his guests to talk with one another. All of them praised Margaret in her efforts to speak German. She learned a number of useful phrases at every meal. She spent many pleasant hours on deck in front of the cabins chatting with the gentlemen, who were traveling to Magdeburg on business, and with the women, who were a pair of sisters who had taken their children to visit their parents north of Hamburg.

The captain kept them all apprised on where they were. Late on the second afternoon, he came to the group with the ship's chart in his hands.

"We have entered USE territory," he said. "We will reach Magdeburg within two hours."

Margaret kept her eyes open, looking for any obvious signs of changes in the landscape. She had seen drawings of the sharp contrast in the land where the Ring of Fire had occurred, and longed to go and see it for herself. The town of Grantville, cupped in the palm of mountains, had appeared in the midst of the Germanies like a handful of sunshine, bringing both blessings and changes.

"Will we see Grantville?" Hettie asked, as if reading her mind.

"I've no notion," Margaret said. "I'll be grateful just to see Mistress Rita again."

The sun began to disappear behind them.

Tapping on the door woke Margaret from a light doze on the bunk in her cabin.

"Magdeburg!" a sailor called through the portal. "We will be docking in moments."

Margaret sat bolt upright and blinked at the lights coming through the cabin window. Hettie was already on her feet, holding her coat out for her.

Outside, she saw men in the coverall suits toss looped ropes to similarly dressed men on the bank. With a few sharp jerks, the ship came to rest against the dock. The unearthly scream of the steam whistle pierced straight through the walls of the cabin. Margaret made a face.

"I won't miss that," she said.

"Neither will I, mistress," Hettie said.

She followed the other passengers to the gangplank. A junior officer assisted her down. The dock was bright with light from gas lights so excellent they did not even flicker.

"Margaret!"

She looked up at the call, and smiled. There was Rita, waving from the other side of a metal fence. She waved back with excitement and relief.

"Well, thank Heaven for all its blessings," Hettie said, climbing down after her.

A porter met her with her cases on a two-wheeled cart and followed her out beyond the barrier. Rita met her at the gate and gave her a bone-crushing hug.

"Oh, it's great to see you!" she said. "You look wonderful. Did you have a good trip?"

"We had a lovely journey," Margaret assured her, squeezing her back. "We enjoyed it so much, except perhaps the pirates. I am so looking forward to telling everyone at home all about it. Thank you for obtaining the tickets for us. Pray allow me to reimburse you for the cost."

"Not a chance," Rita said, laughing. "It's the least I can do." She stopped before saying more, glancing at the crowd around them. "Not one thin dime. It's my treat."

"I was happy to be of service," Margaret said. "I hope... the gentlemen and the lady remain well?"

That evoked another laugh out of Rita. "Harry Lefferts falls on his feet more often than a cat. But, yes, the others are fine. Come on! We can talk more when we get you checked in."

She beckoned to the porter to follow her. The man wheeled the heavy cart toward an elegant landau and loaded the trunks onto the rear below the driver's stand. The carriage curtseyed under their weight, and the horses danced. Margaret felt her cheeks burn. She knew she had packed too much, but she had gifts for her friends as well as her goods and Hettie's.

"I wish I still had enough gas for my pickup truck," Rita said. "I'm just not a priority, to be honest. The horse carts are nice, but they are slow, and I worry about the horses getting overworked. Maybe once we get the refineries really up and running, we'll be able to expand motor vehicles for everyone."

As if to underscore her statement, a small, boxy vehicle, roofless and painted in green enamel, no horses attached to it either front or back, passed them with a roar and turned a corner ahead of them. Margaret stared. Four people sat in two benches, one in front of the other. The man in the front left clutched a round wheel like a ship's tiller.

"Oh, mistress," Hettie said. "Look at that! Wouldn't you want to ride in that?"

"I would," Margaret said, filled with delight.

Rita laughed. "I'll ask someone to take you for a spin," she said.

Even in the darkness broken only by moonlight, Margaret almost broke her neck turning from side to side to look at everything as they rolled through Magdeburg. Like Hamburg, the town was surprisingly clean, and workers using more traditional lanterns, largely men, but with some women among them, seemed to take pride in moving muck off the streets almost as quickly as it fell. Small gardens divided the street from walkways adjacent to the buildings so she was aware of the scent of flowers rather than refuse and filth.

"Hygiene is an ongoing problem," Rita replied to Margaret's question, as they traveled through the handsome streets. "Most down-timers were never taught the basics. Now that we've got regulations and laws in place about sewage and trash pickup, and pushing education everywhere we can, it's helped a lot to combat illness and infection. We still don't have enough vaccines to inoculate everyone, but we're working on it. One thing we have got enough of at last is soap, which helps. I keep telling my brother that he can construct all the machines and buildings he wants, but he's going to end up with no one in them if he doesn't think of health care." She chuckled and let out a sigh. "He has too many things to think about, but he's a good organizer. I'd say he was great, but he *is* my brother."

Margaret laughed. "I might say the same for my own brothers and sisters," she admitted. "I wouldn't want them to think too highly of their own skills, lest they stumble on their own feet while reaching for a star."

"I'd forgotten you were our little Shakespeare," Rita said, leaning over to hug her again. "I've missed you!" She glanced up at the building they were approaching. "Look, we're here."

Margaret stared at the massive granite edifice ahead of them. It stretched long gray arms out both ways along most of the street, and hulked at least four floors in height. Small ornamental gardens were laid out before it, where statues, too new to have acquired a coating of verdigris, stood. It looked larger than the Palace of Whitehall, and had the same imposing air of majesty and command.

"You . . . you live here?"

"Oh, no!" Rita laughed. "We're just visiting. This is the Presidential Palace. Mike lives here, for now." She wrinkled her nose. "He's been trying hard to shed the title, but no one will let him go yet. It's the center of government for the USE. Most of it is offices, but there are rooms on the upper floors for residences. Tom and I stay here when we're in town, which hasn't been that often in the last year. When you wrote, I was happy to find an excuse to come home and visit. When I'm in Ingolstadt, I'm always on duty."

Reassured by their driver that her bags would find their way to her quarters, Margaret and Hettie followed their hostess into the grand entrance. The soaring hallway echoed with their footsteps. Only a few others were present, moving to and fro by lamplight.

"Business hours are over for the day," Rita explained. "They told me are a couple of receptions are going on tonight. People will be there bending Mike's ear. If you can manage it after that long train ride, I'll be happy to bring you to meet him. If not, I'll arrange for some food, and you can take it easy tonight. I have so much to show you!"

Margaret stopped in dismay.

"None of my clothes are suitable for formal receptions," she said.

Rita waved a hand. "Mike doesn't stand on ceremony. You can come in whatever you've got. He is dying to meet you. Okay, this is yours." She swung wide the black-enameled door on the left side of the corridor, and urged Margaret to enter.

When she thought back to the cramped cabin that she had occupied on board the *Meadowlark*, she could hardly believe the enormous accommodations to which Rita had shown them.

Rita had pretty much pushed her in the doorway, and lit a lamp by the door. The broad window shed what meager twilight was left upon a handsome sitting room with carved wooden furniture upholstered in a handsome shade of russet brown. Doors were open to reveal two shadowed bed chambers and a dressing room.

"This is yours. Two bedrooms, one for each of you. You have your own bathroom, too. The plumbing's not bad, even if it's a little noisy."

Margaret couldn't help but gawk like a common urchin. Hettie was speechless to have a bedroom of her own.

"Surely this is for visiting nobles," Margaret protested, all but tiptoeing into the sitting room as though she didn't want to leave footprints on the beautiful Turkish carpet.

"No, but we consider you a visitor of importance," Rita said, with a warm smile. "You're kind of an underground hero in these parts, and we still feel we owe you."

Margaret didn't say anything. She felt almost as though she

was going to commit betrayal by requesting another favor from her friend sometime in the next several days, but surely Rita had more than an inkling of her main purpose for making the long journey.

"And look!" her friend continued, drawing her to a table by the window and kindling a lamp standing upon it. "Melissa Mailey wanted me to make her apologies. She's off rabble-rousing, so she won't see you this trip, but she went through the Grantville Library, the high school, and the college library to find everything we've got on weaving and spinning. There was way more than I thought there could be."

Margaret hadn't registered what the rectangular mass on the table could be until it was pointed out to her. Then, she couldn't keep her eyes off the stacks and stacks and *stacks* of bound books. She had scarcely ever seen so many in one place, and all on one subject? The visitors from the future were unbelievably fortunate to have the knowledge of ages. She held her breath as she reached out to touch the top book on the nearest pile.

Tomes from the future were so strange in comparison with the leatherbound volumes in her father's library and in Lady Pierce's sitting room. The first book was called *The History of Handweaving*. It had a smooth paper cover that was folded around the book itself, and had a picture painted on it—not painted, precisely—of a woman with her back turned to Margaret sitting at a standing loom. The image was so realistic that she could barely touch it for fear of alarming the woman. She looked a question at Rita.

"It's a photograph," Rita said. "I had this explained to me by the high school science teacher, because I knew you would ask, and you're not the first down-timer to wonder what these are. You take a piece of paper that is coated with chemicals so it's sensitive to light, then expose it very briefly to an image, like this woman. You take the piece of paper and use more chemicals on it to develop it, and you get something like this. I had a friend in nursing school whose brother was a hobby photographer. He had a darkroom in their basement."

"It's *amazing*."

Rita waved it away. "It's technology that we are already reintroducing. It's too useful not to have, and all you need are a lightproof box with a clean lens, paper, and a bunch of chemicals that we can synthesize in no time. I'll show you a camera later."

"I... I'd be honored!"

"But that's just the cover of the first book," Rita said. "Wait until you actually *read* them. I started one of them last week. I'm not even that interested in weaving, but I couldn't put it down. I think it was that one." She pointed to a huge book like a church missal that had a very colorful *photographic* cover. "I wish I could let you take them all home. I can't, but you're welcome to spend all the time you want reading them here."

"I understand," Margaret said. "Too many questions would be aroused by the presence of books from the future in such a humble place as my home."

"I doubt it's humble, from what you told me," Rita said, dryly. "Someday, I hope to get a chance to visit you and meet your family. They sound pretty interesting."

"They... each have their own stories," Margaret offered, drawing heavily on tact. She knew from their year-long correspondence that Rita would surely understand. "We would be delighted to welcome you, when that becomes possible."

"I'm looking forward to it."

Margaret kept running her fingers again and again over *The History of Handweaving.* So many people had said the Americans were otherworldly. Having met them, she had dismissed the notion, understanding them to be ordinary people, but this square of paper under her very fingers was enough to fling her back among the whispering masses.

"This rivals the works of the greatest artists," she said. "She looks as though she could turn around and speak to me."

"Well, it's not art," Rita said, with a dismissive twitch of her lips. "I mean, you can take photographs that rival art, but just pictures—" She stopped and shook her head. "We take everything we had for granted, and we shouldn't. Not any longer. We're starting all over again, everyone from Grantville. What we had is gone, left behind in the twentieth century. But we have the knowledge, and we're here to share it. That's what matters now. Open the book. Go on."

Margaret obeyed. The stiff cover underneath the photograph seemed to be made of pasteboard, but with a waxlike surface. Within, the creamy white pages had been trimmed perfectly smooth and square at the edges, like a *Culpeper's Herbal* such as Doctor Trumbull possessed. They felt cool and crisp, like the skin of an apple. She picked up another book, smaller and slimmer than the first. *Rigid Heddle Weaving* was the title. At least that term was familiar. But on the verso side of the title page, it had a nest of small print, with the term © 1987. Three hundred and fifty years from then! She let her hands drop. She should not be delving into such secrets! At any moment, lightning would strike her, or the ground would split and swallow her down to the flaming depths.

"Don't worry," Rita said, with a little laugh. She pushed the book close, and flipped the pages until she came to a cluster of shinier pages that had more photographs on them. "You'll have to look at these to see if much has changed from your time to mine. Maybe basic weaving hasn't become that much different."

In truth, to see from the photographs, the machines were familiar enough. According to the *captions* (another word from Rita that Margaret committed to memory), they had the same names, though many more of the looms were made of metal than the weavers in her father's sheds and in the halls of the guild masters, and looked all alike. She kept flipping through the shiny pages, feeling as though she was looking through a window into Fairyland.

"Hey, I think this one will be helpful to you." Rita pulled another book from the stack and opened it to the title page: *The World History of Spinning and Weaving.* "I remember learning about the Industrial Revolution in school. It wasn't such good news for small businesses like your dad's. But why should your business *stay* small?"

"But how can it grow, when we have the same number of people?" Margaret asked.

"New machines. Well, new to you. Old to us. Take a look."

Margaret began to read. She thought that weaving in England had begun at the time of her ancestor, Sir Wemys de Beauchamp, whose father had obtained the grant of land from the king he served. But according to the crystal-clear print in the section marked "Prologue," the skill dated back before the time of Our Lord. She kept coming back to a phrase again and again, "two thousand years of fiber history." Two thousand years!

Her eye swept down the text line by line. Industrial Revolution was repeated again and again. A revolution sounded so dangerous, but Rita clearly believed it to be a good thing.

Though her brain spun at the torrent of information she was trying to cram into it, Margaret couldn't stop. She sat down on a chair and devoured page after page. There were places and names, and tiny numbers above those that referred to what Rita called "footnotes," more doors that opened to information that would be priceless to her father and the Barlaston weavers. She tried to cajole all the facts into staying in her mind, the names of men and machines and what they meant to the trade, but errant details kept retreating from her grasp, necessitating rereading pages she had already reviewed.

"So, what do you think? Would you like to come to tonight's reception?" Rita asked.

Her voice snapped Margaret out of her trance. Her arms had curled possessively around the book, and her forefinger was already under the top corner of the page to flip to the next. She didn't want to let go of it. She looked up at Rita.

"I'm sorry, what did you say?"

Her friend laughed. "Never mind. You stay here tonight. You'll want to rest up from your trip anyhow. I'll send someone with food later on. You can meet Mike tomorrow. He'll be in his office in the morning. I'll get someone to bring you down to him." Rita squeezed her shoulder and smiled at Hettie. "Make sure she gets some sleep."

"I'll try, my lady," Hettie said, with all the indulgence of a mother hen. "But you've given her a book to read, and taking those away has never been easy."

With another chuckle, Rita retreated, leaving Margaret alone with a library of wonders and her thirst for facts and details.

# Chapter 12

Diarmid O'Connor saw the sails of the packet boat coming into the Hamburg harbor long before his companion did.

"Fitz!" he hissed, poking Oisin Fitzroyce in the ribs. The other man, dozing on a stack of boxes in the early morning sun, awoke with a start and a snort from his long nose.

"What in all the hells?" he sputtered.

For answer, O'Connor pointed.

"Ye think that's it, after all this time has passed?"

"All this time? It's been no more than ten days, and ye know it," O'Connor said, weary of his companion's griping after four months in Europe with him. He knew the shape of Fitzroyce's complaints as well as he did the man's prominent black side-whiskers, in which Fitz took enormous pride. "It took us longer than that to come away from Amsterdam two weeks back, and well ye knew it. We were lucky to catch the outgoing ship to take our messages then. I'd have preferred to stay in the Lowlands, but it's too hot for us now."

"Ach, well, that's so. His lordship won't have been pleased with our report."

The two men, along with seven or eight others, had been in the direct employ of Finnegan, his lordship's favorite confidant and man of all work. Afterwards, well, O'Connor was ready to give it up and return to Ireland, but his lordship had dangled a purse before them, and sent them all out in search of connections to the Americans. How twenty people, some of them children, and all their goods, had vanished into thin air like spirits, not showing a trace of their passage, had enraged his lordship to the point where he was spending money like water to find their accomplices and bring them back to London, to what was left of the Tower, for justice.

Since the previous spring, he and Fitzroyce had gone from one European city to another in search of witnesses who could state that they'd seen the Americans come to shore, and who had assisted them. They had chased rumor after rumor through various ports. In O'Connor's own opinion, it was no use chasing down individual Americans. They were everywhere on the continent. If not actual visitors from the future, then people whom they had influenced. Almost everyone for whom O'Connor had bought a drink or with whom he'd struck up a conversation had an opinion. Americans were largely popular, mainly for their often absurd levels of generosity. Although he did find that there was a mild undercurrent of disdain for the manner in which they had seemed to take over and change things, with or without the will of those who came to be affected by those changes. It was like the story of the juggernaut, from the Bible or some such, running over anything in its way. Still and all, the general opinion was that the advent of the Americans was a good thing.

O'Connor had months ago come to the realization that his lordship would have been better off calling the whole kettle of fish a loss and turning his attention elsewhere. Considering the firepower that O'Connor saw brought to bear in the Baltic during the war—over the loss of a single American, or so he had heard—the English could not possibly win against them if a war was declared. The Americans had explosives to spare and the will to use them, as well as some devastating tactics.

What forced him and Fitz to flee from Amsterdam was pure bad luck, in his opinion. Someone had noticed that they were still asking questions about the damage to the Tower of London, when the attention of the whole country seemed to be turning to the dispute between Sweden and Denmark. Their curiosity seemed out of place. In sober retrospect, they had not paid attention to the mood surrounding them, and drawn attention to themselves.

Poor excuse for spies, that's what they were.

Well, to be honest, they were not naturals at espionage. They'd been hired from the west of Ireland, from County Tyrone, to be bully boys. That, they were good at. When they could get someone alone, away from help, any secrets that the victim possessed were soon in the hands of Fitzroyce and O'Connor. Fitz was especially good with the razor-sharp knife he kept in the back of his belt. O'Connor prided himself on being able to make a weapon out of anything on which he could lay his hands. That had included a potato, once. No one dared to laugh at him about that except Fitz, of course. That was why they got on so well.

They'd managed to get a message out to the Earl of Cork on a trading ship leaving for Tilbury and London, letting him know they were going onto Hamburg. That was the nearest port town to Magdeburg, the Americans' capital. His lordship had said that it was the most likely place to gain information. A few of his spies had already infiltrated the city and the surrounding countryside, though the two who had claimed they had made it to Grantville had dropped out of contact completely. O'Connor reckoned that they had been discovered and put to death. It's what would have happened in England or Ireland. Why should the new country be any different?

It had been a slow and difficult slog to traverse the three hundred miles in between. They had walked from Amsterdam to Volendam, taken passage on a trading ship to Bremen, then took shank's pony again from the port until they flagged down a passing wagon. An unlucky peddler had been kind enough to pick them up not far outside Bremen town. Unlucky, because he had been unwary about keeping his money concealed from his passengers' eyes. They'd robbed him and left him tied up in the trees. A while later, they'd abandoned the cart and horse at a posting inn a day's walk out of Hamburg. O'Connor consoled himself that at least they hadn't killed the boyo, leaving him where his cries could attract the next traveler's attention to rescue him.

So far, they had been able to live well enough on the peddler's coin, though they needed his lordship to send them money along with further orders, if he had any. O'Connor was weary of traveling and had half a prayer that his lordship would simply tell them to return to London, or even go home to Ireland.

The deep harbor at Hamburg droned with business like a beehive. Morning brought in near as many ships as evening tide. The trading clipper on which they had their eyes fixed flew a British flag. When it got closer, O'Connor could read the name on the prow: *Meadowlark*. The crew shouted to one another as they made ready to dock, and German longshoremen moved close, hoisting looped hawsers for the *Meadowlark* to make fast. With efficient movements, they got the ship moored, and began to help the deck hands take cargo ashore.

The captain came down the gangplank, and the harbormaster's man approached him. They had a loud and energetic conversation that O'Connor guessed was about harbor fees. Yes, that was it. At last, the captain pulled his purse out of his belt pouch, and handed over a trickle of coins. O'Connor's mouth watered to see the glint of gold among them. But he didn't want to rob the man. Who knew whether they would have to board this ship one day to make their escape from Hamburg?

The captain was done with his negotiations, and turned away to oversee the unloading.

O'Connor made his way toward him with a smile on his face.

"Captain, sir, are ye carrying any mail? We're expecting a letter from London."

"My lieutenant is in charge of that, man. See him." The ship's master pointed up the gangplank to a spry-looking youth—a boy, really—with light brown hair. The lad was seeing to the debarking of a couple who looked bent with seasickness, and their servant, who was in much better trim.

"Have ye any post from London?" O'Connor asked the mate. "I'm looking for a letter."

"Yes, yes, we do," the young man said. He sounded as though he was from the English countryside, but had some education under his belt. Officer material, then. Why was he not in the Navy? O'Connor wondered. "Let me see these passengers on their way, then I will look through the box for you." He escorted the couple to the bottom, where a cart awaited them.

"James, we're ready to go!"

Another passenger, a young, fashionably-dressed woman, appeared at the top of the gangplank. Young, pretty, proud, with light brown hair, which O'Connor realized was much the same shade as that belonging to the mate. Brother? A boot-faced girl in a bonnet was at the woman's shoulder. Servant, surely.

"A moment, Margery," the mate said. He dashed upward and disappeared behind the gunnels of the ship. In a moment, he returned with a leatherbound box and carried it down the gangplank. The box was full of folded letters, small bags, and a few wrapped parcels.

"What name, please?" he asked O'Connor.

"Seamus O'Flaherty," O'Connor said. They changed aliases on a regular basis, in case anyone intercepted the post and went looking for them. The boy nodded, and extracted a thick letter written on plain foolscap and sealed with a plain blob of wax. No way to trace that back, neither. O'Connor accepted it, and pressed a small guilder into the mate's hand. Even though it was a small tip, perhaps smaller than was really decent for safe delivery, the mate accepted it graciously.

The two ruffians retreated a few yards away, and O'Connor broke the seal. A small, tightly wrapped paper packet fell out. It lay heavy in the hand, meaning there was coin inside. Ah, thank "Divine Providence," here was the money!

The young officer swung up the side of the bobbing wooden walkway to escort the two women down.

"What's it say?" Fitzroyce asked.

O'Connor had his letters, but wasn't the best of readers. He always preferred to have someone tell him what they wanted him to do. But the Earl of Cork's secretary's script was as plain as speech.

"Not happy that we withdrew from Amsterdam. Seems as though there was valuable information to be had about the Americans' armaments. As if we were going to get any closer to those giant ships than the Danish did. Curse him, he has no idea what we went through."

"What else?"

O'Connor grimaced. "Only to keep our eyes open, which don't we always do just that? And we're instructed to go into Grantville and ask questions. Ah, may the Good Lord give him mercy, he's not leaving off."

"We'll need to do with more subtlety than Amsterdam," Fitzroyce said. "My left ear was nearly shaved off in that last *discussion*."

"Aye, we will." A thought struck O'Connor at that moment. He glanced up at the three people behind him. "England's no friend to Germany at this moment, are they?"

". . . No . . ."

"Then, what's a slip of a girl from the Midlands doing here?"

O'Connor raised a sandy eyebrow. "Surely that's worth investigating, in his lordship's eye?"

Fitzroyce grinned. "We might have found something that will please him, then. Write him back and tell him what kind of a scent we're on."

"And send the letter back on the same ship that brought her here?" O'Connor said, with a deep laugh. "That's a jape that even his lordship would appreciate."

The two of them retired to a nearby inn to write a letter. O'Connor foresaw praise and more money in return, although not much of either, knowing the Earl of Cork.

# Chapter 13

A gentle hand pushed at her shoulder. Margaret pried open her reluctant eyelids to see Hettie standing over her with a small tray.

"It's morning, mistress. Do you recall where we are?" The maidservant set the tray down on the small table that stood adjacent to the bed in which Margaret inexplicably found herself.

"Of course, I do!" Margaret said, sitting up. "I didn't drink any wine."

Hettie took the large book that was splayed out on the coverlet, page side down and snapped it shut. "You were drunk on words, mistress. Do you recall me helping you out of your day dress?"

Margaret looked at the sleeves of her cambric shift and shook her head. Drunk on words, indeed. She did have a headache like one from overindulgence, and her eyes burned with strain from hunching over the books beside the lamp. Her mind spun with wonder, completely overwhelmed by the vision of the future. Watermills driving spinning wheels, hundreds and thousands at a time! Horse-powered looms—no, water-powered looms, churning out cloth faster than anything that her father or any other textile owner ever dreamed of. If only such massive machines could appear in their sheds!

Oh, but what would the weavers say? Some of them still left milk on the doorstep for the fairies, not that any of them had failed to see the village cats drinking from them nightly. They couldn't see the future as she did, right here, in these books.

She sighed. "It's so frustrating! These marvels are right here in these photographs. Factories turning out the finest of weaves in minutes to clothe thousands without the backbreaking labor it takes now. It's a dream, but I have no means of making these dreams come true. It all depends upon machines that don't yet exist, nor will they for at least a hundred years."

"Why not, mistress?" Hettie asked. "Who is to say that these Americans don't have a way to help make looms move faster? Didn't Mistress Rita say these are in their far past? We've the river so close to the weavers' sheds. Giving them the power to run all night and day with perhaps a boy to mind them. They must have something that makes their clothes for them. You ought to ask."

"There's another party tonight," Rita said, when Margaret came to meet her for lunch in the *employee cafeteria*. Hettie insisted that Margaret should go by herself, so her maidservant could get to know others of her station in the vast building. Rita and Margaret lifted trays from the long metal shelf that led along stations for meat, vegetables, bread, and beverages, as if each was a tidy little shop devoted to that item. "You should come. If you're worried about looking proper, I can find someone who will lend you a gown, but I think you'll be fine. Did you bring the dress you were wearing when I met you? I think that'll impress people. It was so pretty."

That, at least, was within her luggage. Despite her misgivings, Margaret pulled herself away from her books, and let Hettie fit her out in the woolen gown. It took some shaking out to rid the heavy dress of the inevitable wrinkles it had suffered in transit. She hadn't worn it since before undertaking the journey to Liverpool to take ship, and the long sail around the southern coast of Great Britain.

Margaret had a thousand questions on her tongue when they went to attend the reception that evening, but they fled, leaving her speechless, as soon as she entered the grand ballroom at the center of the presidential palace. She had let Hettie adorn her hair with silken bows at the top of her fashionable curls and dress her in the handsome woolen gown that she had worn to court in London. It didn't feel so dowdy as it had when surrounded by silks and velvets. Most of the people of Magdeburg didn't seem to indulge in luxurious fabrics as the king's courtiers did, or so she deduced from the crowd around her chatting in the wide corridor.

She approached the entrance to the great hall with Hettie at her ear like a conscience.

"You look fine, mistress. Straighten your spine! Think of Lady Pierce."

Margaret took a deep breath and stepped forward.

"Mistress Margaret de Beauchamp!" a tall man bellowed to the milling crowd already present.

Margaret felt too insignificant for such a grand introduction. Part of her wanted to retreat and flee back to her quarters, but Hettie poked her in the back. She almost turned to protest, but the intense training she had received at Lady Pierce's hands came back to her.

*Shame the devil*, the old woman had said. *Keep your head high.*

If she had been prepared to speak with an anointed king, what did she have to fear from ordinary mortals? But Mike Stearns was as good as a king. He ruled a principality as large as England itself, and had the wonders of the future at his fingertips. Still, he was Rita's brother, and was kindly disposed toward her. She had rehearsed and rehearsed her greeting to him, both in English and Amideutsch.

Keeping her hips forward, she glided into the room, with Hettie scooting close behind her. As others glanced up from their conversations, Margaret smiled at them. They went back to talking, paying her no more mind. Now what should they do? She didn't know the protocol.

"There you are! Hi, Margaret! Hi, Hettie!"

Thank heavens, here came Rita. This was the first time that Margaret had seen her in formal clothing, and was pleased and impressed. Rita wore a long green gown with a gem-edged neckline, which revealed a modest decolletage, and embroidered overskirts. It both shouted and whispered of wealth and power. One could be completely unaware of the wearer's importance, but gradually realize the subtlety of how well-made and expensive the dress had to be, and know that they had almost certainly underestimated its wearer.

"Thank you for inviting me," Margaret said.

"You've got an open invitation to any of the parties and soirees that are going on here," Rita said. "Is there anyone that you want to meet?"

"I wanted to ask you, is it possible for me to have a word with the Prime Minister?" Margaret asked. She hesitated to say why in a room crowded with other people who would no doubt have their own requests for him.

Rita looped her arm through Margaret's and squeezed it. "Mike is entertaining the duke of Saxe-Weimar right now, but I saw Becky talking to a couple of visitors from Amsterdam. Come on. I'll introduce you."

Rita wove her way expertly through the crowd, nodding to some visitors, and giving effusive greetings to others.

"She's fantastically intelligent, but she's more in John Simpson's point of view," Rita said, whispering to Margaret as they passed an elderly woman in black velvet. "Mike's been trying to bring her around to our way of thinking. I don't know whether he will succeed, or that they'll kill each other. I'm taking bets on her."

They came to a large circle of people smiling and chuckling at whatever was going on in their midst. Rita drew Margaret with her through the first tier, only to encounter another ring of onlookers.

"Excuse us," Rita said. "*Entschuldigung.*"

The other guests made way for them. Margaret hung back, but Rita hauled her into the inner circle. At its center stood a slim woman with dark, curly hair and laughing brown eyes so dark they were nearly black. She turned to look curiously at Margaret.

"Becky, let me introduce the honorable Margaret de Beauchamp, my friend. Margaret, this is Rebecca Abrabanel Stearns, my sister-in-law. Margaret came all the way from England to visit us."

Margaret felt shy, knowing that this was a member of two important families. Not only was she the wife of the Prime Minister of the United States of Europe, but a daughter of a powerful family that had influence all over the continent.

"I am honored to meet you," Margaret said.

"I have heard so much of you," Becky said, taking her hands and squeezing them warmly. "Thank you for all you have done." She had an accent that Margaret couldn't quite place. It sounded Spanish, but with the flavor of something else. "We are in your debt. I hope we will be friends."

"I . . . it would be my pleasure."

Becky introduced her to the other guests nearby. Margaret barely absorbed a single name, but curtseyed to each with her skirts held wide, and vowed to ask Rita for a list later. Becky kept hold of her hand while she talked, so Margaret couldn't withdraw. The group had been speaking in German when she arrived, but they politely switched to English.

". . . And what do you think my very literal-minded daughter did? She climbed right up into the landgravine's lap and took her spectacles from her face. Why? Because Mike commented in private that the woman was blind. Sephie thought that meant she wouldn't see anyone steal her glasses." She laughed. "We must not speak so freely in front of her."

Margaret listened, smiling and laughing along with the others. Rita had said Becky charmed everyone she met. Her skills at hospitality and diplomacy were the equal of anyone she had met in the English court.

After a little while, Rita pulled Margaret away.

"She hasn't had a chance to meet Mike yet," she told the group. "I just saw him stand up. Let me catch him before someone else does."

"Of course!" Becky said, squeezing her hand once more. "Welcome again."

"Thank you." Margaret felt quite dazed.

Once out of the crowd, Hettie caught up with them. She looked Margaret over with concern. "Are you all right, mistress? Do you need to sit down?"

"No, I'm all right."

Mike Stearns didn't look impressive when compared to an English lord, or even to his wife. A big man, he eschewed elegance in his dress, and had a hearty laugh that echoed off the high ceiling of the ballroom. He would not have been out of place in a common public house or a gathering of workers at the edge of a field, but that, Rita told her, was exactly who he was.

"What you see is what you get," she said.

And Margaret had to agree. He might have been the most real person she had ever met. He immediately made her feel at home, asking her to sit with him in one of the small groups of upholstered chairs around the edge of the big chamber. Rita perched on the arm of Mike's chair. One of the men in modest clothing stood at a slight remove from them to steer anyone away from interrupting. Margaret suspected that there were also guards of some kind to protect his person from assault, though he absolutely looked like a man who could defend himself well.

"It's a pleasure, Your Excellency," she said, keeping her back straight and her demeanor formal. Lady Pierce would have called her posture impeccable. Mike sat back at his leisure.

"You can call me Mike. I've been waiting to meet you a long

time," he said. "We owe you in a big way, and we consider you a friend for life. You helped get my sister back for me, but I'm not holding that against you."

"Go to hell," Rita said, but without rancor. Margaret was horrified at the casual blasphemy, and stared from one sibling to the other. They both laughed. "Sorry. What you see is what you get with me, too. You ought to know that by now."

"Melissa Mailey said you're here for information," Mike went on. "All of us are happy to help you out in any way we can. I'm glad to have friends in England. It hasn't worked out so well with your king. Not that he's been in communication with anyone much. Just the Earl of Cork, and I wouldn't trust *him* as far as I can throw him."

Margaret was both titillated and horrified at the same time to hear him denigrate the king's minister, but privately, she agreed, and he knew it. She understood that he was very much like his sister: blunt, friendly, very intelligent, and not afraid to speak his mind.

"So, your family manufactures wool cloth. How's business going over there?"

She had no secrets to keep from Mike. Rita told him he knew the circumstances of her previous interaction with the prisoners in the Tower. His gaze was frank. She appreciated a listening ear.

"...The prices aren't going up even though our expenses are," Margaret said, warming up to her topic. "Although our product is very good, the circumstances do not favor us. The Churnet House weavers won't be happy with what news I will be bringing back, and there will certainly be worse news to come. They will expect raises in pay, but after three bad years in a row, how can we ask them to sacrifice with us any longer?"

Mike drummed fingertips on the chair arm. "Maybe you need to include them in your successes, Margaret. Have you ever heard of collective bargaining or profit sharing?"

She was baffled. The conversation wasn't going in the direction she thought that it would.

"No, I haven't come across either of those...phrases in my reading."

"They won't be in the books Melissa set aside for you. They have to do with employee relations." Mike smiled. He glanced toward a courtier dressed in dark blue, who shook his head. "Looks like I have a little while before the next wave of petitioners comes over to bend my ear. Margaret, I was a union steward in the miners' union in the USA. Among other concessions it negotiated for us, our organization had a contracted agreement with the mine owners to give their employees a portion of the profits above their salaries according to their work, so everyone got something out of the business. When times were good, they earned a nice bonus. When there's no profit, no one gets any extra, but they found that when employees have a stake in the success of a business, they'll work harder to make sure it succeeds. They'll be happier when things are hard, because they can look forward to when they get better. The carrot makes for better productivity, not the stick. It helps to incentivize your workforce. Make them feel ownership in what they are doing, and they will rise to the occasion. You would be amazed how well it lifts the spirits of the workers when they feel that they're being heard."

Margaret frowned. "I see what you mean, but I am not at all certain that I would be able to get anyone in Barlaston to agree to a bargain like that. Not a one, not my father, not the guild masters, not the dyers or spinners. It's not the way it has been done."

"Things change every day, you know." Mike sat up and put his hands on his knees. "If you offer your workers a piece of the action before they learn about collective bargaining, it might go better for your dad if he begins to have trouble keeping your assets together. And, in my experience, offering a potential bonus in lieu of a raise in pay is something that the mining companies have also had some success with." He smiled. "I won't say that's the most ethical way to go, but I've learned a lot about the management side of business dealings since I took this job."

"It would mean a very small amount of money for each of them," Margaret said, thinking hard. "A *very* small amount."

"I think you'd find that even a minor stake makes people work harder when they realize their own labor produces those results. Might even make them come up with ways to increase productivity."

"Thank you for the insight. I will have to think about that."

"I know it's a lot to absorb, Margaret. You're not thinking as a worker right now, even if your heart is in the right place. Treating people like they matter *works*. They'll give you their best effort when they believe that they're being heard."

Hettie grunted.

Margaret turned to her.

"What do you think?"

Hettie opened her mouth, but before she could speak, Mike Stearns let out a bellowing laugh. "You think you don't agree with me, Margaret, but you're already doing it. Hettie works for you, and you value and act upon her input. You don't dismiss her like the German aristocrats do. Even some of them are changing to accept the humanity of their employees. You're doing it out of instinct because it's the right way. I'll bet you learned that from your father."

"I . . . I think I must have," Margaret said. Memories of Sir Timothy conferring not only with his reeve and craftsmen, but with humbler folk, who felt that he was someone they could trust, as he trusted them. She felt proud of him all over again. "And my mother. But may I ask you—?"

A gentleman in elegant bronze-colored velvet moved nearby and spoke in Amideutsch to Mike's aide. The aide tapped a strap tied to his wrist. Mike grimaced.

"I'm sorry to cut this short. That's my next meeting. The resources of the USE are at your disposal, Margaret. Thank you again for . . . all you've done. Enjoy your time here."

The flunky helped her from her chair. Her back twinged as she rose. She didn't realize until then how stiffly she had been sitting, and her back protested. Rita gave her a pat on the arm and vanished into the crowd.

Men in elegant suits with hats adorned with astonishingly fluffy plumes eyed her when she edged past them, no doubt wondering who this ordinary young woman was who had monopolized the attention of the Prime Minister of the United States of Europe for such a long time. Hettie strutted in her wake. Margaret wondered how long she had been *equalizing* her situation out of instinct, as Prime Minister Stearns had said. It did feel natural.

That gave her important food for thought as she and Hettie made their way back to their quarters.

Once the door of their chamber closed behind them, Margaret realized that she had never brought up with Mike the matter that had brought her to Magdeburg. True, she wanted to visit with Rita and the others whom she had last seen in London, but she wanted to discharge the duty with which her father had entrusted her as soon as she could. Mike had been so friendly and easy to talk to that the dread that had been building up inside her about broaching the subject of trade had faded. Now, she began to feel impatient with herself.

The formal introduction had been made. Instead of imposing on Rita again or one of the other servants—no, *employees*—she went in search of Mike's office the very next morning.

The palace was huge, as sprawling as Whitehall, albeit not as elegantly appointed. She supposed that was to be expected, as the American palace was new and had been erected very quickly. No ornate carvings decorated the walls or ceilings. The floors were plain but clean, always clean. Thought had been put into the construction so that the thing one needed at that time, a light, a step, a door handle, were exactly where one expected them to be.

Hettie had put her finger on part of the difference between the so-called *up-timers* and the people of her time—the ease in which people lived. They didn't seem influenced by the omnipresence of royalty or religion. They made decisions for themselves, without having to worry whether they were exceeding the boundaries of their rank. In every decision, she could not help but think that she was under the authority of her father, to begin with, and thence to the will of His Majesty the king, who held the Duchy of Lancaster since the ducal seat itself had been abolished. Above all, or perhaps beside it, her duty to God kept her in fear that her actions might evoke displeasure and leave her in a state without grace.

She had attended worship services there in Magdeburg at a Baptist church beside Americans, who seemed less to fear what was above them than to rejoice and take comfort in His divine presence as a loving father, even a companion. Allowing the thought to be formed in her mind made her tremble, yet lightning didn't strike her dead. And since Divine Providence had placed her in the path of these people, was she not meant to be with them? If her Heavenly Father approved of these Americans and their new thoughts and ideas, could she not begin to accept that comfort, even pass along the concept to her family?

They also extended the notion of family as much more elastic than did people of her time. Rita had made it clear that they saw her as a relative. She didn't dare consider herself a sister or daughter to them, but perhaps a distant cousin? Once created, the bond persisted. Margaret was flattered and perhaps worried by how swiftly and how fast the connection was made. Americans lived at a speed far greater than that with which she was comfortable. New ways of living as well as new ways of thinking would take her time to absorb.

A plaque on the wall—again, exactly where she needed it to be—directed her to the executive offices. She made her way down a couple of broad staircases, collecting curious but friendly glances as she went, discovered yet another plaque with arrows, and entered a hallway that had doors to either side and a somewhat grander portal at the end. That, according to the plaque, was her destination: the office of the Prime Minister.

No guards stood at the closed door, but to her left was an open office. A man took his hands off a strange device and stood up from the wooden desk inside.

"May I help you, Mistress de Beauchamp?" he asked. At her surprise, he smiled. "We know who you are, Fräulein. I am David Zimmerman, Herr Prime Minister Stearns' secretary."

"If you please, Herr Zimmerman, I wish to speak with the Prime Minister. I have a matter to put before him. An important measure I hope he can address." She didn't know how much to tell him.

He pursed his lips. "Your forgiveness, Fräulein, but His Excellency is very busy today. Matters of state occupy him most pressingly. Is your matter urgent? Must I interrupt him for your query?"

"Oh, no!" Margaret said. Her appeal was such a small one by comparison with *matters of state*. "I do not mean to interfere."

"You do not interfere." He picked up a flat leatherbound folder and opened it. "He has room for appointments in . . . ten days' time. Would you care to call upon him at ten in the morning? I can send a messenger to bring you here. If that is not soon enough, I will see what I may do."

Margaret felt a rush of gratitude. "No, sir, that is time enough. I thank you most sincerely."

He made a slight bow. "If that is all, Fräulein?"

"Yes, that is all. I . . . thank you."

He smiled and returned to his work. It was a dismissal, but not a rude one. Margaret withdrew. She was content to exercise patience. After all, there was a town to explore, more receptions to attend, and books to read. In fact, she couldn't wait to return to the latter.

# Chapter 14

The books from the Grantville Library were such a joy. She had composed a letter to Lady Mailey thanking her effusively for the trouble that the scholar had gone to, and would gladly pay a messenger to get it to her, wherever she was. Every single volume that she had set aside for Margaret contained wonders without number. Even more wonderful was that they discussed innovations of the past, according to the Americans. More than a hundred years had gone by for the people of Grantville since power looms were introduced. The new machines had been made to eat up thread and spit out cloth at a rate no one had yet dreamed of. If it was possible to bring even one type of machine to Barlaston, her father could rebuild their fortunes in a matter of a few years. But which one? The carding machines that removed debris and straightened out the fibers? The powered spinning machines that transformed the wool into thread or yarn? The looms themselves? But did any plans for these devices exist within the library of Grantville? From what Rita and the other up-timers had told her, their collection of printed knowledge was extensive, but not complete. Large gaps existed in topics that were of no direct use to the inhabitants. Their bread and butter was earned from mining and refining of ore.

At Margaret's question, Rita had been fairly certain that no one owned a loom of any kind, most especially not a powered loom. She believed that Magda Stone, the dyemaker's wife, had a spinning wheel, a relic from Tom Stone's first wife, but it was an old-fashioned one, from a *commune*, whatever that was. In other words, of a kind that would look familiar to Margaret. That didn't help.

She made countless notes on what she had read, so many that she had run out of the ream of paper she had brought with her, and had to ask to buy from the storeroom in the palace. Father wouldn't cavil at the cost; he had taken it into account that she would have expenses that neither of them would have foreseen. All of the notes would benefit Sir Timothy and the Churnet House weavers in the end, though the extra outlay stung now. Even more, she resented her impulsiveness in buying that square of brocade. Her mother would love it, certainly, but it cut into her purse's contents.

Not that she had much in the way of other outlay. Their meals were brought to them, or she and Hettie were welcome to help themselves in the *employee cafeteria*. A young woman in a white apron came by to clean their rooms and replace their bedding every few days. Margaret was astonished by that. Often enough, when she had reason to travel from home farther away than one day, she would sleep on a bed at an inn that had been vacated only that morning by another party, and would be occupied by yet another body the night she left, without a change of linens. The young woman also took soiled clothing and brought it back cleaned and pressed, never expecting payment. Margaret was grateful, if embarrassed, but any money she brought home again would go back into the coffers, meager as it was.

If she didn't succeed in doing business with the USE, the de Beauchamps would almost certainly have to sell off the southernmost estate to the gentleman who owned the three properties that flanked it. Half of the tenants there were already working part of their time on the other manor's fields. In their hearts, they probably felt that they would be part of that demesne before the next lambing season. Losing them would be a wrench, since the families had worked for the de Beauchamps through as much as three centuries.

Hettie interrupted her studies, holding out a handsome folded white card with Margaret's name on top.

"Another party, mistress," Hettie said. "Ten of the clock tonight, if you please."

Margaret read it in surprise. "I've not been to so many events in one season, ever! Prime Minister Stearns must be exhausted, having to entertain day in and day out."

"I'd rather you had had notice of this busy a calendar," Hettie said, her face set in a disapproving mask. "Your good chemise is clean, but the overgown is the same one that you've been wearing. I can freshen it, but what will people say, seeing the same dress over and over?"

Margaret shook her head. "I doubt truly that anyone will notice. Or mind. That doesn't seem to be the way people here think."

Her assumption proved correct. By now, she had made the acquaintance of numerous people. The ones she recognized made room for her in their various groups. Not one of them so much as glanced at her dress, only her face. A gentleman at a round table near the refreshments vacated a chair, indicating with a wave that she should sit with him and his party. Margaret nodded her thanks, but kept moving.

She was enjoying Magdeburg, but being so far from home and in a place so different was beginning to take a toll. It had been three weeks now, seeing new things and being busy every day. Once Margaret had her meeting with Mike Stearns, she had no good excuse to stay any longer and impose upon Rita's boundless hospitality. One day soon, Margaret hoped that times would be different in England, and the Americans would be welcome to enjoy hospitality at her family's manor. In the meanwhile, she wanted to absorb all the impressions that she could, to take home and share with her mother, Lady Pierce, and in letters to Lady Ann. Her letters were already so long that she had taken to cross-writing on every page to make sure she left out no details. Hettie gave her a look that asked for permission, and Margaret tilted her head to show that she understood. Her maidservant wanted to stand with the other employees and share gossip. She would have her own stories to tell when they returned to Barlaston. Margaret only wished that she could be a fly on the wall to listen to Hettie's tales, and see the reactions from the rest of the household staff.

She had already met so many people that her head spun. Margaret nodded to a few with whom she had conversed, and accepted a glass of punch from a large man in all black with hair to match. He gave her an odd look, and she wondered whether he was expecting a tip. That would have been odd, since no one who worked in the palace ever did seem to have his or her palm out for a coin. What a change from England!

With her cup in hand, she drifted into a circle of people dressed in what she would have considered working class clothing. The men and women gave her a cursory glance, but carried on with their conversation. A very small part of her was outraged that they didn't notice her rank, and a much larger part was gleeful that they did not. She had been thinking deeply about Mike Stearns' explanation of equality.

Such seemed also to be the subject of the conversation of her current company. She found herself listening with her slowly improving Amideutsch to a powerfully built woman with blonde braids wound around her head and an impressive figure that would have fought against the constraints of any corset. Margaret felt like a scarecrow beside her.

"Innovation," the woman declared, to the nods of the others, then dropped back into a rapid spate of German that Margaret couldn't follow.

True to her training in society matters, Margaret nodded and smiled. But that word stayed with her. She was all for innovation, though she didn't know how or what to innovate upon.

Rita was also present at the gathering, so she excused herself from the group and made her way to the tall woman's side.

"There you are!" Rita exclaimed, putting an arm around her shoulders. "I bet you feel like I've abandoned you."

"Not at all," Margaret said. "You've left me in very good company." When Rita glanced over her head toward the blonde woman with a look of surprise, Margaret laughed. "No, although she is a very interesting person. The ones I speak of are between stiff covers. What marvels are still to come in the future! I only wish that I could see them come to pass in my time."

Rita laughed. "The books! It's funny, though, because most of the people from our time have forgotten everything that provides the things we took for granted, like cloth and paper and canned food, let alone television and computers. They have—had—no idea what struggles our ancestors, your descendants, had to go through to come up with the inventions. It's all become invisible to the ordinary person. I know that cloth came down in price a ton after the machines in your books came in. We all learned about Eli Whitney and the cotton gin in school, but after that it's a blur. You've probably forgotten more about the clothes on my back than I'll ever learn."

"With that in mind," Margaret began, "I've made an appointment to see His Excellency on the business matter entrusted to me by my father."

Rita nodded. "We thought that might be coming. How bad is it?"

Rita did understand. How obvious had it been when Margaret had accepted Rita's invitation to visit that a financial matter was troubling her? She felt tears of shame starting in her eyes. She looked around at the knots of people conversing. A few of them were close enough to hear her, although they appeared to be engaged in their own affairs. She looked around. Some of the people near them tried not to look as though they were eavesdropping, but clearly were. Gossip was a way of life here, as it was everywhere else.

"Forgive my boldness, but I would prefer not to speak of these matters in public."

Rita looked apologetic. "You're not bold at all. I'm being tactless. Let me check in with Mike. All right? Are you going to be all right?"

"Yes, thank you for your kindness."

Once again, Margaret felt overwhelmed by the care that the Americans were showing her. The connection had grown beyond the assistance that she had given them in London. They acted as if they were the dearest friends she and her family had in the world. She blinked hard to drive back the emotion that bubbled up inside her.

Hettie had started over from her post near the wall with a small handkerchief already out of her reticule. Margaret accepted it and retreated to a space behind a pillar to dab at the corners of her eyes. The room was getting very hot from the number of people present, and she felt out of her depth.

The few people that she recognized from previous evenings smiled and bowed to her as they passed. They did not stop to remark upon her red eyes and nose. She was grateful for their forbearance. Margaret took a deep breath and composed herself. How many stories she would have to relate to her family and Lady Pierce! With careful omissions, of course.

"Mistress, look!" Hettie whispered, with an urgent note in her voice. "There, behind the punch table."

Margaret turned, ever so casually, as if she was prepared to rejoin the group, and allowed a glimpse toward Hettie's concern.

Two young women in the loose bodices that seemed to be

the style of the Germanies beamed at party-goers who came to ask for cups of punch or refreshments. It couldn't be those that worried her maidservant. No . . . ! She turned her head back again as if looking for someone. Then, she spotted them.

They were clad in black, as they had been in Frau Engelmann's tavern, and she couldn't mistake the man with dark, wavy hair and the long nose. Beside him, his shorter, fairer companion met her eyes just for a moment, then turned away with apparent disinterest. Margaret felt her heart pound.

"They cannot possibly be the same men from Hamburg, can they?" she asked.

"I'd have said, without a doubt," Hettie replied, after another peep around the pillar. "Them or their twins."

"Did they follow us here? What are the odds that they would end up in this place at the same time?"

Hettie set her jaw. "Why would they be following us? What cause would they have? It's a coincidence, mistress. It has to be. You saw that great beast of a train. And it has traveled up and back to Hamburg several times since we came. Many people come and go from Magdeburg, so it seems. They had business here, same as your good self."

Hettie clearly wasn't satisfied with her own words. Neither was Margaret. She'd have to make careful enquiries as to the identity of the men, if she could.

The next day, a young man in neat breeches and a vest over a spotless white cambric shirt came to call upon her just as she and Hettie returned from morning services at the nearby church.

"Fräulein, I mean, Mistress de Beauchamp?" he inquired, in very good English, although flavored with the German accent. "If you will, His Excellency the Prime Minister will see you in the half of the hour. I will you escort. Along with you the samples of the fabric of your origin you bring, *bitte*?"

"Yes, thank you." Margaret couldn't help but feel fire rise in her cheeks. Rita and Mike both knew she had come to bargain. They had, after all, talked about such a possibility while the Americans were still held prisoner in London. She was determined not to mention the debt until she had to. Business only. All business. "I will be ready when you return."

He smiled and bowed again.

Margaret threw open the lid of the heavy trunk that held her personal goods. She and Hettie removed all of her clothing that was not already in the standing cupboard, as well as the gifts for her family that she had obtained in the last few days. At the bottom lay three rectangular muslin-wrapped parcels that were heavy for their size. Margaret set them on the table with the stacks of borrowed books.

"I feel like a spy," she said. "Smuggling covert woolens under false pretenses."

"Now, now, mistress," Hettie said, comfortingly. "All they can say is no."

Margaret summoned up all the steel she had and concentrated it in her backbone. She gathered up the parcels, and pictured Sir Timothy's hopeful face as he had sent her off in the goods wagon.

"Well, Father, wish me luck."

The office of the Prime Minister of the United States of Europe seemed austere and forbidding with its plain walls and clean-swept floor. Upright metal boxes of gray, brown, or black with many drawers were lined up along one wall. Margaret could only contrast his office with the ornately decorated small den in which the Earl of Cork had met her. Prime Minister Stearns sat in a large leather chair that rather resembled a throne. His sister perched on the edge of a mighty carved desk, her denim skirts swirling around her ankles.

They weren't alone. A gentleman with curly gray hair and twinkling blue eyes behind gold-rimmed spectacles stood at Prime Minister Stearns' side. And another man of the same age, very trim and upright, with barbered, silvering hair and wearing a perfectly tailored uniform that immediately drew Margaret's attention and admiration, stood at a distance from the two of them. She had glimpsed both at the evening gatherings.

"Thank you for agreeing to see me, Your Excellency," Margaret said, curtseying.

"The pleasure's all mine," Mike Stearns said. "Let me introduce you to Admiral Simpson, head of the USE navy." The man in uniform gave her a curt nod. Stearns aimed a thumb at the man in spectacles. "And this is Herr Mullen, head of procurement for my government. So, what can we do for you?"

Margaret held her head high. "I have come to discuss a matter of importance to my father. While I was in London, Lady Rita made a suggestion which was impossible for me to accept at the time, but..." She hesitated, and Rita made a gesture for her to continue. Margaret swallowed her pride. She had come too far to back away. "...I bring some of the finest cloth that our weavers have produced, with the aim of offering the services of Churnet House to help clothe your new armed forces. I promise you that the goods will suit any use to which you choose to put them, and we are eager to make changes according to your needs. My family has been making quality wool fabric for over three hundred years."

Mike gave her a warm smile that disarmed her. "Yes, Rita mentioned it. You impressed her and our other friends."

"I've nothing to do with it, sir. It's our goods that I hope will impress you," Margaret said, a trifle embarrassed.

"Don't discount personal connections," Mike said. "You may have the best merchandise in the world, but sometimes it's who you know that will get it looked at."

Herr Mullen came forward to take the bundles of cloth from Hettie. He brought them to the Prime Minister's desk and undid the twill ties holding them closed. Once freed, the bolts of wool slithered over the desk with an inviting hiss. Margaret was very proud of the weave of each, and the evenness of the deep indigo blue in which they had been dyed. Each bolt represented a different weight. The first was a heavyweight wool, the second a flannel, and the third, a very lightweight woolen, was twilled.

Herr Mullen drew from his waistcoat pocket a small eyeglass and peered closely at a swath of one piece after another. Admiral Simpson stepped close and fixed a keen eye, not on the fabric, but on Herr Mullen's face.

"*Sehr gut*," Mullen said. He spoke in clipped Amideutsch that Margaret had trouble following, although he kept shooting her friendly glances to try and include her in the conversation.

Admiral Simpson asked a question. Mullen held up a length of cloth and offered him the small eyeglass. Simpson waved it away with impatience and barked out a question. Mullen replied in phrases that made the others nod their heads.

At last, Prime Minister Stearns turned to Margaret. "I apologize for holding a conversation in a language you're not familiar with, but it put the rest of us on the same page. Rita has been telling me how good your family's materials are, and Herr Mullen agrees. He says it takes approximately five to six yards of cloth to make a uniform, not including lining. Does that sound right to you?"

"Yes, that is what we would use for a suit of clothes for a gentleman," Margaret said. "We are not tailors, but that is often what drapers order from us. I believe it would be much the same for a uniform like the ones I saw the crew wearing on the *Metahelios*."

Admiral Simpson cleared his throat. His precise voice fitted his appearance.

"We expect over time to grow the force to several thousand men, Miss de Beauchamp. How much can Churnet House supply, and how soon?"

Margaret produced a paper that her father had written out, containing the output that the de Beauchamp weavers were able to make over the course of a year, and handed it to the admiral. He looked it over and frowned.

"What do you think?" Stearns asked him.

"Perhaps fifteen percent of our requirements, probably less," Simpson said. He glanced up at Margaret. "Are you looking to gear up in the future?"

"Yes, sir," Margaret said. "I've been reading books lent to me by Lady Mailey on the marvelous machines of the future. If the USE has plans with which we may construct any of them, I am sure my father will want to make use of them to become more competitive. I realize that we are at a disadvantage, being two overland journeys and a sea voyage away from you. Farther and a little costlier than the weavers in the Netherlands. Still we wish to make progress." It hurt her pride to admit it, but business was business, and she would have to deal with the obduracy of the weavers later. An order for thousands of yards would no doubt smooth out many bumps in the argument to come. "We would be pleased to weave to your order, for what portion of your needs that we can furnish."

Herr Mullen looked over the document from Sir Timothy, and spoke to the Prime Minister. Stearns turned to Margaret.

"We'll need to discuss this, Miss de Beauchamp. Thanks for bringing this to us."

Rita shot her a glance that had a clear question. Margaret shook her head but withdrew. The page escorted them back to their quarters.

# Chapter 15

"I think they liked the cloth, especially the lightweight twill, mistress," Hettie said, as they wove through the maze of corridors. "Admiral Simpson is the one you have to convince, I can tell. He's a stickler."

"Yes," Margaret said, lost in thought. "They have no real need other than friendship to buy from us, and I have no guarantee that I can make the guild masters agree to make use of the machines from the future. I will almost certainly end up having to ask for a loan from the Americans instead. No. We need to think as though we were from the future ourselves, and find a solution that everyone can live with. That's the only way forward. Come with me. Let us delve back into the books, and see what steps we really can take."

But every page in the history books brought new revelations, and made Margaret feel as though her family's business was rooted in almost biblical times, as far as their machinery went. The looms were driven by foot pedals, and the heddles were raised and lowered by foot, and the shuttles sent flying by hand.

To incorporate the water looms and spinning jennies she had seen in the books would require very detailed plans, as well as the assistance of master blacksmiths and turners, probably more than were employed by the manor in any of the small villages around them. But how to tie them all together? Though she knew the ins and outs of weaving and spinning, she couldn't picture the means of making looms and spinning wheels into the massive facilities she saw in the books.

She pushed away the book before her and let her head sink into her hands. All these ideas were beyond the capabilities and the temperament of the Churnet House weavers. Nor did they in fact address the problem that was at the bottom of it all: even at full capacity, they couldn't promise that they would be able to provide fifteen percent of the woolen cloth required by the USE, not without reaching out to other manors for fleeces or thread, which would be an extra cost. Add in the need to hire and train other spinners and weavers, fullers and dyers. But subtract the cost of shipping the goods to Magdeburg, and more red ink splashed the accounting ledger. Not only that, they couldn't possibly raise the rates for the cloth to cover all of their costs, because it had become clear from their visit to Christiansen and Schwartz that their goods were no longer competitive with woolen cloth coming from the continent, a mere wagon journey, train trip, or barge trip upriver.

So, even at full capacity, with all things being perfect, what the manor could produce couldn't pay enough to meet expenses, make even a modest profit, and still pay the tax that the crown required. There would be nothing to share with the weavers, who would undoubtedly begin offering their services to other manors, even leaving the county.

They were in a trap from which Margaret could not see escape. Sir Timothy and James no doubt realized the same thing, which was why James did his best to trade other goods for the commission he could bring home to his parents. Sooner or later, and most likely sooner, the manor would fail, and they would lose everything. Hundreds of years of family history, gone! She never dreamed that she would see the day.

Margaret felt a warm arm slip around her shoulders and squeeze gently.

"Stop looking at the books for now, mistress," Hettie said. "Come out for a walk. We've not seen much beyond this room and a few parties. We shouldn't waste the time we have here, since it's likely to be the only time."

Margaret straightened up in her seat and sighed. She put her hand on Hettie's and squeezed it.

"Bless you. You've been my true friend. All that Prime Minister Stearns said about you is true. I must not take you for granted."

Hettie blushed. "Ah, mistress, you never do. But let's get you out of here and into the fresh air. All these closed windows are letting bad humors cloud your brain." She took Margaret's cloak off the peg and fastened it around her mistress' shoulders. "I've got a little surprise for you, if you will. I was talking with the Senator's maid, and she told me there's a chocolate room not far where women are permitted same as men! Where have you heard of such a thing?" With a look of daring, she donned her own cloak and opened the door.

"There are so many new ideas in the USE," Margaret said, following her. "Many more than may fit in my poor head."

As they came down the main stairs, a strongly built young man with curling brown hair and wearing plain but good ochre-colored trousers and tunic over a gleaming white shirt spotted them. He had a sword hanging from his belt. With gestures of apology, he left the knot of those with whom he was conversing.

"Fräulein de Beauchamp," he said in barely accented English. "I am Stefan Lauter. Frau Stearns has instructed me to escort you this day to enjoy the chocolate. Will you permit?"

Margaret turned her gaze upon Hettie in horror, who held up her hands helplessly. "I hate to impose upon Madame Stearns' kindness, sir."

"It is not an imposition," he said. "If we had known you would like to see more of the attractions of Magdeburg, we would have made arrangements sooner. But, as Herr Prime Minister Stearns will say, 'better late than never.' May I show you the way there?" He held out his arm to her. He extended the other to Hettie, who backed away in embarrassment.

Margaret felt color rise in her cheeks as Stefan brought her out of doors and turned to the right.

"I never asked for anything, mistress," Hettie said in an undertone, walking at Margaret's other elbow. "I vow that I only heard about the shop. Her servant must have mentioned it to her. I had the directions myself." She held up a slip of paper.

Stefan threaded his way expertly through the busy streets, chatting to them all the while. Despite being early spring, delicate blue and white blossoms poked their heads up through the soil in the red-brick flower beds in the center of the wide avenues near the presidential palace. More flowers adorned the center of the open squares that surrounded the imposing building, but something overwhelmed their scent. When asked, the driver drew their attention to the factory buildings that were in sight down the streets toward the waterfront. Smoke rose thickly from the chimneys, and Margaret smelled burning coal. A couple of ships stood at harbor, unlike any that Margaret had ever seen in Liverpool or London. Their sides appeared gray instead of brown.

"What are those, sir?" she asked Stefan.

"The new warships, Fräulein," he replied. "Admiral Simpson's designs. Most remarkable. Metal hulls. They acquitted themselves bravely in Denmark."

Magdeburg bustled, not only in business, but in relaxation. In every square stood a public house of some kind. As it approached noon, those filled up with customers chatting over mugs of beer and shared platters of food. As the weather was fine, most of the customers sat outside at long wooden tables. Some of them smoked long wooden pipes, the tobacco of the Americas.

She noticed that men and women alike occupied the squares and the gardens, talking to one another as though it was nothing in the world. What would her mother say to such unchaperoned interaction? Lady Pierce would be scandalized. But...

"I wish that Lady Ann was here," she found herself saying. The red-headed aristocrat would almost certainly have joined in the conversations without hesitation. Margaret tried to commit to memory every detail of the scene around her, so she could send off a letter to her friend. The world was changing, and Magdeburg was the center of the pond in which a stone had been dropped, setting rings of influence outward, for better or worse.

For better, she corrected herself. She wondered whether she and Hettie would have been allowed to go to the chocolate room alone, but decided, yes, they must. Someone like Rita or Lady Mailey or even Juliet Sutherland would refuse to be kept away from pleasant places just because of their sex. It was fact that, in her world, women of Hettie's class were able to go about their business individually, yet she was expected to have a companion, a chaperone, or a male relative with her, overseeing every action. Oh, of course, the working classes had their constrictions, under the authority as they were of the gentry and the nobility, yet they seemed more free.

These were thoughts that might have wended their way through her mind from time to time in the past, but she would have dismissed them outright as being improper. Prime Minister Stearns' words echoed in her ear: she had already begun to think of the way in which she and others lived, not considering the ramifications of those strata each class occupied. It was a dangerous notion. Had the code by which she lived been a good one or a bad one? Or could it be judged so easily? The prospect was terrifying as well as tempting.

A rich yet flowery aroma tantalized her nose even before Stefan spoke.

"The chocolate room is just here, Fräulein," he said, guiding her over to what looked like yet another public house, but the tableware was different. There were no great ceramic steins with foam sloshing over the lip. Instead, small copper pitchers with long stick handles protruding from the side and white ceramic cups smaller than her fist were borne on trays by rosy-cheeked, white-aproned men to the waiting customers. Chocolate was a new craze among the well-to-do in some of the great cities. It had come to Europe from the New World, brought back by some of the American and Spanish explorers, and was much enjoyed in France in particular for many decades. But the public establishments in which it was consumed had been for men only. Outside, this building was much the same, but inside, yes, there were women customers.

Margaret gulped deep mouthfuls of air as though she was consuming a delicacy from the atmosphere.

"That smells marvelous!" she declared. Stefan chuckled.

"Shouldn't we try it? As we're here? Wouldn't Lady Ann say we ought to accept new experiences?" Hettie asked, with eyes that gleamed with mischief. "Not to make decisions for you, mistress, nor to speak above my station."

Margaret shook her head. "You're like the conscience in my ear. Of course, Lady Ann would say to try it, and to send an account of it to her. You shall help me to remember every detail."

"I shall, mistress," Hettie said.

"Come, then," Stefan said, laughing. He held open the door of the establishment for Margaret, who felt shy but walked in as though she had been specifically invited.

To her great relief, women were indeed patronizing this place, those of every walk of life. A cluster of girls about her age but wearing head scarves and voluminous aprons sat around a small round table near the door. The small pitcher in their midst suggested that these serving girls had pooled their wages for the treat. Further in, elegant men in tall, peaked hats and the soft ruffs that Margaret had admired in Hamburg poured the dark brown liquid from individual ewers. They sampled the contents of their cups with all evidence of satisfaction. Margaret could not get over the tantalizing aroma, and hoped sincerely that it would taste as good as it smelled.

A portly gentleman with a handsome curled mustache and clad in fine, russet-colored coat and trousers spotted them and came to bow before Margaret.

*"Meine Damen und mein Herr, wilkommen! Darf ich dir zu einem Tisch führen?"* he asked.

"I . . . I am afraid my German is not very fluent," Margaret stammered.

"Ach, your pardon I beg!" he said, smiling broadly. "I the English speak. With me come and a table to you I will show!"

He edged his large frame expertly in between the customers. Instead of large, rectangular tables as in the taverns, the chocolate room had been furnished in small, round tables covered in white cloths. Three men rose near the back of the room, and a man in shirt sleeves and an apron rushed to whisk the dishes and cloth away onto a tray. He spread out a new cloth just as the host escorted Margaret, Hettie, and Stefan there. The porter helped both ladies into chairs, pushing Hettie's close in with a playful "oof!" Hettie blushed, and they giggled.

*"Drei schokolade?"* the host enquired to Margaret.

*"Ja, bitte,"* Margaret replied. The host departed. Margaret looked around her. The women customers had given them a quick, curious glance and gone back to their conversations. The men hardly spared them any attention at all. It was as though she and Hettie belonged, and not just because Stefan was with them. Not a single expression of disapproval to be had. She leaned over and pitched her voice low. "This is delightful. I feel so *improper*."

"Should I be at this table with you?" Hettie asked Stefan. "Perhaps I need to be with the servants near the door."

*"Nein!"* Stefan declared. "The Americans do this as their ordinary practice. All may enjoy together."

"I have been talking to the other servants—the employees," Hettie said, shyly. "Those who work closely with them find them to be, not quite friends, but conscious that they are worthy of appreciation? I don't have the words to describe it, and I don't speak the new language like you do."

"I don't have words for all this either," Margaret said. She gathered in all the impressions she could for later consideration. No wonder the king felt the Americans were dangerous. If workingmen could dine side by side with royalty, princes would be little higher than merchants or seamen. Or women, Margaret thought boldly.

No. She dismissed the notion. Or should she? She bantered with her brothers as equals in the confines of her home, yet outside the family, men listened to James and the other boys, even though all of her surviving brothers were younger than she and had less experience in matters of business. Margaret was respected by the guild masters because of her knowledge, she knew, but was openly considered to have less authority because of her sex. She read fiercely and absorbed what she read, yet the hidebound men who worked for and with her father respected her, but would not really listen to any innovation she offered. That was one of the reasons she preferred books. *They* didn't know if the person reading them was a man or a woman.

Her late Majesty, Queen Elizabeth of England had always held herself with the authority of one anointed by God, of course, but had refrained from marrying lest she lose her inheritance. What was the Latin term that her tutor had used to describe the way things were and ought to be? Oh, yes, *status quo*. Well, a pox on status quo.

She turned the new notions over on her tongue, much as she did the warm, bubbling chocolate that the server offered her. She would carry those memories and those thoughts home with her.

Ian Callaghan and his mates enjoyed the bustle of the city from their point of vantage at a table before the Yankee Clipper Inn. The ale was good, just adding to the pleasure of being at liberty for a few hours after the drills that had begun at dawn. Working for the USE was going to be hard work, that was for certain, but they'd been provided with uniforms that fit, for a miracle, and good, sound boots. The wool fabric of the uniform might be a little heavy for the season, as it was far warmer in Germany than it was in Ireland, but the quartermaster promised he'd be grateful for it later. He was learning to speak Amideutsch, though it sounded harsh to his ears. Wages were nothing to be sneezed at, either. He had coin in his pocket.

One of the barmaids had exchanged glances with him. She'd even gone to the length of coming within the curve of his arm when she came to refill their cups, and accepted a tip from him with a smile. Patrick Flynn and his other newmade friends teased him a bit when the girl had sidled up to Feldwebel Schmitt, their sergeant-major right afterwards. Ah, well, fortunes of war, so they said. He'd find a Fräulein. Or more than one. He was a good-looking man, in good shape, with a future. Magdeburg was a fine city.

Across the way was a building the likes of which he had never seen in his life. It looked like an ordinary inn, but either side of it was flanked by wooden arches painted yellow. People, mostly of his own class, came and went from it in a businesslike manner. To be sure, they were drinking, just like himself and his fellow troops, but it seemed there was more going on than just idle conversation.

"Should we join them for a glass?" he asked, pointing idly at the other inn.

*"Nein,"* Sergeant-Major Schmitt said, sternly. "Do not going there. They are the Committee of Correspondence. They have nothing to do with you."

"Private establishment, then, Feldwebel?" asked Patrick.

"Of sorts." That was as much as they ever got out of Schmitt. Ah, well, why move from the spot they were in? Ian could smell wurst frying inside the inn. That'd go well with the beer.

"Hey, there, Ian, isn't that the lass from the ship?" Patrick asked, nudging him with a playful elbow. He nodded up the street.

The freckle-faced colleen? Indeed it was, walking this way! Ian immediately righted himself and brushed imaginary crumbs from the front of his uniform jacket. And the noblewoman with her, as well. As they approached, he stood up. Hettie, for it was she, recognized him and smiled.

"Good day to you, ladies," he said, tipping his hat.

"Good day, Master Ian." Hettie giggled, but Mistress de Beauchamp only inclined her head in a dignified manner. The gentleman with them eyed Ian. Ian eyed him right back. Looked like a man who knew his way around a sword. "And how are you this day?"

"All the better for greeting you," Ian said. His friends laughed, but he ignored them. "And where have you been today? Do you care to join us?"

"Does this man trouble you?" the swordsman asked, his face turning fierce.

"No, no, he and some of these gentlemen were acquaintances on the ship," Mistress Margaret explained. "He saved us all!"

The swordsman nodded. "I honor you, sir. We must return now."

His tone brooked no disagreement. Ian thought about risking a peck on Hettie's cheek, and decided against it. Instead, he took off his hat and bowed.

"It brightened the day to have seen you, Mistress Hettie. And you, my lady."

Hettie reddened with pleasure at the courtesy. "Farewell, then," she said, and followed her mistress away. The swordsman nodded and followed them. Ian sat down again.

"A charming Fräulein," Schmitt admitted, as soon as the women were out of earshot.

"She is, that," Ian said. "She bound up me wounds when we encountered pirates."

"And how is that so?" the sergeant-major asked. "Pirates?"

Ian began to recount the story, continuing his glance after Hettie's sashaying form. He stopped in mid-sentence as a handful of figures detached themselves from the shadow of a building half a block away as the women passed it. A glint of metal caught the sun.

"Wait, then," he said. "Did you see that?"

"What?" Patrick asked.

"Footpads!" Ian said, springing to his feet. He signed to the barmaid to preserve his drink, and strode after them. Patrick and some of the other lads followed.

"Are ye certain o' what ye saw?"

"I am," Patrick said, grimly. "And they've only the one man with them."

Magdeburg might be safer than almost any town he had ever visited, but petty crime was impossible to eradicate. Anyone abroad who looked like they might have money, even a bit, was a target for those who had none.

The ladies rounded a corner ahead, and turned into a street Ian knew to be on the narrow side. He opened up his pace.

The corner was just ahead. The street, a residential lane with tall houses leaning toward one another over cobbled pavement, seemed unusually vacant. Perhaps it was the time of day when *hausfraus* were preparing the evening meal, and the children had returned from their lessons. But he could see the ladies ahead, and their sinister shadows skulking behind them. He started to call out to them, when he heard a strangled noise from behind.

He turned, just as tight fingers clamped down upon his sword hand from behind, and another hand went around his mouth. Ian flexed, prepared to throw off his attackers, but cold steel touched his neck. Cold blue eyes, inches from him, bored into his.

"*Nein,*" a voice whispered. "*Danke Schoen.* Ve vill take it from here, *meine Bruder.*"

Ian, furious at being thwarted, tried to break away. The blue-eyed man, a muscular brute in his late twenties or early thirties, took the knife from his neck and pointed ahead.

Suddenly, the shadows behind Mistress Hettie had shadows. Ian gaped at them, then at the man holding him. Other men, in plain but good clothes, had surrounded the rest of the Irishmen and their sergeant. The blue-eyed man nodded. His counterpart, the one holding Ian's sword hand let him go. Ian shrugged him off, and turned back toward Hettie and her mistress. They were at the end of the narrow street, and made a left turn into the next avenue, safe and sound with their sole escort.

The shadows were nowhere in sight. And when Ian looked around for answers, the blue-eyed man and his cohort were gone. The Irish soldiers stood in silence for a while.

"Didn't know Magdeburg was haunted, did we?" Patrick asked, his eyes wide.

"Let's go back," Ian said, swallowing hard. He still felt that steel against his neck. "I need a drink."

"So, did you like it?" Rita asked. She had invited Margaret to join her for a private dinner in her own apartments. The suite set aside for the sister of the Prime Minister and former ambassador to England was, naturally, far more elegant and well-appointed than guest rooms. It had an air of being lived in, for all that it was clean and tidy. A free-standing wooden bookshelf stood at a convenient spot beside the settee on which Rita plumped herself. The assortment of books reminded Margaret of a marketplace, where the gentry and clergy circulated among the common folk. She longed to thumb through them and see what lay between the colorful cardboard covers of the small, hand-sized books and in the larger, stern-looking volumes bound in ochre- or brick-colored cloth. "I love chocolate. I miss being able to buy my favorite bars in the convenience store. We took so much for granted. It's the little things you miss."

"We enjoyed the chocolate room immensely," Margaret said. "I believe there is one in Stoke-on-Trent, but I wouldn't be comfortable going there myself. Here feels *different*." She hesitated to say why, but Rita understood.

"I thought you'd sense that," Rita said. "Where we come from, men and women can mostly move freely among one another. It's not perfect, but it's better than it was here when we arrived. And, to be honest, it wasn't perfect in the twentieth century, either. But think of all the talent we'd lose out on if half the population was ignored. Or more." She grinned at her own words. "I'm not here to proselytize, though. I thought you'd like to know that I talked with Mike after you left. John Simpson really liked your fabric. That was genuine. Simpson doesn't lie. He's not thinking of buying from your dad just because of the debt we owe you. It's high quality. Anyone can see it. Even I can, and I didn't do that well in Home Ec. So, he's prepared to do business with you. But I saw that look on your face when they were calculating the percentages. I'd be willing to bet that you don't think the numbers add up."

"I fear you are correct," Margaret said, a rush of hopelessness overwhelming her as it had in her quarters. "Things have been so uncertain on our manor. I work closely with my father and with our reeve to manage the estates and the businesses. Ever since my elder brother Julian died, Father has relied upon me more and more. I do my best to learn what he had been taught since Julian was small. I am fortunate that I have a gift with numbers, and I can see sums in my mind's eye." A small but humorless laugh escaped her lips. "We try to keep efficiency, but I feel that so much is wasted. We lose sheep and lambs frequently, then find ourselves counting on those animals even though they are no longer there. And sometimes our workers do what they will, but not what they can. I wish that I could keep a closer eye on all of it."

"Sounds like you need a computer," Rita said with a chuckle.

"I don't know that word."

"Computers are machines that we put data into to analyze, depending on what you tell them you need. We have a few computers still running here and in Grantville, but we're switching some of the basic functions and easy equations to aqualators. They're using them here in the Treasury. They look pretty weird compared with electronic computers, and they run much, much slower, but they work. Or so I'm told. You want to see some in operation?"

"Oh, yes!" The thought of a device to calculate and keep track of all the bookkeeping of the manor for her sounded marvelous.

Rita glanced at a handsome wooden clock on the wall. "I can't do it now. I've got to talk with a couple of people, and run some errands for my husband, Tom. Meet me tomorrow afternoon in the east wing, and I'll take you to see them."

Margaret could barely contain her excitement.

"Until tomorrow, then," she said.

# Chapter 16

Despite the attraction of the books still to be read, Margaret's attention kept wandering. What would these calculating machines look like? Her tutor had explained calculus, and that it had originated with a genius mathematician using small stones, or calculi, to explain his theories. Her imagination even stretched into her dreams, creating fascinating engines like the drawings of Leonardo da Vinci, who had died a hundred years before she was born.

When she and Hettie met Rita in an echoing hallway the next morning, she had designed and rejected a thousand magical machines in her mind.

Somberly dressed employees made their way up and back with stacks of paper or leather folders. The area felt rather damp, as though they were approaching a marshland. In fact, Margaret smelled water ahead.

"This is the accounting department of the Treasury," Rita explained. "No real money is kept here, just the ledgers and records."

A couple of guards armed with long, narrow-barreled muskets stood to attention when they saw Rita approaching.

"Friedrich, Oskar, how are you?" she asked. They murmured shy replies, and unlocked the door for her. Margaret heard water running somewhere ahead of them, as if a stream flowed through the building.

The office was larger than she thought it would be. The

walls were plain red brick, with no ornamentation, paintings, or sculptures on display, as there were in myriad other chambers in the palace. The sole exception was a wooden clock with black chains hanging down from its body to wind it. Small wonder, as the moisture in the air would have deteriorated any delicate works of art. She felt as though she had just wandered into a light rainstorm. Moisture settled on her face.

Several men and women in shirtsleeves were hard at work over large ledgers, but some also minded devices attached to stacks upon stacks of gray ceramic trays about a foot across but half as tall. These were the aqualators? They looked nothing at all like the fantastic images in her mind. Not even close!

Margaret went close to look at the gray trays. Water dripped rhythmically through them and down into a catch basin. An outflow pipe went out again from the basin through the wall. It reminded her of a clepsydra that was in a museum of curiosities in Stoke, which tolled out the passing hours a drop at a time. This was a much larger and more complex system than that simple water clock, sending streams and dribbles at different rates. The water seemed to drive myriad small bronze wheels, causing numbers to appear on a flat tray set upright before the seated clerks. Once in a while, a clerk turned a knob, and a rectangular box near the door squawked and produced a sheet of paper with numbers printed on it. She couldn't make sense of what information the clerks gained from the trays.

"Looks like some kind of water-witching," Hettie said. "It's not right."

Margaret didn't agree. She didn't know how to read the droplets as the clerks did, but she watched them interact with them, trying to gather clues to the system.

"There just aren't enough computers to go around, and electricity isn't that reliable yet, so they set up this array here in the Treasury," Rita explained, her voice echoing weirdly in the damp air. "They do the books for the whole US of Europe."

"But what exactly do they do?" Margaret asked.

"They calculate," Rita said, sounding uncertain, an unusual admission for her.

"How can these trickly things calculate?"

"I don't really know how they work. We'll ask the bookkeepers."

"They calculate for us," one of the workers said, when Rita

asked him. He seemed to be of Lady Pierce's age, with damp white hair slicked back over his head. "We use them for the bookkeeping. We take the numbers given to us by the various departments and put them into the correct array. The array sorts the numbers and gives us the credits and debits, and thus we are able to keep the finances of the Treasury accurate. To the penny," the man added proudly.

Margaret gawked at the dripping trays. "They keep the ledgers for you?"

"That's right," Rita said. "Since we're not capable of producing microcircuitry yet, these are a fairly steady substitute. For now."

After thumbing through countless books from the Grantville libraries on the mechanized systems of the future and the streamlined devices that sat upon nice, dry desks, this one seemed to be primitive, harkening back centuries from her own time. Perhaps they were closer to the works of Leonardo than she had first anticipated, but it was still ages away from anything that she had ever seen.

"The concept amazes me. How do they work?" Margaret asked. The clerks shook their heads.

Rita shrugged. "They're users, not programmers. We'd have to ask a programmer. Who set up these aqualators up for you?" she asked a woman filing papers in a chest.

The woman smiled. "It is Aaron Craig. He set up the array. He's brilliant. He understands all of the ins and outs of the machine language. None of the construction makes sense to me."

"Where is his office?" Margaret asked. "May we speak to him?"

"Aaron's a teenager," Rita said. "I think he's about fifteen. He's an honors student at Grantville High School."

"He takes college courses alongside his regular studies," the woman said. "Engineering and programming at the I.C. White Technical School. That is where we send a message when we need him."

Rita nodded. "That's pretty typical. All of the computer nerds I know are kids. Oh, yes, that would be perfect. He'd be able to explain everything, and figure out if a computer system would help you at home." She glanced at the clock on the wall. "Just before three-thirty. Grantville High School should be just about ready to dismiss classes for the day. Let's see if we can catch Aaron and have him come here to meet you. Come on, let's go send a message. I don't want to miss him."

Rita turned and headed for the door, with Margaret and Hettie hurrying in her wake. She took the nearest staircase up to the top floor of the building. Margaret's thighs burned by the time they reached the top. Rita headed straight for a room that proved to be a corner chamber overlooking the street at the front of the building.

When she opened the door, Margaret heard a strange metallic clicking noise. A man with shaggy blond hair sat at a table, a black stick with a puffy top on a stand just under his chin. He frowned at the pad of paper under his pencil point. He had two black circles affixed to the sides of his head over his ears, and was writing as fast as he could as a strange device with a shiny black button suspended over a metal plate tapped furiously all by itself. Hettie gasped and squeezed Margaret's hand.

"It looks like magic, mistress," she whispered.

Just as in the Treasury office, Margaret couldn't discern any importance to the pattern. The man waited, and reached out to tap the button himself. Then, the button started moving again, and he resumed writing. When he was finished, he took off the black circles, which were connected by a flexible headband, and realized suddenly that he was not alone.

"Frau Simpson! What a pleasure!" he exclaimed, extending his hand to her. "How may I be of service?"

"Margaret, this is Fritz Pennemacher. Fritz, let me present Mistress Margaret de Beauchamp," Rita said.

"Fräulein," Fritz said, taking her fingers gently. His hand was smooth, except for calluses on the tips of his forefinger and thumb.

"Fritz is one of our communications staff. He's an expert telegrapher and radio operator. That's his microphone. He can send a message to Grantville to have someone find Aaron for us."

Margaret put two and two together even before Rita could say anything. She pointed at the . . . the microphone.

"Is this how Master Lefferts knew the details of . . . ?"

Rita laughed. "You are so quick, maybe you should learn to be a programmer yourself. Yes and no. We actually had a radio in the Tower, meaning that we could transmit voices through the air. We lived in absolute fear that the yeoman guards would go through our possessions and find it. The very least they would do would be to destroy it. I was afraid they might burn us at the stake as witches." Fritz chuckled.

"What does the moving button do?" Margaret asked.

"The telegraph requires wires to connect it to the next station, but it's small and can be installed anywhere. He listens to the code, which is a series of short and long pulses and transcribes it. It's used to communicate with locations along the train lines."

"Vould you like to try it?" Fritz asked. Margaret nodded.

He put the circles over her ears. Inside, she heard faint but rapid clicking sounds. She handed the circles back to him.

"And from this you distinguish words? How do you tell one sound from another?"

"Practice," Fritz said simply. "I presume that you did not climb all the way up here just to show off the device, Frau Simpson. How may I serve?"

"Please get on the radio to Grantville High School. Ask Herr Trelli at the Technical School to ask Aaron if he would be willing to come on the next train to Magdeburg. Once Aaron checks with his parents, he can be here by tomorrow morning, and give you a rundown on computers. If Effie won't let him come by himself, Martin is welcome to come along with him. I'll cover the fares and make sure they have somewhere to stay if he has to be here overnight."

"*Ja*. I vill haf to get their attention first." Fritz placed the black circles over his ears and began to move the black button. He waited, then started again. After what seemed like a year, the device began to twitch by itself, clicking furiously. Fritz pulled the black stick closer to his mouth and spoke in a quiet voice. He listened for what seemed like a very long time, then turned to Rita.

"He vill be here tomorrow."

# Chapter 17

O'Connor and Fitzroyce watched the English girl coming and going around the Presidential Palace as easily as if she was at home. O'Connor was delighted, as it meant they had news that the Earl of Cork would appreciate knowing. The tall woman with the commanding manner who escorted the Midlanders from the train station was familiar to the Irishmen. They'd seen her in the prisons of the Tower of London. She had been the one overseeing cleaning and sanitizing rooms, and giving medicine to the sick people, especially children. Ruth Simpson, or something of that order.

So, there *was* a clear connection between the girl from the Midlands and the Americans. Since it had been the Americans' first visit to London, O'Connor put two and two together. He thought it was an almost certainty that the English girl had met them while they were guests of His Majesty. Could she have had something to do with the escape, or had she been present during the planning of it all? It didn't matter. Ah, O'Connor could already smell the rewards he and Fitzroyce would reap. His lordship was wild to solve the mystery that was still exercising his spleen, even as he scrambled to rebuild the riverside wall of the Tower of London, on top of having to cope with the queen's death, and the renovations to the Palace of Whitehall that had already been promised His Majesty, including a mural to be painted on the ceiling of the great dining hall by the Dutch artist and diplomat, Pieter Paul Rubens. London was a beehive, and every stinger was turned toward their master. They'd be able to assuage one of his wounds, if they could get any solid information.

They needed to find a way to hear what the girl and Lady Simpson were brewing between them, but just word that they were connected would have meaning for his lordship. If they could get Mistress de Beauchamp alone for just a short time, they'd certainly glean all the information she possessed. If not with charm, then with threats. Then, they would disappear like shadows, and return to England.

Ah, but the girl was almost never alone.

They'd followed the girl's carriage from the depot to the Presidential Palace, and heard Lady Simpson describing the sights as they went. Her voice carried easily from the open-topped cart to theirs in the echoing street. It had required no jump of intuition to see that the girl and Lady Simpson were good friends, of an acquaintance that extended at least as far back as the Americans' residence in London. O'Connor and Fitzroyce had exchanged pleased glances. There was meat on this bone yet to be savored. After the dry spell in Amsterdam, they'd struck a freshet.

For all that it was the office and residence of the Prime Minister of the new country, the watch wasn't as anywhere near as vigilant as it surely would have been in other royal domiciles. Not a single guard stood at the wide-open door near the kitchen. The two men strode in as though they belonged there, and donned aprons from pegs near the doorway of the busy scullery. Joining the throng of servants was no trouble at all. In fact, the busy woman in the headscarf who was assigning tasks seemed to pay them little mind, just two more sets of willing hands. She put them to work hauling in baskets of vegetables from wagons lined up in the rear of the building.

"Think there's a chance at a meal?" Fitzroyce asked. O'Connor looked longingly at the rows of cheeses on shelves in the dairy and the sides of meat hanging from hooks in the butchery. The warm smell of fresh-baking bread wafted temptingly through the air.

"Do what the others do," O'Connor said. "Ye had a good breaking of the fast afore dawn in the pub on the quay."

"That was hours ago," Fitzroyce whined.

"Keep your voice to yourself and your eyes out on sticks," O'Connor warned him. "It's not like we can just walk in and ask them where the English girl is bestowed."

Though they had very little German or the new language Amideutsch, the Dutch they had picked up while traveling through the Lowlands was good enough to allow them to understand instructions. Apparently, servants and workers came and went from there often enough that no one remarked upon two strangers in their midst. That was all in order to what the two Irishmen could have wished. They didn't want to speak too much, for there was no disguising the fact that the two of them were Irish the moment they opened their mouths.

The head housekeeper, or so they thought of her, barked orders out in both English and the pidgin German. Everyone seemed to understand one or the other, and if the Irishmen didn't understand, someone else was quick to push them in the right direction. They picked up the meat of it, though. A reception for some notable was to be held that evening. The floors and walls of the grand ballroom, on the top floor of the palace, must be scrubbed clean, brass and glass polished to a gleam, and sconces shined so that the freakishly blue gas lamps would cast the maximum possible light. The big room was hung with tapestries, deeply hued velvet curtains covering the floor-to-ceiling windows, and framed pictures of outlandish buildings and people clad in very strange clothes.

Neither Irishman was a stranger to hard work. They managed to avoid having to wield mops and buckets, but they followed on soon afterwards with the heavy lifting. Carrying trestle tables from a storeroom two floors below, and setting them up was as easy as building a tower out of children's blocks. In fact, they got a few words of praise from the housekeeper. When cold food was laid out on a long table against the wall of the room, she waved them toward it, and gestured that they should eat their fill. The two men helped themselves to slices of a cold spiced pork roast and a couple of bread rolls before being ordered to carry chairs up and set them in groups amenable to conversation. Fitzroyce got enough to fill his greedy belly, and more beside. All they needed to do now was locate the girl and strike up a conversation.

From the talk among the other servants, they gleaned the name of the guest of honor for the evening, then promptly forgot it, as it was a lord with a string of harsh-sounding German names and titles. No one seemed to know a thing about the English girl who was a guest of Lady Simpson, nor did they much care.

Once the room was clean and set up to the satisfaction of a man in all black, they were dismissed to their other duties until nine in the evening.

"And do not be late," he admonished them in English as well as German.

O'Connor was unmoved. He'd been chastised by experts. But they weren't going to miss the chance to take Mistress de Beauchamp aside and talk with her, when she should appear.

As soon as the housekeeper took her eyes off them, they slipped around a corner and threw the aprons behind the nearest curtain. People came and went in this warren of a building without questioning from anyone, so they set out to see if they could locate the girl on their own.

Every corridor looked the same, with the same brass plaques and solid wooden doors. They tried a few doorknobs, but most of those were locked, and they'd no excuses or the language to make them for the unlocked ones. Best not to attract undue attention. The girl must emerge at some point.

The Irishmen appeared back in the kitchen on time as ordered, and were given fresh aprons and instructions to dole out food and drink to guests. As he was also clad all in black, the man in charge picked Fitzroyce out of the line, among others, to carry trays of drink among the guests. The Irishman hoisted the broad wooden trencher as he might haul a hog into a pen. In between, they were to fetch and carry more food from the kitchen as it was needed. That was perfect as far as O'Connor and Fitzroyce were concerned. It gave them the excuse to disappear when they needed to.

The appointed hour arrived. Musicians had already taken their place at one end of the grand hall. Men and women in outlandish and unfamiliar dress, hats, and wigs began to fill the room. The two men scanned the hall for the brown-haired girl, but didn't spot her. Instead, they saw the tall woman, Lady Simpson, walking from one group to another, chatting and smiling.

O'Connor went back to the serving table and seized a platter of small portions of food from a woman who was just about to take it, and began to ply guests nearby with his offerings. While Fitzroyce doled out punch with what he thought of as a hospitable smile, his partner followed Lady Simpson around the room, and tried to hear her conversation.

"Well?" Fitz asked in an undertone, when his compatriot returned.

"Nothing. Enough gossip that she ought to ride a ducking stool. Not a thing about the girl, and nothing at all about London."

"You could start a conversation about it," Fitz suggested, as his partner went by for the second time.

"And start Amsterdam all over again? When hell freezes over."

Fitzroyce kept following Lady Simpson until his tray was empty, and he brought it back to the main serving table.

"You two, get more. Down below." The man in black signed to them to fetch more meats and cheeses. O'Connor gave him a cheery nod and headed for the door with Fitzroyce in tow.

The moment they were on the outside of the ballroom door, they scurried around the corner to find a place to stow the new aprons, straighten themselves up, then return to stand in line to be announced by the page.

"Mr. O'Flaherty and Mr. Domhaill!"

And with that, the Irishmen joined the party. They accepted cups of punch from one of the young women at the serving table, and went to mingle. The girl gave them an odd look, but they returned an icy glare. It seemed the aprons had been as good a disguise as masks. Without them, they were no longer servants, but guests.

The Americans talked very freely among themselves, but they kept a close eye out to see who was listening. It could have been the English court, except that the Americans didn't dress as fancy.

They found Lady Simpson chatting with a somewhat older, more petite, and far better dressed American woman. Lady Simpson noticed the two men hovering nearby, and gave them a polite nod, as if to request that they wait a moment for her attention. O'Connor and Fitzroyce smiled back and faced one another in seeming conversation, but listened as well as they could over the other voices and music that filled the room. Finally, someone was talking about the English girl.

They had her name now: Margaret de Beauchamp. The lieutenant of the *Meadowlark* was indeed her brother, James. The woman to whom Lady Simpson was talking was also a Lady Simpson, the mother of her husband, whom, it seems, was not in Magdeburg at the moment. Ruth, or Rita, as they now knew she was called, would also be a source of information for his lordship. Mistress Margaret wasn't coming that evening.

*"Ach, Entschuldigung,"* said a grand gentleman in green velvet. He had bumped into Fitzroyce. *"Guten abend, Frau Simpson! Und Frau Simpson!"* This pleasantry was followed by a spate of incomprehensible German. The two ladies turned to the newcomer and extended their hands to grasp his outstretched fingers warmly. Several more guests, as richly dressed, bumped their way past the two Irishmen to get to the Simpson women. Fitzroyce looked more and more irritated with each jostle.

"I canna stand the shite that these people talk," he hissed. "Thinking they're as grand as God on his throne! I'd murder the whole lot of them!"

Some of the people standing nearby heard his tone and shot puzzled glimpses toward them. A couple of uniformed soldiers started to move in their direction. Sighing for the lost opportunity, O'Connor grabbed his friend's arm and urged him toward the door.

"Ah, well, ye've had too much to drink, have you not?" he said, shooting merry looks toward the others in the room. "Now ye'll not meet his graflandspeer. It'd be a pure disgrace. Come on with you."

Once they were out of the ballroom, Fitzroyce gave himself a mighty shake.

"Sorry I am," he said. "I don't know what came over me. It felt like the crowd was closing in, just like Amsterdam. My back was to the wall. If you hadn't pulled me out of there, I might have started stabbin' people just to get away."

O'Connor clapped him on the back. "Never you mind. We have the seed of what we require to inform his lordship. The girl won't stay out of our grasp forever. We'll have other chances to get what we want."

The next opportunity came soon enough. In the course of the next few days, they picked up a couple of suits of decent clothing from disused cupboards, caught fitful nights' sleep in stairwells and in empty offices, and acquired a stack of documents and a beaten-up valise from a trash barrel that they began to carry about the building, pretending to go to one appointment or another. They'd learned the art of seeming to be busy in Whitehall, when his lordship wanted them within a shout, but didn't want them hanging about near his private quarters, nor throwing back pints in the taverns.

O'Connor and Fitzroyce also kept their hand in at the kitchen. Donning their aprons, they reported near mealtimes to be assigned tasks. The housekeeper sent them to eat with the rest of the "employees," and put them to work as she saw fit when they had been fed. She never asked for their names. Nor did she address any of the other kitchen drudges by theirs, so O'Connor didn't concern himself with it. He'd just have made up another alias, and hope he could remember which name he was using where.

"O'Flaherty," on the other hand, was an honored guest at the large receptions, of course. The footman, or whatever he was called in the USE, came to know him by sight, and admit him without a second glance.

"Always walk in as if you belong," he said smugly to Fitzroyce, "and no one will question you."

They found their pot of gold at that second reception.

"Fräulein Margaret de Beauchamp!"

The girl entered, the plain maidservant at her elbow, and sailed into the room like a princess. In fact, if it was not for her dress, which was virtually unadorned, she might have been a noblewoman, not just gentry.

"She wouldn't be out of place at court," Fitz remarked, eyeing her up and down.

"Is that it, then?" O'Connor asked, disappointed. "Was she only a lady-in-waiting who met the Americans?" Hell's bells, there went their reward from the Earl of Cork. Plenty of the nobles and their servants went to the Tower to try their luck with the Tower guards. Cost them a coin or two to gawk at the prisoners, but it was no different than seeing a traveling mummers show in Covent Garden Market or a hanging on Tyburn Hill. Still and all, she was there in Thuringia, not back in London where she belonged. That was worth exploring. A queen's woman, for all that the queen had gone to heaven, had no business in the realm of an enemy of the crown. That spoke of subterfuge of some kind.

They tried to keep out of her line of sight, easy enough with the crowd. Both men took their turns getting within earshot to hear what she said to other guests. Truth to tell, it wasn't much. She did far more listening than talking. She had some German language, but it seemed to be limited. O'Connor found it to be a relief when the circles into which she introduced herself switched to the more familiar language. Most of the time, when she did make conversation, she talked about books. Books! Who gave a mouthful of devil's spit about those?

Aha, there was the tall woman again, dressed in green and wearing a lord's treasure of gems on her. O'Connor saw Fitz's eyes light up, and he elbowed him hard.

The Simpson woman moved into the circle of conversation and brought the girl out with her. To O'Connor's delight, he saw them move over to where the Prime Minister was sitting.

The man himself looked formidable, kingly, even, though there wasn't a way in creation that he had a divine right to rule anything. He greeted the girl as though he knew her, and leaned forward to ask her questions. With that, O'Connor didn't need to hear another thing. She was of importance to the Americans. But in what capacity? Was she a spy for them?

"That's something his lordship will want to know," Fitz said. He had written the girl's name down on a slip of paper to make certain it wasn't forgotten.

They edged closer to the conversation to try and hear what they were talking about. A man in plain dress saw them and waved them back. Fitz tried edging around the other side of the chairs, still out of the girl's line of sight, but the courtier was having none of it. He marched toward them, and made a scooting motion. They didn't dare attract overt attention, and backed away.

Frustrated, they retreated to near the refreshment tables. The girl there recognized them and gave them a puzzled look. O'Connor gave her his most charming glance and eyed her up and down with a speculative air. There, that was good. He'd embarrassed her. She retreated to the far end of the table.

At last, another person came to claim the Prime Minister's attention, and he made his apologies to the girl. Her servant came to fuss over her and bring her a glass of punch.

"D'ye think we can cut her out of the crowd?" Fitz asked. "We need to get her alone."

"Not here," O'Connor said, keeping his voice to a murmur. "She must go back to her rooms at some point. We'll follow and get what we need to know. I fancy with all the people leaving the palace after the party, no one will notice us spiriting her away."

Over the noise of the crowd, he heard a sudden gasp. Fitzroyce looked horrified, and pushed O'Connor toward the door.

"What ails you, man?" he asked.

"It's the maidservant," Fitz said. "She recognized us. Get out of here before she raises a fuss."

O'Connor turned to look, but was only in time to see both women disappear behind a pillar. He strode after his companion, and all but elbowed the footman out of the way to go out into the corridor.

"May Judas curse them," he said. "When could she have seen us?"

"On the Hamburg docks? Or on the train? It doesn't matter. The servant knows our faces. We'll have to keep our distance."

They kept their eyes open for another opportunity, as well as a keen awareness of who might be around or behind them. But no one came looking for them after the reception. If the wench had told her powerful friends about them, they'd have no choice but to abandon the palace and Margaret de Beauchamp, and go on to Grantville as they had been instructed. Since no hue and cry had been raised, they decided it was worth the chance of remaining.

The head housekeeper scolded them for not helping to clear the ballroom the night of the reception. She sent them to the laundry instead. Now they had to fetch and carry heavy baskets of linens to the rear of the building to dry on lines. Fitz took the opportunity to make up to one of the young women, filling her ears with sweet nonsense. He persuaded her that he could aid her in pushing carts up and back between apartments and bathing rooms, dropping off clean laundry for the residents and guests.

O'Connor waited for him in the laundry, growing more impatient with every passing hour.

Fitzroyce eventually returned, the blushing young lady tucked in his arm. O'Connor grew even more resentful when he realized what the two of them must have been doing.

"I've been pulling heavy, wet cloth out of one tub and into another, and you've been romping through Cupid's garden?" he snarled.

"Be calm," Fitz said, looking smug. "I've found the girl's rooms. Helga wouldn't let me in to look around, but I know which stair and corridor leads there. Come on."

No one was nearby when they reached the doorway. O'Connor plastered his ear against the portal.

"What is she doing?"

"Bustling around," O'Connor whispered. "They are talking about a chocolate room in the city. They are going out." Fitzroyce grinned.

"We'll catch her there."

They followed her down the stairs. They knew the streets outside well enough to know of a passageway to urge her into for a private talk. Fitzroyce fingered the knife in his belt.

But, no, she did not go alone. A young man met Mistress Margaret and the servant in the entry hall and escorted them outside.

Cursing the ill luck, the two men followed at a distance, keeping at least half a street between them so Mistress de Beauchamp, but particularly the young man, who walked like an experienced fighter, didn't spot them. He had a pistol at his side and looked as though he knew how to use it. His sharp eyes darted this way and that, taking in the entire street. They'd no means of taking him by surprise. But they followed anyhow, in case an opportunity arose. But not a single chance presented itself.

They kept back a good distance and listened, both there and back again to the palace. The two women talked without paying attention to their surroundings. Mistress de Beauchamp was planning to return soon to Hamburg, and thence to England.

"On the train, then," Fitzroyce said. "We've still enough money to follow her. She can't escape from it while it's in motion, and she will be easy prey when she alights in the station near the port."

"Aye," O'Connor said. "Our bad luck has got to break there."

# Chapter 18

With Rita's promise to come and fetch her when Aaron arrived, Margaret returned to her rooms. Even if another invitation to an evening reception appeared, she decided to stay in, perhaps stepping out to dine in the cafeteria for a small, informal meal. Although the computers in the Treasury had not given her good news, perhaps if she took home one of those gray clay boxes, they could use it to make economies within the manor and stave off further losses.

It was nice to have a comfortable evening, curled up with a book. She decided to tackle a thick tome about the history of processing cotton. The inventors' biographical notes were presented in such a slow and dull fashion that her eyes threatened to close every other paragraph, but she forced herself to keep going, in hopes of finding detailed directions on how their devices were made. This period that was yet to come, over two hundred years from then, was a whirlwind of design and competition that rivaled the Renaissance. How the author of the book could make it dull dismayed her.

Hettie had taken out their mending, and sat close to the lamp on the other side to fix the hem of a petticoat that had come unstitched. She glanced at Margaret from time to time, as if anticipating any need her mistress might have. Margaret smiled at her in appreciation.

She reached for a corner of the diagonal-cut sandwich on the shared plate between her and Hettie, when a wild, whining noise made her jump and drop it. She sat upright. The howl reminded

Margaret of a grain mill running out of control just before the windmill vanes snapped off in a high wind. She ran to the open window to look down and see where it was coming from.

Out on the street, a bronze-colored horseless vehicle came weaving through the slower carriage traffic at a speed that rivaled the train engine. It fishtailed to a halt in front of the presidential palace, back end forward, and a trio of boys leaped out of it, laughing. Margaret's eyes shone. This motorcar was even louder than the one that she had seen leaving the train station. Its casing shone, and silver pipes protruded through the lid at the front. What a marvelous thing!

The boys disappeared beneath her view as they entered the front of the building. In a few minutes, a servant came their door. Hettie let him in.

"Fräulein, Frau Simpson requests your presence in the entry hall."

Margaret rose in excitement. "They're here! Rita didn't expect them until morning!"

She almost ran after the messenger, but Hettie dragged her back.

"Your lady mother would make me sleep out in the field with the sheep if I let you go out in such a mess!"

She began to tidy Margaret's hair and straighten her gown. Margaret stood, fidgeting impatiently until Hettie released her, then all but ran toward the great staircase. Hettie came behind at a more stately pace.

As they rounded the lintel halfway to the ground floor, Rita spotted them and waved. The three boys were with her, looking a little sheepish.

". . . And I thought I told you to take the train in," Rita was saying to the middle boy, a brown-haired, blue-eyed lad about the same age as Margaret's brother, Nathaniel.

The tallest boy, a lanky youth in the trousers Margaret had learned to call *blue jeans* and a yellow cambric shirt, cleared his throat. "Well, Miz Rita, when my mama heard you're in town, she wanted me to bring you some of her blackberry jam." He held out a thin brown bag to her that clanked at the movement.

"Well, thank her for me, Trent, but it didn't take three of you to bring it in," Rita said. "And isn't that Mr. Dodge's car out there?"

"Aw, Mrs. Simpson, we just wanted to take a road trip," the shortest boy said, with a winning smile.

"Zachary Cooper, you know better than to waste fuel like that," Rita said. She sighed. "I get it. I was a teenager not *that* long ago. All right. I suppose it'll be easier to for you to take Aaron home again in a while."

"Can we get some snacks?" Trent asked. "We're starved! We all came right after school."

She waved them toward the stairs. "Go to the cafeteria," she said. "We'll meet you there later."

"Yes, ma'am! Thank you, ma'am!" The two boys vanished into the hallway. She turned to the last boy, a youth of medium height with brown hair and a square jaw.

"Margaret, this is Aaron Craig," Rita said.

Aaron wiped his palm down the thigh of his jeans and stuck his hand out to her. Margaret took it and was the receiver of a hearty if awkward handshake.

"I'm very pleased to make your acquaintance."

"Nice to meet you, ma'am," he said. "Miz Rita, the principal didn't say. Is something wrong with the aqualators?"

"No, but Miz Margaret might be interested in some to help run her family's business, and everyone here thinks you're the best person to figure out what she needs. Will you show them to her and explain how they work?"

"I'd be proud to, Miz Simpson!" The boy's face was shining with excitement at the importance of the moment as they walked up the stairs toward the Treasury department. "So, aqualators are water computers."

"I saw that," Margaret said. "What I couldn't understand is how they work. How they accept information and how they produce, er, results."

Aaron was only too happy to explain. "A computer is a machine that asks really simple questions, but several at a time, and analyzes the data that you put into it via these keyboards here. I wish I could show you the *real* computers we used to work on. I've got a Pentium at home, but the unstable electricity in Magdeburg has burned out a bunch of other people's desktops, and I didn't want to risk mine."

"I understand," Margaret said, although she didn't. He went nattering on, throwing in unfamiliar words, and peppering his discourse with stories of his interaction with computers, and how each one he had had was better than the one before.

She was surprised by how young he looked, yet how much he knew. Her own brother Nathaniel, about the same age as Aaron, couldn't possibly have explained anything this complex, even if he understood it. As much as she loved Nat, he was a mystery to his own family. Their father had been trying for a couple of years to figure out what kind of job he could do in the future. He had no gift for scholarship, falling even behind their two younger sisters at lessons. He couldn't do sums, couldn't negotiate or get along with the people in the manor, and he would have gotten himself killed if he joined the king's army or navy. Trying to picture him offering a treatise in an advanced science just could not fit into her imagination.

Aaron went on. "... So, most people who need the power of a computer and don't have access to the electronic ones we still have left are using aqualators. Say what you like, but they are pretty stable. You just have to clean them out with a little brush, at least once a week, or use triple-distilled water in a closed system, because the calculations go funky if you don't, with the buildup of silt. So, Dr. Wetmore and some other people came up with this system, and it works pretty well. It goes back to the earliest of computing systems, which I guess is like almost two hundred years ago—I mean, not now, two hundred years ago." He made an apologetic face. "It's hard thinking in two time periods at once. Aqualators are slower than anything, but they work. The ones here in the Treasury can do about the same work as a HP 12C."

"I don't know what that means."

Aaron looked abashed. "Uh, well, it's a computer that some of us used to use. I belong to the Computer Club in school. There are still a few HPs around, but they won't last forever. But the function is the same.

"Anyhow, these can be made to do complex calculations, depending on how many of them you put in parallel or sequence. It's based on that technology, practically older than civilization. They can operate anywhere there's a steady stream of running water, like I said, or in a closed system using glycerin. I've got an Aquarius aqualator at home I've been modifying. I've been trying to duplicate the video games I used to play." He looked sad. "It'll be a long time before I can get anything like that. And they run really slow, but probably fast enough for your purposes. If you need something like that, like a business computer for record keeping. That's what they have here."

"I don't really know yet," Margaret said. "How complicated would it be to make one?"

"It's pretty straightforward." He led her to the wall of dripping trays. "See? There's one set at each workstation. These are stacks that make up a series, and they're joined together with piping to form parallel arrays. That speeds up their computing power to about double what they'd be capable of on their own. It's easier when you're doing simple mathematical calculation, not design or gaming, so these don't have to have a lot of variation in function."

She found herself listening to his explanation with some degree of skepticism and a large dollop of confusion.

"May I touch one?" Margaret asked. Aaron nodded and showed her one stack that seemed to be nearly dry at the moment. She ran her fingertip along the edge of the shallow tray at the bottom. It was very smooth for a pottery dish, reminding her of the gray ware that was made from deposits in the hills near her home. Most of the pieces that had been bought from farther away in England had visible pinpoint bumps of sand. "So, they are fired clay?"

"Right! They're mostly from St. Malo, where there's a factory set up to cast the trays. Everybody needs at least six for a simple calculator, and probably twelve so they can run in parallel, so there's a massive demand. Everyone who hears about them wants one, and they want it right now! Okay, so, this is how they work," Aaron said. He pulled a ladder from against the wall and propped it so Margaret could climb up a couple of steps and look in the top of the stack. He was tall enough to stand beside her and point.

A very thin pipe let a trickle of water into the tray, where it seemed to flow in pathways like a very tiny box-hedge maze before it dribbled through holes into the tray underneath.

"You see the little bars molded in there? Well, they direct the water to indicate, 'If in this case, yes, then, or if not, not.'" He pointed to each pile of the trays through which water trickled. He showed her the channels and the holes in each, explaining what they were there to do. By the time he had launched fully into a description of "binary," Margaret couldn't take in any more information.

"I cry surrender!" she said. She climbed down the ladder and looked up at him. "Aaron, I give all respect to your expertise, but I haven't even the least means to understand anything you said after 'this is how they work.' Or before that, if I am honest."

Aaron's cheeks reddened. "I'm sure sorry, ma'am," he said.

"Can you make a system for Margaret's father and teach people how to use it?" Rita asked. "With an owner's operating manual written for absolute beginners?"

The boy perked up. "I bet I could. I taught my dad to maintain the system that runs the accounting system in the high school. It does inventory for supplies and materials. He's not a computer guy, so if I can get him to understand it, I could probably teach anyone."

"Can it reckon prices and change coins?" Margaret asked, picturing the ledgers that lined the shelf of her father's office. "Of every woolsack we produce, we must pay a portion of it to the crown. And from that, we owe the spinners and weavers their portion, as well as a fee to the dyers. There is also the cost of transport. . . ."

She found herself spooling out the list of potential debits, credits, and losses. To his credit, Aaron didn't look blank, as she had, but took a sheet of the pure white paper from a stack on a table and began to scribble. When Margaret ran out of credits and debits, potential losses, the cost of feed, and anything else she could think of that went into the production of woolen cloth, it was a daunting list.

After what seemed like a year, Aaron clapped the pencil down on the page.

"It's basic accounting," he said. "That's all. Nothing fancy. Entering a change upstream, if you get it, changes the output to reflect that. We can twist the numbers in all kinds of ways depending on what you need. Then you send the output to the printer, and there's your ledger."

"A printer?" Margaret looked around for a screw-down press, but nothing that large was in the room.

"Uh, yeah, like the one over there." He pointed to a small black box no larger than a pillow. Heralded by clattering noises like faraway hoofbeats, a sheet of the white paper slid out of it. "But they're pretty expensive," Aaron admitted. "And they take a really long time to make. And maintenance is tricky. Uh, maybe just a readout would give you what you need? Write them down yourselves? They're making some small monitors, even though I know there's a waiting list, but it'll be shorter than a printer."

"You probably don't need a printer. You already keep a ledger on paper, don't you?" Rita asked Margaret.

"We do. Perhaps all this can help us to be more efficient," she replied, looking at the list Aaron had scrawled. "We don't do anything 'fancy,' but I know my father would welcome any aid in closing up gaps in the oversight of our finances."

"Okay, I can show you how we run spreadsheets," Aaron said. He put on a winning expression. "Frau Brauner, can you help Miz Margaret out?"

Frau Brauner, a woman with brown sausage curls and a stern expression, snatched the sheet of paper out of his hand.

"It is lucky for you I am not working on the month-ending reports," she said, and turned to Margaret. "There are no numbers here."

"I can only furnish you with estimates from the last quarter-day," Margaret said, a bit taken aback by woman's terse tones.

"Then, do!"

As best she could, Margaret recalled the numbers that Sir Timothy's reeve had entered into the Churnet House journals. As she gave Frau Brauner the information, more variables occurred to her, and added them in, hoping that it wouldn't confuse the calculations. Frau Brauner only nodded and entered them in, adjusting the flow of a number of the water trays. After a few minutes, she wrote down some figures. She pointed to the totals at the bottom of the pages.

"Here is the gross, less the amounts that are tax. These are wages, feed costs, and haulage," the accountant said, pushing the paper toward them. "At the bottom is the net income. It is a negative."

Margaret compared her notes to the sheets. The water machines had confirmed what the reeve himself had told Sir Timothy: that the manor would run into the red, over and over again.

"How close is it?" Rita asked.

"It is exact," Margaret said, torn between woe and admiration for the water tray system.

The calculations did nothing but confirm for Margaret that the situation was as bad as she feared. "Our expenses are so high. We can't lessen the reliance our people have on us. Perhaps with these . . . devices, we can find any way to balance them better."

She knew she was babbling. Her tutor thought she ought to be more conversant with poetry and history, but he could not fault her grasp of mathematics. The figures were right there, confirmed by the water trays. If anything, more expenses kept popping into her mind, driving the deficit deeper and deeper. To buy wool from other manors was to add an expense and court losses for more transportation, as well as negotiations for higher wages from the spinners, dyers, and weavers for the increase in work to be done. It would be a long time before the machines that she had seen in the library books could become a reality and increase Churnet House's productivity without putting a strain on the people who worked for them, who relied upon them, who trusted them. Sheep plus wool plus time plus people plus the cost of bringing wool or cloth to market equaled one number. Sales equaled another number. The latter minus the former left very little, almost nothing. And when the tax was added in, less than zero. The water trays told her nothing she didn't already know.

# Chapter 19

Margaret settled into a chair in the damp room with the paper in her hand, staring at it without seeing it. Their business, her father's business, the one she would inherit and hoped to hand on to future generations, was going to become bankrupt.

What could they change? Most of the parts of the equation could not be altered or omitted. In fact, they would grow, quarter upon quarter, year upon year. Lambs were born, true, but sheep died, so the number of their flock would not increase swiftly enough to provide a surplus that would put the books into the black.

But... but could she do something else with the wool itself? Churnet House woolens were stable, handsome, had a goodly drape and consistent color. Impeccable. Irreproachable. Worn by the gentry and clergy, if not the nobility, and the crown had often taken some of their tax requirements in goods instead of coin. The cloth was the only real variable.

Once, His Majesty the king had worn their goods, but that was a long time ago. Was there a way she could interest the current court in their goods? What could she change that was within their capabilities? New dye lots? Her father had a long coat that came from the weavers in the northern islands of Scotland. *Clò-mòr,* made by the crofters of dyed new wool during the long winters, was as sturdy as wood, and impenetrable to the harsh island winds that blew straight in off the oceans. Father always wore it when he went out to help with the lambing. On his return, his nose and ears were almost blue with the cold, but his body remained warm. Margaret had a mental picture of the weave, called tartan. Within the main colors, she noticed smaller twists of hue blended in, giving it a depth that a simple two-by-two warp and weft ought not to have been capable of. The weave was unmistakable, as false fabrics always lacked the tiny colored threads. His Majesty might see it as a compliment to his family heritage.

But, then again, he might not. The cloth was as rough as the tongue of a cat, and smelled like the backs of the sheep from which it had come, no matter how often it had been fulled and washed. His Majesty was known to like ornamentation and ostentation. His late queen adored French and Spanish fashion. She had never been fond of English design. Without a royal warrant, they would not stand out among their peers.

Styles changed so fast. What had been worn by the upper classes when she left England might look dowdy and backward when she returned. Ribbons in the hair might be replaced by Florentine chaplets, and the curls into which Hettie had been so careful to shape Margaret's hair might have become laughable.

How could she adapt the woolens? By use of colors? Mr. Tom Stone's company produced such marvelous and intense colors. Wool took dye so very well. But, no. Any novel hues she brought back from the dye shops there in Magdeburg could be duplicated in a week or two by their rivals in the Midlands.

Could they do something even *more* different? She despaired as she remembered the fine, bright silks in court as she awaited the Earl of Cork's pleasure. Margaret could almost feel the gorgeous texture of the velvets. The brocades and damasks intrigued the eye. She could not compete with silk.

The more that she considered it, the harder the truth of her realization struck her again. No matter what kind of magic these water-filled boxes could do, they couldn't grow more fleece or raise the price in the market for the goods. If only they could do something fancy, that would stand out and make Churnet House woolens more attractive. If only...

An idea floated up out of her imagination. It must have been there for a good while, because it seemed fully-fledged and complete. Was such a dream possible?

"Hettie," Margaret said, feeling as though she was standing on the edge of a cliff. If she would fly or if she would fall depended on what the young man from the future would say. "Would you be so kind as to fetch the gift I bought for my mother from our rooms?"

Hettie tilted her head, as if trying to read Margaret's mind. "Yes, mistress." She departed on the run, her shoes slapping on the tiles.

"What's going on?" Rita asked. Margaret met her eyes.

"I realized when I spoke to Prime Minister Stearns that no matter what we did, no matter how much of our produce he was kind enough to buy, that I would be coming back here again and again, cap in hand. And to create a computer system for us will only eat up more resources than we can lay our hands on."

"We know you're good for it! You'd make it up when you can."

"With all the will in the world," Margaret assured her, "we would pay you back in coin or goods, but I fear that the debt will mount to the point where a century wouldn't suffice to cover it. Your machine only confirmed it." She turned to Aaron. "You say that you can twist numbers with these devices. Can you make them twist thread as well?"

"What do you mean?" Rita asked. Margaret turned to her. The idea was still bright in her mind.

"My brother and I visited one of our clients in Hamburg. The merchants were kind enough to praise our goods, but told us a hard truth. Our woolens cannot compete on the continent. They are very good indeed, but too ordinary, too similar to what is being produced in the Netherlands and Saxony, but for which we must charge more because of transport. But what if we were able to create something that has never been seen before?"

"Something new?" Rita's eyes were dancing. "Like what?"

The sound of shoes slapping on the floor grew louder, and Hettie hurried in, breathless. She thrust the soft parcel into Margaret's hands. She unwrapped it and held out the length of precious brocade to Rita.

"Like this." The ruby-colored fabric glowed in the lamplight. The gold and red embossing stood out upon it like clouds floating on air. "But made of wool instead of silk. Weaving is weaving. It astonishes me that no one has ever tried to do this before. It's a skill that is currently outside the range of our workers, but they may be able to work with it if there is guidance. Could your water machines tell our looms how to make this?"

"How gorgeous," Rita said, stroking the raised threads with a gentle fingertip.

"Let me take a look at it," Aaron said.

Rita and Aaron bent over the square of cloth, turning it over and over to examine both sides. Margaret was nervous for the remnant's safety, but had to trust her new friends to take care of it as well as she would.

"It looks really complicated to me," Rita said, straightening up. "Even looking at it up close, I can't figure out how you do something like that."

But Aaron's cheeks went red with excitement. "It's a repeating pattern, Mrs. Simpson," he said. "It only goes from here to here." He pointed to two places only a few inches apart. "Then it starts over."

"How do you even see that?" Rita asked. Aaron blushed even more.

"I see repeating numbers, ma'am," he said. "It's just something I do." He glanced at Margaret. "I only ever wove a potholder in Rainbow Scouts, though, ma'am. You're gonna have to tell me how you get the three-dimensional effect where the fancy part comes out on top of the plain part."

"It works like this," Margaret said. She took another piece of paper and inhaled deeply. She set the pencil to paper, and found that the point glided over the sheet, leaving behind a trail of ink. Even the Americans' writing implements were beyond her imagination. She sketched the frame of a loom and began to add the pieces.

"The base is made with a warp and weft," she explained. "The warp is made up of threads that run the length of the cloth, and the weft adds detail. The weaver shoots the shuttle or shuttles from side to side, and the heddles move up and down as the weaver steps on pedals or raises them with cords that hang from the ceiling. To make this, a second layer and possibly a third layer of weft is added, and more shuttles, which cross and link in pattern with the first layer. That is why it's possible to make the damasks in more than one color. Our master weavers in Barlaston can make patterned woolens, but nothing as complicated as this. Could your aqualators instruct them a step at a time to send the shuttles at the right intervals so they need not memorize the patterns?"

"Oh, it could do better than that, Ma'am," Aaron said. "If we hook it up with the right mechanism, it even could send the shuttles back and forth by themselves."

"Like in the Industrial Revolution?" Margaret asked, recalling a photograph in one of the hard-sided books.

"Like what?" Aaron asked.

Rita groaned. "Our educational system is good," she explained to Margaret, "but history has kind of fallen off the radar since we got here and began changing it. It's when people stopped making all goods by hand and started using mass machinery, in the middle 1800s, Aaron."

Aaron shrugged. He seemed disinterested in the past. All he cared about was the novel task at hand. He took the pencil back from Margaret.

"Okay. We'll have to work out commands to express the pattern in a code," Aaron said. He started drawing on her picture, adding little lines that led off to the sides, with unfamiliar symbols. "So, every stitch is set in the right place with the right shuttle movements. It isn't as simple as accounting, because you're including a second level of input from the weft, you called it. It'll use a lot of If, Then, and If, Not gates. At least, I think that's right. It's hard to picture right away, though." He peered at the thread. "And the looms are gonna be a lot bigger than whatever made this, like ten times as big. If you can help me work out the pattern, I am pretty sure I can figure out how to program it. I'd have to have aqualators and the mechanisms made custom for you and bring them over to you. I can get it set up and rolling, and you'll have the best cloth in the world! It might take a while, though, to make the array. But I can't wait to see it all work. I bet I can enter that in my 4-H competition. It'll knock people's eyes out!"

He was all but dancing with excitement, making notes on his paper.

"Hold on a minute!" Rita said. "You're jumping too far ahead. I'm sure it's not all Miss Margaret's decision."

"Aww, Miz Simpson!"

"He's right," Margaret said, with regret. "My father empowered me to conduct business on his behalf, and I would not betray his trust. Even though the rewards could be great, I can see a cost here that we must be able to recoup swiftly. Our finances, as you have seen, are fragile. We could lose everything—our trade, our employees, even our home, if I make the wrong decision. The de Beauchamps have been weaving cloth for the crown for over three hundred years!"

"That's pretty impressive," Rita said. "And what's changed in that time?"

Margaret made a face. "Not very much, as far as I know. My father employs forty-three souls in the weaving shop, and as many who card the wool and spin the thread from the backs of the sheep. He also acts as agent for dozens of other weavers who belong to the Guild outside of our manor. And then, there are the shepherds, the shearers, the dyers . . ." She rubbed her eyes, knowing that her mother would have swatted her wrist for such a gesture. "Nothing truly new has been added to the process for decades, if not centuries. I can tell that so much can come out of what you have shown me today. I can picture the cloth here in my mind, and it is beautiful. It would revolutionize our trade!"

"Not just yours," Rita said. "Weaving everywhere would benefit from computerization."

Margaret tilted her head, and gave a shamed little smile. "You must forgive me if I wouldn't want to share the secret for a while, just until we can get on our feet again. We have been running near to red ink in the ledger for so very long that I feel a little greedy that such a solution is possible."

"They wouldn't have me," Aaron said, stoutly, "and from what you tell me, they couldn't figure it out on their own."

"They'd seek to hire you," Margaret said, frank despite her desperation to hold the possibility of this wonder for herself and her family. "And I would not blame you for wanting to enrich yourself with your skills. Every workman should earn wages for his labor. Still . . . If such a mechanism can work, then it will bring our product into the nineteenth century, if not your twentieth or twenty-first. I must think."

She tried to see into her father's mind. This was an enormous chance to take with the family fortunes, as well as its safety. Not only would she have to introduce a concept that had never before been applied to wool-weaving, she would need equipment entirely new to the manor. Ah, but the beauty of the wool brocade would catch eyes and attract a premium that would race far ahead of the kinds of cloth that they now produced. The disappointment in the eyes of Herren Christiansen and Schwartz had been a true blow. Her father almost certainly suspected that the time of de Beauchamp woolens might be nearing an end, but what did he see for the future? Did he see any?

Likely not. Sir Timothy wasn't a risk-taker. No one could be, with all the responsibilities he had in hand. A wife, five children, so many servants and estate employees, part ownership of a trading vessel, agreements with warehouses in three port cities in England, carters and hauliers who relied on them, and on and on out to the edge of the manor for which he had responsibility. He was the squire, the man to whom everyone in Barlaston took their troubles, asked to adjudicate in disputes, lend money and a listening ear when required. All he had was the income from the wool trade, their faithful bounty for three centuries. He was known to be a steady hand, steering the craft he had inherited, with the full intention of making it last three more centuries at the very least. The manor had traditional customers, who relied on the de Beauchamp mills to produce cloth of a certain quality at a certain price.

The fact that she had been inspired to come up with this innovation did not necessarily make it one he would accept. She was only twenty, after all, and a woman. Whatever new ideas were coming out of the USE, she still lived in a place that had no such inherent social advancements. It wasn't as though they did not employ websters and spinsters alongside their male counterparts, but membership in the influential guild was out of all women's reach. And Sir Timothy had not seen what she had. He knew about brocade, to be sure; everyone in their profession knew of the varieties of cloth made from other fibers. Why no one had ever thought of incorporating the techniques of one in another puzzled her. It took meeting the Americans to make her step outside her realm of experience and dream otherwise. She wished he was there with her, to make the decision himself.

Still, Father listened to her advice. He had sent her to do business on his behalf in the USE. It couldn't only be because she was the one who had met the Americans in the Tower and aided them in their escape. He believed in her. He had always said so. She could convince him. She *must*.

But this was an investment the manor must outlay money for. There was the fee for Aaron's time and trouble, not to mention the cost of the creation of devices to add to the weavers' shed. What did he call it, an array? Would an array be needed for every loom, or could one drive many, as in the photographs in Lady Mailey's books? Could Father picture the new way of doing things, to make wool damask become a reality?

Oh, but he had to! She *wanted* to make this fabric. It would be so beautiful! In one color or two, just like Herr Oberdorn's brocades. Perhaps... perhaps she could commission Aaron to make aqualators for one or two looms, and try out the brocade in a small way. If the investment paid off, then they would make a great deal of money, first for the novelty, then for the scarcity of the fabric, since they could only produce so many bolts in a season. Over time, they could expand to meet demand. She already knew it would take time for Aaron to study the way to make the aqualators work with looms, then to design ones to patterns she had to design before she departed for home. Was there time to make the changes to produce this marvelous cloth in order to catch the fleeting interest of the customers?

But shouldn't she consider committing *all* of the weavers in her father's employ to weave the new brocade, and make as much as possible, before the attraction grew stale? Margaret hated to waste the opportunity to be first to market, to overwhelm the customers and be the only genuine source for this wonderful new cloth, because the moment their rivals saw what they were offering, they would try to do their own version of it.

She couldn't miss this chance!

"We have to do it," she said at last. She felt an optimism that she hadn't enjoyed for a long time. "I don't know what investment we must make in order to bring this enterprise about, but we cannot go on doing what we have been doing."

"Whoopee!" Aaron shouted. "I'll ask my mama tonight!"

"Hold on there," Rita said. "We're not too popular in England right now. I'm not sure Effie will let you go there. And you can't go alone. We'll have to figure out some other way to help Miz Margaret, whether it's installing aqualators, or some other means."

"Oh, I gotta! I have gotta do this, Mrs. Simpson," Aaron said, plaintively. "Nobody has ever wanted me to do something this interesting. Ever. I mean, what's going to make the Industrial Revolution happen, if we don't start now?"

"I'm willing to try," Margaret said. "I do have to convince

my father, but with all the marvels I have beheld here, and the difficult truths before us if nothing changes, I feel that sooner or later he must agree."

Rita laughed. "Introducing computers before the spinning jenny," she said. "We are standing history on its head more than ever."

"We could bring the other machines into our sheds much more easily once we are making brocades," Margaret said. "I think we need something... *spectacular* to shake the weavers from their comfortable perches and allow them to accept broader changes. And we need that impressive fabric if we are ever to afford spinning jennies and other devices."

"You've got a point," Rita said, thoughtfully. "If Aaron can make your idea work."

"I'm sure I can! Do I have to travel all the way to England to see this silk loom?" Aaron asked. He looked eager at the prospect.

"No, indeed. I met a silk weaver in Hamburg, Herr Oberdorn," Margaret said. "This brocade is his work. I will write you a letter of introduction to his sister, and I hope that they will allow you to study their machines. Do you think you can create a... a program to allow our weavers to produce fabric like this?"

"Oh, sure," Aaron said, grinning. "It'll be a snap... No, I'm joking. It's gonna be hard as stink, but I want to do it. Once I get the whole rundown, I can code something that will do what you want."

Margaret stopped herself from exclaiming her enthusiasm. There was yet one more obstacle in the path to success. She took a deep breath. "Naturally, I must pay you. What is fair for a... computer programmer to earn for such a task?"

Rita cleared her throat meaningfully. Aaron might want to ask for the moon, but she was going to make sure he kept his request in check.

Aaron dropped his gaze and studied his shoes. "I dunno, ma'am. I gotta talk it over with my mom and dad. Miz Simpson is right. I have to ask them first before I can go anywhere. Then I need to travel to Hamburg and stay there while I'm studying the weaver. And I need to ask my computer sciences teacher what's fair. And there's all that other stuff, too."

He gave her a hopeful gaze. Margaret knew exactly what he was thinking.

"My family will defray that cost, Aaron," she said, although she knew full well that the coins in her purse wouldn't be sufficient for that.

"Great! You design the fabric you want them to make. And once I know how to make the program, I'll have aqualators made to order, and me and my dad will bring them to you in England. It could take a while," he warned.

*And raise the initial investment still further*, Margaret didn't say aloud, although Rita must have known exactly what she was thinking. "In the meanwhile, my father's weavers will begin to make the cloth for the navy. We will fulfill our obligation to the USE."

"In that case, we'll have to write you another advance against the purchase," Rita said. "Whichever cloth you end up making, we'll buy it. If nothing else, you'll be supplying Admiral Simpson's troops. If your plan works, and you can make brocade woolens, I want to be the first person in Europe to wear them. I am pretty sure my mother-in-law will be the second. No," she paused thoughtfully. "I'd better let her be first. She's a lot more conscious of public appearance than I will ever be."

"Is she like my neighbor, Lady Pierce?" Margaret asked, with a smile. "She was once a lady-in-waiting to His Majesty's late mother, and has taught me so much about comportment and manners, and what is expected in court."

Rita laughed. "I bet the two of them would get along like a house on fire. In the meanwhile, I'll ask Mike's secretary, David Zimmerman, to make up documents to make it all official between us." At Margaret's alarmed expression, she smiled. "This time I can read *your* mind. Nobody has to know that you're dealing directly with the USE. I'll set it up to all be through intermediaries, probably through Becky's family, the Abrabanels."

Margaret nodded. No one who dealt with money anywhere in Europe could be unaware of the influential Jewish businessmen who seemed to be at the back of any great negotiation that occurred. So far, her father had not had to go to them, but without the help of Rita and the USE, the business would almost certainly have fallen into their hands.

Those who were familiar with the de Beauchamp holdings and their issues with the crown would assume that they had to ask the Abrabanels for financial assistance. Sir Timothy might burn in shame, but if her plan was possible, they would no longer have to struggle to be seen among the flock of wool weavers in the Midlands. Churnet House could become world-famous, and their money troubles would at last be at an end.

"Can you diagram out this pattern, or do you have something else in mind?" Aaron asked.

"Roses," Margaret said, after a moment's thought. "Our home lies in Lancashire, and the red rose is our symbol." She turned over the ledger sheet with its bad news and began to sketch on it with the smooth-running pencil. "I'd love to create a lion and unicorn pattern, which is the coat of arms of the crown, or a rose and thistle, but I saw many a silk brocade in London that depicted flowers. I believe that would be the most popular." The truth was that she had already made up her mind. In her imagination, she saw rippling red cloth with roses and leaves picked out on it.

After some not-so-subtle hints from the Treasury staff that they had work to do, Rita herded the three of them toward the employee cafeteria. Aaron picked up a huge tray of food and dove into it, still talking all the while about his ideas.

The other two boys joined them at a table in the corner. Margaret caviled at adding them to the discussion, worrying that her project was reaching too many ears. Aaron promised her that the others could keep a secret. Trent and Zachary swore that they wouldn't let anything cross their lips except between the three of them. In fact, they put forward a few ideas to improve the project. They seemed to know almost as much about computers as Aaron did, but he was clearly the most knowledgeable. The growing cloud of unfamiliar jargon threw Margaret into confusion, but Aaron saw her dismay. He slowed everything down and explained what the three boys were putting on paper.

Margaret had to caution them that it might not even move forward, depending upon her father's approval. Her heart sank even as she said it, because she had become devoted to the idea by then. She couldn't rid herself of the vision in her mind of court ladies dressed in her dream fabric. Even gentlemen might choose a sturdier brocade for their own tunics and coats. Who knew how far it could go?

Zachary brought out paper that was divided by lines that ran not only from side to side, but top to bottom as well. Aaron began to lay Margaret's pattern into the grid, outlining the sections that would be woven from the second weft.

"It'll just repeat over and over again most of the way to the margin..."

"The selvedge," Margaret corrected him. "You know computers, but I know woolwork."

"Right," Aaron said, with a cheeky smile. "We'll both know all about each other's pet topics when we're done with this project."

In the end, they repaired to Margaret's quarters to look over the books Lady Mailey had lent to her.

"I'll read those after you leave," Aaron promised. "Between that and what your silk weaver can show me, I'm sure I can come up with a program that will work on your looms and make this fabric for you." He shook the piece of brocade at them. "Maybe even work out a way you can add in variations without me having to come back. That is, if my folks let me do it." His open face turned glum.

"They will," Trent assured him. "The programming's gonna be the fun part."

"That's beyond anything I learned about computers," Rita said. "It'll be a hard job."

"No, I have one ahead that is harder by far," Margaret said, in resignation, closing the *History of Weaving* book with a snap.

"What?"

"I have to convince the weavers to let him do it."

If Margaret thought her trunks and boxes were heavy on the inward journey, they were now strained to capacity with presents from Rita, Mike, and so many others in Magdeburg. She had to take care to place the square of brocade where she could work on it during the coming sea voyage. Rita let her borrow two of Lady Mailey's precious books and she wrapped them tightly in sheets of borrowed *plastic* and oilcloth to protect them against waves and weather. One of the precious books showed the use of water mills for weaving, and the other was a primer on computer design. The volumes had been written nearly a hundred and fifty years apart, yet both were far beyond anything known to Margaret or her compatriots. If she brought nothing else home to Barlaston, those were the most valuable.

A goods wagon with the symbol of the USE on each side

had pulled up in the foreyard of the palace, and a couple of men began to load the boxes into it. Other people, from the building and the street, hung about to watch.

"I hate to let you go," Rita said, hugging Margaret. "The way you think, you should be here, helping to make the future."

Margaret embraced her with a fierce hug. "I need to go home and make the future begin there, too. Never sow all your seeds in one field, is what my grandmother always said." She sighed. "That's how we ran into the bog in which we are now. I hope to be able to pull us out of it. I can't thank you enough for all the kindness that you've shown to me and my family. The first gift—"

"You earned that," Rita said, holding up a hand. "Don't mention that again. We didn't have a chance without you."

"Having met Harry Lefferts, I cannot believe that," Margaret said, with a self-deprecating laugh. "I only saved him time. He admitted that himself."

"Harry," Rita said, with a kind of sisterly exasperation, "always acts as if he's under control, even when he's drowning in a marsh with a one-ton lead weight around his neck. We didn't really have that time. If you've read the history that would have happened without our arrival, the Earl of Cork found excuses to execute some of our friends. I wouldn't be surprised if he had not been coming up with reasons to make us disappear, as well, diplomatic immunity be damned."

"In that case," Margaret said, "the purchase order, and the letter of credit. That will save us again, perhaps for another year."

"Again, you've earned that—or you will. We expect high quality woolens from you folks, hot off the looms." Rita gave her a conspiratorial smile. "Whatever kind of fabric comes. I'm looking forward to it."

Once Margaret's parcels and cases were packed high, she measured the stacks with an expert eye.

"There isn't room for us," Margaret said, concerned.

"Oh, you're not going in this cart," Rita said. She signed to one of the men waiting with them. He put his fingers into his mouth and emitted an ear-splitting whistle.

From behind the ornamental plantings in front of the presidential palace, a bright red enclosed horseless carriage emerged. It screeched to a halt before them so abruptly Margaret jumped back. The vehicle shone like glass. Its gleaming metal rims and wheel edging were matched by the small figure of a horse that was embossed on the forepart of the car. Trent Haygood jumped out and ran around to open the opposite door.

Rita sighed theatrically. "Trent must have carjacked one of our VIP clients' cars. Again."

The teen gave her a cheeky grin. "This is my dad's Mustang," he said, helping Margaret into the rear seat. "Jump in! I'll get you to the train station before you know it."

"Wheeeeeeeee!" Hettie caroled, as the red car hurtled through the streets of Magdeburg. Margaret, in the cramped rear seat, held onto the edges of the leather seats, worrying that it would crash into an obstruction and catapult them across Magdeburg. Until it did, however, she was going to enjoy it to the fullest.

# Chapter 20

They were in plenty of time to catch the steam tug *Metahelios* back to Hamburg, so far ahead that Hettie had hours to worry over the location and state of their bags and whether the provisions she had packed would last them on the twelve-hour journey. Seated on a wrought-iron and wooden bench near the gangplank, Margaret tried to stop thinking about the machines to come and the new vocabulary she had learned to describe them so none of it would come out in casual conversation on her return journey home. The crowd on the dock grew. To Margaret's relief, most of them had their own business to attend to, leaving her alone with her thoughts.

At last, the men in one-piece suits had finished ministering to the ship's boiler, and signed that passengers could board.

She and Hettie had the other forward cabin that time. Margaret wanted badly to talk to Hettie about the innovations that she intended to bring to Barlaston, and her lofty plans for an empire built on the novelty cloth, but there was no semblance of privacy. Voices carried too well through the wooden walls.

Instead, she forced herself to enjoy the people around them. This time there was a larger contingent of passengers. Many were soldiers, returning home on leave from the USE's military, so they were full of good spirits. They offered drink and food to everyone in the car, even though it was an early-morning journey. No doubt their efforts were to make friends with the bevy of young women making their way to Hamburg to shop for goods for an upcoming wedding. A few of the soldiers had musical instruments, and persuaded everyone to join in singalongs that helped to pass the long trip. Margaret rose frequently to shake the numbness out of her limbs and to work off the nervous energy. So many good things had happened in Magdeburg! She imagined that her memories must be visible on her face like one of the up-timers' photographs.

They were favored by good weather, so there were no delays on the journey. Once they reached Hamburg, they returned on a hired cart to Frau Englemann's about an hour after sunset, and drove through streets lit by the blue flame of gaslights.

She spotted her brother alone at the end of a long table with a tall stein in his hand and an empty trencher before him.

"James!" she called, as she entered the inn. He set down his beer mug and came to embrace her.

"I'm glad to see you back safe," James said. His face looked even more sunburned than when she had left him, a tribute to the brightening spring weather. "Come sit with me. Where are your boxes?"

"Outside with the porters," Margaret said. "Hettie is negotiating with Frau Engelmann's ostler to put it all safely in the box room."

"How did it go?"

Margaret looked around at the other guests of the hostelry and slid onto the bench beside him.

"I've so much to tell you," she said, but turned her hand palm down over the table. James nodded. That was a family gesture to keep matters private.

"We'll have the whole voyage to discuss things," he said. "We sailed from here to Amsterdam. I used about half of the money to buy Delft earthenware, which cannot help but please the ladies of Stoke. That handsome blue glaze draws all eyes. I even sold some to Frau Engelmann."

"Curious that you should mention earthenware," Margaret began, then swallowed her next words. She was so excited about the prospects that she had set in motion that it was difficult to think of anything else. *Don't mention the aqualators*, she kept telling herself.

Behind her in Magdeburg—in Grantville, really, since he had to go back home and to school—Aaron Craig was working to formulate a computer that could weave the brocade pattern that she had sketched out for him. He was torn between certainty that he could create the right ebb and flow that would tell their weavers' looms how to make the fantastic cloth she had dreamed up, and knowing he would fail miserably. Margaret had faith in him, partly because Rita did, but also from seeing his passion and hearing him talk about computers with such intelligence. She didn't think she had ever known anyone who had delved as deeply into a subject that he could present it as the most interesting thing in the world. Margaret had written down as much of his discourse as she could to tell her father, along with the computer book, which she meant to study on the journey.

She secreted those notes along with the purchase orders and the letter of credit in her luggage in among the pages of the mathematics book she had carried from Barlaston. Since it was all too easy to overhear conversations on board the *Meadowlark*, she couldn't tell James all the details until they had made landfall back in Liverpool. She had never thought about her family business having trade secrets, but now they did, and the words danced upon her tongue, demanding to be allowed out.

Still, plenty of details of her journey did not fall under the concept of trade secrets. She happily described her visit to the chocolate room. James had enjoyed chocolate in some of the places in England to which she could not go and they compared notes about the flavors and dishes used to serve it.

"Perhaps we'll begin to trade in it ourselves," he said, seeing a potential outlet for the de Beauchamp enterprise. "It's been growing fast in France. Time is past when it should be wider spread. The room in Stoke has gone without a rival for too long."

The two of them bandied business ideas back and forth, James adding lively anecdotes of his own. As soon as she tried to describe some of the evening receptions to which she had been invited, though, his interest diminished to nothing. Small wonder he was happier on a merchant ship at sea.

"I'll come along tomorrow morning to escort you and your goods to the *Meadowlark*," James said. "The captain is pleased by this voyage, and sees profit at the other end. I'll have good news for Father."

"I hope I will, too," Margaret said.

James kissed her on the forehead and took his leave.

✧ ✧ ✧

In the morning, there was a great bustling in Washington's Crossing. Numerous travelers were making ready to depart on their onward journeys. Frau Engelmann had her hands full serving breakfast and seeing off her guests. Hettie had gone out early to the nearby market and obtained sausages, bread, and preserves for them to take on board the ship.

"I've even got a crock of jam for the captain," she pointed out, displaying the contents of their provision basket. "Lingonberry, whatever that is. It'll be a nice change for what he's been dining on. But we've good white bread. It's better for your digestion than this coarse brown stuff, tasty as it is. There are dry-cured meats. I've tried them, and they're of good quality. And butter. I met the woman who churned it, and she knows her way around a dairy. She recommended this cheese, which is not too salty. It's been cured two months."

"I admire your resourcefulness," Margaret said, with a smile. "You always do your best to smooth the way."

"Ah, mistress, you don't have to keep the fine American words, now that we're on our way home," Hettie said, her freckled cheeks blooming with embarrassment. "Things'll go back to the same way they always were."

"Things will never be the same," Margaret said. "One way or another."

By loitering in the corridor of the Presidential Palace near her room, O'Connor and Fitzroyce had spotted Mistress de Beauchamp emerge early in the morning and make her way out to the pavement in front of the palace in Magdeburg. Her maidservant was with her, and both were wearing bonnets and cloaks. The maid had a basket, and the girl herself had a big, thick book. Was she going back to Hamburg, or onward to Grantville? His lordship wanted them to go to the latter eventually.

Rita Simpson awaited her, along with a large number of the staff of the palace to say their farewells. As soon as the tall American woman started talking about boarding the Hamburg-bound steam tug again, Fitzroyce had gone off on a dead run to obtain them passage on the same journey. O'Connor stayed close by, knowing it would take time to load all the boxes piled beside her. They'd never get a chance to take her aside there, as one of the cursed motor cars came along, and swept her away like a bird on the wing. O'Connor envied her the chance for a ride. Never during the weeks they'd spent in the palace did an opportunity arise, for all their hinting to the drivers who fetched up now and again with guests, or those who drove their own horseless carriages.

Instead, Fitzroyce left O'Connor's ticket in the window with the seller, and had a catbird seat's view as the de Beauchamp girl boarded, followed by her servant. They sat together, as if they were friends, just proving that the Americans' rhetoric could ruin decent folks in just a few weeks' time. The servant ought to know her place.

The two men had gleaned precious little information about her during those weeks except for her name and that the Americans thought highly enough of her to put themselves at her disposal. O'Connor had no confirmation of it, but he knew in his belly that she was deeply involved with them while in London. Whether she had traveled there in order to help the king's "guests" escape, he couldn't guess, but the pieces were starting to go together like reassembling a torn-up letter. The Earl of Cork was demanding more detailed answers. The only way they could get more information was if they spoke to her before she boarded ship. The fact that she had remained out of their grasp for weeks dismayed them.

The amount of money and attention that the Americans spent on Mistress de Beauchamp spoke of a debt that needed repaying. But what? Nothing in her demeanor said she was an explosives merchant, or that she seemed to be a siren who could tempt the king's men into turning away from their duties and joining the enemy to stage an escape. And taking the cursed Cromwell with them, too! She seemed an unlikely ally to the nearly all-powerful Americans, but needs must when the devil drives. O'Connor had heard the predictions from the history books that the Americans had brought with them from the future. Cromwell would enslave their precious Ireland and even execute the king! In no decent way should he be allowed to live, let alone escape and enjoy freedom.

Although she seemed bound for Hamburg, that didn't mean she might not make a run for it at one of the three refueling stations. Every time the ship slowed and nosed inward to a dock on the long voyage, they kept an eye on her and her servant, to ensure she wasn't alighting there. It made for a tense journey.

If it had been possible to take her aside and strike up a conversation, they might have done it. Fitzroyce had a knack for charm, after all. But, at no time were they able to find her alone. A veritable hive of women had taken her under their wing in the train carriage to share food and stories. The women even visited the necessary all together, like a flock of hens. Since there was no hope of taking her aside without being observed, they stayed at the rear of the cabin block with their hats over their faces. Pretending to sleep for twelve hours made them both more tired than actually sleeping.

The wench was happy to tell her new friends that she was taking ship from Hamburg and returning home. O'Connor didn't hear the name *Meadowlark*, but what other craft would she travel on, since her brother was an officer aboard the ship? They couldn't travel on the same boat, no. The entire crew would defend her against any slight. O'Connor had no wish to swim all the way across the North Sea.

So, the sole option for getting information from her had to be in Hamburg before she boarded ship. If she stayed in the same inn, they could try to take her in the night.

They'd no time to arrange for a private place to do their questioning, but when they had stayed in Hamburg before the *Meadowlark* arrived for the first time, they'd snooped around, and knew there were rows upon rows of sturdy, thick-walled warehouses on the quay, many of which were vacant. They'd broken into one not far from the pier and slept in it, despite having some of the money from the peddler left over, because why pay for something that they didn't need to? They could carry the girl to their doss house and ask what they would.

Beyond that, they weren't certain what they would do with Mistress de Beauchamp. They ought to bring her home to London and let his lordship have her, but taking her on board another vessel and keeping her quiet for an entire ocean voyage wasn't going to be easy. Finesse wasn't something with which they had much experience. In a city as big as Hamburg, yes, someone could disappear, but their window of opportunity would be brief. Perhaps best to leave her tied up and wait for someone to come and free her.

But O'Connor couldn't help but think of the entire city of Copenhagen having been laid waste by the USE Navy for the sake of one young man. What would the Americans do if a favorite of theirs was known to have been kidnapped? No, she probably could not be allowed to see the light of day again.

They hated to kill anyone without necessity, especially an engaging young lass like that one. The women on the ship had made fast friends with her.

"She reminds me of my little cousin," he mentioned, seeing her lift a smiling face to yet another new acquaintance.

"Ach, don't be soft," Fitzroyce hissed at him. "Himself wasn't happy in his last letter that we hadn't gleaned anything of use so far, and him already sending us money. We must learn what she knows and if she did anything for the Americans in London before she takes passage. Hamburg's our last chance. She must be made to talk. And she mustn't be able to get a word to anyone afterwards."

O'Connor had to harden his heart. It went against his principles to kill someone whom he didn't have to. But letting her get word out to her friends might cause all hell to be visited upon Great Britain. Even if he didn't care what happened to the English, the Earl of Cork would see to it that the two of them never had a quiet resting spot this side of the grave.

"To hell with her, then," he said.

They followed her to the Washington's Crossing Inn, and had thick, heady beers and solid brown bread not five paces from their quarry. Her conversation was so ordinary, not hinting at all of the treason that they were certain that she had committed. After a time, the girl and her servant went up the painted wooden stairs to the sleeping rooms. The Irishmen waited until the busy common room had all but emptied out, nodded thanks to the landlady, and sauntered out into the street. They found a quiet corner and kept an eye on the building for anyone passing in or out.

In the dead of night, O'Connor crept around the side of the inn. Fitzroyce loitered in the street, keeping a lookout. A half dozen sailors and their plump doxies from the pub at the corner staggered gleefully downhill in the direction of the boat slips. Could be another "son of a gun" or more was going to be conceived on the night. He glanced back.

Fitzroyce gave him a nod. O'Connor had a flour sack over his shoulder, and a couple of torn up rags in his pockets to stuff in the girl's mouth. He had a dagger ready for the maidservant. By the time anyone came into the room, he'd be long gone.

Dogs howled in the distance. A new moon hung in the sky, casting a thin, ghostly glow. The side of the yard had one small gas lamp that shone on the side exit to the inn and on the door to the stable, which was latched closed at that hour. He heard horses shifting from hoof to hoof and blowing out gentle breaths. A moment to listen for ostlers moving around, but there was nothing.

Inside the inn, the landlady and her staff had banked down the fire. Everyone had gone to bed. Even the last drunks had gone.

On soft feet, O'Connor made his way to the rear. Bins reeking of rotting vegetables and vomit were set against the wall. The stench made O'Connor's eyes water, but at least they'd provide a leg up to the upper floor windows and give him an easy stage to move the girl out once he'd taken her.

The men had made sure to note in which room of the four the girl was staying, second to the right as you faced the stairs. Often, there would be many people in each bedchamber, but the frau who ran the house didn't put a woman traveling alone with strangers unless it was another woman. The girl's door was undoubtedly latched from the inside, so even if she cried out, there would be no one to come to her rescue. He grinned. It'd be the matter of minutes to climb up, dispose of the maidservant, and be on his way. When the hue and cry was raised, they'd be well-hidden with their prey.

He counted windows. The second from the left belonged to the girl. O'Connor shifted the bag from one shoulder to the other and slipped between the bin and the ash barrel beside it. Something soft shifted under his foot.

"Ooogh," came a voice. *"Ach, meine kopf!"* It was followed by groaning.

O'Connor jumped back. He peered around the bin.

Hell's teeth, not all the drunks had gone. A big, stout man lay sprawled there. His clothes were stained and torn, and the once-white shirt hiked up to display an expanse of hairy belly. He squinted at O'Connor and pulled himself to a sitting position. *"Was? Hast du bier? Lasst uns zusammen singen! Oh, mein schöner Liebling."* He wrapped an arm around the ash barrel and started singing a drinking song.

The window above banged open and another man leaned out. *"Scheisse! Halt den mund!"*

The drunk kept warbling, attempting to stand up. The angry man above disappeared, and reappeared the next moment. O'Connor spied the jurden in his hand just in time to jump back before the contents were poured on the man on the ground. The drunk squawked, and started swearing and brushing at himself. O'Connor smelled the stench of feces and snarled. Had he been splashed, too?

Frustrated, he retreated, slipping around the rear of the inn to the other side, where he wiped down his shoes with the flour sack and emerged onto the street.

Fitzroyce spotted him.

"What news? Where's the girl?" he whispered.

"Couldn't get to her." O'Connor was too angry to give more details. He marched down the street toward the warehouse where they could doss down. "We'll catch her on the wharf before she takes ship."

# Chapter 21

Early in the morning the *Meadowlark* was ready to depart. Fitzroyce kept pacing up and back on the dock, watching crates, bales, and boxes loaded into the ship under the watchful eye of the master.

At last, the young lieutenant left his duties and came up to the inn to fetch his sister and her belongings. O'Connor kept back a short way, staying amid the busy crowd so he could keep a close eye on them. The goods wagon had departed before cockcrow with her parcels and packages, and there they were on the wharf.

He did his best to remain concealed. So many ships were preparing to move on from Hamburg with the morning tide. A Navy ship flying USE colors had just set sail, its brasses polished to a blinding gleam to pick up the red sunrise. With that much canvas on the wind, it would be out of sight in a matter of minutes. He kept the English brother and sister in sight, staying just behind a wagonload of kegs trundling in between them.

The lieutenant showed her to the heap of boxes on the dock. The boot-faced girl clucked around the luggage, no doubt checking to make certain all the bags and cases were there. Her fussing fixed the brown-haired wench's attention on her.

The lieutenant answered a shout from the bridge and dashed up the gangplank, leaving the women alone on the dock. Perfect. The time had come. O'Connor spotted Fitzroyce already moving toward her. They could take her away before the boy came back.

O'Connor felt for the knife at the back of his belt and hid it in his sleeve. Closer, now. He glanced back to see if the way was clear to the warehouse. Yes, a long line of heavy goods wagons lay between the ships and the town, all the better to conceal his escape.

As the wine cart passed them, O'Connor stepped deliberately close and bumped into her.

"*Entschuldigung,*" the girl said, turning around to offer an apologetic face to him, then paled in shock. O'Connor held the knife to her ribs.

"Not one word, girly," he said. "Come with me."

"Now, you!" the servant shrieked, her voice sounding like the gulls screaming overhead. She drew the knife in her belt. "Let my mistress be!"

By then, Fitzroyce had swooped in and taken the girl by the arms. The servant rushed at them, flailing at them with her basket. O'Connor kicked it, and the contents went rolling all over the deck. The girl struggled, jackknifing and kicking to free herself from his grasp, and attempting to get her hand into the pouch on her belt.

"She's strong as a salmon," Fitz grunted, laughing. "Easy goes there, my lass."

O'Connor threw his arm around the neck of the servant, squeezing hard to calm her down. He tossed his head in the direction of the warehouses.

"Let's go," he said.

But by then, the bustle around them had cleared, and the ship's crew had spotted what was going on. A handful of men scrambled down the gangplank toward them.

"Stop that! Let them go!" one of the men shouted.

Fitz pulled the girl toward the row of carts, aiming to squeeze between a couple and disappear. O'Connor had more of a struggle with the maidservant. She was as slippery as a wet pig, and landed a few blows on his ears and chin, and they weren't love-taps either.

"Back, or I'll gut her!" Fitz shouted at the sailors. The brother, James, signed to his fellows. They kept edging warily toward the two men and their captors, flanking outward to surround him. "Back! You don't believe me?"

He turned the knife upward and pricked the girl's chin with it. A thread of blood ran down her pale skin.

That was too much for the brother. He flung himself over his sister's back, knocking Fitz's arm down. Fitz kept hold of his knife somehow, and turned to slash at James. Cloth tore, and the boy had a bloody streak down his chest. Fitz still kept the girl tight against him in his other arm.

The brother caught him with the point of his knife. It was honed sharp as sharp, and tore through the linen. He was used to using it in fights, so it seemed, for Fitz had to defend instead of attacking.

The girl struggled hard. She'd worked an arm free, and brought her own knife into play. Knocking the brother back with his shoulder, Fitz caught her arm and bent her arm back, back, back until everyone heard a crack. Not a bone, but a tendon. The knife fell and spun away. She dropped to her knees, clutching her wrist. Fitz grabbed her around the neck and hauled her toward the warehouses.

All the time, the servant girl was trying to break free of O'Connor and get back to her mistress. O'Connor nearly had her to the gap between a cartload of osier baskets and a pen of barking puppies, when two of the sailors jumped for him. He punched the servant girl in the neck. She went down, gasping. He evaded the Englishmen's grasp to try and help Fitz.

The brother leaped onto Fitzroyce's back, trying to force the man's head back. O'Connor grabbed for him and threw him off into the faces of his fellow sailors. He took hold of the girl's arm and pulled her upward.

Suddenly, a blinding light was thrust into his eyes, burning like the sun. He wailed a curse and struck out with his free hand. He heard a clatter, as if something metal had fallen, but he didn't let go. He dragged the wench backward, away from the waterside.

All this had happened in moments. Finally, someone got their voice back, and shouted for help.

O'Connor, blinking away the momentary blindness, saw two men running toward them. He gaped. The larger of the two he had last seen lying in filth at the rear of the inn, drunk—no, pretending to be drunk!

The smaller of the two pulled a short stick from a loop on the side of his belt and struck it on the ground as he ran. To O'Connor's amazement, it sprang into a staff.

The burly one ran straight at Fitzroyce. They were well matched as far as size, but the man came in under the Irishman's guard and kicked him in the knee hard enough to knock him sprawling.

O'Connor picked up a huge basket and looped it over his arm like a buckler. He swiped at the smaller man's staff. It caught the top of the pole and dragged it sideways. O'Connor twisted to loose it from the man's grip.

The small man grinned, a death's head smile, and yanked back on the staff. That caused O'Connor to stagger forward. The small man swept the rod free, and brought it around in a circle, striking O'Connor solidly in the kidneys. O'Connor yelled and tried to parry the rod with his basket. The other man pulled it back a couple of feet, then jabbed the Irishman in the guts with it. He was a demon! O'Connor watched his eyes to see where his next blow was going, and evaded it, slashing with his knife. He knew he was being forced backward, away from the carts. Their escape was becoming more and more unlikely.

He realized that he was going to have to win this battle just to get away. The stakes were too high. They could be hanged for spies. One of them had to stay free to get word back to the Earl of Cork.

O'Connor used the only real shield he had. He pushed the girl in between himself and the demon. Every time the man moved, he moved the girl. She whimpered in pain from her wrenched wrist. O'Connor pulled the girl against his chest and put the knife to her throat.

"Let us go, or she dies right here," he said.

The man with the staff backed off a pace. Then, he charged. O'Connor sprang backward another step, staying out of range of the deadly staff. Then, he felt himself falling. The last thing he saw was the man with the staff lunge forward like a stroke of lightning and seize Margaret de Beauchamp by the arm.

Filthy water closed over his head. He kicked to the surface, coughing, spitting and swearing, just in time to see Fitzroyce fall off the pier, too. Fitz wasn't too canny a swimmer. He clutched at O'Connor, threatening to drown them both in his panic. O'Connor swallowed sea water and heaved up his guts.

Ropes dropped down onto their heads. O'Connor realized he'd lost his dagger. Men shouted at him from the pier above. He felt a fool. Tricked into flinging himself into the sea!

He turned to grasp at a rope, and something hit him hard from behind. He looked over his shoulder, treading salt water, and realized that he was only a yard or so from the heaving hull of a merchant ship. It threatened to crush him against the pilings holding up the pier.

"Swim out a few yards!" the small man shouted from above. "Get away from the ship!" Men on board the ship were yelling at them, too.

He and Fitzroyce had to duck underneath the boards a couple of times before they could hold onto a rope long enough to be pulled up. Someone snared him around the body with a gaff hook and tossed him onto the quay. Before he could scramble to his feet and escape, the big bruiser was on him with a pair of shining manacles. He snapped them around O'Connor's wrists and hauled him to his feet by the short chain between them.

Fitzroyce got a similar pair of bracelets when his sodden carcass was dragged up from the sea.

Both of the Irishmen tried to wriggle out of the gyves as they'd learned, but these were tighter than those the constabulary in Dublin used. O'Connor wore his wrists bloody before he gave up. The big bruiser pulled a huge pistol from his belt and held it in front of O'Connor's left eye. The Irishman stopped struggling, wary of the big black O at the pistol's mouth.

"You will go nowhere," he said.

The small man glanced around the pier and picked up a small golden cylinder. He brought it back to Mistress de Beauchamp, and she tucked it away in her reticule before O'Connor could get a good look at it.

"Is she a witch?" he demanded. "She blinded me!"

The small man snorted. "Are you all right, Miz Margaret?" he asked in an American accent. He smiled, revealing those shocking white teeth that O'Connor had come to associate with the newcomers.

The girl, wrapped in her brother's arms, nodded.

"Thank you, good sir," she said. "You dropped from Heaven to save us!"

"Oh, it wasn't by accident, Fräulein," the big man said. He spoke English with a thick German accent. "Frau Simpson told us to watch over you. We have been nearby during your entire visit." He pointed to the Irishmen. "These are the only two who came close to hurting you. We are sorry we were not closer when they have made their second attempt. They will never be able to harm you again."

Two other men sat on the ground with the maidservant, who was recovering from her ill-treatment with the help of a flask and a wet cloth to her neck.

"You!" Hettie said, her voice a croak. She pointed at them with an accusatory finger. "You are the ones who we saw at the reception."

"Ach, *ja*, we did not conceal ourselves well," the German admitted, with a sheepish grin. His compatriot nudged him in the ribs.

"I told you we weren't blending in." He turned to James. "I am Sergeant Matt Lowry. This is Sergeant Leopold Klein."

"I cannot thank you enough," James said, fervently. "Without you, they might have succeeded in abducting my sister."

"They have been watching her since her arrival," Sergeant Klein said. "We spotted them when they began to follow her to the inn. They came all the way to Magdeburg. They pretended to work for the palace, so we allowed them. They had access only to places where they could do no harm. We needed to know what they were looking for."

"Good workers, too," Sergeant Lowry said. "Too bad they weren't honest men. They could have had jobs, as fit as they are."

"Let us go!" Fitzroyce demanded. "We could work for you! We don't have to go back to..."

"Shut your hole," O'Connor snapped.

Klein, whose name was wholly inappropriate for his gigantic size, shook him like a dustrag. "*Nein.* You haf no power to bargain. Now, you go ahead and get on your ship, Fräulein. We'll take care of these...?" He looked at his companion.

"Varmints," said the smaller man, spitting on the pier. "Shooting's too good for them. A waste of bullets. Come on, you."

The Irishmen were forced off the pier, fighting like hell to get free. The small man had O'Connor's pinioned arms pushed painfully high on his back so he had no choice but to go where he was steered.

The officers urged them along through a passageway to one of the warehouses a block off the dock. Sergeant Klein produced a huge key and unlocked the door. O'Connor half expected to see a torture chamber, but instead, the brick-lined room contained a large motor vehicle, larger than any of the cars he had seen before.

The officers pushed them into the rear seat and secured their wrist manacles to a bar attached to the ceiling.

"It's time we found out where you came from," the small man said, climbing into the seat with the wheel before it.

"Where are you taking us?" Fitzroyce asked. "Torture won't open our mouths."

"That's not our problem once we drop you off," the small man said, with that death's head grin. The smile made ice form in O'Connor's belly. "Hell's bells, but your employer wasted his money on you two incompetents."

He turned a key, and the front of the vehicle roared like a bull. The big man closed the warehouse behind them and the motor car turned out into the road.

O'Connor craned his neck to see the *Meadowlark* casting off hawsers. He couldn't spot the girl, but the lieutenant stood on the deck, watching them with narrowed eyes until the car turned the corner and blotted the ship from view. The vehicle surged, throwing the two men back against the rear seat. O'Connor was torn between fear and admiration of the Americans' device.

"Never been in one of these before?" Lowry asked, his cold eyes visible in the rectangular mirror attached to the glass window at the front. "Enjoy it. It'll be the first and last time."

# Chapter 22

***May 1635***

Margaret felt shaken and sick most of the voyage from Hamburg to Liverpool. Hettie clucked over her like a hen with one chick, putting salve and clean lint on the wound the would-be kidnapper had left on her throat. Never had such a thing happened in her life! She was grateful all over again for Rita's forethought, which ran not only to benevolence she had seen, but things that she had not. Her mind would not allow her to think what would happen to those men. Neither James nor Hettie would entertain her speculation.

Though she knew she was safe, and that no one could touch her again, she remained below in the officers' cabin nearly all of the time. She entertained irrational fears that someone might swoop down from the sky and carry her off again.

"Who were those men?" Hettie asked over and over, for all of the first day, and often during the rest of the voyage.

"I've no idea," Margaret said.

"They acted as though they know who you are. But they sounded Irish, not English. There hasn't been an Irish guest at the manor in, oh, five years? And you didn't speak to any Irishmen during the time awaiting the Earl of Cork's pleasure, or you would have mentioned it to me, mistress."

"That is true." Margaret cudgeled her memory to try to picture having seen the men before. She wondered if she had missed them in Whitehall, or in the Tower when she had gone to visit Rita and the others. No, she swore she had not seen them. But...

Irish...the Earl of Cork was Irish. Were these two of his men? Had her secret been exposed?

She had nightmares, picturing his lordship appearing at her father's manor house, arresting her for her part in the escape, even taking the rest of the family down to stand trial for treason. Hettie must not have slept much either during the return voyage, as she was always there when Margaret opened her eyes, offering a cool cloth for her forehead, or just a strong hand to clutch despite her own injury. The bruise on her throat faded slowly from purple to yellow as they neared their destination.

"Do you have regrets, mistress?"

That question took her by surprise. She thought deeply about it. "No. The only one I have is the possibility that I may have put my family in danger. But for the sake of these good people, I would have done more if they had asked me. I'm still in *their* debt, even if they say that the balance is still to my side."

The crew treated her like a porcelain doll, coming by to see to her comfort and health. The captain made certain that she had the best food and wine and entertained her at the table during the evening meal. James, too, hovered as much as he could, in between duties on board the ship. He tried to lift her spirits by telling her how excited he was for her to tell their father about the plans and the innovations that she had set in motion. He was like her, able to picture things in his mind, and had been raised to the loom.

He did persuade her to come up on deck to see them sail into Liverpool Harbor, all colors flying, as people on the docks waited. A cluster of urchins waved frantically, and she waved back. It'd cost her a few farthings of alms when she came down the gangplank, but it was a familiar nuisance, and she could hardly fault them. It felt like a welcome home. Her spirits lifted just a little. She was glad to be back on English soil.

Not accustomed to being fearful, she was reluctant to travel overland by herself, despite going with a carter that she had known for years. With the Master's permission, James took leave to escort her homeward.

The truth was that she couldn't have been in safer hands. The carter who awaited them in the warehouse on the dock was named Ranulf Bracey. A man with shiny black hair like a crow's wing, Ranulf had worked for the estate for years until he could buy his own wagon and horses. He was up to three carts and matching teams of ruddy-coated Suffolk Punch horses, with his two sons driving the others for hire. Ranulf greeted her with a broad grin with teeth split in the middle like a pair of doors standing ajar, and started loading crates and trunks as if they were filled with feathers. James handed her and Hettie up to the seat and swung into place on the outside, to prevent anyone reaching for her from the street. Ranulf bracketed them on the other side and clicked to the near-side horse to set off.

The de Beauchamps knew he was completely trustworthy and would be deaf and dumb as the sister and brother exchanged their stories. Even so, Margaret was careful that the word "American" never passed her lips, but Ranulf would have had to be simple in the head not to figure it out for himself. He kept a lot of people's secrets, but particularly those of the de Beauchamps. He knew which side of his bread the butter was on.

By the time they arrived at the manor, Margaret was feeling much more herself. She waved to shepherds in the stone-fenced fields, and counted the fuzzy backs of the hundreds of sheep contentedly cropping the grass. So many lambs! The flocks looked healthy and lively.

The bells in the church steeple that they could just see over the treetops tolled three of the clock. Ranulf paid toll to a small girl in a plain gray dress to pass over the bridge leading over the busy river toward the manor. It was all so homey, Margaret dared to think that she could relax.

At last, they turned onto the long, tree-lined lane that led from the main Stoke road in between burgeoning fields toward their home.

The elderly gatekeeper, Jacob Damson, grinned his wide, gap-toothed smile at them out of the window of the small stone gatehouse at the edge of their estate. The wagon creaked to a halt beside it. Jacob stumped out in his heavy boots and opened the iron portal for them.

"Welcome back, mistress!" he said. "And Master James, you're lookin' fine as a sunny day!"

James leaped down nimbly to clap the old man on the back. "And so are you, my friend! Is our father at home?"

"Aye, he is. He was out with the shearers this morn, but back again the now. Fine fleeces, all. Thirty done today," Jacob said.

"The spinners'n been telling over them like chickens getting their share of the corn, e'en ere the carders get to them."

Margaret shook her head. Nothing could have been a homier welcome than this. She was grateful to be back.

James helped Jacob close the gate behind the wagon and hopped up onto the board beside Ranulf. The carter tapped the near-side horse with his whip, and they lurched forward. Margaret looked ahead toward Churnet House.

Perhaps it wasn't the grandest home in England. She had seen humbler folk occupying newer and better-appointed domiciles in Hamburg and in the USE. Still, this was where she and three hundred years of her forebears had been born, and she loved it. The warm, golden stone seemed to absorb the spring sunlight. The brilliant double blossoms of proud columbines added spikes of color in the beds flanking the wide front door. That had been freshly painted since she left and gleamed a rich sable in its stone frame. The small-paned windows glistened like jewels, each picking up the colors from the outdoors as if they were stained glass. She sighed with pleasure.

Margaret spotted a couple of groundskeepers in ecru blouses belted over their baggy trousers who were working on espaliered trees in the walled garden. She waved to them. The younger of the two, Noah, dropped his shears and ran toward the house, shouting. Their noise disturbed the family greyhounds, who sprang up from their doze on the sunlit walkway, and came hurtling toward the wagon. The four dogs leaped with joy, trying to get into the cart with them. Margaret laughed as they licked her hands and romped around, barking happily. Hettie, seldom patient with the animals' antics, shook her head and kept her hands in her lap. James pulled his favorite, a piebald giant named Alfred the Great, up onto the seat, where he thwacked Hettie in the face with his tail while covering James with kisses.

Before the horses plodded the rest of the way up the stone drive, a dozen people poured out of the house to greet them: housemaids, ostlers, even the under housekeeper, Liza Grey. Mrs. Ball herself was too grand to step out for anyone less than the king, nor would the reeve emerge. But the others were glad to greet the squire's two eldest children. Margaret found herself lifted almost bodily out of the cart, hugged, brushed down, and scolded as if she was five years old again.

"Your mother will be beside yourself that you don't have your head covered, mistress," Liza said. "The sky could open up at any minute! And you'll ruin your complexion. And you!" She turned on James and pointed at his bare feet. "Put your shoes on, sir! What will your father say?"

James laughed, reaching for his boots. "Now I know I'm home."

The dogs leaped and raced around Margaret and James as they came inside. Ranulf and two of the housemen brought in the boxes and trunks and stowed them in the box room as Liza Grey ordered.

"Don't scratch the floor, none of you!" she shrilled. "And you two, mistress and master, if you will please to come this way. Sir Timothy is in his study."

Margaret breathed in the scents of home, enjoying the aroma of old leather, oil, wood ash, lavender, and meadowsweet. Spring had come in full bloom in her absence and was easing into summer. The housemaids had all the windows open to let in the refreshing breezes, and she could tell that the rugs had all been gathered up and beaten to free them of winter's dust. The greyhounds had even been bathed recently, as they smelled of hyssop and grass instead of dog.

Sir Timothy could not have missed the din coming from the hallway. His study door swung open, and he spread his arms wide.

"There you are!" he cried. He embraced them and set them back a pace to study each in turn. "I'm so glad to see you safely home."

Margaret and James exchanged glances. They'd tell everything in its proper turn, including the assault.

"I'll leave you here, mistress," Hettie said. She was at the center of a cyclone of curiosity from the rest of the servants. They swept her away beyond the green baize door that led to the belowstairs chambers.

"They want to hear the news fresh," James said, with a laugh. "Onward, then, Grey."

Squire de Beauchamp's study resembled the nest of an acquisitive and very tidy bird. Everything was gathered around him so that he could pick it up without reaching too far. No one else understood the arrangement, and even the housemaids had to dust carefully so as not to knock anything over. Margaret and

James had to wriggle their way in between piles of books and papers, and remove hanks of wool, a small tray with the remains of bread and cheese, and one of the family cats off of the chairs in order to find places to sit. Sir Timothy plunked himself into his favorite leatherbound chair and clasped his hands between his knees. If it wasn't for the thinning brown hair on his head and the Van Dyck mustache and beard clinging to his round chin, he would have looked like an eager twelve-year-old.

"My chicks, tell me all! Was this United States as wonderful as we have all heard? You are more fortunate than I. The full information that I have about it comes from the yellow press and wild tales." He gave Margaret a sly look. "Not to mention gossip from supposedly unimpeachable sources."

James crept back to look out of the door to make sure none of the servants were hanging around to overhear their conversation.

"Well, Father," Margaret began, "Lady Simpson treated me to a ride on a steamboat from Hamburg to Magdeburg...."

Three hours later, the sun was beginning to set, sending orange and gold rays through the window at Sir Timothy's back. Margaret had had to skip backward and forward in her narrative as her father asked for more details of one thing or another. He was dismayed and puzzled about the attack on her by the two strangers. He understood Margaret's concern that the assault might have had a connection to the events of the previous year but shook his head when she asked if he was worried about repercussions coming from London.

"We shall have to wait upon news from your friends in Magdeburg to tell whether we need to gird our loins or go about our business, my dear," he said. "If they are as thorough as you have said, they will find out what those men know. I agree that they could not have been common thieves, following you about like that, but if there was any suspicion upon you or us, to be sure we would have had a visit from official officers of His Majesty, not a pair of rowdy thugs attempting to abduct you from a wharf in a foreign land."

"I...I hadn't thought of it like that," Margaret admitted.

Sir Timothy put his arm around her shoulders. "Trust to divine Providence for protection, my dear, and don't borrow trouble until we must."

With an act of will, she pushed the matter to one side, even though it left a sense of worry in its wake. However, the square of silk brocade she had brought home evinced nothing but joy from her parent.

"That is a marvel and a wonder," he said, turning it over to see the way the weave went together and stroking its smooth surface. "What shall you do with it?"

"From this piece directly, I will make a purse for Mother," Margaret said. She took a deep breath. "But before that, I want to use it as an example to our weavers."

"What's that?" Sir Timothy asked, taken aback. "We don't deal in silks. Never have. It's not the outlay, although that's a king's ransom to begin in that trade. We've developed no market for it. Our customers rely upon us for good, solid woolens."

"Father," Margaret began, fixing her eyes on his, "while I was in the Germanies, I learned some very uncomfortable truths. May I share them with you?"

He raised his eyebrows. "More uncomfortable truths? I wonder that I should regret asking you to go in my place. Share away, my chick. Is it something very bad?"

"The first truth is. The second, I hope, will be very good news."

"Well, I am listening."

Seeing his open expression made it harder than she had thought to explain, but she brought out the printed ledger from the Treasury aqualators. Sir Timothy marveled over the regular and smooth paper and the clear typography before reading its contents.

"These figures are no secret to me, my dear. Wasn't that the purpose of your journey, to make a sale to the USE and ease our financial burden? Has Prime Minister Stearns refused to buy from us? That would be very bad news, indeed."

"No." Margaret sighed. She opened the enormous mathematics textbook and handed him the letter of credit and the list of requirements from Admiral Simpson. "They have sent you an offer to purchase as much fabric as we can supply."

"Ah, what a handsome order!" Sir Timothy exclaimed. His eyes widened, and his cheeks turned pink with pleasure. "My, my, they'll take everything we have! We are set for the next year, to be sure."

"But if these calculations are accurate, we cannot find our way out of debt even if they buy everything that we can produce every year from now on." Margaret went on to explain her visit to the merchants in Hamburg, and the discussion with the executives of the USE. Her father's face grew longer and longer as each successive tale added proof to the inevitable demise of the family business.

To have it all set out in black and white caused Sir Timothy's shoulders to bow under the weight of truth. He was silent for a long time, then spoke.

"You are right, Margery. I have averted my eyes every time I came near to seeing this truth. I've moved this expense here and that deficit there in hopes that it would all add up. But what can I do? We have what we have. We shall have to go on as we have until it is all gone. There is nothing else we can do."

"There is," James said.

"There *might* be," said Margaret. "If we are willing to take a chance. We could still lose everything."

Sir Timothy emitted a heavy sigh. "It looks as though we will lose everything even if we don't take a chance. What does this scrap of cloth have to do with rescuing our fortunes?"

From its waterproof wrappings, Margaret produced the book on the power looms in the Industrial Revolution. She explained how photographs were made, and what these particular images represented. Sir Timothy turned the pages, and his eyes grew wide with the marvels set out therein.

"We would become rich, indeed, if we could produce cloth at a speed equal to our descendants," he said.

"But it would be the same cloth," Margaret said. "What I picture is creating machinery that would make brocade out of our wool thread."

That made her father laugh. "That's impossible!"

"It isn't. It wouldn't be. These devices," she patted the book, "are distant history to the Americans. They have more advanced machines that will take complex patterns and cause the machines to run by themselves. We could create textiles that no one has ever seen before. Think of how popular they would be among the nobility!"

"Well, they turn their backs on woolens for court wear, as a rule," Sir Timothy said, stroking his beard with a thoughtful hand.

"Not in the winter. Even palaces are cold in those months. The Palace of Whitehall was uncomfortably chilly even in April when

I visited it. Ladies in velvet skirts shivered despite the beauty of their garments. And they would not reject warm fabrics if they were not plain. Imagine roses or *fleurs de lis*, or even the royal lion and unicorn, but rendered in fine wool instead of silk."

Sir Timothy's eyebrows rose. Margaret could see that the idea was beginning to take hold of his imagination.

"And how will we make this wonder come about?"

Here came the difficult part. It would become no easier to evade the question. Margaret took another deep breath.

"I have commissioned an American programmer to make devices that would cause our looms to weave brocade. He is engaged upon research and design at this moment. Once he manages to *encode* the images that I left with him, he will oversee the manufacture of enough devices for our weavers' shed. If those prove successful, we can buy more through him. He has promised to keep the expenses as low as possible. I believe in him, and he believes in us."

Sir Timothy's normally mild eyes flashed with anger. "What? You have commissioned someone to make machinery for my business without my permission? You have overstepped, my daughter. I did not authorize you to spend the manor's funds on a *dream*, before asking me!"

She held out her hands to him beseechingly. "There wasn't time, Father. I was there, in Magdeburg, with all the people in the world who want to help us. I had the opportunity, the goodwill, and the knowledge, there with me at that time. It would have taken weeks to get an answer from you, and I felt the rightness of what I was doing. You have always taken the chance to make a good deal. Strike while the iron is hot! I *struck*. If I have erred, I can send word to Magdeburg now to tell the programmer to stop what he is doing. James can carry a letter to Hamburg and put it into the hands of a messenger to take it to the USE. It will be weeks from now that Aaron will get word. But, Father, you said yourself just moments ago that we will fail, sooner or later. Let us try, I beg you."

"She's thought it through with care, Father," James put in. "You ought to be proud of her. The Americans are capable of marvels, and they support us in this."

Sir Timothy dropped his eyes. He was silent for a long time. Without looking up at her, he spoke.

"It is almost time for supper. Let me think." As she rose, he added, "Leave the books."

"Yes, sir," Margaret said. She retreated. James closed the door to the study behind them.

"What do you think?" he asked in a low voice, when they were safely on the stairs leading to their bedchambers.

"I don't know," Margaret said. "We saw a new side of him just now. A hard side."

"And he saw a new side of you." James tweaked a lock of her hair. "A brave one, and an ambitious one. He's not accustomed to that. 'Travel and change of place impart new vigor to the mind,' Seneca said. Imagine what he is going through right now, seeing his daughter rising to be the heir that Julian was meant to be."

Margaret looked up at the closed door. "I hope that I will have done more good than harm."

"You have," James said. "And for what worth it may have, I believe in your dream, too. You know too much about our craft to make a mistake on this scale. I can't wait to see the fabric your American engineers for us."

# Chapter 23

"I am so happy that you are home," her mother, Delfine, Lady de Beauchamp said, sending a platter of meat down the table for Margaret to help herself. "Were you able to eat well in the Germanies?"

"More than well," Margaret said, lifting a piece of roasted fowl with the tongs. "I tried so many things. I must describe to Mrs. Ball about hamburgers. They are like a trencher with cooked beef and further bread on top, but small, sized for the hand. They are very tasty, and convenient to eat."

"Food is not about *convenience*," her mother said, with a sniff.

"It can be," Nat said, hardly looking up from his plate. He always shoveled in his food as fast as he could, with an eye toward getting to the remains of his favorite dishes before the others could. He and James both had been eying the same platter of roasted potatoes. From the wicked look on his face, Margaret assumed that James meant to empty the plate before their younger brother could do the same.

"What are the Americans like?" Petronella asked. At ten, she was the youngest, and had had her name bestowed upon her by a godparent who had herself had a difficult childbirth. Another awkward silence fell.

"Why do you think I visited the Americans?" Margaret said at last. Her sister opened wide hazel eyes at her.

"Well, didn't you? Like last year. You saw them in the Tower before they left and the castle was destroyed. Why else would you go to Germany? James does all the trading overseas."

"She has been empowered by your father to do business on his behalf," Lady de Beauchamp said, with a gentle smile. "As she is rising twenty, she should have more communication with our trading partners, like the German merchants, as she must learn to take on more of the burden of our business interests. Until she marries, of course."

Petronella's nose turned red, as it did when she was upset. She knew the adults were lying to her.

"If you never trust me, how will you ever know if I can keep secrets?" she asked.

"There are safe secrets and dangerous ones," Mother said. "We have told you not to mention the Americans outside of the house or where anyone else can overhear." She glanced nervously at the housemaid, Gilly. The girl, eyes carefully cast down, busied herself at the sideboard with a covered dish.

"I don't! And the servants don't count."

Delfine was outraged, and pink rose in her thin cheeks. "Petra! Yes, they do. They are our employees and they are worthy of your respect. As am I and your father. You are talking back, and that is not permitted. Now, leave the table and go to your room."

"Mama!"

Mother cast her eyes toward heaven as if her youngest daughter was too much of a burden to bear. "Go, little one. I will come up to talk with you later about your manners."

Margaret sent an apologetic glance toward Gilly. The corners of the girl's mouth were set in a polite smile. After her experiences in Magdeburg, Margaret was newly sensitive as to how much hurt the language could cause. But the others had not seen what she had, so she put aside the discussion until later.

In the meanwhile, she saw the expression on her father's face. His thoughts were the same as hers. If the smaller children had worked out the truth about her journey, others would have put two and two together, and come up with much the same conclusion. She had only been safe because they were so far outside of London that a wayward word wouldn't cause trouble. Few in the area cared what transpired. They could count upon their friends and employees to keep their thoughts to themselves, for the sake of self-interest, if no other. More likely, pure apathy. No one would waste consideration on whether the squire's daughter had ventured abroad, as long as she came home safely. Where she had been was of little interest, as long as nothing changed.

But she meant for change to come. Everything going on in Magdeburg bettered the lives of the people that it touched. The new technology could bring prosperity to her and her family.

Or not. It might also be an unmitigated disaster to bring Americans to Barlaston. In no time, it would become evident that their new manufacture was using tools that could not have been invented in England. In order to make use of the aqualators that she and Aaron had designed together, the de Beauchamps would have to take more people into their confidence. The more people who knew their secret, the more danger they faced. But the alternative was bankruptcy, disgrace, or worse. Her mother's health was delicate. She might not survive the uproar that would come with exposure and shame.

Margaret regretted her haste in making arrangements that would upset the family and risk its safety. Curse the status quo for its obduracy. She ate the last bites of pheasant and potato on her plate without tasting them, and set the utensils down.

At last, Sir Timothy signaled that his family could rise from the table. He nodded politely to Mrs. Ball. The housekeeper flicked an impatient hand at the other servants, who set themselves to clearing and cleaning.

Margaret retreated to her room with her thoughts. Everything had seemed so clear in Magdeburg! Truth to tell, she had not considered the reality of life in Barlaston. The dreams that reading Lady Mailey's books in the United States of Europe engendered seemed as though they would take so little to make real. However, she had failed to take human nature into account, even her own. What a fool she had been!

"Mistress, will you join your lady mother in the parlor this evening?" Hettie asked, leaning in at the door. "She is sitting up for a time, Elspeth told me."

"No, Hettie, thank you. I think I will just go to bed."

"All right, then. Let me help you off with your things."

Margaret felt rather like a doll as her maid unfastened her overdress and chemise and helped her into her night dress. She sat on the edge of the bed, watching Hettie brushing out the clothes and hanging them on pegs. Back to normal, with no machines, ladies kept out of most public places, and the taxes clipping little bits from them day after day, month after month, quarter after quarter. She sighed. Year after year.

When she had finished with the clothes, Hettie set down the clothes brush and came to untie the curls in Margaret's hair. Margaret closed her eyes at the soothing feeling of the comb passing through her tresses, as if Hettie was drawing out the troubles she felt.

A little voice came from the corridor.

"Margery? I'm sorry."

Margaret opened her eyes. Petra hovered in the doorway. She also wore her linen night dress, and her long brown hair flowed down over her shoulders. Margaret held out a hand to her, and her young sister ran to her embrace.

"It's all right," Margaret said, kissing the top of the child's head. "We can't help it that you're observant. But you must learn to exercise judgement before you speak. One day, you might really say something you shouldn't in front of a stranger."

"I know." Petra's voice was muffled in Margaret's lap. "I wish I could meet an American."

"I think you will get your wish, my little one." Father's voice came from the doorway. He came to sit on the edge of the bed and hugged both of his daughters. "Though no more discussion of events outside of the family at any time."

"Yes, sir!" Petra said. Her cheeks were red with excitement. Father looked a little sheepish.

"Margery, I approve your business proposition. In for a penny, in for a pound. Once we hear from your friends in Magdeburg, we'll call in the weavers and discuss the future. We can't do it without their cooperation. Heaven lend me strength."

"Oh, Father!" Margaret beamed at him. She glanced up at Hettie, who only looked worried.

"Why are you scowling?" she asked.

"Well, mistress, now the real work begins."

# Chapter 24

Philip Haymill tapped on his lordship's study door. At the voice from within, he turned the handle and leaned in.

"My lord? I have today's letters for you."

The Earl of Cork looked up from the piles of papers on his desk. To his servant, the chancellor's face looked haggard and thinner than it had in months past. "Bring them, if you please. I have a short while before I must wait upon His Majesty."

Haymill lowered the tray and transferred the missives to the table. His training under Lord Strafford had taught him not to open anything that was sealed with wax and a signet, but others were to be unfolded and laid flat for perusal. While they had little else in common, this chancellor followed the same practice as his deposed and now escaped predecessor.

The Earl pushed through the pile of papers, looking as he did every day for certain seals. He peered up at the clerk.

"Nothing from Hamburg?" he asked.

"No, sir. I've looked for the fish impression in the sealing wax, but none has come."

"Curse those fool bully-boys!" his lordship said. "Ye've had all the postings from every ship?"

Like any efficient courtier, Haymill had anticipated the question. "Yes, sir. I had two boys waiting on the docks since before dawn every day, sir. You have all the news that there is to have from overseas."

"That is all, Haymill," the chancellor said. He waved a hand and Haymill retreated and closed the door behind him.

Cork broke open every seal, scanned the signatures of each of the correspondents, and tossed the pages aside. No mistake. O'Connor had not written. He threw himself out of his chair and walked up and down the short length of his office.

It was not as though he had no other issues with which he needed to deal. If he only heard petitions from the people sitting out in the antechamber, he could have been busy all day and all night for decades to come. If he sat with the king, who had become obsessed with the histories from the future that other spies had obtained from Magdeburg and Grantville showing that he had only a scant handful of years left to live before he was unjustly executed, Cork would get nothing else done. If he did nothing but oversee the restoration of the Tower, again, it would take all the hours that God sent. Delegating took only a few tasks from his burden.

His head ached with the number of things that had gone and continued to go wrong. He, too, could not help but be obsessed with the visitors from the future. He knew how many missteps he had made. Why had he not executed Strafford and Cromwell while they were in his hands? Logic told him that they had still not yet become the men that the future histories said they would. Why had he not released the Americans and put them back on a ship to the Germanies instead of continuing to hold them?

Because of the king, of course. Charles had been paralyzed and unable to act out of pure fear. The Americans had been prepared to make alliances, or at the very least, form a non-aggression pact. He had found that term in one of the books on political science that had been smuggled to him by a spy in Aragon. The much-copied document propounded some very dangerous concepts, none of which gave him any advantages toward dealing with the all-powerful Americans, Gustavus Adolphus, or the so-called United States of Europe's steadily-growing list of allies. He *had* to know how they had escaped and humiliated him—no, not him, for he was but a humble servant of the crown. How the Americans had humiliated His Majesty, Charles, by grace of God king of England, Scotland and Ireland and all the territories claimed by his predecessors. They could not have escaped alone. He had questioned, some under torture, every person that could possibly have assisted in the enterprise, and received surprisingly little useful information.

From one of the stacked boxes of correspondence, he extracted the last couple of letters from Diarmid O'Connor. It was a wonder that these idiots could actually read and write. That barely adequate literacy was the main reason he had sent him and Fitzroyce abroad to investigate for him, that he would be sent regular reports on what they found. Capable of reading and writing letters, yes. Ability to maintain a coherent and steady correspondence, damn them, no.

The two fools had left Amsterdam months ago in advance of his orders, and turned up in Germany instead, sending a half-apologetic letter to him, and hoping that he would continue to use them. Why hadn't he abandoned them then and there? It sounded as though they had drawn suspicion upon themselves, and were looking for another assignment where they had not soiled the nest. It was a wonder that they hadn't turned up with a knife between their ribs. Not that he would ever hear the fate of a couple of ruffians finding themselves dead in a ditch. He'd instructed them to go to Grantville and look for the clues to the culprits there. Despite their stupidity, they might still come up with the information that had kept him awake and restless for over a year.

The only fact that had persuaded him that O'Connor and Fitzroyce were not wasting his time and money was that girl they wrote about who was so curiously out of place. That "Margarette de Beecham." They didn't say who she was or where she came from, other than she was English. That they had happened upon that fact, even by accident, opened up questions from yet another front that was troubling the king.

What, indeed, was an English girl traveling on her own doing heading for the United States of Europe? Was there a connection to the Americans? What possible help could one countrified vixen have offered to render the wall of the Tower of London into ruins? But the mere fact that she was there in Hamburg, that she was bound for the new country, all that worried him. Why was she there? What possible connection did a young Englishwoman have with the Americans?

The name provoked an itch of remembrance at the back of his mind. He pulled one box of correspondence after another to him and looked through it. De Beecham. Why did that sound familiar? March, February, January... no, it must have been further back, before Christmas. It sounded like an aristocrat's name.

He drew a sheet of good white paper from the previous year's file. Yes, here it was, in April (curse O'Connor's misspelling): the honorable Margaret de Beauchamp, daughter of Sir Timothy and Lady de Beauchamp, baronet of Churnet and Trent, who owned a number of small properties in Staffordshire, begged permission to have an audience with the king. He felt ire roiling in his belly.

Well, where in hell was the king to get money to pay for the defense of the realm without taxes? Boyle almost asked aloud. But that was something that was always evident.

And now that he cast his mind back, the girl *had* come to him regarding taxes. Yes, he had granted her a brief audience. Not with the king, of course. A tiny manor, father a gentleman, merchant class, engaged in the wool trade, as so many of them were in the north, didn't merit an audience. Boyle had a very faint memory of a brown-haired girl with hazel eyes, not plain per se, but not striking in any manner. She had asked on behalf of her father for forbearance of the annual levy, and the Earl of Cork had turned her down. That was the last he'd seen of her.

The de Beauchamp manor was in the north. The north of England had been a thorn in the king's side for a long time now. For the last many months, His Majesty had been growing concerned about the protests. Staffordshire and Yorkshire both had shown signs of discontent. In fact, some nobles and gentry alike had refused to pay their taxes until their voices were heard. They wanted the king to summon Parliament back into session, to formulate new laws and to enforce boundaries between the king and the people. Was de Beauchamp part of the movement against the king's will?

But, no, in the tax rolls that Boyle perused, Trent and Churnet was up to date on his levy. So, he was not refusing to pay. Somehow, he had managed to raise the funds. Probably by selling some assets, or a delayed profit coming in.

Boyle chewed on his thumbnail. Was the baronet's complicity a ploy? Was he trying to allay suspicions about his leanings by seeming to comply with the requirements of the crown, but plotting against it behind a smiling face? The king feared armed resistance rearing in the counties near Scotland. Boyle had had reports of those in the duchies and counties raising armies.

He harkened back to the pilfered history books that he had read. A fearsome time lay ahead, not far at all, and the nobles and men of property of the north were instrumental in bringing about the end of the monarchy—at least temporarily. He must starve them of the resources to foment rebellion. The countryside must be subdued and kept fearful. Ordinary troops would not serve to intimidate fellow Englishmen. No, for that purpose, he would employ mercenaries hired by the crown. And what better way to pay those mercenaries than with the very tax revenues that the gentry so hated paying?

What if he was to pick out certain troublesome nobles and make examples of them? More than a few surely had guilty consciences. Like Churnet and Trent. The coincidence that his daughter had been in London and was now in Germany required scrutiny. Would her father argue that she represented the family's interest in the wool trade? Boyle did not believe in coincidence. It would have to be proved to him.

He slapped a hand on the stack of letters. *Why* had O'Connor not written back with more information about her? Boyle feared that they had fallen afoul of the Americans while snooping through Grantville. Or had they perhaps been unable to find a messenger who would safely and securely carry back a message to a ship bound for London? He was going mad waiting to hear from them.

Were they, in fact, dead in a ditch? What, then, had happened to their possessions? Had they remembered to destroy his correspondence, or did someone now have the letters he had written to them asking for information on the destruction of the Tower and those who had aided and abetted the escape of the Americans?

Richard Boyle slammed a fist on his desktop. He blamed himself. He had tried to make the best use of bad tools, and that was his mistake. It had only been weeks since he had last heard from O'Connor or Fitzroyce. Should he continue to be patient? Or would inaction cause more damage to his position or to the crown? These men had proved unreliable before. Should he send other men to Hamburg, to investigate where the fools had gone? Had they turned coat and volunteered to work for the Americans? He would have their heads!

An impulsive swat by a furious hand sent an inkwell flying into the wall. The black spatter that ran down onto the parquet floor made him angry at himself. He kicked the thick glass bottle across the room, then strode to the door and flung it open.

"Haymill! Get someone to clean this floor."

Instead of waiting to see if his will was done, he stalked out of the room, leaving the mess behind. Thirty or so pairs of hopeful eyes met his as he stormed through the antechamber. Their hope quickly faded even before he reached the doors, which a pair of pages held open for him. Their troubles would have to wait another day.

The war in the Baltic Sea had been a terrible revelation to all, proving that the Americans were fearsome enemies. The king had been of no use at all throughout the crisis, seeing assassins around every corner. Refugees had begun to turn up on English shores and been questioned by his men. No sign whatsoever had been found of the Americans, or of the two traitors, nor of his formerly trusted guards and soldiers.

Should he wait to send spies northward? No, why would he wait? But to throw any more trustworthy men into the maelstrom while Gustavus Adolphus lurked at the very shores of the realm seemed foolhardy.

He hated to wait any longer, in hopes that the fools had a report on its way on another merchant ship. In the meantime, he fretted over the lack of information.

It was time to send someone to Staffordshire and see what was going on there. He had no doubt that His Majesty would agree.

Admiral Simpson led Leutnant Georg Zimmer into Mike Stearns' office. Mike looked up from the piles of paperwork that never seemed to end.

"We'll have to regard this matter as serious," John Chandler Simpson said without preamble, gesturing to the man at his back. "It sounds as though that fool in London is never going to let the situation rest. A year has passed. You would think he has more pressing troubles."

"Maybe not," Mike said, setting aside the budget. "One of the most recognizable buildings in the city left in ruins. But if you ask Melissa Mailey, the greater crime was in destroying the Globe Theater."

Simpson dismissed the latter comment with a wave. "I'm serious, Mr. Prime Minister. It seems as though Cork sent at least a dozen spies into Europe looking for those who escaped from the Tower of London and any collaborators who may have assisted in the rescue."

"And have they found any?"

"No. Of course not. Any of our people who are still in Great Britain are staying well out of his hands. Those who returned here have resumed their normal lives and are spread out across the continent. These two dolts we have in custody have no idea where to look for them. We certainly gave them adequate access to the government building in hopes of discovering Cork's plan by what they targeted, but, clearly, he did not trust them with any higher information or plans he may have. They had a mission, which God knows they have failed, and thank God for that."

"That's a relief, but how much can we trust the word of a couple of spies?"

"Calling them spies is an overestimation of their abilities," Simpson said. "It would be comparing college students to kindergarteners. If they had worked in the mines, they would have had the rough edges knocked off them and possibly become good employees. As it is, they are completely out of their depth. I would almost feel sorry for them, but they can't be trusted. They're both too cunning and too stupid to let go."

"What did they know?"

"Herr Prime Minister, the truth is very little," Georg said. He was the very picture of a hearty farm boy from the countryside, with thick blond hair and blue eyes in a round pink face, a long neck but thick shoulders suitable for carrying a couple of oxen. From Simpson's description of him, the exterior concealed a mind foxlike in its cunning. Mike thanked Heaven that the young man was on their side. The USE Navy was the most functional branch of the USE military. God knew the Air Force was still a few puddle jumpers and spotter planes, and not much else was ready to roll. Thank the same God that that young idiot Eddie Cantrell had been found safe in Copenhagen, although minus one lower leg and plus one royal fiancée. John Simpson had been a changed man since he had returned from the North Sea. If anything, he was more protective of the USE and the people in it. The investigative branch that was growing up, both through the Freedom Arches and Simpson's people, was a harsh reality that the former executive fought for, but Mike knew it was a necessary evil. "They are not very intelligent, of course, but they are observant and cunning. It seems that they ascribed importance to the presence of English and Irish personnel in the USE, and named names in their posts to their master."

"They were meant to go into Grantville. We've had an influx of Irishmen, so they might have passed more or less unnoticed while they were snooping around, but they have been as subtle as a brick thrown through a window."

"What names?" Mike asked.

Simpson pursed his lips. "No one of real importance. They'd become fixated on Miss de Beauchamp, ignoring everything else going around them. They did manage to get a letter out to him in Hamburg before we noticed their presence. Since then, my men tried to drop hints they could have picked up on to misdirect London to fire on targets to which they can't do any harm. Unfortunately, the only actually vulnerable person here is the one they identified to the Earl of Cork."

"My sister will be angry about that," Mike said. Rita was back in Ingolstadt with Tom, and she was already angry that the two spies had been allowed free rein in the palace. Mike had agreed with Simpson's estimation that it was better to see what they were looking for, and had discussed it with her over the radio. Naturally, she was worried about her young friend. So was he. "But they haven't been able to send reports since then?"

Georg smiled. "Yes, Herr Prime Minister. They think they sent many reports by way of travelers who were going to the port, or even on to London itself."

"They *think*."

"*Ja*. We have all of them. They did not at first identify their 'handler,' as Admiral Simpson calls it," here Georg offered a slight bow to the admiral, "but it did not take much persuasion before they gave up the name. We knew already, because of the reports."

Mike leaned back in his chair. "Tell me that they didn't have the envelopes addressed to him directly."

"*Nein*, they are foolish, but not that foolish. Three wrappings, one to a warehouse on the dock in London. One to a man, we think is a messenger. The innermost one addresses the Earl of Cork by name, and is sealed with wax."

"He's as slippery as a bag of snakes. I'm certain that he set up this system," Simpson said. "These two would never have thought of it themselves."

Mike frowned. "What did they learn? What does he know now that he didn't before?"

"By the reports, not very much. They overheard gossip at the receptions that our men let them enter. They were always distracted before they could overhear important conversations, such as your discussions, or those held by my daughter-in-law. They amassed the names of nobles that are in cooperation, but those are not precisely secret. And none of them are friends of England. Charles has been isolated for years, now. We were tempted to let that one slip through, but it had references in context to a previous message that we couldn't let pass."

"They told us everything that they have seen," Georg added. "They were eager to disclose anything that they knew. We did not have to resort to strong measures. At least not much."

"You are very thorough," Mike said, with a wry smile. His mind tried to shy away from the reality, but he pushed it firmly back. "Did they overhear anything of importance from my sister? What she's doing in Ingolstadt?"

"*Nein, mein herr.* Nor would they understand the import of her presence there."

Mike stared at the ceiling for a moment. "Of course, they knew that Rita had returned here. The others who were in London with her are scattered all over the landscape, so they're safe. But they saw her interact with Margaret."

"That, yes," Simpson said. "But those letters are in our possession. None of them reached London."

"So, what hard information on her will he have? He may know that she is a friend to the USE."

Simpson shook his head. "He *knows* nothing. He suspects everything. The king is of no use. Boyle is as efficient as Charles will let him be, which is lucky for us."

"What about the spies? How loyal are they to the crown?

"As loyal as they would be to anyone who would pay them. Spycraft is superior to manual labor."

"Can we buy them?"

"With respect, Mr. Prime Minister," Simpson said, "no."

Mike started to protest. Simpson raised a hand. Not in an

imperious gesture, but one asking for patience. They had had this discussion more than once in the past.

"Damn it all," Mike said. "I'm a hunter myself, but I hate the thought of executions. This is not what we do! Why can't we consider rehabilitation? West Virginia did away with its death penalty long before I was born."

"Nineteen sixty-five, to be exact," Simpson said. "But that was where we came from, not where we are now."

"But we are still the same people that we were then!"

"I'd argue that not to be strictly true, Mike," Simpson said. Fine lines gathered around his eyes, and he looked weary. "For so many reasons. But the important difference is that we came from a rich country, where we could afford to house prisoners serving life sentences. Those resources are no longer as readily available, and Gustav Adolf himself would argue, as would the man on the street, that if you plan to feed anyone for what could be forty or fifty years, let it be someone who deserves it."

Georg cleared his throat. "*Mein herr*, no one wants to feed and house spies. They could live another thirty years, and then what? They could still escape and cause more trouble. This is the way things have always gone."

"To be honest, they expect nothing more from us," Simpson said.

Mike stared at him in disbelief. "If they're not confessing to get clemency, why are they talking so readily?"

"So we will make it quick," Simpson said. "We would anyhow. We do not torture. That's barbarism."

Mike felt a chill in his belly. "I hate this part of the job."

"So do I. It's not an honorable death in battle. It isn't passing away on a deathbed surrounded by loved ones. They're pawns in a dirty game, and they know it. Boyle would knock them off the chess board without a backward thought, except the trouble of where to dispose of the bodies. And your own sister might well have been one of those pawns."

"I know it," Mike said, the grim thought even more chilling.

"Don't go soft on them. Not for a minute. They'd hang any of our people if they could. We need to set an example that shows we are serious."

"Is this the example we want to set?" Mike asked. "Why don't we transport them to one of the colonies?"

"And make these two their problem? Is that fair?" Simpson asked.

Mike gritted his teeth. Another of the realities of being in charge. It was one of the many things that would be on his conscience forever, despite knowing how much damage spies did. If he turned them to the side of the USE, they could turn back again, depending on the threats posed to them by their former master, or how much they were offered.

Mike had no stomach for officially sanctioned murder, but he knew that he had no choice. Yet another good reason for giving up this office as soon as he could. The wheels for that were in motion, fortunately. Very deliberately, he changed the subject.

"How is Eddie Cantrell doing?"

"That young idiot," Simpson said, but his tone was indulgent, or as indulgent as John Chandler Simpson ever let himself be. "I'll let you know if we find out anything else of importance, Mr. Prime Minister."

"Thank you." After they left, Mike pulled a piece of paper out to write a note to be transmitted to his sister in Ingolstadt. She'd want to know, and would probably give him a piece of her mind about it.

# Chapter 25

***July 1635***

The smell of roasting beef permeated the entire house when the family returned from morning chapel on a Sunday six weeks later. Nat lifted his nose as if he would draw in all the aromas.

"I will eat the entire side of beef by myself!" he declared.

The others laughed.

"Well, you had best not," said Sir Timothy, with mock sternness. "We're expecting a good deal of company, and some of them have appetites to match yours."

Everyone sounded chipper and bright, but an air of brittle nerves permeated the household. According to letters conveyed from Magdeburg, Aaron Craig and a cartload of aqualators were expected to arrive within the week. Messages had gone back and forth to Grantville on the *Meadowlark* and other ships. James himself had brought the last one, informing Margaret and Sir Timothy that the mechanisms were ready, and went on the final voyage to fetch the up-timers and all their gear. The household had been in a flurry of activity to prepare rooms for the arrivals. Lady de Beauchamp had overwhelmed herself with fussing over whether the furnishings and amenities would be enough for their guest from the future.

"They will accept anything," Margaret had promised her. "They even offered to share a room, either with one another or with any of us, or to put up in a guest house."

"That won't do!" Delfine had protested. She had made the servants move different furniture in and out of the rooms until it all became too much for her, and she went back to her own sitting room with her embroidery to calm down. Margaret was glad to have her out of the way, although she couldn't help but go in and straighten the bedclothes and count the towels and linens that had been set out for Aaron and Martin, his stepfather.

The date of their arrival was supposed to be on Friday. From Wednesday on, Margaret had been in a spin, keeping an eye on the avenue in case the cart should arrive. She wished fervently for a telegraph or a radio so that she could receive advance notice. Had the up-timers failed to meet the ship? Had the ship met with a storm and been delayed on its passage? Had the cart met with robbers or impassible roads?

In anticipation of Aaron arriving on Friday and having his aqualators up and running in the weavers' shed, Sir Timothy had invited the manor's workers and the Master of the Weavers and Fullers Guild, Richard Blackford, to come to luncheon with them at Churnet House and see the modern marvels for themselves. Alas, no sign of the cart or the up-timers had appeared, so nothing had changed, and no number of hints served to soothe the curiosity buzzing through the neighborhood.

After some discussion with Margaret and James, Sir Timothy decided that food and drink would do the trick to making his workers receptive to new ideas, even in the absence of the mechanical marvels themselves. And to invite Master Blackford was only proper. Though the workers were not independent craftsmen, the four masters among them belonged to the Weavers and Fullers Guild under Master Blackford. Their journeymen and apprentices would become full members in time, but in the meanwhile, their masters were responsible for their education, and for their behavior.

They had resigned themselves that the lunch would take place without the guests of honor. No news of a disaster at sea had arrived, so Margaret had to trust that Aaron would arrive eventually, but they would have to explain the purpose of the celebratory meal in some manner. It all felt so awkward.

Early in the arrangements, Sir Timothy had spoken to Mrs. Ball and the other servants about keeping any information they overheard about the visitors a deep, dark secret. All of them had promised solemnly not to reveal anything, but Mrs. Ball had dismissed the notion as foolishness.

"Sir Timothy, people *will* talk," she said, drawing herself up to her formidable height. "We cannot pretend that nothing is happening. We have a roost full of gossips, and they must have fodder, or they will starve."

"You're right," he admitted. He and Margaret conferred for a moment. "The weavers in Hamburg are famous. My daughter sailed there three months ago to negotiate with our buyers there. She was privileged to observe master craftsmen whose work she felt would enhance our own. Not to take away from Churnet House's weavers, who are renowned for the beauty and durability of the cloth they produce, but to take advantage of innovations that are in use on the continent. We have invited two men from the Germanies who have offered to share their skills with my workers. We hope that you will welcome them with all the hospitality of the house."

Mrs. Ball nodded with dignity and turned to the other servants. "You hear that? There's your story. If I hear otherwise from anyone, you *will* be sleeping out in the coop with the hens."

"Yes, Mrs. Ball!" they chorused.

It had taken a reminder or two, but queries that made their way from the de Beauchamps' friends and neighbors proved that the servants had largely adhered to the story that Sir Timothy had formulated. Nothing about it was untrue; rather, the truth was diluted, and a few elements were left out.

The story, however, didn't satisfy the weavers themselves, who sent a contingent to speak with Sir Timothy. He promised the four master weavers in his employ that they need not fear for their jobs, and that all would be revealed when the visitors arrived. That caused more buzzing in the rumor-hive, but that was to be expected. But, at last, the day had come.

"Squire!" Noah, the undergardener, came pelting inside. "The cart's here! By Heaven, sir, it looks like it's carrying a whole house!"

"Oh, thank Heaven!" Margaret grabbed her skirts and hurried out into the sunshine to meet it.

The goods wagon had only just pulled past the gate house and was trundling slowly but steadily toward them. At the sight of her, James and Aaron stood up on the seat beside Ranulf and waved to her with both arms. An older, larger man was in the rear of the cart, wedged between cloth-wrapped bundles. It must be Aaron's stepfather, Martin Craig. She had not met him, but he had been involved in the correspondence that had been traversing back and forth over the sea. Sir Timothy came panting up beside her. They met the cart halfway to the house. She couldn't believe how many boxes were packed into it.

"Well, I'm here," Aaron said. He hopped down. "And you will not believe how amazing the system works!"

"Oh, I am so happy to see you!" Margaret said. She grasped his hands tightly, then realized how forward the gesture had been. She let go. The boy blushed. She felt her own cheeks burning. "I am sorry. I am just so excited! Please introduce me to this gentleman."

"My dad," Aaron said, proudly.

"Martin Craig, ma'am," the man said, clambering down from his perch. His large, rough hand dwarfed hers, but his touch was very gentle. "My boy and I are pleased to be here to help you. Miz Rita sends her regards, and says to tell you she's back in Ingolstadt, but she'll do anything you need her to."

Margaret introduced her father to them, who clapped them both on the shoulders.

"Come in, come in! You've traveled all this way, and there are people who are eager to make your acquaintance."

Aaron couldn't restrain himself from chattering about the machinery that he had escorted all the way from Magdeburg. The boy had a big, dark green sack fastened with straps slung over his shoulder, which he kept close.

". . . And the clockwork parts that run the heddles based on the encoding embedded in the aqualators, Dr. Gribbenflotz helped out a lot with that, as well as a couple of blacksmiths that work for the USE Navy. I couldn't get all the pieces to line up right at first, but the aqualators are gonna stand on platforms that adjust up and down, depending on how fast you want the shuttles to go. Weavers are still gonna have to manage the beaters. If I had to work out more programming to pull that, you'd have to have a hall the size of a gym for all the aqualators. Until I met Herr Oberdorn, I didn't know weaving was like riding a bicycle while juggling chainsaws. . . ."

Margaret finally managed to squeeze in a word, as the rest of the family spilled into the sitting room. Her mother led the way, gliding like a swan. Three of the servants followed in her wake, bearing mugs and plates.

"Please allow me to introduce my lady mother," she said at

last. Aaron closed his mouth and goggled like a fish as Delfine bore down on him like a ship coming into harbor. "Lady de Beauchamp. These gentlemen are Martin and Aaron Craig."

Mother favored them with a gentle smile and offered her hand. Aaron goggled a little at the delicate gentlelady wreathed in lace shawls and cap. Margaret giggled. She knew he was used to heartier women like Rita Simpson and the forthright German woman who was in charge of the Treasury's bookkeepers.

"Be welcome, gentlemen," Mother said, like an angel bestowing a blessing.

"Thank you, ma'am," Martin said. He wiped his face with a handkerchief from his pocket. "Sorry about the delay. Our crates were too much for the cart axle. It had to get fixed just outside the port. Lucky there was a blacksmith who could take care of it right away. It only cost a few coins. We paid with marks. I thought they might have a problem taking another country's currency, but they were nice about it."

Another expense! Margaret's heart sank as she contemplated how much they were going to need to settle with the people of Grantville. With every extra person that Aaron mentioned, she pictured more red ink on the ledgers. Her father must have had the same worries, but neither of them allowed their concerns to show on their faces. The project must be a success, or everything would be lost.

However, the Craigs were welcome guests in the household, and were given every courtesy. Both of the up-timers proved to be polite and friendly with the children and the servants of the house. As Margaret had predicted, they behaved to the latter as though they were equals, immediately endearing themselves to the employees and scandalizing her parents and Mrs. Ball. Margaret knew that the Americans' familiarity meant that from then on, Gilly and the others would make certain that Aaron and Martin would receive the choicest cuts of meat, the best of the bread and sweets, and generously poured glasses of beer. Mother oversaw the offerings of hospitality with kindness. Margaret was beside herself with impatience, but had to wait until all of the niceties were observed. When Martin set down his mug for the second time, Margaret couldn't help herself.

"Are the devices ready?" she all but blurted out. "Will you be able to make them work before the others arrive?"

"Margery!" her mother exclaimed, appalled.

"It's all right, Mrs. de Beauchamp." Aaron frowned and pulled a thin, hard board out of his green sack. It had a metal clip on the top affixing a sheaf of the white papers to it. "It's gonna take some time, but I could probably get one of them running in a couple of hours."

The clock on the mantelpiece chimed four. The weavers would be arriving soon. Margaret's stomach whirled with nerves.

"Should we begin now? How may we help?"

"It will have to wait, Margery," Sir Timothy said, with a wealth of patience. "The guests will be arriving very soon. We cannot wait the luncheon, or Mrs. Ball will serve us sour porridge and rotten meat for a week. If Aaron would be so good, we can make one afterward."

"That's all right with me. I can explain everything while I put one together," Aaron said. "Your employees can ask questions. I know you're worried about them taking to the machines, but people can accept something new if they get a good explanation."

"That's good common sense," Sir Timothy added. "We have committed to this change. We rise or fall on this moment. One way or another, our lives will change."

"I'll make it sound as positive as I can," Aaron said. "I think they'll be up for it. I think it's pretty amazing. All the test runs were fantastic."

"Pray remember," Margaret pleaded with them, "you may only speak German or Amideutsch. No one must know you are Americans."

"Oh!" Aaron looked abashed. "I forgot. You said something about that when you were in Magdeburg."

"I understand, miss," Martin said, with his slow smile. "You let us know where it's safe to talk between ourselves in English, but otherwise, it'll be no trouble. We'll just ask you to translate for us."

"I hope my Amideutsch is up to it," she said.

"I'll be all right, miss," Martin said, smiling at her. "Once they see what my boy has designed, they won't care if we brayed like mules."

How right he was.

Sir Timothy saw to it that two kegs of beer were brought up from the cellar, and a cask of good red wine. The pantler had barely tapped the first keg when Liza came in to announce the arrivals.

"Master Richard Blackford . . . and others, sir," she said, with a clear expression of annoyance.

Sir Timothy grinned. "Pray admit them, and make certain we have mugs and glasses for all."

"And others" was a dismissive way for the under housekeeper to refer to the weavers and fullers who were in the direct employ of the manor, as being of lesser rank than the house servants. The up-timers were clearly unaware of the distinction. As they were "Germans" and not supposed to know English customs, Margaret had to let the situation take its own course. The Craigs would be resident in Churnet House for several weeks. It was all she could do not to try to hold all the strings as if she was a puppeteer in a mystery play, controlling every little motion of her characters. She couldn't manage every interaction. It would tear her to pieces like a piece of bread caught in a whirlpool. If Martin Craig's easy-going nature was any indication, whatever strictures that she or Sir Timothy put on them would almost certainly fall by the wayside in little time. She would have to trust them.

Master Blackford entered first, wearing his Sunday finest, a black velvet coat and matching breeches, highly polished boots, and his heavy gold chain of office. He was a grand-looking man, with long, dark hair and beard worn in a style echoing His Majesty the king's. Sir Timothy greeted him and showed him to a place of honor beside the fire. The burning logs were barely necessary, now that it was getting toward full summer, but the symbol of hospitality meant a lot to the Master.

He greeted the children fondly, as he had known all of them since birth. He shook hands solemnly with James.

"Good to see you returned safely from the sea once again, Master James."

"I thank you, sir," James said. For once, Margaret's brother had been forced into his best boots as well as good clothing borrowed from his father's linen press. Their mother had been horrified at the condition of the clothes in his sea chest: stained, faded, torn and much mended, and daubed here and there with ineradicable pitch and paint. The borrowed tunic, several inches too large, was belted tight around his midsection. She had thrown up her hands at his hair. "Providence has been good to us."

"I'm glad to hear that," Master Blackford said. "You know what rumors are like. No one escapes them. Like death and taxation." He chuckled at his own witticism.

The de Beauchamps, knowing they needed his good will, laughed along.

"And you, Mistress Margaret, your trip abroad has brought roses to your cheeks." Master Blackford patted the side of her face. Margaret forced a smile. It had only been two months since her return.

"Thank you, sir," she said.

"I look forward to hearing what you saw on the continent," Blackford said. Margaret felt ice form in her belly from nerves. The Guild Master progressed to Lady de Beauchamp, who received his handshake from the seat opposite the one prepared for him, on the other side of the fire. "Delfine, you have never looked more beautiful."

Her mother smiled at the compliment. "You are too kind, Guild Master."

Close behind the Guild Master was Master Fred Wilkinson, the eldest of the master weavers, stocky and broad-shouldered, fading blond hair and beard, with his three eldest children. Samuel, Alder, and Ivy had grown up in the trade. Samuel, born the same year as Margaret, had already taken his journeyman's examinations, and was a member of the guild beside his father. Alder was a sound workman. Ivy, the others said, should have been born a man, for she was more talented than any of her siblings, and plied the shuttle as if it was an extension of her hand. She had a plait of barley-gold hair down her back and bright green eyes the color of her namesake plant, and was not yet married.

The weavers and fullers filed in and found seats on the chairs and benches set out for them. As the eldest and most senior of the weavers, Fred saw to it that all of his workers were served beer before he accepted one for himself. He held up his mug to the assembly.

"Squire, Guild Master, may Heaven's blessing be upon us all."

They toasted him and drank.

"Thank you for your kind words," Sir Timothy said. "You are all welcome in our home. No doubt you are curious about the two strangers in our midst. These are craftsmen from the continent. From, er, Hamburg. Herr Martin Craig and his son, Aaron."

At the sound of their names, both of the visitors stood up and waved at the assembly. Margaret expected them to bow, but mentally cut the puppet strings holding onto them. They wouldn't know the customs. No one would expect them to. Hettie kept close to her mistress, fearing that she was going to worry herself into a tizzy.

To her great relief, the Craigs played their parts well. They pretended to look puzzled at most of the conversation during the meal, and kept their conversation to a few low exchanges, all in German. Ivy shot a curious glance at Aaron. He caught her eye and smiled. She blushed and turned her attention to her plate. The boy kept shooting glances her way every time she looked up. Margaret smiled indulgently, feeling as though she was Aaron's mother, instead of barely older than he was.

After the lunch was finished, Sir Timothy rose, glass in hand.

"I wish to express my gratitude for you all. We have been together through thick and thin—perhaps not that thin." He patted his round belly. Everyone chuckled. "But truly, the last few years have been challenging ones. You have all risen to face those challenges, and I cannot tell you how much that has helped to keep the de Beauchamp name alive. I bring you here today to let you know of a tremendous opportunity that has come to us. You will be playing a part in history. I want to explain it to you, and ask for your forbearance in not revealing any details outside of this room until it comes to pass. Do I have your word on it?"

The workers murmured among themselves, but only Master Blackford raised the question.

"What details, Sir Timothy? You know you may rely upon our discretion, but truly, what is there to be discreet about? Our craft is not a new one. Indeed, though those present are of the highest level of skill on these shores, they have perfected what their forefathers have passed down to them."

"Yes, all that is true," Sir Timothy said. "But we live in more comfortable surroundings than did our ancestors. We have the benefit of modern learning—science!—passed along to us by enlightened minds. Why should we not incorporate that into our craft and take a step toward a future that our forefathers would have been proud to live in?"

Master Blackford gestured toward the Craigs. "And is this why your visitors are here?"

"Indeed. I have commissioned from them a mechanical wonder that will give our fabrics a twist"—Sir Timothy chuckled at his own witticism—"to lift our work above that of the textiles for sale on the continent. To be sure, you will have noticed that we are not getting the remuneration that we have in the past for sales beyond these shores."

The Guild Master frowned. "Yes, indeed, I have. I have admonished the weavers to make fewer mistakes and produce a higher quality cloth. That is all we can do to compete with our rivals overseas."

"That may not be all," Sir Timothy said. "And why I must swear all of you to secrecy, or ask you to leave at this time." He looked around the room at the weavers and fullers. Margaret admired the way that he had built up their curiosity. None of them would have risen from their seats at that moment to save their souls from perdition. She had to keep from smiling. "Do you all give me your most solemn word?"

Fred cleared his throat. "Squire, I do." All of the workers nodded, their eyes wide. Sir Timothy looked at Master Blackford.

The guild master threw up his hands.

"Oh, very well, I do, too."

Sir Timothy turned to the Craigs. "What help do you need from us?"

*"Bitte?"* Aaron asked, with just the right expression of polite confusion. Margaret could have risen up and kissed him. James released a spate of German that she could just follow, and Aaron nodded.

"We will to the looms go," he said, affecting a thick accent. Ivy looked on him with shining eyes, and Margaret watched her with a combination of worry and indulgence.

# Chapter 26

"Careful with those crates!" James admonished the workers, as they helped to unload the cart inside the weavers' shed. Fred oversaw the men carrying the boxes. Ivy, his daughter, tied her long braid up in her kerchief, and helped lever open each of the crates with a flat pry bar.

"Ooh, what are these?" she asked Aaron, then slowed down her words. "What. Are. These?"

"Aqualators," he said. In Amideutsch, he set out exactly what they did. Margaret and James understood him, but no one else present could, and they did their best to provide a simple explanation. Every face looked blank. Oh, well, then, they would have to wait for the demonstration. Margaret hoped that Aaron was correct in his estimate of two hours to set one up.

"Careful!" he admonished Seth, one of the apprentice weavers, who picked one of the small flat trays from its bed of straw and went to fling it down. "*Nicht* break!"

"They're fragile," Margaret said. "Pray handle them with the greatest care."

"Sorry, mistress," Seth said. He put the tray down with exaggerated movements beside the nearest loom.

Aaron and Martin began to empty out cartons marked with a white circle and stacked the trays in groups of eight according to a few pages attached to a small hard board. James assisted them as the weavers watched.

*"Ach, nein!"*

Aaron looked at the contents of the second-to-last box and turned a stricken face to his father. He held up a pair of gray trays from it. They'd been split into two pieces, probably from the impact of the crate being set down too hard.

"It's all right, boy," Martin said, in Amideutsch. "Six will be enough to start. You only have to build one right now, to get things going. We can send for replacements."

Aaron nodded and set to work.

"What is the purpose of these aqualators?" Master Blackford asked Martin.

Martin launched into a spate of Amideutsch. From the words Margaret knew, the older man was not talking about anything having to do with weaving or calculating. The guild master looked puzzled, and turned to James, who smiled.

"Pray be patient, wait and see, guild master."

It became evident that the weavers thought that Martin was the chief architect of the mechanism and Aaron was his apprentice. Margaret should have realized that.

Once the pieces were sorted, they moved on to the second group of boxes. These contained thick metal wires bent into weird angles, with cylinders and gears incorporated into their shapes, as well as a quantity of narrow gray metal pipes and what looked like miniature water wheels. They arranged those in sets, too. Margaret noticed that there were six intact groups in all.

"*Wo ist der wasser?*" Aaron asked.

"Water," Margaret translated.

Fred pointed a thick finger toward the rear wall of the shed. "River's by there," he said. "Behind yon wall."

Martin took careful measurements along the wall, using a cloth tape. Then he hefted a red enameled box and an armload of pipe and trudged out of the door. A few minutes later, they heard a grinding noise.

"Me wall!" Fred exclaimed, horrified. As quickly as he was able, he hobbled outside. Everyone else followed him to see what was going on.

They found Martin with a hand drill creating a hole in the wall of the building a couple of feet above the ground. The whitewash coating the wattle and daub structure had had circles the size of Margaret's palm drawn on it at intervals that approximated the location of each of the first six looms in the lofty chamber, both at waist height and within a few inches of the ground. Plaster dust and wool strands drifted around his feet.

"Good limestone here," Martin said, in Amideutsch. "The water is pure."

Martin completed the hole, and passed a length of narrow pipe through it to Aaron. He brought the other end down to the river. Margaret watched him assemble what looked like a miniature water wheel and attached it to that end. The current picked up the tiny cups and began to spin them around. That part of the mechanism must have been concealed behind the wall of the Treasury. Herr Craig, for so she must refer to him in front of their weavers, shouted through the hole in the wall, and Aaron called back to him. Margaret heard a grinding noise, as if something was being slid over the floorboards.

The others rushed back inside. Aaron had moved the big loom closer to the wall and was fitting some strange pieces made of stiff wire to it. The dozen or so aqualators piled by it had been stacked into two boxes with pipes sticking out top and bottom.

"Can someone get this loom set up to go?" Aaron asked Margaret when she reappeared. "I'll be done attaching the mechanism to it, then we can *run a demo*." The first part of his query was in Amideutsch, but the last three words were in English. All of it was still incomprehensible to the others.

"*Ja*, I mean, yes," Margaret said. "If you please, will one of you wind the threads on the warp beam? And wind two bobbins for the weft shuttles?"

"Two?" Fred asked, narrowing his eyes. "What witchcraft are ye tryin' on me looms?"

"Fred, if you please," Sir Timothy said, much less patiently than his daughter. "Three yards should be enough for now."

Muttering about waste, the elder weaver picked up a huge spool, and threaded the wool in and out of the healds in between the teeth of the reed. Fred was arguably the fastest on the manor, and preparing for such a short run of cloth was easy for him. Within a brief time, the loom was ready. As soon as Fred set down the shuttles, Aaron picked them up and attached long wires to each side, then tied into a separate block of aqualators that drove their own small wheels.

"What are ye doin', then?" Fred demanded.

"Wait and see," Master Blackford said.

"The beater will have to be run by hand," Aaron said. "I couldn't get it to work without blocking total access to the loom."

Margaret translated his words to the others. "Who would like to try it?"

Most of the weavers were reluctant to touch the loom with its bizarre attachments.

"Not I," Fred said. "I don't want to get tangled up in all them wires."

"I'll do it," Ivy said, with a smile for Aaron. "What do you need me to do?"

"Pull it just like you would if you were throwing the shuttles yourself," he replied, in Amideutsch. James translated it for him.

"Does he understand me, then?" Ivy asked Margaret, her eyes wide.

"Hamburg has many people who speak English," Margaret said. "He, er, understands more than he can say."

"Oh!" Ivy shot a shy gaze at Aaron. "If I may, shall I teach him our language, then?"

Aaron looked as if nothing would please him more, but Martin clicked his tongue at him. The youth hastily turned to his job. He signed to Ivy to sit down on the stool before the loom and indicated that she should take hold of the beater. Then, he turned the stopcock on the thin pipe that led into the aqualator.

Everyone held their breath as the shallow trays filled up, then the loom started to move by itself.

"Witchcraft!" Fred growled, but Ivy followed the raising and lowering heddles with her eyes. Then, as the shuttles shot across the shed, she pulled the beater to her. The shuttles moved back across the warp, and she repeated the action.

Margaret watched with delight as the heddles rose and fell in line with the diagram she had created. She'd daydreamed about seeing the pattern come to life, and here it was happening in front of her!

"What's it making?" Cedric Hollings asked, watching the dance of the wires as they lifted different threads in turn.

"Brocade," Margaret said, feeling triumph well up in her heart.

Cedric sputtered. "Who ever heard of wool brocade?"

"No one." She turned to face the other weavers. "Not until now. We're making it. Right here."

Sir Timothy looked absolutely delighted as the pattern began to emerge on the loom. "Come and look at it, my friends! Bless my soul, roses! Isn't that it, Margery?"

Margaret's heart filled with excitement. "Yes, Father. Roses it is."

The top of the blossom and leaf pattern that Margaret had devised so many weeks ago was finally coming into shape on an actual loom, not just in her imagination. As the two shuttles danced across the shed, the details emerged. It looked even finer than Margaret dared to hope. Aaron had been a truly good student of Herr Oberdorn. Instead of ten or more blossoms on the breadth of the fabric as it was in the silk, the thicker thread meant that only five blossoms set in a wreath of leaves could find room on the smooth, plain background, but it was still unique and unprecedented. The weavers gathered close to watch, murmuring to one another. Some looked skeptical, some worried, and some as delighted as Margaret herself. Every tiny detail excited.

"Aagh! No!"

Unfortunately, Ivy also became interested in what she was helping to produce, and lost her rhythm. She didn't pull the beater in time, and the two shuttles crashed into it and flipped off the loom. One hung from the wires on the side, but the second shot off across the floor and disappeared underneath one of the other looms. Its bobbin fell to the floor, unwinding what was left of its thread in a tangled mess.

"I'm so sorry! I'm sorry!" she wailed, scrabbling to retrieve the parts.

"It's all right," Aaron said. "Honestly, it's all right." He ran to turn off the stopcock, then retrieved the missing shuttle and started to put the bobbin back into it. Fred gave him a fierce look and snatched the two pieces out of his hands. Margaret held her breath, hoping no one had noticed the slip of the tongue when Aaron spoke in English. Fortunately, no one seemed to have made any note of it. The American's native accent sounded strange enough to the British ear. Aaron gave her an apologetic glance. She nodded. He would be more careful.

Fred rewound the thread and clapped it into place. "There ye go, lass. If this foreigner can make it run again, keep your mind on the task."

"Yes, Pa," Ivy said, chastened.

Aaron reattached the pieces of the shuttles to the wires and checked the parts of the loom to make sure that the warp tension hadn't been upset. He compared what had already been woven to the papers on his board and set the shuttles in place. He gave Ivy a nod and moved to turn the water on again. The loom started moving, and Ivy bent to her task, her face set in concentration.

Line by line, inch by inch, the pattern grew. No one else in the room moved at all, so fascinated as they were by the miracle that was happening before their eyes. Ivy fell right back into the rhythm, even humming to herself as she worked. In a short time, the first row of roses was complete, and the men clustered around and murmured their approval.

"Are they using suchlike in Germany right now?" Master Blackford asked.

"It is not yet widely used," Margaret said, mentally crossing her fingers against the lie. According to her conversations with Aaron, the aqualators were just taking hold in the USE for calculation and industry, but no one but she had thought to combine them with weaving equipment. She thought for a moment that in exchange for his help, Aaron would have extended the technique to the Oberdorns, then dismissed it at the thought of overwhelming that pristine workroom with gears and water. She would have to ask Aaron later. "We will be the first in Britain to produce such."

"If I permit it," Master Blackford said, in an austere tone. "I will have to consult with the guild council."

"Your pardon, guild master," Sir Timothy said, not at all apologetically. "These folk are in my employ, and they will obey my commands."

"But they still cleave to the guild! They are subject to its rules!"

"Master Blackford," Sir Timothy said. "What you have seen here will benefit all weavers in time. I don't believe that we should go backward. New inventions come along every day. Leonardo da Vinci's science a hundred years ago proved that we have not yet explored all of the potential that God has put before us, and we have advanced since then."

"Do you dare speak of the divine with these instruments of Satan?"

"Now, now, my friend," Sir Timothy said, pursing his lips. "You don't really believe that, do you? You saw the pieces go together yourself. None of it was made of anything unnatural, only metal, clay, and water, like a small water wheel, but one that drives a loom instead of a mill. How marvelous that our

German friends had the ingenuity to combine them in a way that advances our craft!"

Margaret hung close behind Ivy's shoulder, watching the aqualators work. Her dream had come true. An inch at a time, she saw the means of rebuilding the family's fortune. She glanced at the men and women clustered by her. They were half-listening to the argument going on behind them, but their eyes were fixed on the rise and fall of the heddles, and the swish-swish of the twin shuttles passing over the warp. A narrow band of plain fabric bounded the first set of roses. Now a second set of leaves was beginning to take shape. Ivy ratcheted the cloth beam toward her, and the pattern was clear as it rolled up onto it. Margaret let out a breath she didn't know she was holding. Then, the second part of the pattern began to take shape. These rose clusters were offset from the first row, forming four instead of five. It looked really neat. Up until the moment he saw it happen, the wool brocade had been mostly theoretical. As soon as the blossoms began to form, Aaron clenched his fist in victory.

"Yes!" he hissed. The others cheered and came to slap him on the back.

"Well done, my friend," Margaret congratulated Aaron in English. "It's everything I could have prayed for."

He smiled at her. "Thank you, Fräulein Margaret. I'm glad to do it. It was fun!"

"Why congratulate this boy?" Master Blackford asked, looking from one to the other. "Surely he's the apprentice, and his father is the master."

*"Nein,"* Martin replied. *"Mein boy ist der Meister Computerhersteller."*

"What, then? Now the whole world is going mad!" the guild master declared. "Where children are the masters and fathers are the apprentices!" The other senior weavers added their sour agreement. But Martin favored them with a contented smile.

"I am proud of my boy," Margaret translated for him.

Journeyman Daniel Taylor cleared his throat.

"Is it all right to try it?" he asked. "The akalabors?"

Ivy looked up at Aaron, who nodded. He moved to turn off the stopcock, and the shuttles slowly came to a halt.

"Everyone should get a chance," he said in Amideutsch. No one needed a translation for that. They were eager to try.

One by one, the weavers sat down at the loom. With Aaron's gestures, they began to follow the rhythm of the loom, and the design on the cloth grew. He stopped the flow of water in between, letting each have their turn. Even when the water was turned on, he kept the trickle slow so the crafters could learn the pace of the twin shuttles.

The master weavers were skeptical, hanging back while the apprentices and journeymen took turns. It looked as though all of the senior craftsmen but Fred were against it.

"It will take all the skill from our hands and put it into this... machine," John Mayhew grumbled, lowering his eyebrows all the way to the bridge of his nose. "We'll be reduced to beating the cloth against the warp end and nothing else! All the work we put in to master our craft, and for this?"

"Nay! It's a good thing."

"Why not accept the gift?"

"What's the harm?"

On the other hand, the majority of the apprentices and journeymen liked the aqualators, because it was less work than throwing the shuttle and dancing on the pedals themselves. The experiment wasn't an unqualified success, as the most junior of the apprentices, Diccon Linden, a small and skinny eleven-year-old, couldn't keep time, and lost control of the beater. His face went scarlet as Aaron and Ivy had to stop the contraption and set it to rights all over again. The others laughed at him. The boy broke away from the stool and hid behind the farthest loom, picking up shreds of fleece into a basket.

"Come, come," Fred said, with exaggerated impatience. "Not everyone will need to work these. We've got regular looms still, don't we, squire?"

"That is true, my friend," Sir Timothy said, nodding.

"But can't we attach these akalabors to the other looms to make ordinary cloth?" Lily Dale asked. Like Ivy, she wasn't an official member of the guild, but had worked alongside her father and her brothers since she was small. "Look what the loom could do for us! You don't lift the threads with your hands. You're already using the foot pedals to lift the heddles now. Think how fast we can go!"

"Aye," Daniel added. He eyed the loom with one eye slitted in speculation. "I'd bet that we can get a bolt done in a day instead of a week."

The masters scoffed. "Fifteen yards in a day? That's a daydream!"

"Would you care to put money on it, eh?" Daniel asked. He scanned the group. "No one? I'll gladly learn the tricks of the water way, and the fine cloth that we'll be getting out of it. The results should be obvious to all of yer. This fabric is amazing, and the customers won't be able to pass it without buying." He patted Aaron on the shoulder. "It's good! I like it!"

"*Sehr gut,*" Aaron agreed. He grinned at Margaret.

"Such a thing should be brought under the aegis of the guild," Master Blackford said, thoughtfully stroking his beard. "This machine is part of the loom, so it falls to us to dictate its uses."

"No!" Aaron protested. "It does many more things. It does not belong just to the weavers."

Margaret translated his words to the guild master. Blackford frowned.

"But what else can it do?"

"Calculating, directing other machinery, creating designs, running games . . ." Aaron reeled off. Margaret and James did their best to render the terms into English. The weavers looked even more puzzled.

Fred threw up his hands. "I do not see how this run of pipes and wires makes any of that come to life."

"That's of no importance, because it does one thing that we *can* see," Sir Timothy said, trying to pull the conversation back to the matter at hand. He patted the raised flowers on the loom. He could not seem to stop touching it. "Look at it! *Look* at the fabric. We can make our fortune by bringing this beautiful textile to market. It could make our fortunes! What do you say, my friends?"

"Well, one pattern doesn't make a new market," Cedric put in, his mouth twisted as if he was biting something sour.

"We can make different patterns later on," Margaret said. She turned to Aaron. "Can't we?"

"*Ja,*" he said. "I can change the gates to match other designs in new aqualators. I'll show you how to read them and change them out when you want. You'll have to learn basic programming, but that should be easy." Margaret explained his words to the others.

"Amazing," Fred said, shaking his head. He was absolutely converted.

"Then we shall proceed," Sir Timothy said. He put out his hand to Master Blackford. "Are we agreed, sir?"

Master Blackford did not reach out to him. Instead, he fixed the squire with a gimlet eye.

"You do understand, sir, that the guild has not received a rise in pay for three years, now? And with this new cloth in the offing, it will bring in superior revenue to the standard weaves that we have been producing all these years."

"Aye," Daniel said, with a raised eyebrow. "We have to learn this new machinery. Especially since it's not guild machinery, but some foreign stuff brought in to change good English labors."

Margaret stared at the men in horror. This was an obstacle that she had not foreseen, even with all the other troubles over which she had fretted.

Sir Timothy, too, was taken aback. "Gentlemen, I am at a loss to understand you! We have not made a penny on this yet. Let us see what the market will provide."

"Nay, I cannot agree," Master Blackford said. "These akalabors . . ."

"Aqualators," Margaret said faintly, not recognizing her own voice.

". . . Aqualators must fall under the auspice of the guild, and any profit to be made therefrom needs to be controlled by the council before any of this cloth is woven, let alone sent to market! Squire, I appeal to you in your role as Magistrate to hear my case, or must I bring it to the king's court?"

That was it, Margaret realized. He was going to make her father both judge and defendant in a case. The other weavers were paying close attention. Not that they cared who controlled the new mechanisms. They had heard the word "pay," and that was where their interests lay.

"My friend, there is no need to litigate this matter," Sir Timothy said. "This mechanism will benefit us all. It works so swiftly, as you have seen, and we will be able to bring the goods to market soon."

"But we'll be paid the same," Daniel insisted. "And you'll earn so much more than that!"

"But you won't," Margaret said, and bit her tongue when all the men turned to look at her. "You'll earn more, too." She shot a look of apology to her father. She had put off discussing

Mike Stearns' philosophy with him, as she hoped that it wouldn't become an issue so soon. It looked as though there might be a work stoppage if she didn't prevent it, just as they were about to weave their way out of disaster.

"So, you're *offering* a rise in pay, then?"

"Margery!" Sir Timothy bellowed.

"Better," Margaret said, mustering all the confidence she could display. She hoped that she would be able to explain it adequately. "You are right that you should benefit from the new style of cloth that we will be making here. Can you imagine how people will respond to seeing it?"

"They'll scoop it up," Fred said, grinning wide enough to show the missing molar on the left side of his jaw. "It should fetch top price. Double or more than, if I don't miss my guess."

"Yes! And the better it does, the better for all of us. Father, gentlemen, we are using the same thread, only formed into a new and more attractive configuration. So, wouldn't it be fair to say that the difference between the higher price and the base price is a bonus that should benefit all? What if..." and here she swallowed, regretting the bewilderment on her father's face, "what if ten percent of that difference should be divided among all of you as a reward for learning the new skill and bringing our new brocade to market?"

"Ten? Should be twenty," Cedric said with a snort.

"But we are not asking you to absorb the extra expenses, Master Cedric," Margaret pointed out. "If you are willing to pay out of your share toward having Herr Craig design and build the aqualators, and travel all the way here from Hamburg, to set up these mechanisms and teach you all how to run them, then I believe you will end up with far less."

The weavers pulled away from her and went to talk in a corner, Master Blackford in their midst. Their voices started as a murmur but quickly rose to shouting. The women and apprentices hung around the perimeter of the inner circle.

"Margery, what in the name of thunder are you on about?" Sir Timothy demanded, pulling her aside. James and the Americans joined them on the other side of the altered loom.

She lowered her eyes. "I am so very sorry, Father. Prime Minister Stearns talked to me about this notion when I spoke to him. He said it would work as a tool to encourage laborers to put more of their effort into a concern if they shared in the benefits it produced."

"Such a thing is unheard of!"

"Profit sharing is pretty common in the USE," Martin told him. "It helps motivate workers to do their best. I don't think you'll miss a small amount like that."

"They won't accept such a strange notion!" her father protested. "They'll want a rise in pay! That's a certainty, not this bizarre notion." He made a spinning gesture in the air. "I know we have fallen behind over the years. Master Blackford is correct that their forbearance ought to be rewarded. But ten percent of the profits . . . Margery, this will thrust us into bankruptcy faster than going on as we have."

"No, sir, it won't," Aaron said. He flipped the top paper on his clipboard over and pulled a pencil out of his pocket. "Look, sir, let's pretend the gross profit is a thousand pounds. If you calculate expenditures, including wages, cost of raw materials, machinery, and taxes and subtract them, say three hundred pounds, you'll come out with the net profit. Say you make fifteen hundred pounds from the new fabric. They don't get ten percent of that, they get a percentage of the difference between that and what you would have made anyway. So, it's really a small deduction." The pencil flew down the page. Sir Timothy, from whom Margaret had inherited her facility with numbers, followed him quite well. Margaret saw him nodding as each figure appeared. "And if you want, you can expand it to ten percent of full net. I'd wait until the brocade was for sale, if it was me."

"By heaven's light, you may be on to something." Sir Timothy eyed the other conversation going on. "But, Margery, you should have discussed this with me before. It is wrong for me to hear you make promises in my name without my having even the slightest notion of what I was promising."

"I know, Father, I am sorry. I was being forward. Pray forgive me. It just slipped out when it seemed as if they would not agree."

Sir Timothy grimaced. "They may still not agree. I don't see this ending soon. James, run up to the house and have Mrs. Ball arrange to have a keg of beer and mugs for us. I'm dry as a desert." Margaret's brother headed off at a run.

The weavers continued with their argument. Occasionally, someone would send an angry look over their shoulder toward either the Americans or the aqualatored loom. The four masters were definitely in disagreement with one another. Master Blackford held himself aloof, not seeming to agree with one side or the other. Again and again, he called for a vote. First, one hand went up. In the second casting, another joined it. In the third, yet one more, Master Walter Twelvetrees, but in the fourth vote, his hand went down again. More discussion followed, growing ever more heated. The Guild Master beckoned to the younger members of the guild and asked for their opinion in a calm, measured voice. The masters weren't pleased with that, and the argument rose to shouts again.

Margaret was beside herself with frustration. Didn't these men understand that they stood on the threshold of greatness? Half an ell of cloth that represented the future lay on the loom between them.

Before she could step into the midst of the fray, she felt a hand come down on her shoulder, both gentle and firm.

"No, Margery," Sir Timothy said. "You've wound up this clock. Now we must see if it chimes the hour on its own."

After several more minutes of discussion, during which the servants of the house arrived with beer and lanterns, as the sun had nearly set, Master Blackford held up his hands. The weavers ceased talking as though someone had turned off the stopcock. He led the procession back toward the de Beauchamps.

"Well, then, Sir Timothy," he said. "Your daughter certainly has some strange ideas that she has brought back from . . . Germany. In my long life I've never heard of such a thing. We of the Weavers and Fullers Guild are accustomed to receiving a fair wage, not engaging in speculation as to whether we will get paid or not." He gestured to the crowd. "We have reached an agreement . . ."

"A tentative agreement," Cedric said, frowning. He had been the last dissenter, and had not changed his mind throughout the discussion.

"Enough, sirrah! Your point has been noted. Sir Timothy, we will accede to the terms you stated, to run the looms for this new fabric. But we want ten percent of *all* additional proceeds as well as fair wages."

"My dear sir! I can't see my way to agreeing until we have product to sell!"

"Isn't that just what your girl just offered us?" Blackford gestured to Margaret, who felt her cheeks burn.

"Guild master, we are starting from a negative position," Sir Timothy said. "I'd be turning over an empty sack."

Master Blackford nodded. "Then, five percent of net until the real profits start to come in. All moneys will be accounted for through the guild. The council will take half a percent until then—ah, ah!" He held up a hand to still protests from his membership. They saw part of the profit sharing being taken away from them before they even had it in their hands. "And one percent thereafter. For working expenses and adding the skills to the roster of mastery."

Sir Timothy had a counter of his own. "Only for the weavers who are actually working on the brocade. The others add no especial value to the common fabric. They will be paid their fair wages."

Master Blackford wasn't having it. "No, all of them! They will *all* be trained, and can step in to run any loom on the estate and in the cottages in the rest of the manor. And beyond it, as more akalabors—aqualators—are added. If the mechanical shuttles can go on any loom, we can make ordinary fabric much more quickly. That is value, indeed."

Sir Timothy looked crestfallen. "But no one will speak of it or bring any of the mechanisms out of here until we give permission. All will keep the secrets revealed here today, under pain of dismissal from the manor."

"And from the guild," Master Blackford said, looking sternly at the assembled workers. "This benefits us all. Secrecy, until we two say otherwise."

"Agreed," said the squire.

"Agreed," said the guild master. At last, they shook hands. The rest of the weavers, save for Cedric and his hangers-on, nodded. Margaret felt like dancing, but held back from making a spectacle of herself.

"Well, well, then have a drink on me, my friends!" Sir Timothy offered, gesturing to the keg of beer, now tapped and waiting.

Master Blackford smiled. "Always the host of the moment, Squire. Here's to profit!"

Everyone hoisted a glass. Aaron gave Margaret a conspiratorial grin.

"Well, this has reached long into the evening, Sir Timothy," Master Blackford said at last. He shook hands with the baronet again. "I appreciate the hospitality. And this glimpse into a new textile that I agree will set tongues a-wagging."

Sir Timothy clapped his hands on his belly. "By heaven, I hope so! We want word to spread so that every scrap sells."

"How soon can your Germans set up the other looms?"

They turned to Aaron.

"Tomorrow," he said.

"As Heaven wills it," Master Blackford said. "Then, I wish you a very good night, sir, Mistress Margaret."

"Guild master," Margaret said, her heart filled with gratitude. If he had not agreed, their plans might have foundered at the outset.

The weavers departed, all talking among themselves. Cedric and the other dissenters murmured darkly to one another. They still weren't happy, but since the guild master had spoken for them, they had to adhere to the agreement. Margaret knew her father would have to use his much-vaunted skills at diplomacy to smooth ruffled feathers until they saw the benefits of working with the new mechanisms.

"Well, I don't know about you, but I feel as if I have run all the way to Scotland and returned again," Sir Timothy said, with a hearty sigh. "Pray allow me to escort you all back to the house. I need a good night's rest. And thank you, Master Aaron and Master Martin. You are about to make our fortune for us."

"We hope so," Aaron said.

"Come on, son," Martin said, putting his arm around the boy's shoulders. "You have to do your homework before you go to bed."

"Dad!"

# Chapter 27

Margaret drifted on a warm, cozy cloud over a landscape woven of green wool, with tufts of brocade sheep rolling over it. In the distance, motor cars frolicked like spring lambs. But as they got closer and closer to her, their engines shrieked in her ears and vibrated her bones in her body.

"Mistress! Mistress!"

Her eyes flew open. A single candle in a bronze candlestick illuminated two faces: Hettie and Liza.

"What's the matter?" she asked.

"Spirits!" Liza said, her eyes huge in the candlelight.

"Noises, mistress," Hettie said. "Coming from the rear of the house. The visitors must have stirred up something uncanny. Perhaps they've roused your ancestors?"

Margaret flipped back the coverlet. The frosty night air chilled her legs and feet. Hettie immediately stooped to put slippers onto her mistress' feet and tucked a woolen wrap around her shoulders.

"I very much doubt that. Are all the doors still locked tight? And the dogs have not raised the alarm?"

"Yes, mistress. No one could have entered. No one *earthly*."

Margaret sighed. "Has it disturbed my parents?"

"Nay, but it might!" Liza said. "The longer it goes on, the more uneasy your lady mother will lie. You know how poorly she rests." She wrung her hands.

"I'll go see if I can find the source," Margaret said. "You were wise to ask me. Pray go back and make certain that my parents are not disturbed."

"Yes, mistress!" Eliza took the candle and disappeared into the hallway.

"Shall I come with you?" Hettie asked, although she looked uneasy at the thought. She went to light a taper at one of the few red embers remaining in the banked-down bedroom fire and placed it in the holder on Margaret's bedside table.

"Follow me," Margaret said, suppressing a small smile. "You can run and awaken James if something ill befalls me."

The big old house made odd noises at the best of times. Most of them disappeared in the hustle and bustle of daytime, but once the sun was down and the household went to bed, any creak or crack seemed amplified. As a small girl, she had fretted over the low wailing of a lost soul trapped in the wall of the room next door, only to brave the noise and discover that it came from a reed trapped in the window that caught the wind when it was in the west. Since then, she had been the one to investigate anything uncanny or weird.

She tiptoed from door to door, listening. Nothing unusual. Her youngest sister talked in her sleep, and both brothers snored. Margaret went through the low-ceilinged passage and up a couple of steep stairs to where the Craigs were staying. Those were part of an annex that had been built by the ninth or tenth Baronet to accommodate his very large family, and had the benefit of privacy.

As she mounted the second stair, she heard it. No wonder it had sounded like spirits to Eliza. The faraway wail was definitely coming from one of the rooms. The flicker of candlelight was visible underneath the door. Margaret tapped on the wood.

"Aaron?"

The door wasn't latched. At her touch, it drifted open.

Aaron sat on the floor with a book and a pad of paper on his lap, reading by a candle above his shoulder on the small end table. As she came in, he dove for a blue-sided box at his side to conceal it, but not before she got a good look at it. The box, about the size of a hen's nest, had a thin black disk almost the same size spinning on its top. A flat stick zipped across the disk. The noise stopped with a sound like the chain being pulled in a wall clock.

"Cornflakes!" Aaron declared, examining the disk. A faint

streak marred the gleaming surface. "I scratched it! My mother is going to kill me."

"I'm sorry," she said. "I knocked, but the door was ajar. May I come in?" She tried to glance around him from the corridor, but he put as much of his body between her and the . . . device? . . . as he could. She and Hettie moved inside and closed the door almost all the way. It wouldn't be seemly to be in the chamber of an unrelated gentleman at night. "What is that?"

He looked abashed, then moved so she could see it. Now that he had removed the disk, she could see a round plaque with a peg sticking up from the center. "It's a record player. It plays music. It belongs to my mom. I thought I was keeping it quiet enough."

"Not quite," Margaret said. "The servants thought that the house was being haunted. They approached me as being the only one who is brave enough to face ghosts."

Aaron looked as though he wanted to laugh, but also ashamed.

"I'm sorry, Miz Margaret. I've got all this homework that I have to finish before I go home. I work better when I can listen to music."

"And this sound, this music is . . . stored in these flat disks?" she asked, looking at the black circle he held to his chest. "How?"

"Oh, that's easy, ma'am!" He launched into an explanation of how a vinyl record was pressed from a master with grooves, and that the stylus that was lowered onto the revolving record produced an electric signal that was carried to the amplifier in the player. Margaret held up her hands for mercy.

"Stop, I beg you. I should have known better than to ask. This makes as little sense to me as your explanation of the aqualators. So, it contains songs from the time you come from?"

"Yes, ma'am." Aaron gestured to another box that sat in one of the small shipping crates like the ones that had carried the aqualators from Magdeburg. It appeared seamless, bright coral on the outside and smooth white on the inside. It held a number of wide but very thin cardboard boxes. "I mean, it's not really from my time, but my mom's. And my grandmother's. Most of these are *old*. I mean, not as old as your kind of music. But not the stuff I really liked listening to, but Mom wouldn't let me take my CD player with me. Those are really delicate because they have a laser in them and they're more prone to water damage, and we were coming here by sea. But they're pretty good. Do you want to hear some of it?"

"Oh, yes!"

He consulted a device attached to the record player that had a glass-topped square on the front. Behind the glass, a red light like a demon's eye glared at them. He nodded.

"What's that?"

"The battery pack. At home I just plug it into the wall, but anywhere else I need a power source. This one's rechargeable. I made it from an auto battery. I rigged it up so I can charge it from one of the river dynamos. It'll run for about six hours on a charge. I'm counting on using one of the water wheels we made for the looms at night when no one is weaving. I've got about an hour of charge left on this one."

"I'm impressed by the endless resourcefulness of your people," Margaret said, shaking her head. "You come up with so many ideas and adapt them for other uses as well."

"You kinda do that, too," Aaron said, then his cheeks went red. "Even Herr Trelli was impressed with your ideas. If you wanted to come to Grantville and take classes with him, you'd probably do great." He selected one of the flat boxes from the red container and slipped the disk from it. "This one is really good. I'll put the volume down real low. If you two can get close to the speaker, I don't think anyone else will hear it."

"No, thank you, sir," Hettie said, politely. "I will stay by the door and make sure no one disturbs you."

"Thank you, Hettie," Margaret said. She thought that her maid was much more likely to be avoiding too much contact with the up-timers' devices. Apart from motor cars, their sojourn in Thuringia didn't make her maidservant much more trusting of technology than she had been when they left. "That is very thoughtful." She sat carefully on the floor beside Aaron. He set the turntable spinning and laid the stylus at the outermost edge of the disk. Immediately, sound began to come through the round pattern of hatch-marked piercings next to the knob that turned the device on.

She heard a cultured man's voice speaking, though she could not entirely understand what he was saying, followed by some rapid notes that sounded as though they were played on strings, and two voices began to sing. She attempted to follow the lyrics, but found herself frowning.

"It sounds very pretty, but why does it go so fast?"

"Do I have it on the wrong speed?" Aaron glanced at the setting. "No, it's right. This is what it's supposed to sound like. It's rock and roll. Here, I can slow it down for you." He changed the setting underneath the edge of the disk, and the results slowed down to something that approximated more of what she considered to be music. Now Aaron made a face.

"I like it, I think," Margaret admitted. "Who is the singer?"

"It's a group of men called the Beatles."

"Beadle? Guild officials? Like the man who obtains livery for Master Blackford? A choir? They don't sound like any choir I have ever heard."

"No!" Aaron laughed. "It's a joke. They made up their name to sound like the bugs, beetles. I don't know why. My granny probably does."

Margaret had stopped long ago trying to work out the logic of the up-timers. "Where in the Americas do they come from?"

"Well, they're not American. Or they won't be, when they're born. They're English. They come from Liverpool."

She gaped at him. "Liverpool? Our Liverpool? The port city, into which you sailed?"

"I guess so." Aaron's eyes danced. "I never made a connection to that at all. You say Lye-verpool, and we say Liver-pool, so I didn't think they were the same thing. Wait 'til I tell Mom."

"Were they . . . important?"

"Mom says for a while they were the most famous people in the world."

"Musicians? Whatever you do, don't let my brother Nat hear you say that," Margaret said with a laugh. "He has a knack for music, but no practical skills whatsoever. He attended university, but he's done nothing with his education thus far. If he feels he can make such strides in the world as a musician, we'll never get him to focus on industry."

"You know, there's a place for everybody somewhere," Aaron said. "He could do great things just playing and singing."

Margaret didn't correct him. She had had to rethink almost everything in her world since she had met the Americans. Wasn't she turning everything on the manor upside down with notions that had been born in their kingdom? What was one more strange idea? Why shouldn't Nat hear the music of the future? It might speak to him.

"Then I see no reason not to. Nat, for all his seeming not to care for a thing in the world, is trustworthy. He would very much enjoy hearing your music and learning about how musicians are regarded in the future."

"Thanks, Miz Margaret!" Aaron said. He beamed. "It'll be great to have someone I can talk to. It's kind of lonely not being with my friends. I mean, I appreciate the chance to be here and be doing all the cool stuff we're doing. But it's different."

"Having joined you in the USE and been surrounded by those who spoke in German and Amideutsch, I understand completely," Margaret said, with heartfelt sincerity. "Have you ever had a dream where you were speaking, saying something of urgent import, and no one seemed to comprehend your words? Or to pass by people and have them not see you as though you were a spirit? To experience that while awake was just as disorienting. I'm sorry you have felt isolated here. We will endeavor to better ease your loneliness."

Aaron smiled.

"I'm fine, Miz Margaret," he said. "We're making the Industrial Revolution happen here, remember?"

"I remember," Margaret said, and touched the back of his hand. "Thank you, Aaron."

"No problem," he replied.

She went on listening. Each of the songs was separated by a few moments of silence. No two were anything alike, and they all had different voices and instruments. But her eyes widened as a familiar sound echoed in her ear.

"That sounds . . . like the organ at our church!" she exclaimed. "To hear it contained in a flat piece of glass . . ."

"Plastic," Aaron corrected her. "Vinyl, really."

". . . Plastic, is a miracle that I feel privileged to hear."

Aaron shrugged. "It's nothing, ma'am. We used to have these everywhere. We even had different kinds of music boxes, and instruments that don't even look like old-time instruments. I mean," he said, his face going red, "maybe not old-time to you."

She kept her ear close to the round grille and listened to the last short song before the stick moved to the center of the black disk, and the sound stopped. She sat up.

"Thank you," she said. "I enjoyed that. Please thank your mother for the gift."

"I will." He took the disk off the turntable and tucked it into the colorful cardboard sleeve. When she looked curiously at it, Aaron handed it to her.

She turned it over, reading the words and looking at the pictures. She felt a connection to these young men from the future. Somehow, knowing that they came from a town not that far from where she now sat made her like them more than ever. She studied the photograph on the cover again, and pointed to one of the men. "Who is that? He is as beautiful as an angel in the stained-glass windows at church."

"Paul McCartney," Aaron said. "That was his voice you were hearing, except slowed down."

"I like it. I liked them all, even the ones that I did not understand. And I will try to become accustomed to them at their proper speed. I would love to hear more, but you must keep it very low, or play it when there is other noise in the house. We're already being accused of practicing wizardry with the aqualators. Music from the future would bring out the witch-finders. Nat will keep your secret, but please don't frighten my servants anymore. If our staff think the house is haunted, they'll tell people in the market, and word will spread everywhere! I will keep your secret if I can, but you need to warn me so we can contrive a convincing story."

Aaron looked abashed. "I will, ma'am. I wish I could use headphones, but I don't have any here. I should've thought of that, but I didn't. I'll be careful."

"Well, good night to you, then. And thank you."

She left him doing the rest of his homework, and went back to bed, thinking about countrymen of hers who were yet to be born.

# Chapter 28

"I want to work on this one," Ivy said, all but leaning over Aaron as he lay on his back on a bench, screwing a bent wire to the side of the loom that would control one of the shuttles on Loom Number Two. "You'll snug it in as tight as tight for me, won't you?" She wriggled just a little closer to him, her leg brushing his. Her bodice was laced more tightly than usual, squeezing her modest assets up provocatively against the material of her camisole.

The men in the shed laughed. Aaron kept his scarlet face underneath the machine and concentrated on his task. She was carbonating his blood. Not that he objected, exactly.

"You'd best watch yourself, girl," Master Walter said, taking his turn on the second completed loom under Martin's watchful eye. Fred had the third loom's warp partially strung with his sleying hook. He intended to begin on a full bolt on Loom Two as soon as Aaron was finished, despite what Ivy wanted. "Mistress Margaret said he understands more than he can say."

"He's coming along well enough," Ivy protested. "Except that he keeps mixing up warp and weft, and he says 'varp' and 'veft.' He knows the difference, but I think he's teasing me."

"That seems to go both ways, then," Lily Dale said with a smirk, winding weft bobbins with rose-colored thread. Ivy stuck her tongue out at her friend.

Daniel Taylor sat at the first loom, his eyes fixed on his work. Aaron listened to the soothing rhythm as the shuttles ran back and forth. Daniel turned the cloth beam and handled the beater like the expert he was, adjusting his speed a tiny bit at a time. Aaron was pretty pleased with the smooth way the machine was running. Not a harsh sound anywhere in it. The aqualator was doing its job, lifting and lowering the heddles as the shuttles zipped back and forth.

Aaron had taught himself to look at weaving critically, both by reading the books that Miz Mailey had left for Miz Margaret to read, and by a kind of apprenticeship under Herr Oberdorn. If he was right, Mr. Daniel *would* be finished with the bolt he was working on by the time the sun went down, or by noon the next day at the latest. In fact, all the weavers had adapted to the change in the looms really quickly, a lot faster than they kept saying they would. Partly, Aaron thought it was competition, with themselves as well as with each other. But it was also because they were on fire for the idea of the new pattern. Now that he had seen the actual cloth, he understood Miz Margaret's dream, and they shared it. The weavers, for all the protests of the night before, wanted to be the first in the world to make this brocade.

The initial piece that had been woven, about three feet long, was bound off and pinned to the wall of the shed for all to see. The weavers, one and all, couldn't help but go over and touch it, turn it to see the back, and comment to one another on the way the weave went together. Aaron was pretty pleased with himself for getting Miz Margaret's design just the way she wanted it. She had an expert's eye, just like he did for a page of code. Weaving and programming did have a lot in common.

Once he got the connections made, Aaron crawled out from underneath the loom to hook up the pipes. That part of the design always took a little adjusting. The edge of the pipe slipped and a spray of water hit him in the face.

"Turn it off!" he shouted, feeling for the stopcock. He sputtered and wiped his eyes with his sleeve. Everyone laughed at him.

"Don't drink too much, son," Martin called through the wall in Amideutsch. "We don't have a lot of medicine to stop you up again if you catch something."

Ivy's dad said much the same thing, except in English. Aaron was looking forward to not having to pretend not to speak the language himself. He rubbed his face, almost grateful for the cold water cooling his hot cheeks.

He tightened the stopcock and went back to check all the connections between the aqualator block and the loom.

"Okay, Dad! It's hooked up."

Martin returned to the workroom, dusting his hands together. Master Fred had finished his work on Loom Number Three and made his way toward Loom Number Two. Ivy started to sit down at it, but Master Matthew pulled up the stool, keeping it away from her. He gave her a stern look. She seemed dismayed, but made way at once for her father. At a wave from Fred, she retreated to the side of the room with the apprentices. She'd told Aaron herself that Loom Number Two was his special pet machine, and no one used it without his word, not even his own daughter.

The older man took hold of the beater and gestured impatiently at the Americans.

"Make it go, then," he said. Martin turned the little brass handle, and water began to dribble through the aqualators. In a moment, the shuttles started to fly. Fred pulled the beater toward him with a thud, then pushed it back again. Within a handful of passes, he fell into the rhythm, and the cloth began to grow on the loom.

"I wonder if playing music would keep them on the beat," Aaron said to Martin. "Maybe something with a steady beat like "All Together Now"?"

"Oh, no, boy," his father said, with a look at the others to make sure no one could understand them. "I warned you when you packed that record player that it was to be kept out of sight. We're risking enough just by being here."

Aaron sighed. "I'd have liked being able to listen to music while I'm working."

"No! You know better. Don't get Miz Margaret in trouble. She's trusting us. Don't go too far."

Aaron sighed. "I won't, Dad."

"Need to refill the shuttles," Daniel called.

One of the apprentices dropped what he was doing and ran to turn off the water. The shuttles slowed to a halt. The boy plucked the two empty bobbins from their "boats," and hurried to the big spools near the wall to wind fresh thread into them. Master Blackford came over to watch him as he clipped the ends and set them back where they belonged.

Aaron watched, realizing how much work went into something

simple, like a length of cloth to make one piece of clothing. So, this is what the world looked like before the Industrial Revolution. His history teacher was expecting a paper on the comparison as soon as he got back.

The guild master had been underfoot since early morning. Aaron had seen the avid look in his eyes as he sized up the looms and their new attachments. It reminded him of the way his friends eyed each other's computers or collectibles. Master Blackford wanted these devices, too, as soon as they could be imported. *He* saw the possibilities, just like Miz Margaret did. Master Blackford was being converted to a modern man. The other masters were more than a little afraid of change, but even they could see money in the new cloth. Master Blackford saw a lot more. Aaron longed to ask him what was on his mind, and maybe discuss what other applications he could design for them. Maybe after the de Beauchamps made enough money, his next programming job could be for the local guild. From the man's fancy clothes and gold jewelry, Master Blackford looked like he could afford it. Aaron would have loved to make enough to buy his mother some jewelry, or bring home some of the nice fabric the weavers were making. Not the brocade, not yet. Miz Margaret had plans for every piece for the foreseeable future.

Miz Margaret herself flitted around, checking over each of the looms as Aaron and Martin finished fiddling with them. Aaron didn't realize, not really, until he was there, how much she had risked on him and his skills. Though Sir Timothy was generous to a fault with hospitality, it wasn't without an eye to keeping everything in balance. Aaron was sorry then that he had charged Margaret anything for his coding. After all, he had learned a lot that he could take away from learning to program looms and use it for other applications. For her sake, he vowed to make sure nothing would go wrong.

But, of course, it did.

Mr. Fred had no trouble keeping up with the rhythm of the aqualators. He fixed a frowning stare on the shuttles, and Aaron saw his free hand twitch again and again. He must be doing all he could not to slam the shuttles himself. But Fred was wary of all the wires. He kept adjusting his shoulders so as not to interfere with the mechanism. Aaron knew how he could widen the space and adjust the tension on the wires, which almost sang their frustration, but every time he started to move toward Fred, the older man snarled at him like a guard dog. Oh, well, he could wait until Fred stopped, and fix it for the next day.

Even though Mr. Fred seemed cranky, he kept nodding at the growing breadth of fabric. A little smile crooked the ends of his mouth every time another feature of the pattern appeared on the field of red, a leaf here, a petal there. When the motif had finished forming, Fred put his lower lip out in what looked like an expression of satisfaction. Everyone noticed his expressions but didn't draw attention. They all seemed to know him pretty well.

Aaron had to admit that at a distance, the woolen cloth looked as smooth as the silk Miz Margaret had shown him. Master Fred was the best of the weavers he had watched so far. Small wonder the others put up with his grouchy attitude.

Clump, clump. Swish, swish. Creak, creak. Thud, thud. The shuttles flew from one side to the other and back again, propelled by the framework Aaron had set up. The cloth being wound up on the big spool in front of Fred's chest grew steadily. There was no way he could overtake Daniel's progress, but he wouldn't be far behind him, despite having started over an hour later. Aaron found himself grinning as he worked to attach the mechanism to Loom Number Three. Ivy crouched beside him, pretending to pick up pieces of lint. She sure was a pretty girl, smart and ambitious.

"Hey, there, my friend," Master Matthew called. "Fred, tha's makin' an eerie noise."

"Shush," Fred snapped at him. "It's nothin'. The loom's old. My granda made it with his own hands a hundred years ago. It's bound to sound as creaky as my old bones."

"And it complains as much as you do! Hold back. No need to race her as though she was a yearling!"

Fred lifted his eyes from his work to glare at the other master. "There's naught wrong with my loom, I tell ye! Despite the blacksmith's construction attached there'n. It's fine!"

Master Matthew shook his head and retreated. But Aaron started paying attention to the noises. The heddles were shaking in their framework. The wobble wasn't normal, although he had to admit his experience was limited. It wasn't the fault of the aqualator. He saw Miz Margaret close by and wriggled out from under Loom Number Three.

"What's wrong?" she asked.

"Something's going loose in the loom. I think it's coming apart. Mr. Matthew can tell there's a problem, too. Everyone seems to hear it but Mr. Fred. Please make him stop so I can take a look at it."

"Master Wilkinson," Margaret said, in a gentle and conciliatory tone, moving toward Loom Number Two. He favored her with a momentary glance and went back to concentrating on the shuttles. "Your work is exemplary, but I believe that Aaron needs to make adjustments in the mechanism."

"It's workin' fine, I tell ye!" Fred said. But his back looked tense. The loom was making some alarming noises.

"I beg you to slow down," she pleaded.

"I don't need to slow down. I know this old girl as if she was my wife."

Aaron smelled something burning. He hurried to the stopcock to turn it off.

"Don't ye touch that!" the weaver snapped. But almost as soon as he spoke, the tension pulling on the frame caused it to creak like a car going around a tight bend. The shaft harness containing the heddles lurched out of place. The speed was too much for the old machine. The warp suddenly flew upward, tangling the shuttles in the half-finished cloth. Attached to the moving framework, they tried to pull themselves loose. Aaron twisted the stopcock to close off the flow of water, but it was too late. The old loom seemed to collapse in on itself, then burst with a sound like a gunshot. Pieces flew outward. Fred ducked, but a splinter of wood the length of his hand grazed his scalp. Margaret turned away in time, but was pelted by small pieces. The heddles sprang loose like pickup sticks and hung on the warp threads running through them.

"Curse ye, now see what you've done!" Fred shouted. "Look at my old girl!" Blood ran from the cut over his ear. Ivy grabbed a handful of lint and came to press it against the wound on her father's head. He ran his hands over the ruined loom, looking distraught. "Curse ye, Germans! If it weren't for your infernal machine, there'd be no problem here. Oh, poor old girl. Poor thing!"

"We can fix her, Fred," Matthew said, kindly. He gathered up a handful of small parts and started to sort through them. "She's from the last century. She never thought to be a modern lass."

"I meant to have Alder take her over one day," Fred said, laying his hand on one part after another, as if mourning them. "And now look at her."

"I couldn't get her to go like that for me, Dad," Alder Wilkinson said, soothingly. "You're the only one with the touch. No one else could get the work out of her that you have. She'd sit up and beg for you, but none of us can run her without having snags. She's too tetchy. Look what you've done already." He patted the length of rose-adorned cloth, already three yards long. "See, Dad? We can fix it. It'll be as good as the day Great-Grandad made it."

"I am so sorry, Herr Fred," Aaron said.

"We'll do what we can to make it right," Martin added.

Fred waved them away. "She'll never be the same again."

Master Blackford came over to inspect the damage.

"Let's get her out of the way, then, Fred," he said, with sympathy. "Apart from the broken upright, there's nothing that can't be mended." He looked up. "We can take one of the other looms and put it here in the meanwhile. Come ahead, man."

"This is what happens when ye try wild ideas," Master Cedric said, sourly. "The old ways are the best ways."

"I am very sorry," Aaron repeated. He tried to help move the pieces of the broken loom, but the other weavers waved him off. He sent Ivy a helpless glance, but she only gave him a sad smile. Her brother directed her to pick up the scattered pieces and put them in a pail.

Together, the apprentices and journeymen hoisted the frame and brought it to the end of the workroom near the open door.

Fred's son, Samuel, unpegged the splintered piece of frame and examined it. "Ashwood, a hundred years old," he said. "It'd bend if it was younger, but it just broke under the pressure. I'll cut a new piece for it, and it'll be good as new."

Aaron felt as shattered as the loom. He knew he wasn't to blame, but he felt guilty.

Miz Margaret was kind. "Keep working on the others, please, Aaron. It'll be all right. Please. We need to keep going. It was an accident."

He felt terrible. The Wilkinson family wouldn't look at him, except for Ivy, who shot apologetic glances over her shoulder. The other weavers, though, were impatient for him to get the rest of the looms updated. Some went to help Fred and his family fix the old loom, but just as many encouraged Aaron to get back to work.

"I want my chance!" Mr. Matthew said, clapping the teen on the back. "I never thought I'd live to see the day when anything new came out of this old barn, and I want my name in the books as one of the first to do it. Ye should be proud, boy."

The truth was, Aaron was proud of what had been accomplished. Taking a deep breath, he went to put the last connections on Loom Number Three. He turned on the stopcock and ran a test, and the heddles lifted and lowered as they were supposed to. The wires that would control the shuttles danced as if eager to get going. It didn't creak at all.

"That's the stuff," Matthew said. "Just don't make mine burst apart, eh?" But his eyes twinkled.

Aaron felt sheepish.

"*Nein*, it vill be right."

"Ach, ye almost spoke the decent tongue! Come now, boys, let's get her moving!

Matthew's apprentices helped him load the bobbins into the shuttles. The master weaver sat down on the stool and nodded to Aaron to turn on the aqualator. The shuttles started crossing the warp.

"There ye go, boy. It'll be right." Matthew nodded to his journeymen. "Help him take one of the idle looms and put it where Fred's ought to be."

The young men went to fetch the nearer of the unaltered looms. Aaron hurried ahead of them to shift all the unused aqualator parts to a corner where they wouldn't get stepped on.

"Can't you put these together?" Lemuel, one of the apprentices, asked, as Aaron stacked the loose trays.

"*Nein*," he said, indicating the broken sections. "Leak."

"Ah, well," the boy said. "With eight akalabors, we'd be flying like gulls, and Sir Timothy would be as proud as Lucifer."

Aaron bit his tongue, unable to explain in make-believe pidgin English why comparing their employer to the Devil was not much of a compliment, but he just grinned, shook his head, and set to work.

Together, they moved a loom into place that had been occupied by the broken one. Aaron took one more look at the damaged aqualator tray. Each of the broken ones had an unusually thick gate close to the drainage hole, which meant that it would slow down the flow into the one underneath it. The crack in the plaque ran alongside it. He'd have to send a message to St. Malo to fix the mold when he got back to Grantville, for when Miz Margaret ordered more. Maybe they could find a local guy who worked in ceramics to make a mold here to cast a replacement?

He shook his head over the rejected pieces. His long suit was programming and software design, not hardware. From Herr Trelli, he knew that clay shrank when you fired it, but how much? What proportions? How, when he wasn't supposed to be able to speak English, could he explain to a local potter how to make an aqualator tray that would fit into the stacks?

Frustrated, he went back to what he *did* know how to do.

# Chapter 29

By late afternoon, the last of the six intact sets of aqualators was up and running. At last, Ivy got her chance to sit down and work the revised loom. She had to take turns with Lily Dale, but the two of them did pretty well. Aaron went over to watch them. He was impressed by how skillful they were at managing the weave. Ivy caught his gaze, then lowered her eyes as if she was shy. Aaron felt disappointed. He wanted her to look at him. It wasn't often that a pretty girl paid attention to him, and he wanted to enjoy every minute of it. There were always better looking or more athletic guys in his school. The geeky ones like him got ignored almost all the time. If he and his friends didn't band together, they'd probably have gotten bullied by the jocks. That was just life in high school. But here, he was the big man on campus, the guy with all the answers. That felt good.

"So, what do you call these?" Ivy asked, gesturing at the roses in the pattern with her free hand.

*"Rosen,"* Aaron said, with the "R" far back in his throat.

"Wosen," Ivy said. Her bright green eyes tilted up to meet his, and he felt his heart skip. *Don't make a mistake now*, he cautioned himself.

*"Nein,"* he said. "'*Rosen.*'"

"Now, you say it in English. 'Roses.'"

Aaron let out a big, theatrical sigh. "Roses."

"See! You can do it. You know the difference now."

"I do," Aaron said, careful to keep the accent because it

was expected, and would be until they left for Hamburg. The thought of going away from Ivy suddenly made his heart drop into his stomach. How could he be getting a crush on her? He'd only known her two days! He really wanted to open up to this very nice girl, but he was afraid of her father, as well as making trouble for Miz Margaret and her family.

The teasing look in her eyes faded. "It's got to be hard for you, living in a different country like this, with people speaking a whole different language," Ivy said. "I know I'd feel strange being swept away from everything I ever knew."

*You don't know the half of it*, Aaron thought. He opened his mouth, but his father gave him a look of caution.

Aaron let out a huge sigh. He'd been a small boy at the time of the Ring of Fire, but he missed so many things from before. In an instant, the town had been dragged into the past, and their whole lives had changed. What they had come to depend on was all gone, all at once. Mike Stearns and the other people who were in charge had had to regiment everything, all the resources. Suddenly, no TV, no rides in the country, no candy or peanut butter, soldiers in weird uniforms marching through their town, like being in a movie but never being able to get out of it.

He and his friends had adapted pretty fast. His mom, Effie, said it was because they were children, and children coped with change. But he wasn't sure that was true of everyone, and it was like there was a small part of him that hadn't changed, either. He knew what the English people here felt, getting this new technology shoved in their faces, and having to accept it or lose their jobs. It wasn't fair. But it would do them so much good once they accepted it and learned how to use it.

"You are right," he said, in English. "But I am learning."

The weavers nearby nodded their approval. Not only was he "learning" English, but they were picking up Amideutsch words, too, which they threw around like slang especially when they were sure he could hear them. Dad thought it was funny, and told Aaron it was their way of making the two of them feel welcome.

The humming of the looms was hypnotic. Once there was nothing to do but watch out for problems, Aaron sat on a bench and drifted off. After all the anticipation of learning the skills needed to code aqualators for weaving, overseeing the building of the equipment, getting ready to go and traveling by ship all the way to England, and putting the mechanisms together, all while pretending only to speak Amideutsch and doing his homework late at night, he had used up all his energy. All around him, people were working like bees in a hive, and the sound put him into a trance.

Suddenly, a number of voices rose in a shout, rousing him from his doze.

"It's done!"

"Stopcock!" barked Daniel Taylor. His apprentice hurried to turn off the water to the aqualator. The shuttles drifted slowly to a halt. People crowded close around the loom, murmuring in wonder.

"God bless my soul!" Master Blackford said, crossing himself.

Hands grabbed Aaron and pulled him off his bench. They hustled him toward the first loom. Daniel Taylor sat on the bench, a look on his face as smug as if he just won an Olympic gold medal.

"There, ye see, gentlemen? Did I not tell you such a thing was possible?" He thrust his hand toward the cloth beam. A thick roll of cloth clung to it, and the last of the warp was stretched out over the knee beam. On the field of ecru fabric, the pattern of five-and-four roses and leaves across was complete. Daniel scanned the room. "Mistress Margaret, will you do the honors?" He took a massive pair of shears from a peg on the wall and handed it to her.

Miz Margaret came forward, her eyes shining, but she didn't take the big scissors.

"The honor should go to my father," she protested. Sir Timothy laughed with delight.

"Indeed, no," the squire said. He brought the shears to Aaron and closed his hands around them. "This young man has traveled far and made a marvel appear before us, my friends. Do you not think he should be the one to cut free the first of the brocade that will make our fortune?"

Aaron looked around in confusion as the room erupted in shouts of acclaim.

Not all the faces were smiling. The one master, Cedric, was no longer skeptical, but still looked displeased. A few of the others matched his expression. The rest looked excited.

"Everything's changed now," his father murmured. "Go ahead, son. You've earned it."

Very carefully, as he had watched Herr Oberdorn's apprentices do on fabric that was almost as precious as the one before him, Aaron clipped the threads against the warp beam to leave enough to tie off, and eased the loose end of the cloth onto the beam. He couldn't help but pat the loom as if it was a faithful dog. It did a good job. The weavers cheered. With the help of his apprentices, Daniel unhitched the ratchet and folded the newly crafted bolt with the brocaded side out, showing the roses and leaves.

"There, my friends," he said. "There's the future for ye."

With six brocade looms in operation, each with the potential to make a bolt in a day or two, Sir Timothy became full of plans.

"The dyers have the first lot now," he told Delfine at the dinner table a few days later. "And once it's been treaded, fulled and dried, I want to send it all to Master Bywell in London. He'll know the best eyes to put it before, so that it will attract attention from the court."

Margaret swallowed a bite of food and opened her mouth to say something, then thought better of it. Lowering her eyes, she cut another piece of meat and speared it with the fork. Unfortunately, her father had noticed her expression.

"What is it, my kit?" he asked. "Do you think that I've forgotten your promise to our benefactors?"

Margaret felt her cheeks burn.

"I did promise Lady Rita that she—or rather, her goodmother—should have the new fabric to wear before anyone else. She has been so kind to us. They all have."

Sir Timothy sighed. "And I'd be more than glad to oblige her, but we need capital. In order to fulfill the orders from... from there," he said, cautiously, "then we will need more raw materials. Abbot Lincoln has a surplus of thread from his spinners. He was going to sell it on to merchants on the continent, but I believe we can make an advantageous bargain. You have created a new problem for us, gentlemen," he said to Aaron and Martin, who sat at the table between Margaret and Nathaniel. "We suddenly have more capacity to weave more wool than our sheep can produce. The spinners' fingers are wearing to the bone trying to keep up."

"That's good for everyone," Martin said. "By and large, your weavers are on board with the new program. They're very impressed, although it sounds like they wouldn't tell you straight out. Most of them are already daydreaming about what they'll do with their bonuses." Sir Timothy looked a question at him, and the other man laughed. "I'm a high school janitor, sir. People talk in front of me all the time. I'm used to it. They think I'm not listening, or I can't understand. In this case, the weavers think I don't know much of the language. But you have a couple of dissenters in the flock. Master Cedric and his friends. I don't know whether they're jealous, or they just don't like bringing in something new."

"My goodness," Sir Timothy said, alarmed but amused. "I didn't realize I had imported a spy." He raised a hand to stay outcry. "Pray do not take that amiss, sir; you're giving me valuable information that I would rather have than not. What about Master Blackford? It is important that he supports us. To go against the rules of the guild would ruin us swiftly."

"Oh, him? I get the idea that Blackford wants to hold onto his post, but benefit from the new technology. He wants credit for *allowing* you to introduce it. More than anything, he's afraid that it won't fall into his purview, as the aqualators bear no resemblance to anything ever used in weaving before."

"As indeed they do not. I had hoped that would be his view. Thank merciful heavens for his alliance. I'll make certain to cultivate his agreeableness and include him in decisions." He glanced at Aaron. "But you, young man, you look as though you, too, have something on your mind. Is there a concern with the aqualators?"

Aaron's mouth worked, then words just spilled out of him. "No, sir! That girl, Miss Ivy. She's awfully sweet. But she comes on pretty hard. She wants to teach me English, you know, and I'm willing to let her help me. The sooner I can stop having to speak nothing but Amideutsch, the happier I'll be. She's asked me to dinner some evening, and promises me she'll get me speaking English like a local in no time." Margaret chuckled, and Nathaniel snickered loudly. "But I dunno. What's the right way to act around her? I'll be completely respectful, I swear."

"Bless you," Delfine said, shaking her head, and regarding him with a motherly look. "The question, my child, is not whether you behave respectfully toward her, it is how she will behave with you."

That comment made Aaron's face go beet red.

"Don't worry about it!" Nathaniel said, adding to the teasing with a wicked smile. He and Aaron had formed a friendship over Aaron's hidden stash of records. They'd gotten to the point where they could razz one another. He gave Aaron an outrageous wink. "Just let things go naturally, and I'm certain it will all work out well."

"Nathaniel!"

"She's got a lot of talent," Aaron said, fighting through his embarrassment. That evoked another snort from Nathaniel. "I think I could teach her to draft patterns for the aqualators."

"Really?" Margaret asked, surprised.

"Oh, yeah. She's really smart. It's too bad the guild doesn't admit girls."

Delfine smiled. "I would love to see all her energy channeled into a useful skill. She's not a bad girl, just a little willful. It's a shame she wasn't born a boy."

"Mother!" Margaret exclaimed, surprised.

"My dear, I may not be strong of body, but I am not weak of mind. I see what people do, and what they are capable of. Enjoy your time with her, Master Aaron. If you can teach her how to use these devices better, you'll be giving a gift to all of us."

"Perhaps later," Sir Timothy said, shaking his head. "We are putting a mighty cart before what is at the moment a very small horse. I have spoken to Master Piers about arranging transport. The bolts will be on a wagon to London soon. May divine Providence favor us."

In order to gain even more of Heaven's grace, Sir Timothy asked the vicar of St. John the Baptist's Church, the Reverend Peter Olney, to give a blessing to the covered wagonload of woolen cloth as it departed.

The family and Churnet House's weavers gathered around the cart as though it was a ship about to sail into unknown waters. All of the workmen wore their Guild finest. Over his black velvet suit, Master Blackford had on a cope of lace with his golden collar on the shoulders. His beadle, Paul Thornton, stood at his shoulder, an elegant feathered hat balanced on his arm. Mr. Olney's sonorous voice was caught by the high ceiling of the weaving shed, amplifying it as though it came from the speaker of Aaron's record player. Margaret kept her head lowered so that James could not catch her eye. She didn't know whether to be angry with her brother or laugh along with him at the absurdity of invoking heaven for the brocade as though it was a newborn baby. On the other hand, she had fought so hard for this that she felt she should appreciate the invocation. But it was hard. Nat had chosen the latter, to the dismay of their mother. He wriggled around more impatiently than their two younger sisters, stifling snickers. The house servants, too, did their best to contain their merriment.

"Shh!" Mrs. Ball snapped. Nat subsided, and Margaret had to swallow her own giggles.

"...And may this work of Your Hands gain favor wheresoever it shall go, and send blessings back to this place and these, your faithful servants. Amen." Mr. Olney made the sign of the cross and bowed his head.

Everyone echoed the final word and gesture, then the men clapped their hats back onto their heads. James said his farewells to the family and climbed into the cart. Ranulf Bracey's elder son, Lewis, clicked his whip. The cart rolled toward the manor's gate. Margaret felt a part of her heart going with it. Since the fabric had been finished, she'd barely let it out of her sight. She, Ivy, and Lily had draped it against themselves, imagining grand gowns all covered with the roses.

*Godspeed*, she thought. *Let others see what I saw.*

"Thank you, Vicar," Sir Timothy said.

"My pleasure, Squire," Mr. Olney said. "I have never seen anything like this textile. If it was not for the sin of vanity, I wouldn't mind possessing a coat of it, myself."

"We would like for it to become so common that it is no more extraordinary than the fustian you are wearing now, Vicar," Sir Timothy said, heartily.

The vicar ran his hand down the front of his modest black vestment. "I do not wish to twist the Lord's words to find excuses, sir. But if such a thing does come true, I will agree that we are all to be equally blessed."

Fred Wilkinson grunted. "Back to work, then."

# Chapter 30

"Is that the home of Sir Franklin Leigh?" asked the man with the pockmarked face, swinging off his horse.

One of the men-at-arms who was waiting to spar again on the Upper Nobut village green with the thirty or thirty-five men there lowered his sword and turned to him. Behind them in the distance, visible in the broad gap between a coaching inn and a smithy, stood a grand house with seven chimneys made of local limestone and red brick.

"Who is asking?" he inquired, looking the well-dressed man in the dark blue suit up and down as if judging whether they'd be evenly matched in a fight. The ease at which he stood said that he believed that he'd be the winner. He wore a metal helmet and a thick leather jerkin.

"My name's Ben Sandown," the man said. "I bring a message for him from London."

"London, is it?" the man-at-arms asked, his thick brows rising. "Go over and ring the bell, then. We'll see whether the squire wants to hear tidings from London."

Some of the other fighters near him laughed. Ben laughed, too.

"We'll see, then," he said. "Remember me, won't you?"

The man gave him a strange look. "Are ye worthy of a place in my memory?"

"I will be," Ben said. He raised his chin to the man in the polished breastplate on the horse beside him. He turned away and walked his own steed up the lane toward the house. The men looked after him for a while, then went on with their exercises.

"May I ask your business, sir?" the footman asked, when he answered the door. He was dressed in breeches, a good linen shirt, and an embroidered waistcoat. His employer must pay well; such a thing would cost a month's wages in the East End of London.

"I bear a message for Sir Franklin from the king," Ben said. "May I enter?"

The footman looked impressed. Hardly any emissaries from the crown had come here in a long while, and that was half the problem, according to Ben's employer.

"Squire's at table," he said. "Will you wait here?" He gestured to a door to the left just inside the foyer.

"No, I'll see him in the dining room," Ben said. He pushed past the footman, and listened for the sound of cutlery on crockery. "It's this, isn't it?"

He twisted the handle of the elegant mahogany door and swung it open. Give credit where it was due for the Leighs' management, the hinges didn't make a single sound. Hence, the lady being helped to chops from a silver platter only noticed him because of the unfamiliar movement. She looked up in annoyance.

"Who are you, sir?" she demanded.

By now, the gentleman of the house, Sir Franklin, had risen to his feet. He stood the same height as Ben, but carried a good deal more weight. Again, more signs of prosperity that was not being shared with the crown.

"What do you mean, coming in here like that? Get out of here!"

Ben was undeterred. "I come on behalf of His Majesty the king," he said, standing at his ease. "You have not paid this year's taxes. So far, you have ignored three letters requesting you make good on your obligation. It is time to pay."

For a moment, Sir Franklin looked apprehensive or guilty. It didn't matter which. Then his face turned red.

"Leave my home, sir!" he said. He strode to the doorway and shouted through it. "Phillips! Call the men!"

"His Majesty has been more than patient," Ben went on as though nothing was happening. "Your taxes go to support services that benefit the duchy as well as the royal estates. The roads, the security of the realm, ministers to oversee all the aspects of life for all of the king's loyal subjects."

"And to pay mercenaries like you," Sir Franklin said. He snatched a walking stick from a tall jar near the door and made for the messenger. Ben neatly sidestepped it.

"Oh, where is Phillips?" Lady Leigh asked. The children, five in all, none older than twelve years, had abandoned their seats. The younger four fled to their mother's arms. The eldest, a gangly boy who had the first few silky strands of a mustache beginning to grow beneath his nose, came up to confront him with the meat knife gripped in his skinny hand.

"You are not welcome here, sir," he said. To his credit, the voice didn't squeak.

"I am not addressing you, sir," Ben said, not bothering to hide his amusement. "Go back to your mam's teat."

"How dare you!" Lady Leigh protested.

Possibly emboldened by her words, the boy sprang at Ben. The man sidestepped neatly, grabbed the boy from behind around the neck and the wrist, and squeezed until the knife fell on the floor. The boy snarled, and this time his voice did break. Ben spun him away. The boy crashed into the wall and fell down. One of his sisters ran to him.

"I suggest you send for your strongbox, Sir Franklin," Ben said.

"I will not pay such rapacious sums!" the gentleman said. "Taxes have tripled in the last two years. How am I supposed to support my estate on what is left after the king milks us dry?"

Ben shook his head. "That's not His Majesty's concern. Perhaps you can undertake economies? You are surrounded by fine things, many of which could be sold. Or perhaps not feeding so heavily at the trough, eh? Your waistcoat needs to be let out at the seams."

By now, the footman came scrambling into the room. "Sir Franklin!" he exclaimed, out of breath.

"Where are the men?" his employer demanded. The footman gibbered and pointed toward the door.

"Oh, yes, about the men," Ben said, lightly. "They will not come."

"What?" The squire turned on him in a rage. "Why not?"

"Because *my* men are keeping them busy. This is your last warning. Now." Ben fixed a cold gaze upon him. "You must pay up and satisfy the king's requirements of you. Or you will be in arrears, and a claim might be put upon your manor on behalf of the crown."

Sir Franklin still stood firm, both hands clutching the upraised walking stick.

"And if I do not heed that?"

Ben shook his head. "Ah, I was hoping you wouldn't say that."

He swept up one of the side chairs from the table and brought it down on Sir Franklin's wrists. He heard a crack, though he was fairly certain it wasn't breaking bones, only bruising. The man let out a scream of pain, falling to his knees. Before Sir Franklin could recover enough to defend himself, Ben threw the chair aside and latched onto the squire's shoulders. He hoisted the man to his feet and hauled him bodily out of the dining room, down the hall, through the front door, which stood ajar, and down the brick steps to the drive.

In the distant square, it looked like chaos, but was in fact organized and managed. Fifteen pikemen on horseback rode around the villagers, keeping them herded together like sheep. From Ben's perspective, they hadn't had to harm any of them yet, not substantially. One of the horsemen doled out a solid bang on the helm of a man trying to break through the cordon.

"Let go of me! What are you doing? Who are they?" Sir Franklin shouted.

A couple more of Ben's mercenaries rode up.

"Family's in the house," Ben said, tilting his head toward the door. The men swung off their mounts and dashed up the steps.

"Leave them alone!" Sir Franklin protested. He fought to break free. Ben let him stand up, then delivered a solid punch to the man's wobbly gut. Sir Franklin doubled over. Ben joined both his hands and brought them down on the upturned back, dropping the man to his knees. Then he began kicking him. The man fell on his side, trying to protect his face. He tried to crawl away, but Ben hauled him back and continued striking and kicking him.

"My husband! Pray let me go to him!" Lady Leigh screamed, as one of the armored men brought her outside. The children were herded down the stairs by the other.

Of course, the elder boy had to throw himself to his father's defense, pummeling the attacker with both fists. Ben backhanded him. The boy fell down the stairs and landed on the gravel drive. He looked like he wanted to cry, but came barreling back in again. Ben had to admire his spirit. He was already twice the man his father was. He swatted the boy back. This time, one of his lieutenants, a broad man with greasy black hair, grabbed the youth and held onto him with an iron grip.

Lady Leigh huddled against the doorframe, trying to shield her younger children from the fray. They screeched at Ben to stop, but he ignored them. There was nothing they could do. A lesson had to be taught, not just for one minor landowner, but for everyone he knew and would tell later on.

When Sir Franklin lay on the fieldstone terrace, still awake but not moving, Ben crouched down to meet his eyes.

"You're evicted, Sir Franklin Leigh, you and all your family. This manor and the lands belonging to it are now the property of His Majesty the king. Next time, if there is a next time, you will obey His Majesty's concerns."

Sir Franklin hauled himself painfully to a sitting position. He bled from his nose and one eye socket, and bruises were starting on most of his face. "But you can't displace us like that!"

Ben felt in the pouch at his belt. He fished out the writ that the chancellor had signed and threw it into the man's lap. "I can. The Duchy of Lancaster belongs to the crown. If you had paid up on time, you would have been spared. But since you have been heard to voice sedition—"

"I never did! I am loyal to His Majesty! My family has served for generations. . . ."

"Ah, but your men have heard you state your opinions. They talk about it in the tavern, or didn't you know that? His Majesty demands absolute fealty."

Now, Sir Franklin was coughing blood. Ben doubted it was a sign of anything fatal. "I have always given the king all honors."

"But that is not all he requires from you. Your estate now belongs to the crown. You have an hour to remove necessary belongings and move on. His Majesty is merciful in not setting torch to this house." The Leighs gasped, but Ben remained impassive. He had no intention of burning it. It was too fine a place, and His Majesty would find it to be a good foothold in this area. If in fact the Earl didn't buy it instead. Ben knew that he had bought up a few of these distressed properties. "You'd best begin as soon as you can."

Such evictions served so many purposes: putting down potential rebellion, to forestall the disaster that was rumored to befall the king in the future history books, and to enrich his most loyal minister in the meanwhile. Also, Ben thought with a grin, to line the pockets of his faithful in the meantime with rewards for each successful eviction. There was no downside that he could see. He stood guard on the doorstep with his men, keeping an eye on the church clock.

Lady Leigh, released from the grip of the dragoon, ran to her husband, crying her eyes out, wiping the blood from his face with a lace handkerchief. She sent one of the children running. The tot disappeared around the rear of the house. In a short time, she came back with two men and a horse-drawn cart and a carriage.

Ben gave it some thought. Should he prevent them taking their carriage? No, there was nothing more piteous than displaced gentry showing up on the steps of a neighbor with all their goods behind them, begging to be taken in. Let him have that.

The eldest boy helped his father up, wiping the blood from his lips. Ben saw the look on his face. The rebellious glare. Ah, here it came. The youth came charging toward Ben, who had learned his craft as a mercenary in Europe and had practiced it in the taverns of London. The boy swung wide. Never learned to fight, did he?

On the lad's next charge, Ben stuck out his foot, tripped the lad to the ground. With a few well-chosen punches, the boy lay still, winded, a sound bruise growing on the side of his face. Ben had taken the fire out of him without doing unnecessary damage.

"You'll thank me later for my mercy," Ben said.

"I'll kill you," the boy snarled.

"When you grow up, perhaps we'll meet again," he said. "But I'll have learned more tricks in the meanwhile. You'd best help your mam before the clock runs out. I'm not so patient as to wait past the church bells' chime."

He watched them pile things onto the cart, silks and silver, paintings and rolled tapestries. What did it matter if they took fine goods with them? Their biggest asset was gone. According to the tax rolls, this gentleman owned another very small house to the east of this one. Ben could take possession of that, too, as the tax was as of yet still unpaid, but the lesson had been taught. He had all the time in the world to make his point again next year. But he would have taken a solid wager that the taxes would arrive early then. In fact, he would be surprised if it took more than a fortnight to make his debt good to the crown, but the Earl of Cork would add hefty interest on top of it to rescind the eviction.

Patiently, not letting the grin he felt show on his face, he waited until they had packed everything on the wagon that they could. He watched them roll away. Once they were out of earshot, he called his men to him. The horsemen let the would-be army escape back to their homes. It looked like there were plenty of bruised bodies and egos, but no dead, and no major injuries.

He assessed his ragtag force with an expert eye, and nodded to the captain of the company, Johann Rawl. Rawl stood forth at the head of the band of mercenaries.

"You are now stewards of the king," Ben bellowed. "Some of you will live in this house and respect it as if His Majesty was about to visit. Do not loot this place by as much as a penny piece. Do you understand me?"

"Aye. I do," the men chorused. Ben wasn't convinced, but he trusted Rawl's judgement.

"Choose a handful of men to remain here to guard His Majesty's property."

Rawl surveyed the squad. "Reggie Deer."

Reggie, a wiry man in his early thirties that Ben had signed up when he saw him win a dirty fight in a tavern against four other men, shifted the pike in his right hand to his left and scratched his ribcage. "I ken ye well enow."

Ben was in no mood to deal with insubordination. He grabbed the man by the ear, dragged his head down, threatening to pull him out of his saddle, and put his knife to the lobe. The point penetrated the soft flesh, making one ruby drop snake its way down the blade. "Do you understand me?"

The face, now inches from Ben's own, wore an expression of alarm and instant respect. "Aye. Sir."

Ben thrust him away. The horse danced a pace backward. "That's better."

Rawl reeled off four more names, and the men wheeled their horses to stand beside him. Ben addressed them.

"This is now an asset of the crown of His Most Sacred Majesty, Charles, by right of heaven lord of this land. Do not let anyone in you do not know. Let the servants leave if they want to, but let them know that their master is now the king. I'll send you word when anything changes."

"Wa' abou' them?" Reggie asked, pointing at the servants who huddled in fear on the doorstep. Ben shrugged. The servants usually stayed. Where would they go?

"If they want to stay, let them," he said. "If they serve you well, pay them. You'll be hearing from me. I'd best not find anything amiss when I return."

Ben unwrapped his horse's reins from the post where he'd tied it and rode off to the west with the remainder of his force. He had a letter to write to his lordship and other prospects to watch. Men like him were spread out across the landscape, making the Earl of Cork's point that rebellion wouldn't be tolerated.

They'd save the king from the headsman's axe, and make a good profit in the meanwhile.

As the king signed his approval for his guest to depart, he watched as Meister Pieter Paul Rubens retrieved his broadbrimmed hat from the stand beside the door of the grand sitting room and bowed deeply to him. The king never noticed that the artist had been careful to wear only self-effacing black to visit Charles.

"Your Majesty, it has been the utmost pleasure and privilege to speak with you. I am so delighted that the commission is progressing with your approval. I only wish to please you."

King Charles, clad in russet velvet and priceless Bruges lace, gold buckles on his shoes, and long hair scented with the finest and most exotic perfumes of the Orient, sat at his ease in the upholstered and gilded chair beside the ornate fireplace. He smiled, having enjoyed a pleasant hour of not only flattery, but a deep and detailed conversation about art. He knew a good deal, but had few courtiers who were as immersed in the study as himself. To have one of the most important painters of the day spending months in his palace was a coup to other heads of state.

When visits should resume between other nations, he would be pleased to show off his newest acquisition: the ceilings of the Palace of Whitehall. It was an expensive enterprise, to be certain, causing his chancellor to moan often about the costs to feed and house the army of apprentices and servants that Rubens had brought with him from Amsterdam. Charles dismissed all of the complaints, which he was amused to share with the artist himself. The glorious paintings in the coffered ceilings each paid tribute to interests of his: mythology, nature, the hunt, the pleasures of the table. Many of the main pieces were dedicated to his late, beloved wife. Henrietta Maria, his dear Maria, so tragically ripped from him. He stated that he would never get over her loss, but at least he could bask in her image. Rubens was happy to oblige him, as it would give him many weeks' unfettered access to the palace.

Rubens had met her, and thought her a silly, spoiled woman, whose adherence to her Catholic faith had caused her to miss out on the most important moment as a queen: that of her coronation. Since she declared that she could never be crowned in a Church of England by her Protestant husband, she was queen in name only, not affirmed under God. He was sorry to hear about her death. Although he hinted broadly, a commission to paint a memorial portrait was not forthcoming. His Majesty was satisfied with the life-sized paintings of himself and his wife that Van Dyck had done. Rubens had applied an expert's eye to these portraits, and, professional jealousy aside, had been satisfied as to their quality. Their four children were still very young. Rubens had offered to paint them as well, but Charles wanted to wait until they were older. The artist had done a few quick sketches for five-year-old Prince Charles, which amused the boy greatly.

Most of His Majesty's courtiers were honored to have Rubens among them. It tickled him that a few of the youngest and richest affected tableaux in their best dress and jewelry to try and capture his interest. A few of them were worth painting for their own sake, and he incorporated some of Charles' favorites into the ceilings and the murals. Flattery was a currency that he was happy to be able to coin. He warned his employees not to make promises on his behalf, no matter how much silver crossed their palms, but only to suggest that they would whisper the courtiers' names into Rubens' ear when the opportunity struck. He made it known he was also open to other whispers, ones that applied to his secondary profession, that of conduit of information that benefited his royal masters in Amsterdam.

With opportunity in mind, he traversed the hallways in the direction of the working side of the palace, greeting his newfound friends and hangers-on. With Parliament out of session for so long, there were far fewer people in Whitehall than there would have been. Most of the decisions, Rubens knew, were coming from Charles through the Lord Chancellor. He'd had a passing acquaintance with the previous holder of that office, Thomas Wentworth, and had found the scandal of the man's imprisonment and escape as titillating as the rest of Europe did. The current inhabitant of the chancellor's office was a grim and greedy man. Rubens didn't trust Richard Boyle. He didn't trust any politician, but in Boyle's case, he was even more cautious to keep his interactions polite and bland. Flattery would get him nowhere. Boyle was not a man who could be turned by offering to immortalize him on canvas or plaster. If that obduracy had come with a staunch loyalty to his sovereign, that would be almost acceptable, but his eye was turned only to the main chance, to enrich himself, and only secondarily bestow advantages upon his master.

However, the supporters of the office of the chancellor were ordinary men, as prone to praise and bribery as any other. They generally remained in place, no matter who held the title. Phillip Haymill had replaced Wentworth's aide, but had been a courtier before ascending to his place, and knew the palace inside and out. Rubens was well aware that the most important information passed through the chancellor's hands, so it became worth his while to cultivate the acquaintance of those who served him.

On his first visit to Boyle's office, he deliberately went when he knew that the man had gone out. Rubens' great celebrity was enough to gain entrance to the outer offices, and Haymill's natural cupidity made gaining his cooperation more than easy. A few coins, the promise of a sketch or a cartoon of one of the ceiling images, and the secretary not only cared little what Rubens investigated within his master's chambers, but often set aside particularly interesting missives that he just happened to leave exposed upon his desk while chasing a fly, or sending a servant for refreshments for his distinguished visitor. Paper for paper, Rubens liked to call it.

"Greetings, my young friend. Is your master in?" Rubens enquired, as Haymill opened the door to his tapping.

"Alas, no, sir," Haymill said. His long, fair face became wreathed in welcoming smiles. "I believe that he has gone out from the palace for a time. The day's correspondence seems to have spoiled his mood."

"A shame that is, for it is a fine day," Rubens said. "I have just been chatting with His Majesty, and I wished to share the details with his lordship."

Haymill's eyebrows rose, for a chance to hear royal gossip was like a saucer of milk to a cat. "And how is His Majesty today? Well, I trust?"

"Very well he is. Ah, but I must not try you with dull conversation." Rubens made as if to go.

"Oh, sir, pray do not!" Haymill protested. He pulled his own chair around for the artist and gestured for him to sit. "May I offer you a cup of wine?"

Rubens smiled as he settled into the leather upholstery. "My throat is slightly dry. I would welcome refreshment. Thank you, my friend."

Haymill moved to the door, a knowing look on his face. "I will see to its speedy service. Pray forgive the untidiness of my desk. I have many papers to file for his lordship, and correspondence that I have just opened for his attention when he returns."

"Take your time," Rubens said, with a smile. "Take your time."

The moment the door closed behind the secretary, Rubens took up the handful of documents that Haymill had indicated. His artist's eye was expert at taking in an image in an instant. Most of them were begging letters, asking for a favor from the king. No surprise there. Every court received barrow-loads of those every month. Nothing of real interest was there.

Instead, Rubens glided, as much as a man of his elder years could, into the Earl of Cork's personal study. This was a room where things got done. Behind the desk and underneath it were boxes of correspondence. Rubens had investigated it many times, and his keen memory allowed him to dismiss documents that he had already perused.

A box beside the desk was used for discards. One letter attracted his attention, as it was signed by many names. He scanned it.

The letter was from a group of guild masters of weaving guilds. Rubens didn't necessarily recognize all of the names of the towns or cities they represented. They appealed to the king to step in and make more fair distribution of some magical device that one guild had acquired from overseas to make luxury woolen cloth, or remove it from that guild pending import of more devices for all. Rubens wondered why it would be up to the king to deprive an ambitious craftsman of an invention that benefited only him. Ah, well, petty jealousy was no new thing. The weavers argued that the import of such a device grossly unbalanced trade, and such a thing should not be allowed. They demanded that the matter go to the assizes to determine damages owed to them by the lone guild. That was unlikely, but one could bring suit for anything, if one had the funds.

He was curious as to the source of the mysterious device. It smacked of something that had originated in the new lands, in Grantville. What it was doing in the English Midlands aroused his curiosity, as it would surely do to the Earl of Cork, but the weavers' suit did not. Either Boyle would ignore the letter or have Haymill send them a polite refusal for the Crown to take any notice of the suit.

It seemed that Rubens might already have seen this luxury fabric around London. A nobleman and his wife had appeared at soirees wearing garments cut from rose-tinted, textured fabric of complicated pattern that was clearly not silk or linen. Rubens had noticed the costumes, and had remarked upon them only because of the discomfort of wearing wool in a London summer. Perhaps he should have paid more attention to the pattern. Indeed, he observed expressions of envy in a number of nobles who attended the same event. He acknowledged the value of experimentation, and that it was indeed handsome and eye-catching, but why would anyone want scratchy wool when smooth, supple silks and velvets were available? Honesty made him admit that wool would not be ruined if it was rained upon, and if there was one constant in London, it was rain.

One letter after another begging for the king's intervention in matters of property. His masters in Amsterdam were curious about rumors that the taxes imposed upon landowners were growing ever more onerous. That did seem to be true. A nobleman in the Duchy of Lancaster sent a missive that pleaded for restoration. It appeared that his estate had been attached by the Crown for nonpayment of tax. The nobleman in question insisted that he had paid everything that was required of him as of June quarter-day, and no more was owing. He complained also of the "bully boys" who had entered his home and evicted him and his family, causing much damage and distress, especially to his wife, who was now fearful of miscarriage.

Another missive, not on fine vellum, was written in such a coarse hand that Rubens had trouble deciphering it. A spy, of course, and in the same part of the country as the dispossessed gentleman, it would appear. The "parcel" was now ready for "receipt," should his lordship care to take ownership of it. Rubens assumed that the matters were connected. The correspondent also spoke of the financial troubles of one gentleman in the north, who suddenly showed signs of prosperity. The spy was continuing to observe that gentleman as the Earl of Cork had instructed him. He would send further reports if anything came of it, and suggested that it could become another "parcel" to his lordship's benefit.

All of these letters were returned to their precise locations on the desk by the time Haymill returned with a decanter of fine red wine and crystal goblets lined with gold on the rim. No doubt the secretary had used his name when obtaining them. Rubens tucked the information away in his memory to be sent to his masters in Amsterdam, and settled himself to give Haymill the reward of gossip that he desired. Rubens made a further mental note to beg Amsterdam to send the information onward to Magdeburg. Had they sold such a device to England, or had it been extracted without permission? He wondered if he would ever discover the truth.

"Well, my friend, His Majesty wished to discuss art," Rubens began.

# Chapter 31

"Did you have a pleasant meal last evening?" Lady de Beauchamp asked Aaron, when he returned to the family table for lunch a few days later. His face turned red to the ears. "Mrs. Wilkinson is a fine cook. Her bread is delightfully light and fluffy. And I suppose you were able to spend some time with Ivy?"

"Yes, ma'am." The youth shifted uncomfortably in his chair.

"Doesn't Ivy have a beau?" Nat asked, his attention on his food. "I thought one of the journeymen, Sam Crowforth, had set himself on her. I didn't think she cared a fig for him, though."

"She never mentioned him. She was more fixed on telling me the names of things. I didn't know there were so many names for sheep!" Aaron sighed and bit into a chunk of bread. "I wish I could just *talk* with her."

"That's not going to work, son," Martin said, sympathetically. "She's got to be fooled, just like everyone else. It's only for a little while more. We're not going to be here that long. I don't want the two of you to fall for each other when we'll be back in Magdeburg by autumn. We can't leave too late. I don't want to run into rough seas when winter starts coming on."

Aaron's shoulders sagged. "I know, Dad."

Margaret sympathized, but the truth hit her hard in the belly. She had come to admire the Americans even more than before. Martin, with his kind soul and wise mind, had become a genial uncle to the people on the estate. Aaron everyone admired as though he was a lightning bolt that had come to Earth. Small wonder that Ivy, and a few of the other girls around the estate, had noticed him. He wasn't the handsomest, nor the most charming, but he was friendly, intelligent, and eager to share his knowledge. But why should he be lonely for the time he had remaining here?

"I suppose there's no harm in spending time with her. She's a nice girl. Escort her to church, if her folks let you." Martin patted his son on the shoulder. "Sounds like her parents don't mind you getting to know her. If you can teach her something about program design, that's all good for business."

That seemed to be the answer to getting more time away with Ivy. Aaron didn't neglect his duties in the weavers' shed, taking care of the looms and cleaning out the aqualators when they silted up, and showing the apprentices all the little things to do to keep them running smoothly. But he spent all his free hours sitting with Ivy underneath the trees or around the corner from sight of her vigilant father, Fred, or anyone else who might tattletale to him. Supposedly, they were talking about work, but there was a lot of time for some necking, as well. He was getting paid for his work with the weavers, but this was his real reward.

That afternoon, they sat on the ground near the stream, their shoes and socks off, dabbling their feet in the cool water. A stand of bushes shaded them from sight. Aaron knew she had chosen the spot deliberately and didn't object. She sat cuddled against his chest, making his blood bubble. She smelled of flower petals, although the scent was almost overpowered by the odor of raw wool, something none of them could escape from.

"So, the little bars in the akalabors are called 'gates'?" Ivy asked, her fingers busy weaving a wreath out of flowers. "Why is that?"

"Just as gates between fields," Aaron said. "Open for right data, close when wrong."

"But what is *data*?" Ivy asked, then giggled at the frustrated expression on his face as he struggled to remember what words he was supposed to know in English. "Perhaps you shall teach me German, and then I can understand you."

"*Ja*," Aaron said. "If you vish it."

"Wish, I tell you for the ninth time, *wish*!"

"I wish," Aaron said, gazing at her lovely green eyes. She leaned closer, her lips very close to his.

"I wish, too," she said, her voice very low, and set the crown of flowers on his head. Their lips touched. He heard a rustling noise not far away, and drew back a little. Ivy ignored the sound. She pressed her mouth against his for a deep kiss. Skyrockets went off in Aaron's brain. He'd never been kissed like that in his entire life. No girl at school had ever seemed so interested in him. No girl in his school was as pretty, either. Her mouth tasted of fruit and flowers. He kissed her back, hard, and she giggled again without lifting her lips from his.

Suddenly, she put her hands against his chest and pushed him to the ground with her on top of him. He realized that his legs were more than halfway into the stream. He struggled to get higher onto the bank. Ivy all but climbed his body, giggling like mad. They went on kissing. He put his arms around her and squeezed, not wanting to let go, ever. Her mouth moved on his, and her tongue licked between his lips, touching his. The rest of his body went into a frenzy, wanting to caress more and more of her. She encouraged it, wriggling against his hands. His body surged against the tight denim of his jeans, and he couldn't do a thing about it.

Then, the distant noise grew closer.

"Boy! Where are you? Aaron! Come here, then! Ivy! I know you're out here! Come here!" It was Mr. Fred, Ivy's dad.

Alarmed, Aaron sat up. Ivy went sprawling, and laughed out loud. The bushes parted, and Fred looked through and down. His brow lowered.

"Get out of there!" he barked. "Straighten yoursel's up! Put your shoes on! Aaron, come by the shed this minute. And you, daughter, get home with ye."

"Aye, Father," Ivy said, not looking even a little ashamed of herself. She reached for her shoes and shoved them onto her wet feet.

Aaron was grateful for the thick fabric of his trousers as he scrambled up. Ivy blew him a kiss and set off home. He picked up his shoes and followed the master weaver into the high-ceilinged room, his head bowed in shame. Diccon Linden elbowed him in the ribs and pointed to his head. He snatched the wreath off and hid it behind him.

To his surprise, no one made fun of him or teased him about being caught with the girl. In fact, every loom was at a standstill. Instead, all the weavers and their apprentices were gathered around Master Blackford, Sir Timothy, and Miz Margaret. The squire held up a leather pouch. He shook it. It jingled with the unmistakable sound of coins. Martin stood behind him, a broad grin on his face. Beside him, Piers Losen, the reeve, held a tray with trestle feet, which he planted in the middle of the workroom. On it, he set a small strongbox with a stout lock on it and a thick leatherbound book.

"From London!" Sir Timothy announced. "Master Bywell sent us the good news by swift horse messenger so we would not have to wait. I wanted all of you to behold the beginning of our good fortune!" He undid the neck of the pouch and poured the contents out into the wooden tray. The coins clattered out like a waterfall, glinting silver. The weavers gasped.

"By heaven's mercy!" Master Matthew declared. "That is far more than the value of the woolens. We may as well have sent them silk."

"Here is the receipt that accompanied it," Sir Timothy said, holding out a yellowish piece of paper. Aaron couldn't read the copperplate script upside down. His own handwriting, like everyone in his school, suffered by comparison with the way people wrote in the current day—those who could write, that was. "Once he displayed Churnet House brocade to the company of drapers who sell to those tailors who make up garments for the court"—the word excited murmuring among the weavers—"they began to bid against one another to obtain as much of the cloth as they could. They paid up to five times the value of good suiting per yard!"

Daniel Taylor threw his cap in the air. It was followed by a scattering of others. "Three cheers for Sir Timothy!"

"Nay," the squire said, his round face glowing. His eyes went around the room. "Three cheers for all of you. To my daughter, who set this sphere in motion." Miz Margaret beamed, her cheeks red. "You, my skilled workmen, who have my respect always. And to you, Master Aaron and Master Martin, for bringing us the wonder of the age." He turned to the guild master. "Now, Master Blackford, if you will?"

The guild master pulled up a stool to the low table and began to organize the coins. "Master Piers, pray note down the sums?"

"Of course." The narrow-faced reeve never did say much. Aaron hardly ever spoke with him. After Sir Timothy, he was the highest authority on the estate, and kept the books. He was a great organizer and cared deeply for the family. He and Aaron's dad had made friends almost right away when they had arrived in Barlaston. Of course. Dad made friends with everybody.

With deft fingers, Master Blackford stacked the coins, mostly silver shillings, into columns of ten. Every eye watched his hands. Two stacks represented one pound, a large amount for the day. Piers tapped the top of each with the non-inked end of his pen, adding them up. He made notes in the ledger book in his flawless handwriting.

When the counting was finished, Aaron estimated that there was between forty and fifty pounds on the table. The weavers murmured in astonishment.

"Now the share for the guild," Master Blackford said, with a pleased expression.

"Alas, no, my friend," Sir Timothy said, raising a warning finger. "Do not forget that we have expenditures that must come first. For the mechanisms that have made this success possible, Master Piers has the sums."

The reeve opened to a different page and read out numbers in his sonorous and nasal voice. To Aaron, he sounded like the preacher. He shifted coins toward himself as he spoke. "Educational courtesy, Herr Oberdorn, five guilders. Design and fabrication of the aqualators: twenty-three marks, fifteen albus, nine pfennigs," he said. "Transport of same, seven marks, twelve albus. That is not to include passage to and from Thuringia for Master Martin and Master Aaron, the sum of eight marks. As for food and lodging..."

"I will absorb that," Sir Timothy said, waving a hand. "We do not stint on hospitality."

"As you say, sir." He reeled off a bunch of other expenses, each of them accompanied by a shifting of coin. "That leaves the sum of eighteen pounds, five shillings, sixpence."

"And the cost of goods?"

Master Piers moved yet more of the coin stacks to the far side of the table, but it still left a lot of silver in place: the profit on the cloth sold. The weavers twitched with anticipation.

"In the name of the guild, then, I claim one percent of the net," Master Blackford said, looking pleased. Master Piers stacked coins before him. The guild master swept it into his belt pouch.

"Now, what you have been awaiting, my friends," Sir Timothy said, with a smile for the assembled workers. "Master Piers has calculated the number of yards that each of you have created in the shipment, so here are your wages—and your share of the profit."

One at a time, he called the names of the weavers, masters, journeymen, and apprentices. As each stepped forward, he placed silver into their palms. Master Cedric received his with lowered brows, but the eyes of the rest were shining. Sir Timothy even beckoned to Lily and gave her two shillings extra.

She let out a shriek of delight, holding her windfall in both hands. "I'd only expected ninepence!"

"And these are for Ivy," the squire said, holding out three coins. "She worked hard, as well." He looked around, his brow furrowed.

Fred cleared his throat. "I sent her home. I'll give un to her if she mends her ways."

Aaron felt his face grow red. This time the others did laugh. Sir Timothy chuckled. He beckoned the Craigs forward.

"Master Aaron, Master Martin, please take this as a token of my gratitude."

Aaron didn't know what to say, as the squire offered them, not silver, but gold coins from the tabletop.

*"Danke, mein herr,"* he said at last, his voice unexpectedly thick in his throat. *"Danke schoen."*

Sir Timothy beamed at him. "You are welcome and more than welcome. And, last but not at all least in my thoughts, my daughter."

"Oh, Father, no!" Margaret went wide-eyed as her father offered her a couple of the gold coins.

"Yes, my dear. You earned it. Is it not your design that earned us this treasure?" Sir Timothy asked. He caught her hand and tucked the coins into her palm. "This is only the beginning, my friends. The brocade that you have been weaving in the meanwhile," he gestured toward the shelves that held the output of the last couple of weeks, "will gain us more and more fame. We move onward to greater triumph!"

"Hmmph!" grumbled Cedric. But he stuffed his money into his belt pouch.

"We begin again tomorrow," Sir Timothy announced. "We have more orders from London, and we have to fulfill those for customers on the continent. Master Aaron, Master Martin, are the aqualators in good working order?"

"*Ja*," Martin said. "Need cleaning. Tonight."

"I trust you to take care of that, my dear friends."

Aaron groaned. Taking the units apart and cleaning them with a small soft brush or a pipe cleaner wasn't difficult, but it was tedious.

"Come on, son," Martin said, more or less reading his son's mind. "The sooner we start, the sooner we finish."

"Happy, my dear?" Sir Timothy asked, wrapping his arm around his daughter's shoulders as they walked back up the hill to the manor house. "I am not forgetting that you defied me while you were in Magdeburg, you know. And here, when you brought up the absurd notion of *profit sharing*."

"I know, Father," Margaret said, feeling flustered. "I apologize..."

"I'm not at all angry," he assured her. "In fact, I was taken aback for a moment, but every time you have proved that your ideas were right. I am glad that you followed your instinct, and your dreams. If this is a sign of things to come, we shall be well and truly fixed for the future. I shall be content to leave the business in your hands when the time comes."

"Surely that day will be many years away," Margaret said, worried.

"Oh, aye, I am in good health, my dear Margery." Sir Timothy smiled and shook his head. "I only hope that we can find you a husband who will respect your intelligence and drive and support you. So you can raise sons—and daughters—who will innovate and lead, as you have proved you can do. I am reminded over and over again that the Lord created Eve not as Adam's servant, but to work at his side as his helpmeet. I will accept no suitor for you who does not understand that."

Margaret didn't know what to say. In the months, and now years, following the death of her elder brother Julian, her father's dreams had come tumbling down, including making plans for an advantageous marriage for her. Since then, there hadn't been time to think about a husband, or even where to look to find one. She wanted to have a mate, certainly, but all the young men to whom she had been introduced at country dances or at the homes of her father's peers thought as he had, before she had encountered the Americans. Did she want to be tied down to one such as they? She glanced at her father. Having been to Magdeburg, she saw how women occupied spheres of influence equal, or nearly equal, to that of men. Should she ask him if she could find a husband among them, instead?

But her father's thoughts had wandered away already from the subject of her future marriage. He chuckled, a hearty laugh bubbling up from his belly.

"Did you see Cedric's face when I paid him? He nearly suffered an apoplexy! I feared we would have to call for Dr. Morrison!"

Margaret smiled. "He both hates and loves the status quo."

"But it is the status quo," Sir Timothy said. "The others will not let us revert to the old ways, not for anything."

"Nor would I want to," Margaret assured him. "All the expenses for this year could be paid off in four or five shipments!"

"Six at the most," Sir Timothy said. "And didn't our lad say that he can make variations in the patterns? While I am content with what we have for the moment, I would dearly love to be able to offer more than one style. Master Bywell would have to conduct auctions for each, at most advantageous rates!"

Dreams in her eyes, Margaret stumbled over a clod of grass. Her father scooped her up and held tight to her arm. "Be careful, Margery!"

She laughed. "I had my eyes on the stars and not on my feet. Thank you, Father."

"Squire, a moment."

The two of them turned. Master Blackford caught up with them, straightening his elegant hat.

"Yes, my friend?"

The guild master offered Margaret a polite nod, but addressed himself only to her father. He was not of the opinion that her father had lately voiced.

"Sir Timothy, I rejoice in the success of your venture, and wish to reassure you of my absolute support. However, I must inform you that rumors of what your workers are doing here in Churnet House have reached others of my guild. They are curious about the technique and the machinery that have made wool brocade possible. To be blunt, they are pressing me to ask how and when such advances can be made available to the rest of them. I have not yet given them details, as we agreed, but they can't help but know what issued forth from here last week. I realize, after Master Piers read out the costs of the aqualators and the associated expenses and training involved that it is an investment that no individual is capable of achieving." He hesitated, and Margaret realized he was embarrassed. "I acknowledge that the means of attaining these devices is entirely in your hands, through your friends on the continent. If you would be so kind as to facilitate the manufacture of such things and arrange for them to be made available to others in the craft, you would be a benefactor. Naturally, we would expect that you would be entitled to a commission for this, and possibly a royalty for all goods made upon the altered looms."

Margaret drew in a breath in astonishment. Sir Timothy smiled. "Naturally, sir, we would hope for recompense for providing both the design and the devices. And I am glad to promote the widespread use of advanced technology. You cannot be unaware of the growing disadvantage at which we find ourselves with regard to the continent. I would be proud to lift English woolens once again to the level of esteem that they have always enjoyed in the civilized world before this."

Master Blackford echoed his expression. "I see that we understand one another, sir. May I and my fellow guild masters call upon you to discuss further particulars?"

"Of course, but this is only the first shipment. We need to see whether this is a single success or the beginning of an ongoing enterprise."

"I . . . see," the guild master said. "I can't say I disagree, but I am being pressed from several sides."

"I do understand, my friend," Sir Timothy said. "But pray see it from my point of view as well. I would ask you to wait a month or two until we are well established. Pray inform my reeve of when it would be convenient for you to call. Good day, dear sir."

"Good day, Sir Timothy. Mistress Margaret." Master Blackford touched the brim of his hat and stalked off down the hill.

Disappointed thoughts crowded Margaret's mind, but she didn't dare contradict her father, considering what he had just said to her before the guild master interrupted them. But Sir Timothy squeezed her shoulders again.

"Tell me what you think just happened, my dear," he said, continuing their walk up the hill.

"I believe . . . that we cannot hold onto exclusivity forever," she said, choosing her words as carefully as she would pluck flowers from a bed. "But we hoped to build our brand and earn enough that the annual taxes won't ruin us." Then, she smiled, as realization dawned. "But you did not give him a date by which we would order aqualators for the rest of the weavers, did you?"

Sir Timothy laughed. He nodded to Percy, who opened the door to them and bowed them through. The squire continued up the stairs to his study. "You are as sharp as a tack, my child. Precisely. Blackford's not such a fool as to think I can produce aqualators out of the air, but he will have in his mind, as it is in the mind of those who sent him to ask, that he can obtain them before the end of this season. But, oh, my, what with the time it will take to send an order to . . . to our friends . . . and what with weather, and delays, and the difficulty in precision manufacture, for I have heard our young friend Aaron's baffling discourse in an attempt to explain to us the particulars of 'computers.'" He emphasized the last word, as if it was from a foreign language. "He has also informed your brother James on the state of the seas in between October and March, I could not see them arriving nor being installed and ready before next spring. Even the ones we received had flaws, lowering our potential output.

"I expect we have one season of exclusivity, then we will have rivals rising everywhere. As long as we hold the supremacy in variations on the design, we can continue to be the premier source for wool brocade—for a time, at least. All things that are not basic necessities rely upon trends. Look how swiftly fashion changes. I've noticed at least a couple of our journeymen attempting to emulate the indigo trousers that Martin and Aaron wear. They can't copy the front fastenings, but they have made the five-pocket style. Those, too, will almost certainly have their day as well."

"Then how will we ever find prosperity?" Margaret asked, almost despairing. "I had hoped that these water computers would be the answer to rebuilding our trade."

Sir Timothy helped her into one of the chairs and lowered himself with a sigh into his favorite seat. "We walk a knife's edge in this uncertain world, my dear. I hope to have an inheritance to leave you, but it does not depend solely on me. There are, as

Master Martin says, a lot of moving parts that interact, and we dare not knock them too far out of true lest the whole contraption comes falling down about our ears. I expect that there are those who will take the short way to prosperity at our expense, and I am trying to guard against them. In the meanwhile, we continue to produce, and adapt, and hope that today's income is not just a windfall, but a steady stream. The drapers and tailors will remember our name, but only as long as we have innovations to offer them. I think there we will maintain an advantage for a while yet."

"I saw the weavers' faces when they received their profit-sharing," Margaret said, recalling the expressions with pleasure. "They were so happy."

Sir Timothy shook his head. "We've bought their loyalty, at least for now. I'm not such a fool as to assume that a larger purse might not unseal their lips. Now that we've sold the first bolts, the word is out, and we'll have to deal with what comes, the bad along with the good. We've made friends. We need to make more."

# Chapter 32

The door of the Four Alls Inn at Blithe Bridge swung closed behind Master Cedric, shutting out what remained of the fading summer sunlight. He'd spent a frustrating day slamming the beater against the complicated cloth, but none of his other skills had come into play. They weren't needed! What was the use of him, then? The simplest apprentice, that Diccon lad, had proved that he could manage that task, after a fashion, that was. As long as the bobbins were kept filled and the warp wheel taut, the loom did virtually all the work by itself. Both Sir Timothy and Master Blackford looked well pleased with that concept. Did they truly mean to do away with the craft and trust it all to machines?

Aye, the cloth was fetching, and made good money. Weren't the coins in his purse proof of that? But he had naught to do with it! How was he to take pride in his job, if he could be replaced by one more hank of wires? That boy—he hated taking orders from a lad who had been at his wet-nurse's breast only a short time ago—pretended to be humble, but he was taking a man's honest job away from him, and proud to be doing so.

He glared through the gloom and noticed that the bench he normally liked to sit on, the one with the unobstructed view of the door, was full of men drinking and playing a game of flip-the-knife. One big fellow, Thomas Gorsey, a weaver's journeyman he knew from Stone, the village not far south of Barlaston, flicked his belt knife up into the air as his friends shouted wagers. When the blade came down, it buried itself tip-first into the rough and much-scarred tabletop. Two of the others cheered, and the others grumbled as Gorsey gathered up the farthings and stuffed them into the purse on his belt.

As much as he wanted to take his place at that table, he wasn't in a mood to join in the game. He wanted to drink a lot, and keep an eye out for his wife, Dorcas. On payday, she made the rounds of all the taverns in the area, to find him and extract as much coin as she could from his wages before it all went down his gullet. This wasn't the normal day, thank the saints, so he could drink for a while and avoid going home to her and their noisy brood. He wanted to sulk in peace, and use as much of his earnings on himself as he could.

Instead, he had to take a corner of the table nearest the window. The two barmaids, daughters of the landlord, noticed him. The elder, a homely girl named Gaynor who tried to make up for her misfortunate looks by being excessively cheerful, sashayed over to him. Her cheer annoyed him. She swished her skirts back and forth attempting to raise a smile or better from him.

"What will please you tonight, sir?" she asked. "Master Crupper has just tapped a fine keg of ale. Smooth and tasty."

"A pint," he said, curtly. "And don't let my cup run dry."

"Aye. I've not seen Mistress Dorcas yet tonight." With what she must have thought of as a winsome smile, she undulated back to the bar to pull a draught for him. He pressed his lips together tightly and lowered his face so he didn't have to meet any condemning glances. Everyone in the area knew his wife. He couldn't hide from her forever. He gave her plenty, damn her! Was he to enjoy none of his hard work? Was it his fault that they had six children, and every one of them ate like a hog at a trough? No one ever went hungry, not that he'd noticed.

A mug plunked itself onto the tabletop. Cedric reached for it without looking up, but it shifted out of his grasp. He raised his eyes, ready to snarl at Gaynor, but the possessor of the cup wasn't her. Instead, it was the stranger, Ben, who had been in and out of the tavern all summer long. The round-headed man with the pockmarked cheeks grinned at him and hoisted the beer mug in salute.

"What ho, my friend. You shouldn't look as if a pack of troubles was tied to your back! It's a fine summer evening. You should be breathing the sweet air and thanking Heaven for the bounty."

Cedric shook his head. Gaynor came to set down his beer. Cedric fumbled for his pouch and began to extract a coin. The stranger reached for his own purse and took coppers from it. He handed them to the girl.

"You look as though you need a friend," Ben said to Cedric. "I'll buy the first round. Tell me your problems, and let them be halved."

The unexpected treat mollified Cedric. He took a powerful pull at the beer. Once the calming brew hit his belly, he could let go the humiliation of the moment.

"Why would I break my back just to sit and tug a bar back and forth?" he asked the air. "Why did I learn all the secrets of my craft for nothing? I've been a faithful servant to his honor and done me job all these fifteen years to be reduced to a dog turning a spit!"

"Has your rank been reduced?" the other man asked in concern. "Are ye no longer a master weaver?"

"Muck take the squire! I'm still called a master, but it's all for show."

The stranger sat back and took a pull from his own mug, eying Cedric with curiosity. "Ye've been saying these last weeks that ye're in doubt as to the craft of these Germans who've come to help out. Have they not done what they promised? Haven't you been paid an honest wage?"

Cedric spat on the rushes lining the floor. "Oh, aye. My wages and more beside!"

"More?" The other man's eyebrows rose into his greasy hairline. "You received a gift alongside your rightful income?"

Cedric slammed his mug on the table. "He calls it *profit sharing*. It's to buy our silence! But I will be silent no longer on the assault to my pride." He dropped his voice as the door opened again. To his relief, it wasn't his wife, but a number of other weavers from the estate. They were all looking cheerful and expansive, and he wanted no part of them. They joined a huddle of craftsmen from the town to the south at the bar, and struck up conversations, ignoring him. That was just as well. He had to deal with them day in and day out, except for on the Sabbath.

"What silence needs buying?" Ben pressed. "You and your fellows weave the cloth. Your master sells it. He pays you for your labor. All is well."

"Ah, but it's no ordinary cloth," Cedric said, then clamped his lips shut.

Ben's eyebrows rose again. "What's it made of? Moonlight and fairy dust?"

"Nay, it's made of pure wool, off the backs of the sheep in the squire's fields."

"Then what's the cause of the extra money?"

Cedric scoffed. "You're not a weaver. You wouldn't understand the difference."

"I'm not a butcher, neither, but I can tell the difference between lamb and pork. What's going on with this new cloth?"

Cedric was torn between airing his grievance and keeping the promise extracted by the guild master. "Ah, well, it's a complicated weave. Made using machines brought over by the Germans."

"New machines, is it?" Ben, seeing that Cedric's mug was low, winked at Gaynor, who hurried over with a pitcher. She poured more for each of them. Cedric drained half of it in a gulp and belched from his belly. "From the Germans? What business does he have working with Germans?"

Cedric shook his head. "Times be hard, and he's been looking out for anyone who can help him forestay troubles from the tax collectors. That's what he thinks these machines do, taking work from good men and bestowing it on gears and boxes!"

Ben's eyebrows went up. "Something that makes good woolens even better? How do they work? What do the Germans have to do with it? Is Sir Timothy swearing allegiance to them now instead of His Rightful Majesty?"

"Nay, it's naught like that!"

Master Matthew had just taken a mug of beer from the innkeeper. He overheard the question and made his way over to Cedric, leaning his hand in a casual manner on the edge of the table.

"Now, Cedric, you shouldn't be taking Sir Timothy's business outside his premises. We have an agreement!"

A few of the weavers from the manor to the south now crowded around curiously.

"Now, Matthew, we've been hearing rumors," a broad-shouldered man named Master Michael Gooden said. He worked for Sir Alfred Jervis at Meaford Hall, west of the pub in which they now drank. "What's going on that's so unusual? What new machines? Are ye not using looms any longer?"

Cedric shot a look of annoyance at Matthew. "Looms, forbye? Oh, that we are. But it's like sitting in the middle of a clock, with gears all around you like you're the little man who will be pushed out to strike the hour! It has more pulleys and wires than anything I've ever seen."

"Wires? What for?"

"That's enough, Cedric," Matthew said, still patient, at least outwardly. "The ale is striking you harder than usual. Go on home. Dorcas will be here any time, and she'll set us all by our ears for letting you drink up your wages."

"And don't you feel ashamed of yourself?" Cedric snapped back. "Taking money for letting our craft turn into clockwork? Spinning out a bolt in a single day, but ye can't claim you actually *did* anything, can you?"

"What's that?" Michael asked, wrinkling his forehead. "A bolt in a day? How's that even possible? Our guild master has said ye'll have tricks to share, but he's said nothing about that."

"Oh, aye, and it isn't just ordinary cloth," Cedric said, maliciously enjoying the horror on Matthew's face. "We can't even take credit for the skill involved in making a *brocade*, for it's the machines doing it all."

Michael looked astonished. "How in the burning wastes can ye make a brocade on a wool loom? It's as intricate as an orchestra playing."

One of the men laughed, but Ned Bywater, one of Cedric's journeymen, spoke up, his broad red face eager.

"It's a wonder! Looks like pounced embroidery, lifted right off the surface. The wisdom for making it is all enclosed in little clay boxes, like the genie's lamp! We've barely to make an effort, and it turns out the most beautiful of fabrics, with roses and leaves all over it like a *garden*."

"Here, here," Matthew said, shocked. He looked at the other de Beauchamp weavers in alarm. "That's enough. Cedric, your men shouldn't be discussing guild business here."

"And why not?" Peter Chance, a journeyman who had left Sir Timothy's stable to work for a master in Oulton. He often came to drink with his old colleagues at the Four Alls, as if he missed them. "Isn't it all of our guilds' business, anything to do with weaving?"

Matthew stopped and gathered himself. "I misspoke. It's Sir Timothy's business, not strictly our craft."

"And what else could it be used for?" Cedric interrupted him. "You think you can attach one of those akalabors to a cow and make her produce more milk?"

"Tell us more," Peter pressed. "Tell me how you made a bolt in one day."

"I didn't do such a thing," Matthew said, trying to divert the conversation. "And true, there are additions to the looms, but looms they remain, my friends. In the end, we are still weaving wool, as my family has for ten generations. Here's to our craft, one and all!" He lifted his glass. Many of the others matched his toast. They drank.

"Nay, nay, what's going on that's so unusual?" Ben pressed, clearly reluctant to let the discussion die away.

"Sir, I don't know you," Matthew said, affecting a puzzled look. He looped an arm around Cedric's shoulders and attempted to pull him to his feet. "But let me take my friend home again. His wife is surely looking for him."

"Let me be!" Cedric snarled. He shook off Matthew's arm. They were nearly the same as far as strength and endurance went, able to carry bales of wool and manage their machines all day if needed, but Cedric had the advantage of a good load of ale on board. He dodged Matthew's attempt to take hold of him again. "The devil take my wife! She's a hindrance, and so are you!" He turned to Ben. "The unusual is that the whole contraption runs on water!"

"By water? Like a mill?" Ben asked, clearly interested. He jingled the purse on his belt. Cedric felt malicious satisfaction in thwarting Matthew's efforts to still his tongue. He'd get more beer, free, and possibly a tip as well.

"It's not exactly that," he said. How to describe the workings? He glanced at Ned for support. His journeyman opened his mouth.

Master Matthew cleared his throat threateningly, and Ned halted before he could speak. "Cedric, shut your hole. We've agreed, and Master Blackford has agreed. Nothing will be said outside until the guild masters have had a chance to talk amongst themselves."

"To the darkness with Master Blackford! I'll tell what I want to tell and show what I want to show!"

"We all want to see it," Ben said, encouraging him. "I want to see what's so special about it, and what Sir Timothy intends to do with these machines. Take us over there and let us see."

"Perhaps you'd best go home and sleep it off," Matthew said, still trying to appear kindly.

Cedric was tired of people trying to tell him to shut up. Without another word, he threw off the hands of the people and marched out of the door of the inn.

It wasn't full dark yet, and besides, he knew every step of the way if he'd been blindfolded and far more drunk than he actually was. He marched uphill toward Churnet House, and crossed the small bridge over the stream at the rear of the weaving shed.

Diccon Linden was asleep on the floor across the doorway. He glanced up blearily at Cedric.

"Go back to sleep, boy," he told him. Obediently, the apprentice put his head down on his arm again. He wasn't going to defy a master, and sleep was precious. Dawn wasn't that many hours away.

Cedric stumped to the wall and tore down the example cloth. He folded it into the front of his waistcoat and stalked back to the tavern.

The loud conversation that had begun in his absence cut off suddenly as he reentered the room. He walked to the table where he had been drinking and threw the woven cloth down upon it.

"There. Tha's the mystery before ye."

"By all the angels," Michael said, his eyes wide with awe. He reached for it, but Matthew put a hand down on top of it.

"That shouldn't have left the barn, Cedric."

"Don't care what you think. Do you like being turned into a piece of machinery?" Cedric countered. "Shall I treat you like a corncrake or a furnace bellows?"

"Give that to me! I'll bring it back."

"I won't."

The other weavers crowded around the table to examine it, even as Matthew tried to gather it up.

"This is a wonder. How's it done?" Michael asked, turning it over to examine the back.

"With the little machines!" Ned said, ignoring the furious byplay going on over his head. "It made us a pot of money. Look! He slammed his pay down on the tabletop, and the others stared at the handful of coins. "Sold in London, it did, every yard snapped up like fresh pies, all gone in minutes."

"God's troth," Thomas Gorsey said. He kept fingering the rose clusters over and over. "I've not seen anything like it in me life!"

"You all should have these little machines," the stranger said.

"By heaven, you're right," Michael said. "I want these. How much to buy one? Where do you get them?"

"Who owns the one that this was made on?" Thomas asked.

"Sir Timothy de Beauchamp," Ben said, hiding his smile.

Thomas waved a hand. "Ah, well, he's a straight up gentleman, the squire. He heard my cousin's case on some stolen cattle."

Ben pressed his argument. "If he's so good, he ought to share this new machine with all weavers."

"Aye," Michael said, with a frown. He peered at Cedric. "You say that a couple of Germans made the machines?"

"Yes, a man and a boy. But it's the boy who knows how they work."

"*Cedric.*" Matthew was still trying to make him see sense, but he paid no mind.

"A boy? Well, sometimes it's the young ones who see how things go better than us older folks," a white-haired man at the bar said.

"How do we get them?" Michael asked.

"Well, I couldn't say," Cedric said.

"You shouldn't say," Matthew interjected. "Cedric, enough is enough. The guild masters will discuss it in good time."

Cedric raised his voice until he was shouting over his fellow master weaver. "There are six at work in our barn. But there are pieces of two more that never got put together."

"Why should they not be made use of? Eh?" the stranger asked. "I know those who would pay a good sum for something like that."

"Cedric," Matthew said. There was now no trace of friendliness or patience in his voice. "Go home. Go now, or tomorrow I will bring a charge against you with the guild master. You're talking out of turn, not just with regard to guild matters, but with our employer. You should be ashamed of yourself. Out, now!"

"You can't tell me what t'do!" Cedric protested.

"I shouldn't have to," Matthew said. "You're acting like a schoolchild, tattling on things you ought not to be talking about. Master Blackford said he would bring it up to others at the right time. Do you now outrank him? Eh? Do you?"

The thought of bringing charges finally got to Cedric. It was passing through his muddled brain that he should backtrack and stop talking. He sank into his seat and pulled his beer to him.

Matthew gathered up the cloth and tucked it away. The others drifted back to their conversations, shooting speculative glances toward the two master weavers.

But Cedric's new friend wasn't letting it go. Ben put a hand on his arm and spoke in a confiding voice.

"My friend, you've interested them now. There's money in this enterprise, more than you have in your purse, mayhap many times more! How long did it take you to earn today's wages?"

"Well, not that long. It's my due plus a bit of the profits from the squire, as I told ye."

"But you could be paid a lot, if you can work out how to help these other gentlemen. Am I not right?" Ben turned to the others.

"That's not for us to say." Master Matthew was worried, but Cedric put him off with a laugh.

"The news would be spread sooner or later. Why should we not talk about it? It's a triumph for the squire! First man in the world to bring this to market!"

Matthew shook his head. "He won't see it that way."

"And are you going to tell tales like a schoolboy? Let the opportunity go to waste?"

"Well..."

"Ah, there she comes!" came a cry from the front. Near the window, Gaynor gestured furiously to Cedric. Alas, there was no time to escape out through the kitchen.

The door slammed open, and a short, scrawny-faced woman with her graying hair tied up in a white linen scarf bore down upon them.

"Cedric Hollings, the angels will weep for you! Give me your purse. Do it now!"

"Go away, woman," Cedric said, mournfully.

Dorcas Hollings pushed past Ben and the other drinkers at the table. With an expert hand she staved off his attempts to keep her from grabbing the pouch at his waist. "Aha!" She tore it off. "By heaven's grace, I have gotten to it before you've managed to starve your children yet again! Come home now."

Cedric's nose and cheeks were red. "Nay, woman, I won't!"

"Fine, then." She pointed a skinny finger at his mug. "That's yer last drink of the night. And you can sleep on the stoop with the dogs, then." She stalked over to Gaynor and brandished the purse. "How much does that slug owe you, girl?"

Gaynor shook her head. "He's had friends treat him this evening."

"Well, then, that's a wonder," Dorcas said. "I'd never have thought he had friends."

She stalked out of the tavern and slammed the big door behind her.

The other patrons laughed. Cedric didn't raise his face again. He looked as though thoughts were circulating in his mind, but as much as Ben pressed, the weaver didn't say another word. Once the mug was empty, he did go out into the night.

The stranger remained behind, listening and laughing to the conversations and byplay until Gaynor and her sister turned down the lamps, and the last of the weavers staggered out toward home.

Candle in hand, Ben went up to his room on the first floor of the inn. It was a quiet season, so he didn't have to share the whitewashed chamber with anyone else. If he'd needed, he would have slipped a coin or so to the publican, but it wasn't necessary.

From his modest case, he drew a flat locked box and set it on the table next to the broad bed. A few sheets of plain paper, an inkwell, a fistful of quills, a stick of wax, and a penknife lay within. He always burned the letters he received.

By the candle, he began a new letter.

"My lord, something interesting is going on here. Germans are involved. You were right to send me here. My men are available at two hours' notice. I will keep my eyes open to any activity that might interest you."

He folded the note in a complicated pattern and sealed it with a copious dollop of hot wax. He'd entrust it to any merchant traveling toward London in the next day or so.

So, the Churnet and Trent estate was bobbling on the brink of ruin until the Germans came in, and suddenly magical looms were set to make their fortune. No doubt more information of interest to his lordship was forthcoming in the next days or weeks.

Maybe another manor would become part of the crown's holdings. And maybe a new and growing industry would fall into his lordship's lap.

# Chapter 33

***August 1635***

Margaret, Rita's latest letter in hand, marched resolutely up to her father's study. It was time to request even more strongly that they fulfill the promise she had made. More than a month had gone by since the first bolts of the brocade had sold. Surely by now there would be enough to provide Lady Simpson with a dress length.

There was also the matter of a couple of obscure lines in the letter that she didn't really understand, mentioning surveillance and unwelcome incursions. Their tone was concerning. Perhaps her father could help her puzzle them out. She tapped on the door.

"Come in!"

She entered, and nearly backed out again. In the midst of Sir Timothy's usual clutter, Aaron and Martin perched on chairs, making themselves as comfortable as they could.

"Oh! I apologize. I will come back another time."

Her father gestured her in. "No trouble, my dear. We are waiting for Oliver Mason."

"Hettie's Oliver? The potter? Why?"

"We might have a task for him." Her father held up a sheaf of paper of an assortment of hues and shapes. "These are orders! Not only from Master Bywell in London, but directly from drapers and tailors all over England! They want more of our brocade, and they want it at once!"

"We've got a shipment ready to go," Aaron said.

"And every inch of it spoken for," Sir Timothy said, torn

between pleasure and concern. "Two master drapers have been bidding against one another. Robert Bywell has been rather enjoying himself playing the two royal drapers against each other for the best price. I believe they'd parade themselves down the Strand in donkey's ears if it would win them the trade. In fact, nearly every buyer here is prepared to take the entire shipment, even at the high prices that the brocade has been commanding. And more!" He brandished a handful of letters. "I've even had enquiries from Scotland, from the Duke of Argyll's own secretary. These gentlemen are importuning me in an attempt to bypass our agent and buy directly from us. I am cudgeling my brain to express to them in the politest terms that I am grateful for their interest, but Bywell is my agent, and all my affairs must go through him."

"He is enjoying his moment of notoriety," Margaret said. "It's gratifying to see how well the fabric is being accepted. Lady Pierce has had letters from a number of her friends who are still in London about the fashions. Even though it is still quite warm in the City, the ones whose tailors have been able to obtain some of the fabric are already wearing them." She smiled. "It feels very odd to be at the heart of a fad."

"It is indeed an odd feeling," her father said. "But no matter how courteous our would-be buyers are, all that means is that we cannot satisfy even a fraction of the demand. And so, I have perhaps overpersuaded our young friend here to speak to the best man I know who makes pots and dishes to see if he can expand our ability to produce the brocade."

"I still don't know, sir," Aaron said, uneasily. "I'm really not a hardware engineer. I don't know all the tolerances that have to be maintained to get the results we want. I wish I could contact Herr Trelli, or the engineers in St. Malo on the radio and get them to explain the specifics to the people who make ceramics." He lifted his arms and let them drop. "I feel pretty isolated here, not having access to any communication devices. Letters are so slow!"

"I am sorry," Margaret said. "Are there perhaps any of your radios here in Great Britain? Perhaps we can get a message to those people some way. It will be faster than waiting for messengers."

Martin shook his head. "There's no way we can do it without blowing our cover, Miz Margaret, or the cover of the people who are carrying them. We're still not exactly welcome guests here."

Margaret felt a shiver go down her spine, thinking of the former "guests" in the Tower. The nightmares she had had after returning from London cropped up again in her imagination. For a moment, she regretted having ever opened this Pandora's box, but only for a moment.

"The aqualators are only pottery," Sir Timothy said. "Our craftsmen have been making clay goods since before the Romans. I feel sure that you should be able to express to Master Mason what it is we need."

"I'll try, but that's not where my skills are. I wouldn't be able to tell you how to cast them so they do everything right. I can design them, but I never made them. We send our orders to St. Malo and a couple of other places, where they have the right clay. Like I said, I'm a software guy."

Martin agreed. "I don't have the skill, either. I'm just a janitor."

"You're far more than that, my friend," Sir Timothy said. "Your calming presence has allowed my weavers, not an explosive bunch by any means, to accept the new process, and to admit to the idea of a master craftsman who is still a boy. You set a fine example, sir."

Martin looked abashed. "It's nothing. I know how good Aaron is. I'm proud of my boy."

"Aw, Dad."

"Still, I am willing to pay Mason to *try* to see if he can make replacements for the broken trays," Sir Timothy said. "Even if he has to recast them again and again, it will be worth it if he succeeds. We have the funds coming in, and can afford it." He chuckled. "Bless my soul, I haven't thought for years that we had enough leeway to make mistakes. But it would increase our output by a third, and that means something."

"The clay here feels very similar to the aqualators that you brought us," Margaret said. "It's quite smooth, and has a similar gleam when cast, although it appears to be lighter in color. I don't know whether that would make any difference."

"The texture is why I think it's a possibility," Aaron said. "But it's a long shot."

"I am willing to take that shot," Sir Timothy said. "Master Blackford has been hinting more insistently that we open our bounty to benefit other weavers, and sooner rather than later. Hence the urgency to find a way to manufacture more and not wait until spring."

A tap at the door, and Hettie leaned in.

"Oh, mistress," she said. Her cheeks were red and her eyes bright. "Master Oliver Mason is waiting downstairs. He said the squire sent for him?"

"Thank you, Hettie," Sir Timothy said. He beckoned. "Pray bring him up, will you?"

"Of course, sir."

When the door closed behind her maidservant, Margaret let out a little laugh. "Is Oliver your choice among the potters because he has been courting Hettie?"

"I've a number of reasons for calling him, my dear. He is the best in the area, without a doubt. His pots never break, and they're always as sound as can be. We need work that will last a long time. If I am to share our good fortune with another craftsman, it may as well be one that will make someone in our household happy—that is, if you can bear to see her leave your service to marry."

Margaret felt a wrench in her heart—twofold. Her own chances at a happy match had not proven lucky, for one reason or another, and who knew when her father would have time to devote to helping her find a husband? But she was loath to lose her very good friend, for Hettie was every bit of that, and more . . . ? She was Margaret's rock to cling to in storms, but Margaret vowed to be as good a friend in return. "I would never stand in the way of her contentment, Father."

"That's my Margery," Sir Timothy said. "Thirdly, I find him trustworthy, and trust is more scarce than I hoped it would be. Ah, here he is. Master Mason, please come in!"

Oliver Mason was a very good-looking man. He had large, liquid brown eyes that one of the servants had compared with deep peat pools, a long, poet's face framed by wavy, dark brown hair, and beautiful, long hands that attracted the eye. They moved and flowed through the air when he spoke, as if they were dancing. Margaret completely understood how he had caught Hettie's attention. And, as her father had said, his skill seemed to be unmatched in the area, for all that he was still under twenty-five years of age. He'd inherited his pottery when his father had passed away of fever a year ago.

Even when the others stood to greet him, he still towered over all of them. He gave Hettie one more glance as she backed out of the room. She blushed and closed the door behind her. Margaret couldn't help but smile.

"Afternoon, Squire, gentlemen, Mistress Margaret," Oliver said. Margaret had to admit she felt a warm flush when that deep brown gaze met hers. "Hoping to find you all well."

"Sit down, sir," Sir Timothy invited him, hastily clearing a small bench beside his writing desk. A heap of spun fleece, a leatherbound book, and a saucer from her mother's best crockery were shifted to the floor. Oliver sat down, still obviously ill at ease. His long hands dangled between his knees, clutching his hat.

"Is there anything amiss, sir?" Oliver asked. Sir Timothy shook his head.

"No, not at all. In fact, this might be a good thing for both of us. I hope to be able to offer you a commission. Do you know anything of what we have been about here? The weavers?"

Oliver's long face brightened. "Oh, aye, is this something to do with what Master Cedric has been talking about? He went on and on in the tavern the last number of nights, spouting nonsense about gears and water and whatnot."

Margaret saw her father's face stiffen, and the Craigs looked uneasy. Yet another reminder of how precarious their situation remained. Alarmed, Oliver stopped talking. Sir Timothy waved a dismissive hand.

"Do not concern yourself, Master Mason," he said. "You're not at fault for mentioning it to me. I cannot control what anyone speaks of when under the influence of drink." His tone was light, but Margaret knew him too well to think this was going to end well for Cedric. "I hope you are better able to hold your tongue than my unfortunate weaver."

"I hope I am!" Oliver said, and made the sign of the cross. "Whatever you ask of me, I will keep it close, except for my apprentices. I can't keep secrets from them, if they are to do the work."

"And I wouldn't ask you to hold a secret that tightly," Sir Timothy said. "This would be a very important commission for us, and I expect that you will do your best for us. We have always enjoyed the produce from your father's pottery, but this is something different."

"I'm eager to try, sir," Oliver said, his hands dancing in the air. "It sounded like a true marvel. What is it you want me to do?"

"Come down with us all to the weaving barn," Sir Timothy said. "We will show you."

The mood in the weavers' room was professional to the extreme. All eight looms, six brocade and two working on plain woolens, were in operation, with Fred Wilkinson plying his old loom, repaired so well that the damage was invisible, and Ned Bywater beside him, waiting as one of the boys replaced the thin black thread in his shuttle. With approval, Margaret noticed that the two of them were working on fabric for the uniforms in Admiral Simpson's navy. The rest concentrated on overseeing the brocade looms.

She was accustomed to seeing them in operation, but she enjoyed the look on Oliver Mason's face as he took in the new mechanical devices and the steady drip of water passing through the aqualators.

"By heaven!" he said, going to look over Matthew Dale's shoulder at the roses on the growing cloth. He glanced past the loom at the boxes hanging from the wall, watching the water drip into the trays and the gears turning. He gestured at them in excitement. "Is that what's making it happen?"

"Aye," Matthew said, pulling the beater bar back and forth with vigor. "A marvel, isn't it?"

"By heaven," Oliver said again, his eyes full of wonder. The other weavers smiled indulgently, keeping their eyes on their work. Cedric, in his corner, worked on brocade at Loom Number Six with a sour look on his face, as if Oliver's reverence was an affront to him. Margaret shook her head. He needed to get past his resentment. He was in enough trouble as it stood.

"These are a cornerstone to the mechanism," Aaron explained, and Margaret translated for him. "They work in stacks of six, and the stacks are paired side by side." He retrieved the damaged tiles from the unused aqualators lying in the corner. "Do you see the break along the ridge?"

"Aye, looks a bit like underfiring."

"Can you make a pair just like these, but without the flaw?" Margaret asked. The American teen was almost dancing with frustration at not being able to explain better. She patted him on the arm, understanding completely what it felt like. "It must be exact, or it will not fit into the others, and the loom will not work. We trust your expert knowledge."

Oliver turned the pieces of the square tray in his long hands. "I will try, mistress. It's not like anything I've done before. But I swear to you I will try."

"That is all we can ask," she said, smiling at him. "Take it, and let us know when you have succeeded. Now, why don't you go up to the house. Hettie will find you something to eat."

Oliver's long face turned red. "That I will do. Thank you, mistress, Squire. I'll do for you what I can."

He cradled the two trays in his elbow and strode out of the weaving shed. Everyone lifted their heads to watch him leave.

"Our hopes go with him," her father said. Aaron nodded.

Margaret glanced at the pile of bolts growing on the shelves against the long wall, in blue, green, and rose, as well as the undyed ecru. It looked like a lot, though she knew well that it wasn't. Still, it couldn't hurt to ask.

"Father, I have a letter from my . . . friend," she began. Sir Timothy turned to her. She knew he understood exactly what she was about to say, even as she knew what he would reply.

"My dear, I cannot countenance it yet."

"Father, it's a debt of honor," Margaret reminded him. "Two dress lengths would satisfy it!"

"Not yet, daughter," Sir Timothy said, his voice still gentle but firm. Margaret felt her temper rising.

"How long must I put her off?" she asked. "If not for Rita, we may well be living in one of the small houses with our tenants, auctioning off our sheep!"

"Margery, you must trust that I know what I am doing!" Sir Timothy said. His face had turned red. He drew her outside so their argument would not be overheard by the weavers. "Mistress Rita will know how pressed we have been. I thought you understood that I want to gain as much interest as possible among the nobility before we must share our technology with others. Public acclaim is fickle! We can only produce so much, even with the six intact aqualators attached to looms creating embossed cloth. Happily every yard is spoken for before it's made, I cannot in conscience send even a single bolt abroad. Not yet. We must exhaust our resources as far as possible and gain every copper. Tomorrow, someone will begin to make hats out of cloth of gold, and we'll be hard pressed to interest anyone in our goods."

"Would that we had all eight looms able to make the cloth,"

Margaret said, with a sigh. She caught the doleful look on Aaron's face. "I know, Father, I know. I am sorry, Aaron. This is not your fault. Damage happens in shipping all of the time. Our woolens are often subject to water and weather when we send them abroad."

"We are all frustrated," her father said. "Not only among us, but further afield."

Cedric. She glanced through the barn door at the weaver. His hunched back spoke of discontent, although it did not seem to have impacted the quality of his work.

"Has there been any repercussions from Cedric's loose tongue?" she asked.

"I am so disappointed in him," Sir Timothy said, shaking his head. "He came to us at eight years of age, and now look at him, a genuine master of his craft! I can't know yet if we have anything to fear, but I am taking precautions. From tonight, Master Piers is setting a rota with the stouter apprentices, some of the farmhands, gardeners and shepherds to take watch overnight. The shed will be locked tight when no one is working in here. The further word of our devices spreads, the more precious the six we have become. And should Master Mason succeed in creating working duplicates of the broken trays, what will stop anyone from taking the ones we have and casting more?"

Margaret felt shocked. "Do you think that can happen?"

He dropped his voice so that only Margaret and Aaron could hear him. "My dear, people are paying absurd sums for *tulip bulbs.* I've heard from Captain Forest that the *Meadowlark* has had thieves attempt to board, thinking that he is hiding a cache of tulips somewhere just because we trade with the Netherlands. I fear that the scarcity of our brocade could potentially excite the same madness. Master Bywell has said that a nobleman whom he will not name in a letter for fear that it will be intercepted vowed to cut his own throat in the middle of the warehouse should he not be permitted to buy a length of the bronze-colored fabric we sent down last month. But with that in mind, I do not want you, your mother, or either of your sisters to go about without an escort. Nor you, Master Aaron. The looms are worthless without your knowledge."

"Father, no!"

Sir Timothy sighed. "Yes, my dear daughter. We've knocked over the beehive, and the bees are swarming. They want nectar, and they do not want to wait for it. That's the only reason why I have not dismissed Cedric. He and his apprentices are sound workers, and if he hates working on the brocade looms, well, then, he can resign from my service and seek another master, but he cannot take the machines with him. In the meanwhile, I see no problem with the cloth he produces. I've made him take turns with his journeymen on turning out the serge for the USE uniforms instead of the brocade. He sees it as a demotion of sorts, and I understand that. Perhaps I can speak with Lord Cantwell about taking him on. I think Daniel Taylor is coming close to testing for his mastership, and would be a sound replacement, so we would not be shorthanded."

"I doubt Cedric will go," Margaret said, thoughtfully. "Can you speak to Master Blackford about stopping him talking to our rivals? The bees are indeed buzzing here as well, and they *are* getting their nectar."

"Ah, yes, I owe your Mike Stearns a debt of gratitude," Sir Timothy said, slapping his belly with both hands. "The profit sharing has done good by all of us. I've never seen our weavers set to work so fervently. Yes, I have spoken with Blackford. He's prepared to withdraw Cedric's certificate of mastership if he causes trouble. I think he's merely a fool who dislikes change. I hate to think he actually means harm to us."

"It does not mean that he won't cause any," Margaret said, sadly.

She realized much later that evening that she had never brought up Rita's concerns for their well-being. When the moment presented itself, she meant to let Sir Timothy read that part of her letter, and see if she was only imagining a threat, or if there really had been one.

# Chapter 34

Fortunately, Master Blackford was a true ally. On that Sunday, once the family had returned from church, Margaret was making ready to go on a call with her mother to visit Lady Pierce. Hettie was pinning a hat onto her freshly set curls, when her father tapped on the door of her room. He looked a bit sheepish.

"Margery, would you mind not going with your mother? I need you to, er, translate for the Craigs."

Margaret turned to Hettie, who lifted her palms helplessly. Normally, any doings in the household had spread across the servants' quarters, and her maidservant knew everything long before she did.

Sir Timothy watched the interplay and smiled. "I apologize, but this was not of my doing. Master Blackford has arrived rather without warning, and he has a number of gentlemen with him. Master Piers has alerted Mrs. Ball to prepare hospitality in the parlor."

Margaret immediately knew what was about. "Please take my hat, Hettie."

"Yes, mistress. Shall I attend you?"

She thought for a moment. "Yes. I'd feel more confident if you were there, until we discover which way the wind is blowing."

The air was warm in the de Beauchamps' apple orchard, the breeze smelled fragrant, and he was there with a girl. Life could not have been better, Aaron thought. He glanced up lazily at the green pippins on the branches.

"*Sind diese schon reif?*" he asked, pointing to the small fruits.

"Rife? No, it's *ripe*," Ivy said. She lay on her back with her head in Aaron's lap, toying with the ties of his shirt. "And no, they're not. You eat those, and you'll be purging out of both ends!"

"*Ja*, ripe," Aaron said. He smiled down at her. She wound her hand in the ties and pulled his mouth down to hers. This time, he was ready for her kiss, and made the most of it. Her soft lips drove him crazy, and her boobs were almost visible through the white linen of her blouse—camisole—whatever the women here called the long undergarment. He wanted to feel them, but he kept his hands away from them somehow. With one, he stroked her hair, and the other rested lightly on her bodice.

Suddenly, she grabbed the hand on her waist, and brought it upward toward her bosom.

"Don't you want to touch me?" she asked, in a teasing tone. "You're such a gentleman."

"*Nein*, I shouldn't."

She wound her other hand in his hair and smashed her lips against his again. When she let go, she challenged him with a look. "Why not? We like each other well enough. I give you leave."

"*Was*?" he asked.

"It's *what*, as well you know," Ivy said, letting him go with a playful push. "I know you speak English as well as I do. Mayhap better."

"*Nein*, I do not."

She laughed. "Of course you do. You're a couple of Mistress Margaret's Americans, you and your dad."

Aaron stiffened. "Vy do you think something like that?"

She groaned and sat up. "Because you are Americans. Everyone knows it! Well, a lot of us do."

Aaron began trembling. This was the thing his father had warned him about, what Miz Rita had told him to keep quiet, what everyone was afraid would happen. He clutched his hands in his lap. What was he going to do?

"How?" he asked.

"We're not fools," Ivy said, playfully. She put her arms around him and fixed her eyes on his. "Aaron. We know Mistress Margaret met some Americans in London, and came back to tell us all about the explosion. Everyone was talking about it! But instead of seeing them as dangerous or terrible or enemies of England, she was friendly about them. So, that's how *we* came to think of them. And when she went off to Hamburg—that's right next to the United States of Europe, where the Americans are, isn't it?"

"Well, not *right* next to it."

Ivy looked triumphant. "See? I knew you could talk like ordinary folks! All right, not right next to it. But there, close by, with no ocean between them. Anyone could cross from one place to the other, right? And to have you and your father come with such incredible inventions that have changed our life! The Germans have never come up with anything like that, or they'd have been sold here long since. Those must have come from the Americans. From *you*."

His mind spun. He ought to get up and find his dad, let him know they had to leave, but Ivy held him tightly.

"But the king hates us," Aaron said. "Why has no one told him about us?"

Ivy shook her head. "Because we love Sir Timothy and Lady de Beauchamp, and all their family. They are good to us. They are our gentlefolk, running the manor and making sure all is good for us. They secure our future. And we like you and your father. You are truly good souls, beloved of God and working hard to our benefit. Why would we jeopardize your safety? You can trust us." She laughed. "Well, me. And my father and my mother and my brothers. And most of the folk in the weaving shed, or I'm a fool. We will never do anything to hurt you. You're safe here. No one will tell your secret. But it's been as frustrating as can be, teasing words out of you one at a time! I want to know more about your life, what it was like in the future. We hear wild stories told by peddlers and travelers, and we don't know what is true and what is fantasy."

He was still frightened, but the look in her eyes was so honest and serene, he had to believe her. She tilted her head slowly. Now she appeared hesitant, waiting for his answer, for anything. Aaron leaned forward and kissed her. With a relieved chuckle, she kissed him back. Then, she planted her hands in the middle of his chest and pushed him down to the grass. Their kissing became more urgent, and Aaron let his hands wander over her body for the first time. Her eyes closed in pleasure, she moved into his touch. He knew she had had a lot more experience than he had. He had been such a nerd that he hadn't had any real girlfriends, but she didn't seem to mind.

He felt himself getting hard, and shifted away from her leg so she wouldn't feel it, but she did. She put her hand on the fastening of his jeans, a wicked look in her eyes.

"How do you undo this?" she asked.

Instead, he pushed her hand away. "We shouldn't," he said.

"It's all right," she insisted.

"No, please. I . . . it wouldn't be right."

She moved her hand from his pants up to his face and stroked it. In a way, that felt just as intimate, and his cheeks caught fire.

"If that's what you want," she said. It wasn't, but he knew it would be wrong to take advantage of her. Still, he nodded. She nestled against him. He told his body to calm down, that it was nothing, that it should stop embarrassing him. But that wasn't easy with a beautiful girl in his arms. "Tell me a secret."

"You know the biggest secret I have," he said. He still had a big, icy ball of worry in his belly, but it actually felt good not to have to pretend to be someone else after that many weeks.

"Then tell me another," Ivy said. A thought sprang into his mind, and he laughed.

"Do you want to know a secret?" he asked.

"Yes!"

He jumped up and pulled her to her feet. "Come with me."

By the carriages in the drive at the front of the great house, the de Beauchamps had company. Instead, he took Ivy in through the kitchen. The amused and indulgent look on the faces of the cook and the scullery maids made him blush again, but there was really no judgement in it. Ivy greeted them all by name, and they asked after her mother's health.

"She worked here when she was a girl my age," Ivy explained. "It's where she learned to cook."

"*Ja,*" Aaron said, although apparently all the servants knew the same secret she did.

He and Ivy went up the rear staircase to the annex. He stuck his nose in the other rooms, but no one was there. He gestured to Ivy to sit on the floor next to the box that held his record player.

"What's this?" she asked, eying it warily.

"I'd love to serenade you, like a troubadour from the past, but I can't sing," he said. "So, let me play you some music. From the future."

She had to lean low so as to hear the speaker, giving him too good a view down her blouse. He had to concentrate on playing her the best songs from the albums. Like Miz Margaret, she seemed to like the records slowed down from 33-1/3 to 16, but that was okay. He was getting used to hearing them like that.

"This is wonderful!" she said, her eyes shining like stars. "Those Beadles are lovely!"

"Oh, yeah, but wait until you hear Pearl Jam. You'll go crazy for them."

She leaned into him as he changed the record, and their lips met. They were only half-listening to the music when the door flew open.

"Dad!" Aaron blurted out. Ivy tilted her head back lazily.

"Hello, Master Craig," she said. "Aaron was just playing me some Pearl Jam."

To his credit, Aaron's father didn't waste time berating his son. Like he'd often told Aaron, he had once been a teenager.

*"Guten tag, Fräulein,"* he said with his usual friendly smile, and added in Amideutsch. "Aaron, you are needed down in the parlor."

"Oh, it's all right," Ivy said. "I already know you're American. You don't have to pretend with us."

Martin shook his head. "We need to keep pretending, Ivy. It's not for us. It's for Miss Margaret and her family. Aaron, Master Blackford is here with a number of other guild masters. Straighten yourself up and come downstairs right away. Ivy, can you sneak out of here without being seen?"

Ivy brightened up, realizing he wasn't going to scold her. "I know every inch of the house, Mr. Craig." She turned around and kissed Aaron chastely on the cheek. "See you tomorrow."

Martin laughed and put his arm around his son's shoulder. "Come on, boy. That's some girl. She's more than she seems, isn't she?"

"She sure is," Aaron said, watching her flit down the rear stairs. "I'm lucky she likes me."

# Chapter 35

Margaret was relieved when Aaron entered the parlor. She stood at one end of the room as if she was presiding over a magistrate's court, much as she had seen her father do many times. The three strangers eyed the Craigs with curiosity. She wondered what they were thinking. When the Americans smiled, at least one of the guild masters started. It was the teeth; the perfect, straight white teeth. That always struck the *down-timers*, as Aaron called the people of her day, as the most astonishing thing about them. Considering how few of them had ever left Lancaster or Staffordshire, they must now think all Germans had such beautiful teeth. Margaret kept her amusement to herself.

Paul Thornton, the beadle, stood back from the group with deference. He nodded to Margaret, and she returned the courtesy. His presence meant that the visit was important to the guild. Not just the local chapter, but perhaps the whole county.

"Mistress Margaret, I trust I find you well?" Master Blackford greeted her with the same avuncular friendliness as usual. He gestured the visitors to come forward. They were all dressed in the finest woolen cloth, almost gleaming in its smoothness, and lined with shining silk. The tallest man's elegant hat had a peacock feather in it.

"Very well, sir, I thank you."

"Sir Timothy, Mistress Margaret de Beauchamp, I want to make known to you the guild master from Stoke-on-Trent, Master Phillip Melton, Master Bernard Green, guild master of Uttoxeter, and Master Reese Denby, guild master of Stafford Weavers and Fullers Guild."

"Gentlemen, I am honored!" Margaret said, curtseying as Lady Pierce had taught her. The men all swept off their hats and bowed. "These are Herr Martin Craig and his son, Herr Aaron Craig. They come to us from the Germanies, and have been of great service to us." She rendered the introductions to the Craigs in Amideutsch, who smiled and nodded to the visitors.

*"Guten tag, Meine Herren,"* Martin said. The visitors bristled.

"Do they speak no English at all?" Master Denby asked, looking peeved. The peacock feather in the hat now clutched by his side bobbed with annoyance.

"Yes, they have been learning," Margaret assured him, not wanting to meet Aaron's eyes. He looked as though he was going to laugh, and that would have set her off, too. Behind her, Hettie cleared her throat with a warning. "But they understand nearly everything you will say. How may we serve you, gentlemen?"

Master Blackford looked embarrassed.

"I apologize for the abruptness of this meeting. It was meant to be some weeks or months from now, but thanks to some... *interference*, no amount of persuasion is enough to delay it further."

"We want to know about the akalabors!" Master Green interrupted him.

"Aqualators," Master Blackford said, with a sigh. "Sir Timothy, while he is in your employ, Master Cedric Hollings has been talking widely about the devices and the novel fabric that is being manufactured with their assistance, and that is an infraction against the guild itself. Master Matthew Dale approached me with an official complaint, and that is being addressed separately, but the damage has already been done. The confidential agreement that you and I made has been breached."

"Yes, I know," Sir Timothy said. "I find myself embarrassed that this has come to light. We must have a discussion regarding him, and the sooner the better."

"I agree, sir, but it has precipitated some urgency in other quarters. Now that the word *has* spread, these gentlemen are here to make a proposition to you."

"A proposition? Nay, a demand! You've no right to keep guild secrets from others of our craft," Master Melton said, pushing forward, his face red. "Surely you are aware of the competition from the continent cutting into our profits and threatening to put us all out of business!"

"Indeed, I am, sir," Sir Timothy said. "Like you, I have enjoyed greatly reduced revenue from any goods that we send overseas. Even some of our sales in London are less remunerative than they have traditionally been. It has always been our intention to share the knowledge that has made our new fabric possible, but it is not yet a perfect system. We have errors to correct first before those are distributed widespread across the land. I would also point out that we have a right to recoup the *considerable* expenses incurred from our outlay before allowing others to profit from our hard work and innovation. While I would never accuse anyone here..." The sudden rising hubbub overwhelmed his voice for a moment, but he spoke louder, "...of undercutting prices or making deals as though we were rival manufacturers. There have been times when I have sent my goods to market only to discover that my buyers have been made a better bargain than I can afford to."

From the expressions on the faces of the visitors, her father had scored more than one painful hit.

"Sir, you cannot expect us to sacrifice ourselves for the sake of—"

"But is that not precisely what you are asking of me? Times have indeed been hard for all of us over the last several years. I have held back on sharing the process because I can't. Even now, we are not sure if it's completely viable..."

"But it does work! We've seen the goods!" Master Green declared. "...Well, one man I know has seen it: the fellow who drove me here today." He gestured vaguely toward the window. "It's quite remarkable to have revived the wool trade with innovation, and you deserve all the credit for bringing it about. But we want to make it, too, sir. It's all the talk!"

"That is so," added Master Denby. "We've had news from London, through a supplier of iron goods with whom we do trade. Sir Thomas Bowes has been seen walking out wearing a suit made of your brocade, and his lady in a matching dress. It's the talk of the town! You are to be congratulated, sir."

Margaret felt her cheeks flush with pleasure. Sir Thomas was a noted man of fashion, and had been known to spend large sums on clothing for himself and his family. Sir Timothy looked pleased at the revelation.

"You can judge that everyone wants this miracle fabric, sir," Master Blackford said. "Everyone wants more. We come to you, I and my fellow guild masters, to make it possible for all weavers to create it. These gentlemen want you to share the secret of its manufacture." He had the grace to look apologetic. "That is why we wanted to have these gentlemen present, to explain the mysteries." He nodded politely to Aaron and Martin.

"But it isn't something that you can start up from nothing, sir. The devices had to be created abroad and brought here at colossal expense, I might remind you yet again. They are not easily duplicated."

"But they can be made and imported?" Master Blackford pressed. "The guilds have put forth the notion of offering you the exclusive on licensing and providing the devices, and even paying you a royalty on yardage produced in this way. Times are hard, indeed, but if you were to offer a way to redress the imbalance by allowing others to share in the bounty, you would still be better off than you were before."

"We cannot yet make enough to satisfy all orders," Sir Timothy reminded them. "And the devices do not maintain themselves. Our guests from Hamburg have had to instruct my workers in their operation, and they are having to make constant adjustments as we determine what changes need to be made."

"Yes, but if you shared the machinery, then we could all be making it!" Master Green said.

"Sir, that is true, but I can't just provide it out of my pocket. It has to be designed and sent for. You may not even want it when you see how tricky it is to operate."

"Bah," Master Melton said. "All weavers need to learn every peg and pedal of a loom to begin with. What's another piece or two?"

Denby snorted. "My man tells me that once running, all a man has to do is pull the beater bar back and forth, nothing more. We can run them just as well as you. And if you won't share it, perhaps it is that no one should have it!" He threw himself out of his chair and breasted up to Sir Timothy. Margaret's father did not move from his seat. He met the visitor's eyes.

"Are you... threatening me, sir?" he asked in a mild tone.

Immediately, the other guild masters began to argue with Denby, their voices all but echoing off the high, painted ceiling.

Margaret, alarmed, withdrew into her chair. Martin set a hand on her shoulder. When she looked back, he gave her a reassuring look.

Hettie disappeared from her post. She reappeared in a few moments with Percy. The boy wasn't of the subtlest nature, as he had a poker hidden insufficiently well behind his back, and he had thrust his sheathed knife awkwardly through his belt. Margaret sent a questioning glance toward her maidservant. Hettie nodded at the window. Through it, Margaret could see some of the gardeners and farmhands gathering in the drive with their tools. She knew that in a crisis, they could summon thirty or more men to come running to their aid, and more from further afield. If there was going to be an altercation, it would not go well for the visitors. She gave Hettie a grateful smile.

Master Blackford looked wary of the actions and stepped between the visiting guild master and Sir Timothy with his hands raised in a placating manner.

"Please! Everyone is keen to find every advantage available to protect the trade. Let us behave as civilized men. We all want something from one another. Let us negotiate, please, gentlemen."

"I offer you my apologies, Squire," Master Denby said, stiffly. "It has indeed been a series of poor seasons, and my passion for renewing our craft got the better of me."

"Accepted, sir." Sir Timothy accepted the offered hand graciously. He had noticed the gathering outside the window and glanced back at Margaret. He shook his head, but Margaret felt it better to be safe than sorry.

The temperature in the room had cooled down, and the visitors were looking a trifle ashamed of themselves. Master Blackford thought it best to take a hand. "My friends, might these gentlemen see the looms in operation?"

"Why not?" Sir Timothy said. He drew Margaret's hand through his arm and patted it. Hettie gave her a hesitant look. Perhaps best to keep their impromptu force on hand in case another altercation arose. Hettie stayed close by. Percy abandoned his poker, but he followed along.

Outside, the manor's workmen had scattered, and appeared to be laboring in the gardens close to the house, though still vigilant. In the drive, the guild masters' carriages awaited. A couple of men in each helped their employers into the conveyances. Sir

Timothy chuckled, and walked down the hill with his daughter and the Americans. It took only a few minutes to reach the barn door, but somewhat longer for the wagons to traverse the pebbled road that led down from the manor.

"How much do you want me to tell them?" Aaron asked, while they waited.

"At this moment, whatever they ask," Sir Timothy said. "As Master Blackford said, the damage is done. We are no longer operating in secret."

He escorted his guests into the weavers' shed.

To Margaret's eye, everything was running smoothly. Old Fred Wilkinson was just about to take a bolt of black serge off his loom and looked for some praise from the guild master. Blackford greeted him offhandedly, and walked past to where Master Walter was indeed pulling the beater bar and producing a length of brocade dyed with brilliant purple, a purchase negotiated from Stone Dyeworks that had arrived only a week ago. Fred looked sour. Margaret stopped to speak with Fred.

"That is so very fine, sir," she told him. "I know that our buyers will have nothing but praise for your skill."

"Aah," he said, shaking his head. "I think I know my craft. Forty years and more, man and boy, not that anyone's appreciating the hard-won skills any longer."

Cedric, glowering from behind the other unaltered loom, seemed to agree with him. Margaret gave him a pleasant smile and hurried to join Aaron and her father.

Alongside the guild masters, the men that had accompanied them on their journeys from their hometowns came in to gawk as well. Ben had made himself acquainted with the guild master from Stafford, and had ingratiated himself so well that it seemed natural that he should accompany Master Denby to Churnet House. Though Ben stayed in the midst of the crowd, he knew that Cedric had spotted him. He made a casual gesture with his hand that the weaver should not acknowledge their acquaintance. Best to steer clear of Master Matthew, who would almost certainly recall him from the Four Alls tavern.

The foreign youth was speaking. He seemed delighted to have an audience, and launched into a complicated discourse featuring many lengthy and complicated words in German that he could not begin to parse out. Fortunately, Sir Timothy's daughter understood everything, and translated to a rapt audience, Ben among them. He was as curious as the rest. Not that he hadn't snooped in the shed before, but it was the first time anyone present could explain what he was seeing.

"... So, the left stack of aqualators contain the pattern for the brocade, and the right propel the shuttles on their way."

"Why do they need water to run through them?" Master Green asked.

"That is how the aqualators tell the mechanisms when to lift and lower which sets of heddles," Margaret said.

"Do they count drops?"

The girl hesitated. "In a manner of speaking. The boxes contain the program, and feed the correct information to each part of the loom it controls at the right time."

Aaron launched into another spate, gesturing with his hands in excitement.

"Slow down!" Margaret admonished him. Apparently, he could understand some English, or read her expression, for the tumbling words slowed to a trickle. The translated words didn't make much sense to Ben. Instead, he watched the small wheels turn as the water dripped into them, and saw the pieces of the loom move as though by magic. He made a mental note of every detail. Such a thing might be of use to his lordship, though he didn't yet know how. He needed more information.

"This is Journeyman Daniel Taylor," Master Blackford said, with a smile for the young man at the first loom near the door. "Though I fancy not to remain a journeyman for long."

The other masters moved close to see the cloth.

"It is all the marvel that we have been led to believe," Master Melton said. He felt the tautly stretched expanse of fabric. "Not as smooth as silk brocade, of course."

"No, sir," Daniel said. "Though Squire's sheep do produce a good, long fleece, it's not the same staple as silk." He was delighted to show the visitors what he was doing, and how he was doing it, pulling the bar to himself and advancing the warp wheel every few rows. Master Denby let out a snort.

"Don't you feel as if you've taken a step downward in your craft, letting a machine do the work for you?"

Ben smirked. It was a question he had taken the trouble to

prime the guild master to ask. He hoped he could provoke an argument, but he was disappointed.

"Not at all," Daniel said, with a laugh. "I'm proud of what I'm helping to produce. Look at that! When it's treaded and fulled, it's got the smoothest hand and suppleness of a linen."

"Aren't you displeased that your hard-won skills set you to minding the wheel like a dog turning a spit?" Ben asked, scornfully.

"I've seen you in the tavern, sir," Daniel said, with a dismissive wave. "You're a master at causing arguments. I still use my skills."

"But any apprentice could learn to do what you're doing now! Most of the skill is in those little boxes, not in your hands."

Daniel smiled. "And should I go back to the oldest of looms and weave the shuttle in and out by hand instead of using heddles?" he asked. "This is only another convenience taking the trouble out of making good cloth."

"And good it is," Master Green declared, shutting down Ben's argument before it could grow. He retreated. "My weavers have heard the rumors. Now that I see that they are true, I want these in my shop as soon as possible, and I know every man in my guild will say the same!"

"Aye," agreed Master Melton. "So it is. I see that the pattern is roses and leaves. Can it be changed to, say, wreaths of bay, or the unicorn of Scotland?"

"*Ja,*" Aaron said, followed by another discourse in German.

The girl stepped forward to translate. "The trays would have to be changed out. Each of these stacks of trays are in six parts, and one or more would have to be replaced to change the pattern, but it could be done. We have discussed having more patterns made for next season, once we have the funds."

That evidently reminded the guild masters that they were there to strike a bargain.

"What is the cost to get these devices here to the rest of us before the end of the year?" Master Denby asked. "We'd pay a premium if need be. And more beside."

"Sir, it's not the cost," Mistress de Beauchamp said. "It's the time that it takes to make them."

"I don't want to wait until next year! I've had customers asking me for the brocade. Disappointing them costs me dearly."

"Gentlemen, please!" Master Blackford said, holding up his hands.

"I count six," Master Green said, looking up and down the shed. "Would you be willing to part with one or two?"

"No, sir, I would not," Sir Timothy said.

"Have you no more to sell? Not in another barn elsewhere on the estate?"

"*Nein,*" Aaron explained. "I brought eight, but two are broken. One of the local potters is working on replacements for the damaged pieces. He has brought a couple of samples to try this morning, but they have not yet been tested." The girl explained again, rendering the German's words into good speech.

Master Green frowned. "Can we buy the two broken ones? See if we can make shift with the damaged pieces?"

"They will do you no good if they are incomplete," Aaron pointed out. "The system requires a steady flow throughout to drive the pistons moving the heddles and the shuttles. It is a gentle movement, but throwing off the amount of water going through them disrupts the pattern."

Ben and the others heard the words, but even in English they made no sense to him.

"We would be happy to try, with your aid, Master Craig," Master Green said, jingling his purse. "There would be a goodly reward for you helping us."

Aaron let out a sigh and led them to the far side of the barn. There on the floor was a number of pale clay trays. He pointed at a couple of them that looked exactly like the others: little barricades set up like a wild-mouse puzzle with holes pierced through here and there in no pattern that Ben could discern. "They must be intact to function, but there are flaws in two of the pieces that causes errors in the system."

"Did you create this . . . system?" Master Green asked.

"With the help of Fräulein de Beauchamp," Aaron explained. The girl tried not to look too proud, but she was. "And many other people in Hamburg, who brought our designs to reality."

"Well, then, if nothing can be accomplished without delay, then let us discuss particulars," Master Melton said.

"Certainly," said Sir Timothy. "Allow me to escort you back to the house. Gentlemen, ladies, I thank you. Margaret?" He put out his elbow and his daughter came to hold his arm.

They went off talking, the guild masters hoping out loud for the very slight chance that the promised aqualators could be in

England before winter set in, and weaving over the cold months would keep everyone warm. The prospect had all of them feeling cheerful, slapping one another on the back and laughing. Even the German boy's father looked relaxed. Everyone but Master Denby. Ben was pleased about that. He had planted seeds so deeply in the guild master's mind that he continued to be suspicious of Sir Timothy's motivations. And so he should.

Ben hung back and sidled up to Cedric.

"So, the boy is the key to all of this?" he asked in a tone low enough not to carry over the noise of the working looms.

"Aye," the weaver said, sullenly. "His father defers to him like he was the younger and the boy was the elder. Bad enough that we are made to listen to a mere girl, as her father wants her to command good craftsmen, but a foreign stripling?"

"Is it true that the broken pieces don't work? Or is he holding out for more money?"

Cedric sneered. "Would not surprise me. He acts too good to be true. No one is that holy."

Ben eyed the pile of clay tablets. "We could sell those two sets. I could arrange it."

"But we don't understand how it all goes together."

"Then the boy needs to come with it," Ben said.

Cedric gave him a wild-eyed look. "No, I'll not be involved in that."

Ben offered a beatific smile. "We only want the information he has, my friend. Once he divulges what the lucky buyer needs, then he can return to Germany. But in the meanwhile, someone else can make their fortune with the wonder fabric. And you will have made it happen, so there surely will be a reward for you. Perhaps your own weaver's shed, away from these unimaginative dolts." His smile turned sinister. "Maybe even a royalty."

# Chapter 36

With eyes watering from the stench of fresh paint, the Earl of Cork read the latest missive from Ben Sandown. Germans in Lancashire? And living on the same estate as the English girl who had traveled to Hamburg on her own, leading to the disappearance of two of his own agents?

He threw down the letter and clenched his fists on his desk, watching the flesh on his knuckles lose all color.

Richard Boyle did not believe in coincidence. For all that the Baronet of Churnet and Trent was paying lip service to the crown and sending in his taxes and levies on time, it was beginning to sound as though Sir Timothy de Beauchamp was at the center of some kind of empire building. Too much money! There was too much money circulating in the northern baronies and estates.

Boyle did not believe for a moment that the "magical boxes" running complicated patterns that Sandown spoke of had been created by anyone from Hamburg. No, in the absence of a Leonardo, a century dead, that would have required a jump of several decades, if not centuries of innovation. It seemed even more certain that Americans were behind them. The United States of Europe must be establishing a foothold in the Midlands. The presence of two men suggested scouts spying for their masters. If it was easy enough for them to infiltrate, more and more of them must be preparing to land and secrete themselves about the landscape. Any day, they would have enough allies and wealth accumulated to challenge London. Perhaps even under the command of Oliver

Cromwell. Of whom there was still no sign! How could such a divisive figure have remained hidden all that time? What was he planning? Where? And with whom?

Boyle could bring the rumor to the king and ask for a force to take over that manor and the ones surrounding it. Fearful of any signs of insurrection, Charles would almost certainly allow him to send a small force to send a message. According to Sandown's letter, craftsmen from several towns had been flocking to the de Beauchamp estate to make lucrative deals. He could not believe that they were interested only in futuristic looms. No, those aqualators had to be a cover for something.

Superior weaponry? No, from Sandown's account, they actually did make cloth. He'd seen it on some of the most fashionable figures of the court. A trifle flashy, in his eyes. Frivolous, like nearly all fashion. It seemed to him, though, that these machines were an overly large mechanical advance *just* to make cloth. So, what other use could they have? Other than justifying the presence of the Americans in Lancashire, of course.

If only those two fools in Hamburg had carried on sending reports! Boyle had lain awake far too many nights wondering how much information they had given up before they died. And if they were not dead, he would kill them himself, slowly, for robbing him of sleep and peace of mind.

The smell of paint invading his office was giving him a headache. The artist Pieter Paul Rubens had come and gone as he pleased, adding to his "masterpiece" in the palace's ceilings. The commission had come from the queen, rest her soul. Instead of ending it while Charles was grieving her passing, Rubens had talked him into continuing as a tribute to her memory. The king had agreed, approving all the decorations and flourishes that the artist had continued to add. That meant that the Dutchman had been underfoot all summer long. His skills as a diplomat had made him a favorite among the other courtiers, but Boyle could not escape the feeling that Rubens was watching everything too closely. Was no one what they seemed in this world?

Asking the king to commission mercenaries to send a suitable message was the proper approach. If Sir Timothy de Beauchamp had nothing to hide, then he had nothing to fear. Sandown had met with notable success in reminding dilatory lordlings that they were not their own masters.

Dashing away tears brought to his eyes by the smell of spoiled milk and spirits of pine, Boyle reached for his inkwell and penned a terse letter to Sandown. Let him find out the truth of the curious devices. He was to use his discretion—but if that didn't serve, then brute force must.

A crate marked with the word FRAGILE on every side arrived at the gatehouse of the Churnet estate and was conveyed to the house by Jacob Damson's son-in-law as though it might explode.

"Addressed to the German gentlemen," the young man explained to Mrs. Ball, the housekeeper. She motioned him impatiently toward the side of the house. "Peddler that dropped it off said it's lingonberry preserves. Whatever a lingonberry might be."

"You know deliveries do not come in through the front, Andrew Catlow."

"Yes, ma'am," Andrew said. He frowned. "What's that odd noise?"

The housekeeper sighed and shook her head. "Master Nat. He's come up with some new tunes, and they're painful to the ears. I've no idea what "yeah, yeah, yeah," means, but I suspect it has to do with Aaron Craig."

"Some German country song, then, mistress?"

"If it is, then I hope the rest of them stay in their country! Now, to the rear door with you. I will inform the senior Master Craig that he has a delivery. Don't do this again. I don't want to inform the master of your infraction. It won't end well."

"Yes, mistress," Andrew said. To give the German tune credit, it was actually pleasant to listen to, although of a fairly fast tempo for a country dance. It sounded as though Master Nat was also singing, though he couldn't discern the lyrics. No matter. He'd hear it sooner or later. Master Nat liked to play his compositions to everyone.

The master of the estate, seated with the reeve in his study, looked up as Martin Craig tapped on the door lintel.

"Sir Timothy, I've had word from Grantville." He held out a sheaf of white paper.

"That printing is superior to anything I have seen from a press," Piers Losen said, admiring the typography. "No mistake as to what is written here."

"That's how pages look when they come off a printer," Martin said.

"How can we obtain one of those?" the reeve asked, enviously.

"It could be a long while," Martin admitted. "The technology is pretty primitive—for us, I mean—and you need a dedicated computer to run it. That all runs into some solid money. Even I couldn't afford one. We have an electronic printer that we used in the house before the Ring of Fire, but it's getting old.

"So, here is the contract for the aqualators for the other guilds. I put in orders for the Stafford guild, in spite of Master Denby complaining about the prices and delivery times. I figure he was going to come back looking for them anyhow, and thought I would head him off."

"Well done, my friend," said Sir Timothy. "And you are right. He came a few days ago, asking to buy the two unused aqualators. I turned him down, and he gave me a piece of his mind. He seemed sincerely distraught. I believe that the weavers in his city suffered as many downturns as we have had, and he was hoping to steal a march on his fellow guild masters. I'd help him if I could, but I do not like to be caught in the middle of a war between guilds. I watch Master Blackford walk a tightrope as neatly as any traveling acrobat, and I do not wish to emulate him. But what is this I hear about a delivery of lingonberry jam?"

Martin laughed. "It's a way of disguising correspondence," he said. "Especially long documents like this one. Thieves are looking for valuables, not food. They couldn't give a possum's hind end about a box of jelly. But it's tasty stuff. I turned it over to your kitchen staff. I bet you'll be getting it for breakfast."

"What is the delivery on the new systems, and when do they require to be paid?" Master Piers asked, always the most practical of men.

"April at the earliest, more likely May or June. The engineers in St. Malo have a big back order for Gustav Adolf," Martin said. "He gets priority for everything. The same goes for replacements for the trays Oliver is trying to work on. Sorry not to have better news. The deposit you sent will hold them until they're ready to ship. They'll take a letter of credit on a Hamburg bank. The Abrabanels will make it good for them."

Sir Timothy was crestfallen. "I'd half a hope that we could placate my rivals with the possibility of delivery this year. Alas, I do not want to lie to them, or they will be asking me any time a wagon appears at my door if their brocade devices have arrived. Was there anything else hidden away in the crate?"

"A letter for Miz Margaret," Martin said. "If you don't mind, I'll take it down to the weavers' shed. I want to check on Aaron."

"Ready!" Daniel Taylor called through the hole in the wall at Loom Number Four. When the squeak of the dynamo submerged in the stream came through from the other side, Margaret waited impatiently for the trickle to come down the small pipe. Already an expert on the sounds made by the system, Daniel nodded, and twisted the stopcock.

Seated at the loom, Ivy waited with her hand on the beater bar. The shuttles had been wound and rewound several times in hopes that this time, the substitute trays would work. Oliver Mason had been backwards and forwards from his shop, trying this way and that with new moldings that all of them hoped would hold—and work. He hovered nearby until Daniel elbowed him in the ribs to make him move back.

Master Blackford sat on a bench near Margaret, who was keeping well out of the way. Everyone in the shed kept an eye on the proceedings. Like Sir Timothy, the weavers were aware of the press of orders coming in from all quarters. Merchants had even visited the de Beauchamp estate, keen to put their names in ahead of everyone else. Every order meant more money for all of them. There probably wasn't a worker in the room who hadn't begun to make a wish list of everything that they could buy with the upsurge in revenue. Samuel Wilkinson had begun to pay court to a girl from the estate's dairy. Margaret thought the girl a bit dull-witted, but she was sweet-natured, and would make a good wife, once Samuel could support one.

The shuttles and the heddles began to move. Ivy pulled the beater close, then thrust it away, keeping her eye on the moving boats. Aaron came in to watch, wiping his hands on a towel.

Five rows. Six. Margaret held her breath in anticipation. The flow seemed to be right. The weavers, even the ones working the other looms, began a murmur of pleasure. Then—

"It's happening again!" Ivy exclaimed. She pointed at the loom. "They're not lifting the heddles in the right pattern, and it's causing raised lines right across the cloth."

Between the trays of the aqualator, water began to leak, first a drop, then a trickle, and finally an unmistakable overflow. The heddles began to dance uncontrollably.

"Cornflakes!" Aaron exclaimed.

Daniel leaped for the valve and shut it off.

"I'm sorry, Aaron," Oliver said. "I thought we managed to close that gap."

"To blame you are not," Aaron said, regaining his senses. He went over to examine the stack.

"What is this, the fourteenth?" Daniel asked.

"Sixteenth," Fred said, from behind his faithful old loom. "It's a shame, isn't it?"

Thankfully, he exhibited no sarcasm. It wasn't the extra money coming in that had finally convinced him of the benefits of the altered looms, but the pleasure of stealing a march on the other weavers in the area. Also, he could no longer deny the beauty of what the aqualators produced. It was an honor to be connected with something so popular. Margaret felt that way herself. But, at that moment, she sympathized fully with Aaron. He felt so frustrated for not looking over the trays more carefully before they had departed from Grantville. He knew all this could have been avoided, and blamed himself.

"I'll take them back and try again," Oliver said, glumly.

"It is difficult," Aaron said.

Daniel was already disconnecting the pipes from the stacks and lifting out the substitute trays.

"We'll get it, my friend," he said. "It's a new thing, this, having to cast a mold so precisely."

"Aye," Oliver said. "I feel like I'm making clock parts, thinking in tolerances so small I can't see them."

"Picture that on your wall, a big clay monstrosity," Fred said with a cackle. "Clanking the hour, isn't it?" The others chuckled.

Ivy gave Aaron and Oliver a sympathetic smile.

"It went for a while," she said.

"I know. It's not enough. We will get it. At the worst, we will send for substitutes from St. Malo. They will be here in the spring."

"Why didn't you simply bring more of these with you?" Walter Twelvetrees asked, not for the first time. He was hard at work on Loom Number Three. Many of the others chimed in, talking over one another. Margaret, wishing for peace in the workroom, held up her hands.

"You know why he did not, Master Twelvetrees," she said. "This enterprise was not guaranteed to succeed. We had to make an outlay we could afford in case it was a loss. And eight was the number that was within our budget."

"You're forgetting what it was like before, Master Walter," Daniel added. "And you had a lot to say about the aqualators not being worthy of the trade."

"You speak above your station, sir!" Walter said, miffed. "Don't dare to contradict me."

"Gentlemen," Master Blackford said, stepping in between them. "Do not fight in front of the lady." He bowed to Margaret. "We are all enriched by the additions. I look forward to more. Did I not hear you discussing the possibility of further patterns with young Herr Craig?"

"Yes," Margaret said. "We have been making plans to expand."

"What will it be?" Master Matthew asked, as eagerly as a boy. "More flowers? Or a heraldic shield?"

"No one wants to wear someone else's coat of arms," Fred said, dismissing the idea with a wave. "Especially the nobility. Can you imagine each demanding their own? We've not the time nor the tools to serve that. Something holy, then? Doves and olive branches?"

"How about the lion and unicorn?" Ivy suggested, coming over to hang on Aaron's arm. "Or a unicorn and maiden?"

"Not that you'd get anywhere near a unicorn," Sam growled, but she ignored him.

"What will it take to bring in more images?" Master Blackford said, pleased that the discussion had turned so readily away from the argument.

"I can probably do it in two trays per system," Aaron told Margaret, and she conveyed it to the others. "You will have to write the pattern as you did before, and I will translate it into code."

"Agh, that snippity language," Cedric Hollings said. "Speak good English! You've learned enough from all of us!"

"*Was*?" Aaron asked. "Slow talk, *bitte*?" Margaret bit her lip, refusing to let the laughter out.

"I shall consult with you, gentlemen, and make the design you think is best," she said. "You know the business well. Master Wilkinson has been in service to my father since before I was born."

Old Fred, pleased to have his expertise recognized, put out his lower lip in a thoughtful manner. "It'll take some thought, aye."

"Don't forget the rest of us!" Matthew said. "I reckon I can come up with better ideas than this old gander." Fred erupted in outrage.

"I will trust all of you to discuss it," Margaret said, soothingly. "That is another part of collective bargaining. My father will be pleased to grant credit to those who originate any design that becomes popular with our buyers. It will be to your honor and the honor of our establishment."

Martin came into the barn at that moment. By the pleased look on his face, he had heard the last thing that she had said. She smiled at him.

"Master Craig, welcome," she said. "How may I help you?"

"I have a letter for you," he said, extending a large white envelope to her. "It came today."

"From . . . from Hamburg?" she asked, in excitement. It must be from Rita.

"*Ja.*" The others eyed her curiously, but most carefully tried not to appear to be staring.

"Do you know what is in it?"

"*Nein.* I had my own letter. The contract for aqualators for the other guilds has been accepted."

"Oh, that is good news!" she exclaimed, and conveyed the news to Master Blackford.

"Well, thank the good saints," the guild master said. "That will appease some of the weavers. Not all of them, I fear. With every order of brocade that leaves this place, their resentment grows."

"I am afraid that they will have to be patient." She turned the folded paper over and over in her hands. News from Rita! She couldn't wait to read it. "Will you all excuse me?"

The letter was full of interesting gossip, all of it couched in terms that she and Rita had agreed upon. A case of two popes, one yet to succeed the other. And a marriage had been contracted between the Danish princess and an American naval officer. Many more pieces of news beside tickled Margaret's imagination. She wished that she was closer to the center of intrigue, but was grateful not to have to guard and protect against becoming embroiled in it. Here in the Midlands, four days' drive from London, she was as safe as she could be.

The most worrying thing, though, was a further warning

about the men who had attempted to capture her on the docks in Hamburg, the spies for the Earl of Cork. That fact she had known from previous letters. Admiral Simpson had learned that they had mentioned her by name in at least one report to London. What she didn't know was that they had been ordered to find out more about her. Rita assured her that no further word from them had ever or would ever reach their master. Margaret felt a sinking feeling in the pit of her stomach, knowing what that firm statement must mean.

It was her bad luck that the two spies had spotted her debarking the *Meadowlark*. Had she been even an hour ahead or behind in her arrival, her presence would never have been remarked upon, and none of this would have caused a moment's worry.

The nightmares that she had contained since the year before came back in full force: disgrace, fear, even... death. She needed to discuss her concern with her father. What could they do? Nothing had happened in these many months since the escape, or in the few months since she had visited Magdeburg. Couldn't the Earl of Cork simply have dismissed the report as of no importance? After all, she was there on business for her father. It could be construed as innocent, a contact with merchants who sold their wares on the continent. The trouble was that his lordship had received other correspondence about Churnet House, and he had shown some curiosity about them. Margaret wondered how Rita knew about that, and realized there were cogs revolving inside wheels spinning inside wheels that she would never know or understand.

Rita had had words with her brother, but they were agreed on one thing: they wouldn't allow anything to happen to Margaret or her family. They still insisted that they owed her a debt of honor, and she was family now. She had referred the matter to the new prime minister, William Wettig. Rita swore that nothing would happen to her friends. She had set gears in motion, and to trust her. Margaret shook her head. She wished that they didn't feel so obliged toward her. The conversation with Robert Bywell had been a simple introduction, nothing more. But she was grateful that the Americans wished to protect her. At that moment, she could see neither how, nor from where a threat would come. The fear preyed upon her.

They must be vigilant.

# Chapter 37

Dinner had been a quiet meal. Despite Lady de Beauchamp's attempts to draw everyone into casual conversation, too many of the people at the table were mired down in their own concerns. The only ones who seemed to be positive were Nat and his two younger sisters.

"I am gaining mastery of another new song," he said. "It is a narrative about a man in his later years and his life with the woman he loves. I think it's charming."

"I like it," Petronella said. "I could listen to you play it over and over again." She had been making up dances to Nat's newest tunes.

"But Aaron dismisses it as not being enough 'rock and roll.' Don't you, my friend?"

Aaron stared down at his plate. Usually a hearty eater, he picked at the meat with one tine of his fork.

"Aaron," Delfine asked gently. "Do you not care for goose?"

"I'm sorry, ma'am," he said. "It's delicious. I just can't stop thinking."

"Is there anything that we can help you to decide?"

"Nothing for me to decide, ma'am. I feel guilty that I can't make the two extra sets of aqualators work. I blame myself for not checking over everything. I guess I thought that all of them would be right. I feel I've let everyone down."

"That's not true, son," Martin said. "Look what you've all accomplished! The others are working great. Everybody is impressed."

"Young man, I feel as if I am in the center of the Renaissance, and you are one of the great minds that brought scientific advances to light. Is that not right, my dear Margery?" Sir Timothy turned to Margaret.

She had caught her name in time to look up from her plate and away from her own thoughts. She had left the letter from Rita in Sir Timothy's study, awaiting a moment to take him aside and discuss it. Her head had been on a swivel since reading it. She worried about her family, and the possibility that their name would have at last come to be associated with the escape from the Tower.

"Yes, Father. It has been a dream come true." She tried to put the good things in mind that had happened because she had met the Americans. True friendship, exposure to new ideas and new places, experiences that she had never dreamed of, such as riding in a train and a motor car.

Unbidden, the memory of the men on the dock returned to her, and she shuddered. Her mother put a gentle hand on hers.

"Why don't I put you to bed, my dear," Delfine said. She smiled at her eldest daughter. "So much has been going on. Perhaps you need an early night. I will come and sit with you for a while."

Margaret looked into her mother's eyes and found understanding. Because of her delicate health, people often overlooked Delfine's observant mind. Lady Pierce had once said that Delfine could sense what was going on in a person's heart. Margaret felt an outpouring of love for her mother. It would be so very nice to be coddled for an evening as though she was a small child once again, and not the captain of a growing industry.

"I would like that so very much, Mother," she said.

On her way to bed, she left the letter on the desk in Sir Timothy's study.

All the dogs in the house were barking wildly. The brass knocker on the front door was being wielded as though it was a blacksmith's hammer on the anvil. A housemaid, in cap and wrapper, came to pull it open. Diccon Linden all but fell inside, out of breath.

Everyone came hurtling down the stairs from the family quarters and the servants' rooms and into the foyer. Diccon's huge eyes reflected the flames from the candlesticks.

"Sir Timothy!" he exclaimed. "The shed! People broke in! Dozens of them!"

"What?" his employer asked. He had a coat on over his nightshirt. "Who were they? Where did they come from?"

"I don't know, sir! I was asleep on a bale of wool in front of the door. I had a bale hook to hand. Then, I heard the door creaking. They were forcing the latch open! I threw myself on it to hold it down. Then it flew up in the air, and I was flung back. They came through the door, all of them! They had knives, sir. I called for the men, and ran up here."

"Good boy," Sir Timothy said. He kicked off his slippers and stomped into the boots next to the door. "Nat, go get the gardeners. Tell them to bring axes and billhooks. Percy, run down and see what's going on."

"Yes, Father," Nat said.

"Yes, Squire!" The two youths set out at the run.

"I'll come, too," Margaret said, reaching for her boots.

"No, Margery!" Sir Timothy said. "You stay here. Defend your mother. I must go check the looms." He beckoned to the footmen. "Come with me."

Margaret and her mother and sisters huddled together in the sitting room. They heard shouting and banging coming from down the hill.

"It was only a matter of time," Delfine said, her arms wrapped around Margaret. "No one could resist the aqualators. They are the only ones in the country. They envy our good fortune."

Martin came into the room, blinking sleep from his eyes.

"What's all the commotion?" he asked.

"Someone's broken into the shed," Margaret said.

Martin ran out. She heard his footsteps on the stairs. In a few moments, he came thundering down in shoes.

"Have you seen Aaron?" he asked. "He's not in his room."

"Could he have heard the noise and gone to investigate?" Lady de Beauchamp asked.

"I'll check," Martin said. "Stay put."

"We will," Margaret assured him. Petronella huddled against their mother's legs like a chick hiding in a hen's feathered skirt.

The shouting went on. Through the small panes of the sitting room window, Margaret spotted the dancing flames of lanterns and torches. The voices came nearer. She slid out of her mother's embrace and picked up the poker from beside the fireplace.

Sir Timothy, Martin, and all the men came through the front door. Percy locked it.

"The looms are intact, thank Heaven," the squire said. "I have

Noah and Andrew Catlow standing guard tonight. I sent Diccon home to bed. But the spare aqualator pieces are missing."

"Did Aaron move them somewhere?" Margaret asked.

Martin's face was grim. "We don't know. He wasn't in the shed. Or in his bedroom."

Lady de Beauchamp turned to Percy. "Ask the housemaids to see if he is elsewhere in the house, please."

The youth nodded and ran off.

"Did you find anyone else around the shed?" Margaret asked.

"No. By the time Diccon raised the hue and cry, they must have been long gone. I'm troubled because none of the dogs raised the alarm. That means," Sir Timothy said, his face grim, "that at least one of the thieves was someone that they knew."

"You could have used some security cameras down there," Martin said, frustrated. "That's what we would have had around locations with sensitive equipment. But nobody has those anymore. Yet."

Percy came panting back with one of the housemaids in tow.

"He's not in the house, my lady," Liza said. "We've been everywhere about. All of the staff is looking."

"Wasn't he visiting Ivy this evening?" Nat asked. "Could he still be there?"

Margaret blushed at the notion, but her mother nodded. "Percy, please go and see."

"Yes, my lady." The youth went off at the run.

Struck by a sudden chill, Margaret wrapped her arms around herself. "He won't be there."

"How do you know?" Sir Timothy asked.

"I don't know, but I do."

Her dread proved to be true. Percy returned with Ivy and Alder, her older brother.

"He was with us for an hour after dinner," Alder said. "But he said he was coming back here. Said he had *homework*."

"Where could he be?" Ivy asked, wringing her hands. "He seemed to be well enough when he left us!"

"Ask Cedric," Margaret said. The thought struck her out of nowhere.

"Margery, you can't accuse a man of a deed like that," Sir Timothy said, shocked.

"He knows something," Margaret said. "I know he resents

the aqualators, for all that he has been working them well. He's been acting oddly. Anyone could see it. He knows something. Or perhaps someone."

"Get the carriage," Sir Timothy said. "We will ask him."

"Wait a minute," said Martin. He went upstairs and came down with a long, thin tube of metal bent in the middle at a hinge. Margaret realized it was a gun, with a triangular wooden stock at one end and two holes like baleful, black eyes at the other. She hadn't even suspected until then that he had brought it with him from Grantville, or that he would use a weapon. He had always seemed so mild. But even the mildest of men might be ready to kill in defense of his children. "Let's go."

"Are you all right, boy?"

The rough cloth covering Aaron's head was pulled off, and he took a deep breath. The smell of old cow manure and sour milk filled his lungs, and he coughed. He was half-sitting, half-lying on a pile of straw. The walls around him were of split boards, rough enough to catch on the fabric of his linen shirt. It was a stall in a barn, but he didn't hear any animals moving around. His hands were free, but a rope still bound his ankles together. His shoes had been roughly pulled off. He didn't see them anywhere close by.

Crouching before him was a small man with tousled light brown hair and pockmarks that underlined rounded cheekbones. He had a lantern beside him. He handed Aaron a leather jack.

Aaron waved it away.

"It's all right. It's only water."

The man was speaking German, but with an odd accent.

"No, thank you," Aaron replied in the same language. "I want to go home. Please let me go."

The man let out a sigh of regret and looked off to the side. In the dancing shadows of the lantern, Aaron saw at least three dark forms with hoods pulled down to conceal their faces. He gulped.

"I cannot, boy. These men have questions for you."

"Who are they? Who are you?"

The man glanced up again, then returned a worried gaze to his.

"I am a peddler," he said. "I sell small iron goods, useful things, and other little items to people who need them. I like to travel around and meet people. My name is Osti. I come from Rotterdam, where my brother owns a smithy. What is yours?"

"Aaron."

The figures seemed to nod.

"And you are from?"

"Hamburg." He had gotten so used to saying the lie that it came out without hesitation.

"I know many languages," Osti continued, "so they have offered me money to speak to a foreigner, they said. I did not approve of them taking you against your will. A man deserves better treatment. I am sorry for you."

Aaron's body ached from the rough handling. From the first moment, when he had heard the sound of hoofbeats behind him on the twilit road, strong hands stuffed a cloth in his mouth, put a bag over his head, and lifted him off his feet, to being held down on the floor of a wagon that bumped unsteadily over the ground until it moved onto a lane that crunched under the wheels, to being dropped onto the floor here, he had been treated like a sack of potatoes.

"What do they want?"

"Ah. That I can tell you." He drew the lantern a little to the right, to a squared-off stack of gray pieces of clay. Horror surged through Aaron's belly. Had they taken the aqualators off the looms? No, on second examination, these were the two rejects, with a couple of Oliver Mason's tries at firing substitute trays. "They want to know how to make these work. I admit I am also curious. What are they?"

Aaron didn't want to speak. All he could think of were the man-shapes between him and the door, and how upset his mother would be that he had disappeared in a strange land all alone. What would his dad do now? He wished he could call them and ask what to do.

What if he yelled for help? Would anyone hear him? And what would those cloaked men do if he did? The hiss of metal and leather in the darkness told him that they were probably armed. He wore only his pajamas, and had nothing on his feet at all. The peddler smiled at him and gestured at the ropes around his ankles.

"These are unnecessary," he said, and untied the knots. Aaron watched him warily.

A low growl from the tallest of the men near the wall.

"Be calm," he said in English. "This will take time. Please be patient." He turned back to Aaron, and gestured at the aqualators and asked in German: "What do these objects do?"

"They're a system to tell a loom what pattern to make," Aaron said. His voice trembled. He couldn't help it.

Osti raised his eyebrows. "This is a remarkable notion. Is it like clockwork, to tell the clock when to chime the hours?"

"It's related," Aaron said, unable to get more words out of his dry throat. He wondered if the hooded men were weavers from a rival guild. Master Blackford had told Miz Margaret that others were jealous and getting impatient. After all the months that it had taken him to get these aqualators designed, made, and transported, he wasn't surprised that everyone else wanted to get their hands on them. He never dreamed they would resort to kidnapping. What would they do if they weren't satisfied with his answers?

"How related?" Osti pressed. "How do they chime the hours?"

"It's not a clock, but it works on a similar principle," Aaron said, trying to dumb down the explanation as much as possible. "They are a primitive form of a computer. The ridges inside the boxes tell the system to make choices on which threads to lift, and when to send the shuttles back and forth to make the pattern programmed into the trays."

"What is a *computer*?"

"It's . . . it's a box that makes calculations according to the program inside."

The peddler looked blank. Another growl from the wall.

"They want you to put the pieces together to make them work," Osti said. "They want to see the cloth come out."

Aaron realized in horror that none of the men were really weavers. They didn't understand anything about machinery. Who were they?

"I can't! They won't work without the rest of the system. They have to be attached to a loom and to a dynamo."

Osti patted his hand. Even terrified out of his mind, he knew the peddler wasn't a bad man, but both of them were in a bad situation. Osti didn't look as frightened as Aaron felt, but he was not as confident as his voice suggested.

"What goes into the box?" the peddler asked.

"Water. Only water."

"So, you pour water into it, or lead it in from a pump? Why does it work?"

"The shape of the interior of the box makes it work."

"Is it magic?"

"No, it's science. It works because of scientific principles."

"It makes a design on cloth? It does do that?"

"Yes, sir."

"Why do they want it?"

"I don't know. They aren't men who work on cloth." Aaron didn't want to use the word "Weber" because it was too close to the English word, and he wanted to avoid words that were recognizable in English.

"I thought that as well," Osti said, with a nod. "Can you make it work?"

"These are only pieces of the whole," Aaron tried to explain. "They mean nothing out of context."

"I don't understand. What is *context*?"

Aaron gestured with both hands, but dropped them when the men growled again. "Without everything—the loom, the river, the pipes, the wires, it doesn't do anything. All it can do is contain directions for a certain outcome and produce those."

Osti translated pretty well, and the men shot him another question. Aaron heard it, and his heart sank. Osti turned back to him and fixed him with a kindly expression. "They are trying to understand. Does this *computer* do anything else? Can it be made to achieve other purposes?"

Aaron hesitated, reluctant to explain any more than he had to. "Uh. Not really."

The men recognized his hesitation and barked an order to hurry up. Osti patted the air with his hands. "Please be more patient," he said in English. "Aaron, can this computer be made to do anything else?"

He made it emphatic. "No. It makes a pattern on cloth."

Osti gestured behind him. "They do not believe you."

"I can't help that!" Aaron yelped. The men shifted, and he heard the hiss of metal. Someone had drawn a knife from a scabbard. He felt like pissing in fear.

"What would it take for you to put enough pieces together to show them?" Osti asked.

"I can't do that. These pieces are faulty. I don't know how to fix them. We're *trying*. I designed them, but I didn't make them. I only brought them here."

"From Hamburg."

Aaron hesitated again, reluctant to speak. The sun was beginning to send faint light into the barn through gaps in the boards. Was anyone going to come here, or was the farm as deserted as the barn?

Osti carried on as if he had spoken. "Yes, from Hamburg. I can tell. You have the Hamburg accent. This is a new thing, a marvelous thing, a box that tells a loom how to make cloth." He gave Aaron a knowing look. Without a doubt, he had guessed where Aaron was really from. Aaron felt grateful, realizing that the peddler wasn't going to give them away. "So, these pieces cannot be made to go without the rest, without water?"

"That's right."

Osti translated for their captors.

"Then what good are they?" the tall man in the middle barked. "What else can they be made to do?"

Osti shrugged and conveyed the words in Amideutsch. Aaron's heart pounded. Osti really had guessed.

"Nothing!" Aaron's voice came out in a squeak.

The man in the middle, whose jutting chin Aaron could just begin to see in the nascent daylight, snarled at him. "You're lying. These are too complex to be just looms."

The man nearest the door of the barn, who somehow seemed more sinister than the others, shook his head under the concealing hood. "Cork is sure they are meant to be weapons of some kind. Or something else that will serve to overthrow the government."

Cork? Could he mean the Earl of Cork, the Chancellor of England? The man Margaret was afraid of? Aaron wanted to shout that that was nonsense. On the other hand, computers *were* versatile. How the king would have found something out like that, Aaron had no way of knowing. But he couldn't say anything. His heart pounded so hard he felt a lump in his throat.

"Come, come," Osti said, as casually as if they were sitting together in a bar. "This is a boy! He knows nothing of weapons of war. He assembles devices to make looms move. They are toys, not cannons."

The three men ignored him. Osti fixed his eyes on Aaron's. The gaze was meant to be reassuring, but all it did was send Aaron's imagination into overdrive. He wanted to get out of there alive. He wanted to go home!

"This is treason," the dangerous man said. "Our Baronet of Churnet and Trent must have a plan. This so-called enterprise involves too many people. They're planning to spread these devices across the land, under the guise of craft tools. Get rid of them."

The broad-shouldered man who had not spoken stepped forward. Aaron caught a glimpse of cold blue eyes under the hood. The man lifted one set of aqualators, and let them fall to the ground with a crash. The trays fell into pieces. The man laughed at the horrified expression on Aaron's face, and picked up the top tray of the second set. He smashed it down on top of the others, hammering at it until shards flew. Aaron and Osti shielded their faces.

"Now, no one can use them, for weapons or weaving," said the dangerous man. "They'll do his lordship no harm. I'll report back, and we can catch Churnet in the act of using illicit machines against the interests of the crown."

Aaron realized he knew the voice. It was the visitor, the one who had been hanging around with Cedric. Bob? No, Ben! Ben was a king's man? Aaron did his best to suppress his reaction to the knowledge. He must remain silent. Margaret! She had drawn him into her dreams, and now everything she and her father had could be destroyed. He had to get back to tell them they were in danger.

He glanced at Osti, but the peddler seemed worried about his own fate. The men were talking freely in front of them, as though they had no concerns about being overheard. Aaron's fear was confirmed in the next exchange.

"What do we do with the boy?" the big man asked.

"He's no use," said Ben. "Drop him down a mine?"

The man in the middle cleared his throat. "No pit mines here. Just clay." He sounded frightened.

"Then cut his throat and leave him."

"He doesn't understand us. What can he tell people?" the speaker asked.

Ben snorted. "He knows some English. He's been here long enough. You've no stomach for it?" He turned his head, perusing his companions. "Very well, there's no need for it. His lordship will have to take the shed and its contents if he wants the secret, and the boy will show them all how it works. Or he won't. It doesn't matter. We've enough evidence now to seize the estate."

The big man laughed. "Does his lordship want to go into the wool trade?"

Ben threw back his head, revealing his face as the hood fell away. "Hah! Anything that will make a fair bit of money. His lordship has hungry pockets. I heard these weavers talking about what a yard of this magical cloth is going for. It's not a big fortune, but it could be one in time. Once the squire is off the estate. Then his lordship can peruse the machines at his leisure."

"And how will we do that?"

"I've sent for help," Ben said. "Tie the boy up and leave him."

"And him?" The big man angled a thumb toward the peddler.

Ben spat on the ground and gave them a terrifying grin. "He's of no use at all."

# Chapter 38

"Cedric! Cedric Hollings!" Sir Timothy knocked on the door of the goodly cottage in the midst of a burgeoning garden. The group behind him milled impatiently. Sir Timothy pounded his fist on the panel. "Cedric! I need to speak to you! Come out immediately!"

Margaret huddled in her wrapper, holding onto Ivy's hand. Her heart beat so hard she was certain everyone could hear it. The girl looked as frightened as she was.

Somewhere along the way, Master Matthew had joined the throng. His shirt was tucked only partway into his breeches, and his coat was buttoned oddwise, one too many buttonholes up under his chin.

"I'm sure he's not to blame for this, Squire," he insisted, trying to straighten himself out. His apprentices ran alongside the open-topped carriage. "Cedric's a good man. He would never be involved in anything underhanded."

"He's been against this enterprise from the beginning," Sir Timothy said. "If he hasn't had a hand in the boy's disappearance, by Heaven, he knows who does!"

The door was flung open at last. Dorcas Hollings leaned out, a candlestick in her hand. "What's all this about? Why are you rousing us at this hour? Oh, Squire! Beg your pardon, sir. What may I do for you?"

"Madam, where is your husband?" Sir Timothy asked.

"What, that drunken fool? Only the Lord knows, sir." Dorcas' eyes grew wide. "What's he done now?"

"Isn't he at home?" Martin asked.

Margaret bit her lip, but the goodwife didn't realize that he "only spoke German," and merely answered.

"He wasn't in the bed just now, sir."

"Are you sure he's nowhere in the house, madam?" Sir Timothy asked, more patiently than Margaret would have. "It is vital that we speak with him immediately."

"I... no... well, then, you'd best come in and see."

No sign could be found of the master weaver at first. The Hollings children piled out of their beds and stood wide-eyed beside the banked fireplace. Margaret wanted to comfort them. They were only children, despite the oldest boy being nearly fifteen, the same age as the missing Aaron. The men searched through the rooms, looking under the beds and tapping on walls, as though a secret passage might be found there.

"He's hot-footed it," Percy said, grimly.

"He wouldn't dare!" Matthew exclaimed. "He's no reason to fear us."

A girl with her hair bound in a cap and long shift, barefoot, came sleepily out of a passage from the rear of the house. She must be the maid of all work for the household.

"What is afoot, mistress?" she asked.

"Where's yer master?" Dorcas asked.

"Oh, aye, Master Cedric?" The girl pointed toward the corridor. "He's asleep in the kitchen, up agin the taters, mistress."

The search party didn't wait for Dorcas to guide them. Martin led the way, his shotgun broken over his arm. They edged their way past hanging herbs, and crocks and bowls perched on a well-scrubbed wooden table. The girl pointed down near the kitchen door.

The missing weaver was indeed asleep. Margaret almost laughed at the way the man was slumped, almost as though he was a sack of potatoes himself, his cheek and nose on the flagstone floor, breathing heavily. When she got closer, she could smell the stink of stale beer on him.

"Cedric! What have ye gotten us into?" Dorcas demanded. She gave him a nudge with her foot. Cedric waved it away without waking. "Cedric!"

Between them, Martin and Matthew hauled him to his feet. Matthew took hold of the man's left ear and gave it a solid tweak. That brought Cedric to consciousness instantly, sputtering and furious.

"What in perdition d'ye want, wakin' a man of his honest sleep?" he shouted, fighting against the solid hold on his arms. He immediately moderated his tone. "Curses, it's the squire. Good even t'ye, sir."

"Indeed," Sir Timothy said. "Where have you been this evening?"

"Doin' nothin' wrong," Cedric said, with a guilty look toward his wife. She narrowed her eyes at him. "A few beers with friends."

"Bah!" his wife said. "More than a few, I'd warrant."

Both Cedric and Sir Timothy ignored her.

"Have you seen Aaron Craig?"

"The foreign boy? Nay, I have not. Why? What's he done?"

"He's disappeared," Margaret said. "Someone broke into the weaving shed and took the incomplete aqualators away. And Aaron is missing."

Cedric barked out a laugh. "Best you ask Fred Wilkinson's girl as to his whereabouts. I'm sure she knows exactly where he's been."

Ivy shook loose from Margaret's hand, marched up to Cedric, and delivered a stinging slap across his face. The surprise of it sent him reeling backward.

"Ye'll not question my character when yours is so low," she said, her chin held high. He covered his cheek with a surprised hand. "He left our house at sundown happy and well. What have you done with him?"

"I've done nothing!"

"You had best tell us all," Master Matthew said. "You realize that your membership in the guild, your mastery, are all in danger here."

"Wherefore?" Cedric said. The tweak and slap hadn't frightened the alcohol out of him, but the threat had. "Haven't I plied my trade as I should? Have I not put up with the insult of being made a piece of clockwork? You have no call to be demanding aught of me."

"Do you know nothing about the missing aqualators?" Margaret asked.

That seemed to have struck home to the weaver. He cast a wary eye on her. "I know nothing of that."

"You were talking freely enough of them in the Four Alls," Matthew said.

"That was just talk!" Cedric was awake enough then to regain some of his senses. "I talk to people, and that is all! If you wish to bring charges against me, I demand to have Master Blackford here so all is done right and proper."

"If you insist to have this made a formal inquiry," Sir Timothy said, all warmth gone from his voice, "then it shall be. I am disappointed in you, Cedric. For all the many years you have spent in my service, to refuse to answer questions."

"I don't know aught!"

"You talk to people. With whom do you talk?"

"People in the public house!" Cedric fumbled for names. "Like Ben."

"Ben? Ben who?"

"I don't know his name. That's all."

"I saw him in the tavern, too. He came to visit our looms with the guild master from Stafford, did he not?" Matthew asked. "Showed an uncommon interest in them, for a man who does nothing in the trade."

"What if he did?" Cedric countered. "You call those akalabors the wonder of the age!"

"And you revealed all about them to a chance-met stranger. You talked out of turn, and betrayed the trust of your guild and your employer. Your loose lips are a danger to us all. This is a boy who has been a help to us, and you might have put his life in peril."

Martin hung back, not saying a word, but his eyes flashed with anger. He looked like a firework that was about to go off.

"Where do we find this Ben?" Margaret asked.

"I don't know!" Cedric's voice rose in a wail. "I see him around the tavern. He always seems to turn up of an evening."

"Perhaps he stays there," Margaret said.

"I will go," Master Matthew said. "It's not far. I'll take horse at once."

"I'll go to Master Blackford," Sir Timothy said. "If this Ben wants to know more about the aqualators, it is probably in service to one of the other guild masters."

"Master Denby," said Matthew.

"Yes. Why couldn't the man just wait for spring?" Sir Timothy asked. He seemed in despair.

"Greed," Martin said. His face was stoic. "I only want my boy back safe." Margaret, her mind awhirl, translated for him.

"Let's us spread out to look for him," Sir Timothy said. "Take all the horses from my stables. If it's an innocent disappearance, he might be lost, though I take leave to doubt it. I am so sorry, Master Craig. I believed that you and your son were safe under my roof."

"And me, squire?" Cedric asked, his eyes desperate. Sir Timothy didn't spare him a glance.

"Master Blackford will deal with you later. I've no time for you now."

With that, Sir Timothy turned and stalked out of the Hollings house. Margaret shot a sympathetic glance toward Dorcas, who was just as stricken as her husband. Perhaps Cedric was not directly involved in Aaron's disappearance, but he almost certainly had a role in it. Then, she followed her father and Martin Craig.

Aaron sent a desperate glance toward the peddler. The man didn't seem as upset as anyone would have, just having heard his death sentence. Osti smiled at him and nodded toward the rear of the barn. His hand, away from the cloaked men, gestured in that direction. The movement was so small that it could have been a shadow from the dancing flame of the lantern. Aaron was puzzled. What was he trying to say? Then Osti set his hand upright, and turned it, as if opening a door. A door! What was the matter with him? He'd been in 4-H since he was pretty small. Barns didn't have just one way in or out. But how to get away from the men? Osti was a little guy, a good head shorter than he was, and no match for three big, armed men.

"The boy is hungry," Osti said, as though he had not just heard the threat from Ben. "And thirsty, I will be bound. I would like something to drink as well. Have you anything to eat?"

The three men looked up from their conference. Aaron wished he could hear them. They had fallen into hissed whispers, with angry, jerking gestures toward the two of them. Osti just sat there with the calm smile he had worn throughout.

"Eh?"

"Food? The boy has been woken from a sound sleep. I know when I was that age, I needed constant sustenance."

Ben felt in a belt pouch and threw something at them. It landed in the straw. It gave off the scent of freshly baked bread, both appetizing and horrifying. Neither of them touched it.

"And drink?"

"If ye thirst, ye can drink out of the trough," the big man said, and laughed. "It was no doubt filled a month ago."

"Ah. Thank you well."

He pulled Aaron to his feet and lifted the small lantern.

"No so fast!" the hooded man snapped. "What are ye about?"

"Taking care of this boy."

Osti brought his hand up as he spoke. Suddenly, with a crack like lightning and the smell of burning coal, a blinding light burst out from the lantern. The peddler threw the lamp at the men, grabbed Aaron by the hand, and plunged further into the dark barn.

Behind them, Aaron heard shouting. The lantern seemed to have exploded, and Aaron heard the crackle of flames. The straw must have caught fire from the oil in the lantern.

He didn't have time to think about it. The peddler kept them moving forward. Aaron stumbled. His bare feet found every pebble, every sharp fragment of straw. He didn't dare to look down.

A thin line of light loomed ahead. Osti let go of him and fumbled with his hands along the wall. The creak of a latch, and they were hit in the face with a rush of cold air.

"Come along!" Osti said, his arm through Aaron's elbow.

Aaron hurried out. Ahead was a faint pinkish light, false dawn coming up from the east. Under his bare feet, the pebbled path was overgrown with weeds and grass.

The field around the barn stood knee high with what his dad called "volunteer" crops, straggly wheat or something. Even though it was August, the greenery wasn't high enough to hide in. They'd have to get somewhere before the men caught up with them.

Osti urged him around the blind side of the barn. "Trees there," he said, pointing. A silhouetted line of trees wound around the edge of the field. "Get there. Go home. Safe going, Aaron."

"What about you?" Aaron asked.

Osti smiled. "I run fast. Go."

The peddler took off across the field. Aaron didn't take any more time to think about it. He had to get back to his dad. But he had no idea where he was.

He made for the trees. The soles of his feet weren't as tough as they used to be when he and his friends had spent all day outside barefoot. If he hadn't been terrified for his life, he'd have laughed.

He smelled smoke, but didn't dare look back. The barn must have caught fire from Osti's trick. What had he thrown into the lantern to make it blow up like that? The peddler said he sold iron goods, and "useful things." Was one of them gunpowder?

It didn't matter. Only moving as fast as he could made any sense.

He heard shouting. The sun was coming up fast. He'd lose what advantage the shadows gave him in a moment. Heedless of his bare feet, he dashed into the trees.

Beyond the gray bark lay twisted shadows, like Halloween skeletons reaching for him. The ground sloped suddenly downward. Aaron almost fell down the incline, and found himself ankle deep in cold water. Natural streams often were used as boundaries between farm fields as well as serving as the source of irrigation. Which way was the stream flowing? Could this be the same water that lay behind Miz Margaret's land and the weavers' shed?

Threshing noises came closer and closer, and he heard the nickering of horses. Aaron ducked low and hid underneath a leafy branch that arched over the brook. Something in the water touched his foot. The shock almost made him cry out, but he stifled it. A couple of figures pushed through the bushes and onto the bank. He stayed crouched and as still as a statue, even though his feet were freezing.

He smelled smoke, oil, and sweat. If there was any justice, they had been scorched by Osti's fire. It was too much to hope they'd burned to death. He was surprised how much he wanted to get back at them. His dad would have reminded him about the commandment, "Thou shalt not kill." All right, but he could wish they'd fall into a hole.

"Any sign of the boy? That Dutchman led us a wild chase."

The footsteps swished up and down the bank. Aaron ducked his head down, hoping he looked like a rock in his gray pajamas.

Further down the stream, something went PLOP!

"What's that?" Ben asked. Aaron distinctly heard a sword

come out of a scabbard. Then, to his relief, they strode away from him down the bank. Then, a cry came from one of them, followed by a splash.

"God's teeth!" the man exclaimed.

Ben laughed. His henchman had fallen into the stream, not five feet from Aaron's hiding place. He hauled the man out. Aaron prayed they wouldn't stumble against him. "A fish jumps, and you go in after it. He's run off. I must send a report. Back to the horses, before someone comes asking about the fire."

Aaron kept his eyes closed and counted to a thousand, listening to their footsteps recede farther and farther in the distance. As soon as he was sure they were gone, he stood up and wrung as much water as he could from his clothes, and waded downstream along the shallow brook, counting on the tree cover to keep him from sight. The pebbles under his bare feet were cold and a little slippery, but better than walking on a rough road.

Through the gaps in the foliage, he saw the blaze rising high, sending a thread of black smoke upward. With the sun coming up, he could see the old barn engulfed in flame. No one seemed to notice the fire. Aaron guessed that the farm had been abandoned for some time. It was a perfect place for a villain's murder hole, and might have been, if not for Osti. He sent up a prayer of thanksgiving for the peddler, and hoped he'd gotten away. He just wanted to get back to Miz Margaret's place.

He walked on and on, freezing and sweating with fear, starting at every sound. Was that rustle to his right the men coming back again? Any shadow that passed over the trees had to be them again. The fish that nibbled at his legs, or the birds that flitted into the arched passageway, or the frogs that jumped into the water at his passage made him imagine the intruders all over again. He concentrated on the light at the far end of the green tunnel, and kept walking toward it, hoping he would wake up from the nightmare.

Ivy, her shawl over her hair and shoulders, clung to her brother's waist on the back of one of the squire's horses. They'd ridden miles out to the east of the estate and back again. Now, Alder turned the steed to the south, on the Stafford road. They'd been out looking since the hours before dawn, and her legs and hips were sore.

"He'd surely not have come this far," Alder said over his shoulder.

"Not by himself," Ivy said, firmly. "He could have been taken down this way." She refused to believe in the theory that Aaron had run away. She begged Heaven that he be returned safely. The sun was full in the sky now, having lifted its countenance above the horizon a couple of hours earlier. She felt horrible for Master Craig. The man was distraught. So would she be, if her only son had disappeared. Her heart wrenched. Aaron had become dear to her and to her family. Curse Master Cedric for being a fool! If his gossip friend was to blame for this, she'd see him damned.

"I'll stop in a public house soon and get us some victuals," Alder said.

"No," Ivy said, though she was tired and hungry. Aaron must be worse off. They had to find him. "Keep on, please."

"As you wish, sis."

They enquired of every single person they met if they'd seen a boy matching Aaron's description. All passersby promised they'd bring him back to the squire's manor if they found him. The squire had offered a reward for Aaron's safe return of ten pounds. That had motivated Alder to keep on, even though he ought to be back at the looms. She couldn't give a fig for the money, no!

The horse, a big bay with a white blaze on its nose, covered another ten miles south, then Alder brought him about, heading back toward Barlaston. Then, a boy in a long shirt and gray-green breeches came running toward them.

"Mistress! Master! Me mum's found him!"

# Chapter 39

"Where was he?" Ivy's mother asked, as they brought the shivering Aaron into the cottage. Ivy had wrapped her shawl around his shoulders. Alder had given up his saddle and led the horse with Ivy holding Aaron to her all the way home to keep him warm. She settled him on a comfortable stool before the fire and wrapped his hands around a bowl of broth her mother had dished up for him. Aaron still hadn't said a word.

"Near as I can figure, a ditch near the Hubert farm," Alder said. "A dairy farmer's wife on the Stafford road saw him climb up out of the stream, as wet as wet. The barn caught fire this morning, so it seems. Ever since Mistress Hubert died and they sold off her cows, the place has been empty. Did the fire happen while you were near it, Aaron?" The secret that he knew English had long ago been revealed in the Wilkinson home. Even her father had let his resentment pass. The Americans may be mysterious visiting strangers from the future, but Aaron and Martin were *their* visiting strangers, and no harm would befall them in their care.

Aaron seemed to hear them inside the trance he was in, and nodded slightly. Ivy, overjoyed that he had reacted, hugged him tightly. She couldn't stop touching him, as if she didn't believe he was there with her.

"I'd best go tell the squire and Mistress Margaret," Alder said. "They'll be glad that he's safe. I'll bring his bay back again."

"Don't you dare take that horse out again," their mother

said. "It deserves a rest after the morning it's had. Borrow Hugh Green's plough horse. It'll be fresh."

Alder nodded and dashed out, the prospect of a ten-pound reward clear on his face.

"We've chores to get done with," her mother said, turning to Ivy. Ivy felt stricken. Her mother saw her expression, and her own softened. "Ah, well, you can take care of the boy until we can get him home again. I'll milk the cow, but it's your task for the evening. Get him dry, and take some of Alder's clothes out of the press for him."

"Yes, Mum," Ivy said. Her mother slipped on her clogs and went outside.

Ivy held onto Aaron's hands. They were cold. She willed the warmth of her own body into his. He was so still. He'd been reserved around her, but not like this. It was as though his soul had flown elsewhere, leaving the shell.

"Come back to me," she said. "You're safe here now, I swear it."

She studied his face. It still looked stiff, but the left corner of his mouth turned up just a little.

"There, now," she said, pleased and relieved. She stroked his cheek with gentle fingers. As they passed his mouth, he turned his head and kissed her hand. Ivy couldn't help herself. She took his face in her hands and kissed him on the mouth.

For the first time, he moved. His hands came around her, crushing her to his half-dried, wrinkled and soiled shirt. She laughed, and helped him pull it off over his head. The feel of his bare skin made tingles run up her body. The two of them fumbled with the fastenings of her bodice until the two halves of the stiffened cloth fell open. Then she felt his hands moving down her body, as she had wished he had done weeks ago. Their lips joined again, and Ivy couldn't stop kissing him, on his cheeks, his lips, the sides of his neck. Aaron drew back and searched her eyes.

"I . . . I've never done this before."

"Don't worry," Ivy said. "I have."

She pushed him back on the settle and cuddled up against him, running her hands down his body, undoing the drawstring of his wrinkled trousers. He kissed her frantically everywhere he could reach, and she guided his hands along her torso, sighing when he touched the sensitive skin of her breasts.

"Sorry I stink," Aaron murmured at last. She laughed again. "I don't mind at all."

Margaret sat on the front of the wagon with Martin Craig as Percy drove them, Hettie, and Alder back to the Wilkinson house. When they turned at last into the lane, she spotted Aaron and Ivy sitting on a bench beside the door. They stood up to await them. Margaret saw that they were holding hands. She felt enormous relief that he seemed to be unharmed, but the youth's expression was odd, a mixture of many emotions at once. That didn't surprise her, considering the terrible experience he had gone through, but he seemed . . . happy. She studied him, looking to see if he had been badly injured. He was wearing unfamiliar clothes that were rather too large on him, and no shoes. His feet looked bruised and scratched.

"Those will take some physicking," Hettie said, in a business-like tone, which belied the concern that both of them had had during the long night of worry. "I've got poultices that will lighten those purple marks in a day." Margaret felt a rush of warmth for her maidservant's good common sense. "Are those his clothes?"

"Yes," Ivy said, picking up a damp bundle beside the bench.

Martin hadn't waited for the cart to come to a halt. He jumped off the seat and ran to hug his son. They clung together for a long while. The American spoke in a low voice with Aaron, then guided him toward the cart. Aaron pulled back. Martin looked a question at him, then smiled as Aaron gathered Ivy in his arms and kissed her. The gesture looked a little clumsy and inexperienced, but the girl beamed as though Aaron was a noble courtier.

Margaret smiled. If only they weren't so young, their parents would surely be arranging a marriage for them. She sighed to herself. Thank Heaven that Aaron had been returned safely.

She thanked Fred and his wife for their good care, and presented Alder with a small leather bag containing ten silver pounds.

"We'd have done it for nothing, ma'am," Alder said, his fair cheeks red. "Aaron's a good fellow."

"Let's get you back," Martin said. This time Aaron didn't resist. He climbed up on the cart and waved farewell to Ivy. She touched her hand to her lips and extended it out toward him.

✧ ✧ ✧

An hour later, the Reverend Mr. Olney had a visitor appear in his study at the Church of St. John the Baptist. He looked up from the sermon he was penning and smiled.

"Ivy Wilkinson, be welcome," he said.

The girl looked very nervous. "I wish to make a confession, Father."

"Of course, my daughter," Mr. Olney said. He escorted her into the nave of the church and gestured to the small wooden booth adorned with angels with gilded wings and sympathetic eyes.

He listened through the screen to her outpourings, his heart full of sympathy albeit tempered by the rules of his office. The boy had told her all of the harrowing experiences, and the aftermath between them. He sighed. It was only to be expected.

"God absolves you, my daughter," he said at last, making the sign of the cross. "I exhort you to not step out of the protection of the Scriptures, no matter what the temptation."

"Oh, he won't," Ivy assured him. "He's a good man."

"I'm not talking about him, my dear. It was Eve who plucked the fruit from the Tree of Knowledge. You have learned things in this age that no man has known."

"Oh, I have, Father! I have learned so much from Aaron!"

The vicar was taken aback. "Is it a matter that you must confess? Of sin?"

"No, of the future! The music, Father! He has brought music from the future. Oh, Father, you would love it. One of them is a hymn asking blessings from God's lady mother. It is so beautiful."

Mr. Olney had to gather his thoughts. "Music?" He loved music. One of the greatest joys of his vocation was listening to the prayers buoyed up to heaven on a cradle of song from the throats of his congregation and the huge church organ. He was aware of the sin of pride he suffered for that glorious instrument, so much better than a humble house of worship like his would otherwise have deserved. And to hear songs vouchsafed to this time from the future? "I am curious, my daughter. Do you think he will let me hear it?"

"I am sure he would! Who could he trust more than you?

"Do not attribute more to me than any man, my daughter," Mr. Olney said, abashed. "I am as fallible as anyone else. Only God is perfect."

"Yes, Father. You won't tell anyone what I've told you, will you, Father?"

"Never. The seal of the confessional is absolute. Only our Heavenly Father will have heard what you said today."

"Do I need to do penance?"

"For what? You saved a man's life, and he showed his gratitude to you. Be blessed, my child." He intoned the litany. *And may our Heavenly Father keep her from having a child so soon,* he thought. *She has more growing up to do than that boy has.*

"Come with me, Father. You shall hear the songs."

"I would like to hear the one that seems like a hymn," Mr. Olney said. His mind raced like water tumbling over a weir. She had given him so much to absorb. Americans here in their village! He thought that the wonders that they had already bestowed upon Barlaston were enough for one lifetime. Listening to a song from three centuries hence was beyond what he thought God would ever have in store for him.

At the soft tapping on the door, Margaret stood up from the edge of Aaron's bed. Her brother Nat, on the floor with his five-string guitar, left off his strumming, moved to conceal the record player from view. Hettie opened the door a crack. Ivy peered in, and Margaret relaxed. She had been standing unofficial guard over Aaron since he had been returned to them. Two of the undergardeners were in the corridor, preventing anyone from intruding into the room. That excepted, of course, people that they trusted.

"Ivy!" Margaret felt a rush of affection and gratitude, since she and her brother Alder had been the ones to bring Aaron home.

"May we come in?" Ivy asked.

"Of co— We?" she asked, suddenly on her guard. "Who else is here?"

"The vicar is with me," Ivy said, looking sheepish. Hettie stood between them, looking over her shoulder for Margaret's permission. She had no choice but to accede, and nodded. Hettie, very reluctantly, retreated a few paces. The vicar offered a polite nod.

"Mistress Margaret? Master Nathaniel? Master Aaron, I trust that you are recovering?"

Aaron sat up. Margaret hurried to straighten the pillows under his back. He was in fresh pajamas, and had undergone both a bath and physicking from Hettie. The maidservant sat upright upon a cushion on the floor, ready to leap upon her patient at a moment's notice.

"He's doing well," Margaret answered. "His feet have been rubbed raw, and his mind is troubled by his experience, but he is on the mend."

Mr. Olney smiled at her. "I believe he can answer for himself, can he not?"

Margaret stared in horror. "Ivy!"

"Ye must be able to trust a priest, mistress," Ivy said, looking guilty.

"Please, do not fear, Mistress Margaret," the vicar said. "I am but paying a pastoral visit to one of my . . . temporary . . . parishioners, to offer God's blessing for health and well-being. Consider this room to be now under the seal of the confessional. Nothing that takes place here and now will ever be revealed."

"Thank you," Aaron said. "I'm okay, I guess."

Mr. Olney's smile spread wide across his gentle face. "So the rumors are true."

"The secret seems to spread far afield, no matter how much care we take to keep it," Margaret said. Her back stiffened into its most formal posture. Ivy looked stricken at her disapproval.

"I only want the best for Aaron, mistress," she pleaded. "Surely God already knows and offers His blessing to him."

"That is right, Mistress Margaret," Mr. Olney said. "I am but His humble servant. But I confess to the curiosity of a mortal creature. Learning that we harbor not just visitors from abroad but from the future is like learning that we entertain angels unaware. Do not be angry with Ivy. I'm afraid that I pressed her, perhaps unfairly. Especially when I learned of the music that Aaron shared with her. She told me of the sacred music that one of these future troubadours has written. May the Lord forgive me, but I have an obsession for music, which I consider the language of the angels. I beg that you would allow me to hear it."

Nat started laughing like a deranged cuckoo, and played a cocky thread of melody on his guitar. Margaret stuck her tongue out at him. Mr. Olney looked quizzically from one sibling to the other.

"Of course, Vicar," Margaret said, in resignation. "Pray make yourself at home. Hettie, will you see to some refreshments for our visitors?"

"Of course, Mistress," Hettie said, rising from her seat. Margaret was scandalized to see a twinkle in her eye and understood that she was the only one still trying to maintain the situation. Word of the record player and the black disks had escaped entirely from her control. She simply had to accept it, in light of the other revelations with which Aaron had returned.

Aaron, albeit still looking the worse for wear, began to act as what he called the *disk jockey*, leading the new listener through a playlist of his favorites. He switched from one album to another, accompanied by his opinions, and what his mother had told him about all of the "old time" artists and songs. The vicar, as she guessed he would, was astonished and delighted by the magic of the recordings, and the association with a neighboring city, albeit many years from then. He seemed to like all the same songs that Margaret did, but he went back over and over again to the simple song adorned by the thrill of the pipe organ.

"By Heaven's grace, listen to that chord progression! You are right, Ivy, that would make a good hymn," Mr. Olney said, his eyes shining. He turned to Nat, who was strumming along. "Can you teach Mistress Tamsin the notes?"

"I'm sure that I can," Nat said. "I've learned a number of these songs already, enough to set them down in manuscript."

At last, the automobile battery was beginning to lose its charge, and the record player began to slow down. The vicar stood and made the sign of the cross over Aaron.

"You have done a good thing, my son. Thank you for bringing a new iteration of the word of God to this time and place. And your secrets are safe with me. Mistress Margaret, Master Nathaniel, thank you again. I will take my leave now. Pray give my regards to your parents. Master Aaron, my prayers are with you for your healing." He went to the door and looked back, a small smile on his face. "God does work in mysterious ways. We will take the singer's advice to let all things be."

# Chapter 40

Margaret left her charge guarded by the servants, with an admonition that no one else outside of the household was to be admitted. She saw threats everywhere. Even a simple visit by the vicar brought with it intrusions upon the secrets that they had been keeping.

Once Aaron had returned and was bandaged up, Sir Timothy and Martin Craig had sat him down in the office to glean every detail of the night's misadventure. They had allowed Margaret to sit in on the discussion, though she was too overwhelmed to add too much to the queries. Although Sir Timothy had the same concerns and care as any father would for a boy who had undergone such a terrifying experience, he acted more as the justice of the peace and magistrate that he had been for many years. He led Aaron through his account, point by point, from the abduction to when Ivy and Alder had pulled him up onto their horse and taken him home. Margaret noticed he became a bit vague on what had transpired in the Wilkinson cottage, but Sir Timothy allowed him to elide that passage of time. In truth, it had nothing to do with the matter at hand, nor was it really any of their business.

Once they were certain that they had elicited all they could from Aaron's memory, Martin had entrusted him to Hettie's ministrations. Since then, the two men had been mewed up in the office, deep in discussion. They were horrified by the destruction of the unfinished aqualators, and concerned about the leader's demands to know what else they could do.

"That's something that we don't want gossiped about," Martin said.

Margaret had been more than alarmed by the mention of the Earl of Cork. She had asked Aaron several times to confirm that that was the name he had heard the man in charge to have said.

"I'm positive," Aaron had said, over and over. "He only said it once, but I remember every moment of that night. I'll never forget it."

That confirmed her deepest fears. The wonderful invention that was meant to rebuild the fortunes of her family had drawn the attention of the one man who would be pleased to take vengeance upon her, if he could discover her connection to the Americans. And his henchman had swept up one of those very Americans straight from her home, as easily and stealthily as plucking an apple from a tree.

She had thought and thought about her enterprise, and how much it meant to the people of Barlaston. What wealth and fame it had brought and was bringing, but how much scrutiny had clearly come as well. She had caused this calamity. She was to blame for Aaron's abduction, and no one else. No gentle confession would wash away that guilt.

She tapped on the door of her father's office. The voices inside stopped for a moment.

"Enter," Sir Timothy said. His face brightened when he saw her. "Ah, Margery, pray sit down and join us." Martin was with him.

He had his special cut crystal bottle of brandy on a tray at his elbow. He poured a tot into a small glass and handed it to her.

"It seems as though all the fears that you've had were not an exaggeration," her father said, as she took a sip of the bronze liquid. It burned its way down her throat. "The Earl of Cork does seem to have taken an interest in our small doings, as Lady Rita said in her letter. But it appears that he hasn't twigged to the presence of our friends here. Not as Americans, in any case. We have continued to fool them in that way, at least."

"Not for long," Margaret said, setting the glass down without taking another sip. "That secret is fast making its way around the parish. The vicar has just left. Ivy Wilkinson went to make confession, and revealed all to him."

"He's a man of honor," Sir Timothy said, frowning at her. "He will not endanger any of his flock."

"I am not concerned about Mr. Olney speaking out of turn," Margaret said. She wrung her hands together. "But others have learned, or certainly have guessed, that Master Martin and Aaron are not what we have told them. The secrets percolating away inside them can so easily bubble over. Some will have spoken out inadvertently."

"Or foolishly, like Cedric," Martin put in. "He's not a bad guy. I think he's a damned sight more impulsive than is good for him, but it's not out of malice. He's scared for his job."

"And he should be!" Sir Timothy said, his round face turning red with anger. "I did not think that I would ever have to explain trade secrets to a master of his craft. Yet, he took his misgivings to the tavern, and this is where it has brought us. I cannot apologize enough, Master Craig, for putting your son in peril."

"He's all right, thank God," Martin said. Sir Timothy and Margaret crossed themselves, and Martin looked sheepish. "That's a habit I've got to unlearn, taking the Lord's name casually. I'm sorry. But my boy is in one piece, if a little bruised up. It could've been far worse."

"We can't continue in this manner," Margaret said. "If the king's men are willing to try violence on a youth, then they are acting without morals or ethics."

"Perhaps the king doesn't know what is afoot," Sir Timothy said. "I should write to him, or make the journey to offer an appeal to him directly."

"You will not get past the Earl of Cork," Margaret reminded him. "He is the gatekeeper to what His Majesty hears and sees. There is no aid in that direction."

"Then, what?"

"I could send a message to Grantville," Martin said. "But it will take at least a week to reach anyone on the continent. Could be a lot longer."

"Are there no radios or other machines that can convey the message?" Margaret asked, recalling the room at the top of the presidential palace.

"Most of what we've got is short-range, meaning no more than a few miles, and only in line of sight. The long-range broadcasts aren't set up for two-way communication." Martin sighed. "I sure do miss telephones."

"Then we must send a messenger," Sir Timothy said.

"Who?"

"You," Margaret said, her heart aching with the thoughts that had been building up in her all the night before and the day since. "And Aaron. I believe that it is time you went home. We are so grateful for the time that you have spent here with us. We can go on with the looms that we have, and we will cope with the coming competition once the other masters have received theirs."

"They won't be able to function unless Aaron sets them up," Martin protested.

"We will have to find a way to make them function. I trust Daniel Taylor and Master Matthew to have learned everything they were shown. Aaron's manual has been studied until it is nearly falling apart. Daniel and Matthew know how the pipes are put in place, how strong a flow is needed, and how to clean out the aqualators. If we run into trouble, we can send a message for assistance." She folded her hands around Martin's. "But, please, my dear, good friend, go home and keep Aaron safe. My conscience is hurting desperately for what he suffered. I feel that I am directly responsible for it, and I do not wish either of you to come to further harm."

Martin's brows drew down over his nose. "Ma'am, I don't know what kind of cowards you think we raise in West Virginia, but I promise you we don't cut and run at the threat of violence. We act."

"But there are only two of you," Margaret said. "And, to be frank, if you are discovered, more than the two of you will suffer for it. The Crown will execute women and children as well as men for treason. I . . ." She steeled herself. "I will do my best to keep silent unto death, but who knows what means the king's executioners have of prying open unwilling lips?"

The men fell silent.

"It's no good saying you can come back with us," Martin said, after some thought. "Even though y'all would be a welcome addition to the USE. But I understand. You can't just leave your life behind."

"Too many souls depend upon us," Sir Timothy said. "And we do not raise cowards in Staffordshire, either. Let us use our wits instead of our emotions, my dear. I share your alarm, but the reality can be addressed with cooler heads. The melodrama of threatening bodily harm is only one tool that is at the king's hand. He can also fine me, or compel me to give up our manors, as happened to Sir Franklin Leigh. My fellow magistrates tell me that the grounds for the Leighs' expulsion is a dispute over taxes remaining unpaid. The case is still pending, or so I have heard, as there has been no news at all from the royal court of appeals. The poor man and his family are living in a small house on the outskirts of Upper Nobut while coarse ruffians occupy the historic mansion." He shook his head. "I've heard rumors that more than one nobleman has been threatened or disenfranchised by men claiming to be acting in the king's name. I've been approached quietly by fellow landowners who are displeased with the growing attitude that those of us who live in the north are potential traitors. I do not care to have aspersions such as those cast upon us. None of us wishes to act prematurely, but that day may come when we have no choice. We are loyal subjects to His Majesty, despite his seeming lack of care for us. Curse it, we pay our taxes, as extortionate as they are."

"Think there's any connection to Aaron's abduction?"

"If there is, it can hardly be official court business," Sir Timothy said. "Or they would have approached us in an open manner, asking questions directly of me as the person of authority, or summoning me to appear at court to answer to His Majesty. If there is any further interference in our lives, I shall apply to have our case appealed to the Crown myself. In the meanwhile, we must keep Aaron and you, my friend, safer than we have."

After a couple of days, Aaron was up and around again, his feet well-padded inside his socks. Margaret, Ivy, and Hettie spelled one another looking after him. Noah, the undergardener, had been told to stay with Aaron any time he was out of doors.

"Is that necessary?" Aaron pleaded. "I'm fine!"

"It is, my young friend," Sir Timothy said. He tapped Aaron on the forehead. "You are the only source of the information that make the aqualators run. Despite all the training you have given us, and the manuals that we have copied, it is not the same as the knowledge in your head and the skill in your hands."

"It's embarrassing," he grumbled. Miz Margaret held tight to his elbow as they made their way down the path to the barn.

She swung the door wide to reveal all of the masters, journeymen, apprentices, and women within. As soon as they saw

Aaron, they began clapping. Aaron's face turned pink. Margaret pulled him inside.

"Glad to have you back, my lad," Master Blackford said.

"Thanks," Aaron said. The guild master looked bemused for a moment, then smiled. The secret was well and truly out among their friends, as Miz Margaret had said. He scanned the big room. "Where's . . . ?"

"Cedric?" Master Blackford finished his question. "He and Ned have been given a few days off to consider where their loyalty lies. All here support not only the aqualators, but you and your father. You've been good friends to us."

"Well, then, lads," Master Matthew said, clapping his hands together. "Shall we make it a six-bolt day, then?"

It became a contest, with the masters vying for the fastest and best lengths of cloth. The apprentices had their feet almost worn to nubs changing out shuttles as fast as they could wind them.

"On the rhythm, men!" Master Blackford said, walking to and fro among the looms. He slapped Fred Wilkinson on the back at his precious old machine. Fred still refused to weave brocade, but it had become a matter of stubbornness now, not resistance to the new cloth. If anything, he toasted it with pride in the inn at night. Still, he bid fair to make a full bolt of fine serge by evening. "On with you, then! To, fro, to, fro, to, fro!"

Aaron had a whispered conference with Margaret. She dissented at first, then shrugged in resignation. She sent Hettie and Noah back to the house on the run.

They returned a few minutes later. Hettie held Aaron's precious record player, and Noah the much heavier case of albums.

"Let's have some music!" Aaron declared. "That'll keep the rhythm going."

It was the first time for most of them hearing the sounds and voices of the future. Just out of pure reaction, Fred made a face, but Margaret saw his expression change when he glimpsed the delight exhibited by his daughter. It seemed one could teach an old dog new tricks. Or songs. But the beat of the new music did keep everyone keen. Perhaps it was like the drums on a galley, but with less whipping. She grinned to herself at the thought. Aaron had been right. It was an aid to productivity. She had to learn to relax and let things be.

By nightfall, hands were raw and backs were stiff, but the

workers were jubilant. Sir Timothy was summoned from the house to take account of the weavers' output.

"There we are, Squire!" Master Matthew said, proudly, brandishing the big pair of shears to cut the weaves loose with a ceremonial flourish. "Seven full bolts, and one nearly done."

"It'll be perfect in the morning, sir," Sam Crowforth said, abashed. "Had to replace two heddle wires. It put us behind."

Sir Timothy walked among the looms, stroking a length of cloth here and there, stopping to admire the fine indigo-blue brocade on Master Walter's machine. He came to the end of the long room and clasped hands with Master Blackford.

"I am proud to say that I employ the finest weavers in England," he declared. As tired as they were, the workers cheered. "In celebration, I declare tomorrow to be a half-holiday! You'll all be given full pay."

Alder Wilkinson stood up and held his hands high. "To the best employer in England!"

Everyone roared their approval. Margaret was proud of them all. It was the best day she could imagine. Everyone had surpassed themselves. Aaron was safe, and their future was assured.

"Go on home, then," Sir Timothy said. "Sweep up, and I'll see you all tomorrow afternoon. Come up with us, Master Blackford. Let us drink to our good fortune."

"Gladly," said the guild master. "Master Aaron? After you."

# Chapter 41

Ben Sandown rode west at the head of the company of mercenaries. A distant church clock struck nine. Rain threatened ahead, but it was hours away. Plenty of time to make their destination and do what needed doing. They were making haste. Beside him, Captain Rawl kept his gaze far out on the road. That was why Ben liked to work with him. He didn't like surprises, and did everything possible to gain intelligence in advance. A good thing, too, when dealing with the irregular troops riding behind.

Beginning before dawn, they'd ridden from one to another of the confiscated manors to collect the available mercenaries. He left a couple of reasonably trusted men in each to make sure that the dispossessed families didn't try to enter them in the absence of the larger force. Not only did he have most of his original company, but in reply to his latest letter, the Earl of Cork had given him leave to employ another squad of German and Irish soldiers for pay for this specific enterprise, giving him a force of forty strong men. Although their armaments and weaponry varied hugely, every one of them had at least two pistols with fifty balls and powder. Some had muskets with ammunition. All were armed with viciously sharpened knives. A number had swords, but those were an odd collection from different armies and nations. Strahan, an Irishman who had never been anywhere east of London, possessed a Russian saber that was his pride and joy. To his credit, he wielded it with a skilled hand and fierce glee. Ben was glad that he was the one paying the man's salary, and not his opponent. In all, it wasn't a polished band, but it had proved an effective one. They'd had no trouble fulfilling the orders he had given them.

Most of the defiant northern landowners were a simple eviction and dismissal. He was under strict instructions to make certain that the greatest asset of the property was safely obtained, and kept in good working order. Obeying that instruction was the reason why Ben had kept his position with Richard Boyle all this time. Too, he was curious to discover if indeed the machines in the de Beauchamp weavers' barn contained weaponry or not.

His lordship had a bee in his bonnet over that family, devil only knew why. His lordship had given him a solid bollocking in the last letter he had received over letting the boy escape. It stung a bit, and Ben had held back the information that the peddler he had hired to translate had thrown a fireball at him and managed to get away clean. Not only that, his lordship was unsatisfied by the report he had given on what they had elicited from the boy. Cork wanted to know more. Were the devices simple labor-saving weaving machines, or could they be stretched to other purposes? How many men were involved in the enterprise? Had they had any contact with other landowners? Was de Beauchamp raising an army?

No, he wasn't, at least from what Ben had seen on his visit to the estate. The artisans were hardly soldiers, although Ben had trained up good mercenaries from men like that. They were interested in nothing but their craft, their lives, and their rivalries, like poor old Cedric. Employing a couple of Germans—what of that? Until the American history books had begun to circulate, it was of no moment to see foreigners abroad throughout the country. Any alliances that had been formed in earlier days had fallen away. The isolation was doing Great Britain no real good. If King Charles wanted to make the events of the future come true, he was going about it in exactly the right way. In the meanwhile, Ben had a task to fulfill.

His lordship wanted possession of these devices at once, to give him time to explore their workings at his leisure. Another example set for the northern nobility that the king's fist could come down on them at any time, for any reason, and there was nothing that they could do about it. The benefit of a force like his meant that if something went amiss, his lordship, and the king, had the ability to say that they'd had nothing to do with it.

"Barlaston two miles ahead, sir," Captain Rawl said. His sharp eye had picked out a signpost amid the trees that was only just becoming visible to Ben.

He nodded sharply. "Keep formation. Speak to no one. The manor is on the southwest side of the town."

"Is there a road around the edge of town?" Rawl asked. "We'll draw attention."

"Not a good one. The closest is sadly rutted and has a stream passing over it at the bottom of a hill. The best track is on the other side of town, and we'll be seen either way. Best to go through and shame the devil. There's nothing the townsfolk can do to stop us." Ben grinned. "The weavers'll not even see us, as they'll all be in the barn at work. We'll be on them before they can do aught."

"Orders as usual?"

"Up to a point," Ben said. "Take the house, but make fast the outbuilding down slope where the weavers work. His lordship wants the machines preserved intact."

"And the workers?"

"Dissuade any of them that resist," Ben said. "I believe they'll fall into line if you need to discipline one at the outset."

If Captain Rawl was curious as to what was so special about a room full of weavers, he didn't ask. Another good reason why he was the leader of choice. He'd served for twelve years in the army of the Electorate of Saxony, and moved on when he didn't get promoted. It was all political, as the officer put over him was a cousin or nephew of the Elector, John. Too bad. He should have been a colonel by now. Saxony's loss, England's gain.

At a copse of trees near the next mile marker, they halted for any of the men who needed to adjust their saddles or take a piss. Once they got moving, he didn't want any delays. Rawl rode around the group, taking note of loose breastplates or helmets set too far back on heads and barking corrections at them. A stream running next to the road gave the horses a chance for a last drink. Ben twitched with impatience in his own saddle.

Soon they were on their way at an easy trot. This should be a straightforward eviction, an hour or two at the most to see the squire and his family on their way. A good reward awaited him and his men once he had secured the aqualators for the king.

✧ ✧ ✧

A salamander in fire was the banner fluttering over the horseman at the head of a long double file of soldiers. James Douglas, second son of William, 1st Marquess of Douglas and friend and cousin to Archibald Campbell, Marquis of Argyll, nodded to a passing carter. The man, hauling a load of cloth-wrapped bales northward on the road leading to Stoke-on-Trent, gave a wary look at the ranks of kilted horsemen. As their redheaded leader with the long face and tidy trimmed beard didn't seem hostile or much interested in him, the tradesman smacked his beast's rump with his whip and carried on along his way.

The men laughed as the small wagon disappeared over the hill behind them.

"We'll be a nine-days' wonder to him, no mistake," James said.

"It feels like we've been abroad nine days already," said his companion, Henry Paisley.

"It's no' been that long. Ye haven't had enough time to grow calluses on yer buttocks. But I'll be glad to relax once we arrive."

"I hope they've room to put us up," Henry grumbled.

"Ye've slept on a battlefield before this," Alex said cheerfully to his friend and long-time lieutenant. "At least no one is trying to blow yer head off."

"And that's a small comfort!"

James chuckled. The sun had risen high enough that it was striking him squarely in the eyes as they rode south. He pulled the brim of his hat down to shield them. Three days on the road so far, with another half-day, or so James estimated. He was glad to do a favor for his cousin, Archibald. He hoped that the twenty-four soldiers at his back wouldn't be needed, but prepared was better than taken unawares. They'd all served in the Scots Regiment in France, and returned home again five months before. James had gladly ceded the colonelcy to another Scots commander who was on fire to prove himself in service to the French king. He'd welcomed Archibald's mission, as he had not yet decided what to do with himself since his return. A second son had to make his own way in the world. What was the old saying? The first son was the heir, the second went to the military, the third to the church. He'd done the second, and now had no office to which to return. He'd been raised in the Catholic faith, but was hardly fanatic enough to want to spend his life in holy orders.

Ah, well, he'd see what he would do once he returned to

Scotland from England. From the rumors, all hell was bound to break loose up there with regard to the disagreement between the Catholic Church and the Protestants. Might be a position for a well-trained soldier such as himself.

He let his horse have his head, and set an easy pace southward.

Gaynor, the barmaid of the Four Alls, dropped the dishpan she had been emptying in the rear yard of the inn, and came rushing inside.

"Soldiers!" Her voice squeaked. She took a deep breath. "Soldiers! A whole army! Riding this way!"

"What?" Master Blackford asked, enjoying his second pint of the day. Nearly all of the estate's weavers were enjoying a morning drinking. They meant to take full advantage of the half day off, as Sir Timothy had granted them, and the guild master thought it would be a fine idea to join them. He set down his mug. "You must be mistaken, Gaynor my girl. There's no battles going on hereabouts."

"See for yourself, master," Gaynor said. She rushed to the window and pulled it ajar. Half the patrons in the tavern crowded around her to look. Ivy Wilkinson ducked underneath the guild master's arm to see.

Two men wearing armored breastplates and shining helmets led a double file of riders that seemed to stretch most of the way through the small village. Anyone could see that the men had guns and swords. Their faces were grim set. At the pace they were going, it wasn't a pleasant day's ride out, no, indeed.

"By heaven," Ned Bywater said, horrified. "It's not an army, but there's dozens of them."

"What can their aim be?" Gaynor asked. She appealed to her father, the barman, who watched the parade with a speculative eye.

"They want nothing here," he said. "They're not even looking around them. No, they're passing through this town."

"But where? Where are they bound?"

"There's only one place," Fred Wilkinson piped up from his table near the bar. "They're bound for the squire's manor. That's the way they're heading."

"No!" Master Blackford said. "Fred, you've got to be mistaken."

"I'm not," the master weaver said stubbornly. "There's naught that lies in that direction but Churnet House! He's been worried about the king's men for a long while. Ye've all heard the rumors of other lords being turned out and made homeless. What if that should happen to the squire?"

Daniel Taylor looked appalled. "Why would that happen? He's paid his taxes. And the brocade has been bringing in plenty of money. What we made yesterday would nearly pay a quarter's levy."

"But the taxes have been going up for us all," Master Matthew agreed. "And the squire's been having a rough couple of years. You know our wages hadn't increased until recently. Spring quarter day was months back. If the king's assessors have only just been working their way through the rolls, they could be here for a missed payment."

"But we've been working our way back to prosperity all this summer," Ned said. He sent a guilty glance back toward the corner, where Cedric Hollings was drinking by himself. The fourth master weaver still had not been readmitted to Sir Timothy's good graces yet, nor had his journeyman, but Ned was a more social man. "I'm sure that Piers Losen has sent the money to the king."

"We don't know what goes on in that man's head," Master Walter said.

"Do not speak so of the reeve," Master Blackford said. "Piers is a good and faithful servant, and skilled at his work. It must be another destination they are bound for."

"Stop this knocking about," Fred said. "If these soldiers are bound for the squire's house, it could be the end of our prosperity! No more brocade. No more brocade, no more rich takings."

"As if you gave a care for the brocade," Walter said.

"Master Twelvetrees, this is unworthy of you!" Master Blackford said, shocked.

Fred's face turned bright red. "I give a care for the squire and his family. They've always been good to us. If the estate turns to the Crown, His Majesty won't care who runs the looms. We'll be out of jobs. Better to defend our own than let the king take it all over!"

"Aye," Daniel Taylor said, coming to stand with Fred. "We'll face down the soldiers and find out if it's a mistake that sent them here. If not, I'm prepared to fight for him!"

"Best not to face them empty handed," Master Matthew said, holding up cautioning hands. "Arm up, all of you. Who is with us?" He turned to look into the faces one at a time.

"I am!"

"And I!"

"I'm coming, too," Ivy said. Lily Dale put her arm around her friend.

"And so am I!"

"No, ye won't!" Fred said. "Go home, the both of you."

"It's our livelihood, and our friends," Ivy said.

"Let them come. I will stand with him, too," Master Blackford said. "He has been a good friend to the craft, and to all of us."

With the guild master's endorsement, one after another rose to their feet. They all knew the truth. Sir Timothy de Beauchamp had always had their backs, and he must not face injustice alone.

"I'll come," Cedric Hollings said, his voice hoarse. He made his way to stand beside Fred. "I've made a mistake. I won't make another one."

"And welcome you are!" Master Blackford barked out orders, as if the roomful of weavers was a band of apprentices. "Get home, find what arms you can. We can't get there before the soldiers do, but we'll be there soon enough. Spread the word and let anyone else who will join us come as soon as they may. We have to defend the squire!"

"What in the infernal regions?" old Jacob Damson asked, as the sound of jingling of horse tackle reached his ears. The balding septuagenarian drew himself up from his chair with some difficulty and made his way out behind the tall iron gate. "No one is expected today until the afternoon."

"Is it a goods wagon?" his granddaughter Anne asked. She came out, wiping her hands on her apron. She had been sorting berries for jam on the table in the kitchen of the gatehouse and left red smears on the starched white of her pinafore.

"Ranulf's wagons don't sound like that," Jacob said. His eyes widened as horsemen in armor trotted up the road and halted at the gate. "Soldiers! Who are you?" he demanded.

"Open up!" the first horseman shouted at him. "Open in the name of the king!"

Jacob peered through the iron bars at them. "I do not open without my gentleman's permission, sir. State your name and your business, and I'll put it to him."

The leader signed to a couple of his men. They swung off

their mounts and pulled at the gates, trying to open them. Jacob was glad to have them firmly locked.

"Now, you stop that at once!" he yelled. "Andrew! Go get the squire! On the trot!"

Andrew Catlow came out of the woodshed, the axe still in his hand from chopping firewood. At the sight of the soldiers, he took off running toward the house.

"Stop him," the leader called over his shoulder.

One of the men on horseback lowered a musket to his shoulder and cocked back the hammer. Jacob saw the movement. He threw himself at the iron bars, his hand outstretched in supplication.

"No!" he begged. "No, don't do it! It'd be murder. Please!"

*Bang.* Jacob turned in horror. Andrew went limp and fell full length on the ground. Anne ran to him and turned him onto his back.

"Dad! Dad!"

"No, Anne, no!" Jacob said, hobbling to kneel beside her. "Go to the house. Tell the squire. Oh, Andrew, my boy. Go on!" He pushed the girl to her feet. She needed no further urging, and left her grandfather sobbing over her father's body.

"Over you go," Ben said to the soldiers shaking the gates. "Get the key from him. Move!"

The two men stopped tugging at the wrought iron. One of them put his hands together, and the other stepped into it. He pulled himself over the tall spikes and dropped easily to the ground. With a couple of steps, he reached the gatekeeper and pulled him up by his shoulder. Ben could see that the old man was frail and probably weighed less than eight stones.

"Give me the keys, granddad," the soldier said. "Give them!"

Jacob, still weeping, took the keys from his belt and threw them a dozen feet away.

The soldier put a scornful foot in the old man's belly and shoved him over. Jacob fell next to the still-bleeding body of the younger man.

The gate was well-oiled and swung open without a sound. The rest of the soldiers swarmed into the grounds.

By then, the house had been warned. The little girl had raced toward it, screaming and pointing back toward her grandfather. One of the gardeners, a burly man with a monk's tonsure of gray hair, swept her off her feet and carried her inside. The door slammed shut. Windows that had been open to take in the summer breeze were pulled in and latched. From the rear of the house, a slender man with long legs took off running. He disappeared down a slope.

"He's gone for help," Rawl said.

"That won't hold us out long," Ben said. "Give your orders."

"Dismount! Form up," Rawl commanded. "Four rows. Stay well back until we see if they've got any guns."

"Bah," Ben said. "If the squire ever saw service, it was twenty years back. The most they'll have is a fowling piece or so."

The mercenaries tied their horses to stakes and armed themselves with pistol and sword.

"Be ready," Ben said. "The king's newest asset must be disturbed as little as possible."

# Chapter 42

The entire de Beauchamp family and the Craigs looked up from their plates at the echoing sound. Hettie, who had been helping Margaret to potatoes, set the platter on the table with a thump.

"That's a gunshot," Sir Timothy said. "Are the gardeners shooting at a fox?" He rose from his chair and hurried toward the front door.

Margaret heard the young girl screaming and followed her father out. Nat strode beside her, his long legs eating up the yards faster than she could move. One of the footmen already had the door open. Anne Catlow hurtled toward them, pointing back over her shoulder.

What lay behind the girl was a horror none of them expected to see. A host of men in armor with guns and drawn swords advanced toward the house. On the ground near their picketed horses, Jacob Damson knelt with a man's head in his lap.

"They've shot Andrew," Sir Timothy said, his eyes wide with horror. "Get down into the cellar, Margaret! Take your mother and your sister down with you, now!"

At that moment, Hubert, the head gardener, rushed up, seized Anne under his arm, and all but fell up the steps into the front hallway. Sir Timothy and the footman slammed the door shut and barred it.

"To arms!" her father called out. "Everyone, find any weapons you can muster! Here, Martin," he said, as the Craigs came rushing out into the hallway. "Help me pull furniture in front of the door."

"What about Jacob?" Margaret asked. Her father directed the men toward the bookcase that stood in the sitting room. It was the heaviest piece of lumber in the house. Dumping precious books in all directions, they dragged it and set it up against the door. Martin lifted a cabinet up over his head and pushed it against the rear of the bookcase. They piled chairs against it, hooked underneath knobs and handles.

"They don't care about him," Sir Timothy said, looking about for more barriers. "We must all survive so we can see to his solace later on. Go into the cellars, my dear. Bar the door. Protect yourself."

"We will not leave you to defend the house alone," Lady de Beauchamp said. She seemed to float into the room like a nymph.

"My dear, obey me," Sir Timothy said. "I can't defend the house if I have to look after you as well."

Delfine shook her head. "It is my house as well, Timothy, and these are my children! Margaret, go into the kitchen. I know Mrs. Ball was making soup today. Tell her and the scullery maids to pull the pot up the stairs to Nathaniel's bedroom."

"Right above the front door," Nat said, with a grin. "I'll help them, Mother."

"This is not a game!" Sir Timothy bellowed. He and the others had begun piling other furniture up against the windows. "Run down to the barn and fetch the weavers! Tell them to bring anything they can find to use as weapons."

"You can't," Margaret said. "They're still on their half-day off."

Sir Timothy stopped, looking stricken. "Then get the farmhands, and anyone else you can find."

"I'll go, sir," Percy said, raising a hand. "I'm faster than Master Nat."

Nat nodded agreement.

"Good man. Go!"

The youth spun on his heel and dashed toward the kitchen. Margaret and Hettie followed him. She gave Mrs. Ball her mother's instructions.

"Heavens above, good soup wasted!" the housekeeper declared. She turned to the others. "Well, you heard the mistress! All of you together! We'll need more than one barrage. Liza, fill that with water and set it boiling." She pointed to a large copper pot with a wire handle. "Take cloths, this is both hot and heavy. Not you, mistress," she admonished Margaret.

"Oh, yes, me," Margaret said, in a tone that would not permit argument. "It'll need all of us. Hettie, help me." She took a handful of cloth from the pile of neatly folded towels on the sideboard to shield her hands and helped hoist the rounded-bottom copper cauldron from the fire. Hettie followed her example, as did the other kitchen maids. The savory broth inside it sloshed up and back as they moved it at an agonizing pace at a time toward the rear staircase. Bones and pieces of potherb surfaced and sank again, making *bloop* noises. It was hot, heavy work, and Margaret thought more than once that they would lose control of the round monstrosity. All of them were well splashed with soup by the time they managed to wrestle it up the narrow stairs.

"I've absorbed more dinner than I'll get to eat later," Hettie said. Margaret gave a grim chuckle.

"A moment," Mrs. Ball gasped out, signing for them to put the pot down on the hall carpet for a moment. "I never thought in my life we would have to wage siege warfare in this house!"

By then, word had spread to the rest of the household. The housemaids snapped iron curtain poles and ancient weapons that had been mounted on the walls as decorations and piled them in a heap for the men to take. The footmen armed themselves and took up positions on either side of the door and the windows. The groundskeepers had a few guns, which they armed and handed around.

Lady de Beauchamp was already at the casement of her son's bedroom window. Margaret had to admire her mother's ingenuity and sharp eyes. The sill was exactly wide enough to permit the pot to balance on it.

The women wrestled the broad copper pot into the room, and prepared to lift it to its perch.

"Not yet," Delfine said, holding up a slender hand. "We have to wait until they try to breach the door. We'll boil as many of them as we can."

"Mother, you astonish me," Margaret said, regarding her with admiration. Her mother, whom she had thought of as delicate and beyond physical matters, patted her cheek. Her hands were cool and gentle, as they always were.

"My darling, I don't know why you would be astonished. I've always thought that you take after me."

"They're making a rectangle," Petronella said, kneeling at the window and peering up over the sill. "What does that mean?"

"It means, my darling, that we have to fight for our lives," Lady de Beauchamp said.

"What now, sir?" Captain Rawl asked Ben. The mercenaries had been chivvied into four rows of ten facing the door. None of them looked pleased at the idea of facing an enemy of unknown strength. "Do you want us to charge the door, or try one of the other entrances?"

Ben regretted letting the dragoon shoot the gatekeeper's man. Having to face just a locked gate would only have slowed them by minutes, not hours. They'd lost the element of surprise. Still, the estate was sufficiently isolated to make this an easy enough task. He must not lose sight of the important elements.

"Send men to the weavers' shed, down there," he said, pointing. "That must be secured. If there is anyone inside, take them prisoner. They are the only ones who know how to operate the machinery. And if you see a boy with brown hair, bring him to me. Do not damage anything inside unless I send an order."

"As you wish. Twelve men! Two shillings each to take the woolen mill!" Rawl barked an order, and a dozen of the mercenaries separated themselves from the main body. Pistol muzzles pointing upward, they ran toward the rear of the manor house. Rawl pointed his chin toward the house. "They're watching us. I can see movement in every window."

"Let them watch," Ben said, with a vicious grin. "Maybe it will move them to surrender. I hope so, for their sake. Form up and make ready!"

"Who are they?" Nat asked. He held onto a pike that had come off a plaque in the sitting room. Aaron had its twin. Both of them were frightened to death. "What do they want?"

"Anne Catlow said they were crying out that they were king's men," Sir Timothy said. He held an axe brought to him by one of the gardeners. Every man—and woman—around the estate had come into the house with saws, hammers, pickaxes, garden shears, pitchforks, and every hand tool they could find. But they were no more than forty in number, and no one but the reeve and a few of the old men had ever served as soldiers. Aaron had talked with enough of them to know.

"If that's so, then why didn't they just ask to see you?" Martin asked. He was filling the upper pocket of his shirt with shotgun shells from a cardboard box.

Sir Timothy turned a grim face to him. "This is not an official visit, sir. I am certain this is connected to Aaron's abduction."

"The aqualators?" Martin asked. "They're of no use to anyone if they take them out of the installation."

"They do not intend to take them anywhere," Sir Timothy said, peering out through the bottom of the window. "They mean to be rid of those who are the rightful owners, one way or another. Yes, there they go. A company of them is moving downhill. Thank the Lord that the weavers are not there to be attacked by them."

Aaron felt cold, as though his whole body had been thrown in an icy stream. Every moment of that terrifying night came back to him. He cursed his injured feet. Those were still in bad condition from his forced cross-country barefoot walk. Lady de Beauchamp had spread ointment on them, bound them up in soft lint, and given him a pair of felted woolen slippers to wear over them, but every step still hurt.

With a sinking heart, he realized that he had left his record player and box of albums in the weavers' barn. The battery was charging next to the stream, wrapped in oilcloth to protect it from the weather. The raiders wouldn't see that, but the phonograph was impossible to miss. He couldn't let that be taken. Any up-timer gadget that fell into the possession of down-timers would arouse more questions. Not to mention the fact that his mother would strike him dead if he came back to Grantville without it.

He rose quietly. Nat gave him a puzzled look, but Aaron held up a hand to forestall any outburst. Taking the pike, he made his way through the kitchen.

The cooks and footmen near the doors held kitchen tools and wickedly long knives.

"Where do you think you're going?" Mrs. Ball asked him.

"I've got to go down and get something out of the barn," he said. "It's urgent! It'd be bad for Sir Timothy if they find it."

Mrs. Ball, alarmed, nodded to the nearest footman to unbar the door.

"Hurry up, lad," she said. "Get back here safely."

The twelve men were far enough away not to see him as he slipped down the hill and dashed the short distance to the barn door. It swung ajar. The two people who had been watching it overnight were either in the house or close by, waiting to defend it.

He spotted the box of records near Fred Wilkinson's old-fashioned loom. Funny how Ivy's dad still pretended he hated all things up-timer, but you could tell he really liked Barry Manilow and Carole King when Aaron played them. Aaron gathered the scattered albums and put them into the plastic case. He had just stacked the record player box on top of it, when he heard the sound of jingling and footsteps outside the door.

No time to get away. He shoved the two boxes into the shadows against the wall. As the men came inside, he dove for the shelves of finished woolens and burrowed in among them.

"*Nicht* anyone herein," one of the men said.

"Makes it easy, then," another answered him. "Weavers, eh? Me old uncle was a fuller. Stamped many a length of woolens, he did. Gad damn, the smell would choke ye."

Aaron held his breath. The strong odor of lanolin and dust tickled his nose. He pinched it between his thumb and forefinger. He must not sneeze. His eyes watered. He couldn't hope to outrun them. His heart pounded so loudly, he was sure the men could hear it.

"Breach the door!" Captain Rawl shouted. When no one moved, he looked at Ben.

"One gold pound for each of the first five men through the front door!" Ben bellowed.

At once, a handful of men unlimbered axes they'd been carrying on their backs and dashed toward the house. Another bunch scrambled after them, swords and pistols at the ready.

Shots came from the windows to either side of the door. The mercenaries returned fire, ducking behind the axemen to reload their pistols.

Ben watched with satisfaction as the men set to chopping at the fine old carved portal, splinters and chunks of wood flying everywhere. The squire had been hiding secrets from his lordship and the king. Now he was going to lose everything. It was a handsome house, all red brick with ornate trim, like it had been touched by an artist's hand. Maybe Ben would set himself up as the caretaker. He fancied the life of a country lord.

A gunshot report came from the left window. One of the axemen let out a curse and fell, dropping his axe. The other axemen ducked down, and the pistol-wielding soldiers returned fire in wreaths of black smoke. The solid boom of the door as it was being struck became a squeal of wounded wood being wrenched out a long splinter at a time. One man after another went down from the defenders' gunfire. They fired back, but only God knew if they hit anyone.

"Close in!" Rawl commanded, waving his arm over his head. "The door's almost down! Come on, you mannikins! You'll earn no gold by staying out! Charge!"

The rest of the dragoons let out a war cry and raced to join their fellows.

James Douglas raised his head at the distant noise. It wasn't thunder. No, all too familiar. It came from the south, in the direction they were riding.

"That's gunfire," Henry Paisley said.

"Seems as though we're right on time," James said. He twisted in his saddle. "Ride on! Ride on! We're needed! Douglas to the rescue!"

He spurred his horse. Henry and his steed galloped right beside him. The troop followed, bellowing, "Douglas to the rescue!"

As the mercenaries reached the doorstep, they heard a wrench of wood from above. The ones who looked up to see the source of the noise got caught in a waterfall of brown liquid. Ben was far enough away not to get splashed, but the ones who were drenched bellowed in pain.

"Boiling oil!" one of the men cried, his cheeks bright red.

No, it smelled more like soup. Chunks of carrots, onions, and marrow bones decorated the man's helmet and shoulders. Ben almost laughed at the cheekiness of the householders. Pouring soup on the intruders from an upper window! He couldn't fault them for courage. But it was useless. They'd almost breached the house.

"Keep chopping, boys!" Rawl shouted, as half the door swung off its hinges. "Almost there!"

The mercenaries with the axes kept hacking, but some of them held back. Ben knew half of them were bully cowards who would run off at any sign of resistance. A couple near the rear were sending him side-eyed glances, as if they were going to race back to their horses and leave.

"I'll kill anyone who retreats!" he shouted. He hoisted his pistols. "D'ye want to try me?"

None of them did. They worked on pulling down the door, ducking when they heard more shots. They fired back. A cry of pain came from the right window. They'd winged or killed one of the defenders, at least.

There was a sudden silence from within, and the gunfire stopped. Had Sir Timothy shot his load?

No, he spotted movement above once again.

"Fall back! Fall back!" Ben cried.

Too late. The men at the door got a shower of boiling water and ran away from it, howling in pain and wiping at their eyes. This time some of them did cut and run. Ben fired his pistols at their retreating backs. One of them dropped, shot in the back like the coward he was. The other swung onto his horse and galloped out of the gate.

But the door was breached at last. A wide piece of furniture stood in the way. The rest of the mercenaries were so angry at the attacks from above that they shoved it bodily.

It crashed into the front hall of the manor, and the soldiers poured into the house. They were met by a number of men wielding the most absurd assortment of weapons. There was a noise like a stick hitting a hollow box, and the first man in went down, bleeding from a dozen places. A ratcheting sound followed, and another man dropped with the same wounds.

The mercenaries didn't like being fired on, especially with a weapon that left a dozen holes in the victim. Some of them tried to retreat, but Ben shoved his gun in their faces. It wasn't loaded, but they didn't have to know that.

"Move in, you cowards!" he shouted.

"That's gunfire," Master Matthew said. He rode with one of the apprentices sitting pillion behind him. The boy held a pair of polearms that had belonged to his grandad and Master Matthew's own musket held barrel-up. Master Blackford rode a fine dark bay that pranced like a warhorse. He had a set of silver-hilted pistols in his belt. His beadle, Paul Thornton, had Alder Wilkins behind him on a massive brown gelding.

The others, either crowded into wagons or on their own horses, looked concerned.

"They're under attack at the house," Fred Wilkinson said. He sat on the front of his family's cart beside his two sons. Ivy Wilkinson had argued that she should come, too, but he had threatened to tie her to the doorpost. "We're closer to the barn. Save the looms! They're unique across all of Great Britain!"

The contingent of weavers diverted from the main road and took the lane that led to the narrow bridge across the stream behind the shed. All the while, they heard more sounds of banging, shouting, and further shots fired.

"In with you!" Ben shouted, pushing the men ahead of him. The hallway was blocked by numerous pieces of furniture. He caught a glimpse of men behind them, but he couldn't count how many. Only a few seemed to have firearms, but they wielded other missiles. Pieces of ironwork and bricks came hurtling over the barricades at him and his men. "They've not enough weapons to hold us off! Take everyone inside prisoner! If they fight back, kill them!"

The sound of ratcheting came again. The mercenaries, their eyes wild, crouched in time before the hollow box noise arose. It saved some of them from a broadside barrage of tiny pellets, but the blast was large enough that they were peppered in the neck and shoulders. A couple pinged off Ben's breastplate and struck him in the chin. He hissed in pain.

"Kill them all!" he snarled. "Ten gold pounds for the man who brings me the squire."

The mercenaries let out a wild cry of glee. The injured fell away to bind up their bleeding wounds, and were replaced by more eager hands.

But they were under attack by more than the hollow box gun. A filleting knife zipped through the air toward Ben's face. By pure instinct, he flinched away. It struck one of his men in the arm, who dropped his pistol. Ben stooped for the gun, and shot it over the heap of upholstered chairs to his right. A wail of pain came from behind it.

Ben shoved it over and plunged into the room beyond, and took in the scene with a sweeping glance. The place was defended only by a few men and boys.

Sir Timothy was waiting with an ancient blunderbuss that his father had used to kill wild boars. The moment the heap of armchairs toppled over, he stood up and pulled the trigger. It exploded, throwing him backward. One of the invaders fell, blood gushing from a massive hole in his chest. The squire ducked around the corner to reload the gun.

The gardeners and foresters struck at the invaders with bill-hooks and tree saws. Martin Craig dipped down to reload his shotgun and came up looking for another target. A wild-eyed man came after him wielding a curved sword. Martin had to retreat. He dodged away, letting Noah, armed with a pitchfork, come in between him and the soldier. The two of them tangled. The undergardener, used to wrestling with stubborn briars, was by far the stronger man. He twisted the pitchfork. With a cry, the soldier found his arm being bent back. The sword blade snapped between two tines of the fork. Noah brought the head of the fork around and clouted the soldier in the side of the head. The soldier yelled and went for Noah with both hands outstretched. Noah swung the fork back the other way and knocked the man to the ground. The soldier behind him started to back away. Noah pressed toward his new target with a terrifying grin on his face.

Martin looked around him, his expression one of concern.

"Aaron! Where is Aaron?" he shouted.

"Went down for his phonograph!" Nat called to him.

"He did what?"

At the sound of Aaron's name, one of the men looked up. At that moment, Martin recognized him.

"Ben!" he shouted.

The man turned, and Martin saw the pockmarked cheeks. Yes, it was the down-timer who had come to inspect the weavers' barn with one of the guild masters. They recognized each other at once. Martin drew his shotgun up to shoot, but Ben ducked down behind a couple of the invaders to shield himself.

Martin clambered over the makeshift barricade and went after the man, shoving his way through the melee. No one was going to get away with kidnapping his son. Ben fled, not caring what happened to the people behind him.

Martin pursued Ben out into the courtyard, swatting the invaders aside. There were so many of them compared with the few household staff who were capable of withstanding them. The air was heavy with black powder smoke, making his eyes tear. As he leaped down the stairs after his quarry, Hubert the gardener swung a mattock and connected with the chest of a man in an ill-fitting red uniform coat. That man toppled over and didn't move, but two more men rushed Hubert from behind and shoved him over. One of them grabbed up the mattock and brought it down on the gardener's head. Martin saw that and hip-shot the attackers with a full blast from his shotgun. They went down screaming. But there were more behind them, too many more, all pouring into the house. The women of the household were throwing things down on the invaders, but most of their missiles were doing little damage. Martin loaded another pair of shotgun shells, but it was futile.

In a moment, they would be overrun.

Then, the sound of a horn echoed across the ground. Martin looked up to see another troop of soldiers hammering through the gate on horseback. He drew up his shotgun, ready to make the shells count. Then he hesitated. Unlike the invaders, these were in matching uniforms—and Martin caught a glimpse of bare knees. They were wearing kilts. Scotsmen? What were they doing here? Finishing up the attackers' job for them?

The horsemen hammered across the lawn, coming to a halt nearly at the steps. They swung down from their saddles, swords drawn, and waded into the fray. Unlike their opponents, they moved with practiced skill, defending against blows and striking back on the downstroke.

"Looks like we are dead on time!" their captain said, when he saw Martin gawk at him. "Lower yer weapon, sir. We're here ta help ye."

When the Scottish cavalry appeared, terror started to spread through the mercenaries on the manor house steps. Ben saw some of them pull away from the attack and flee toward their picketed horses. They couldn't face trained soldiers, and they knew it. Their only hope of survival was to run.

"Stop them!" he bellowed at Captain Rawl.

"Ye'll not get paid if you go!" the captain shouted, as one man after another legged it for the horses. There was another scrimmage, as the mercenaries went for any horse that they could reach. The rightful owners fought with them, often getting a knife in the hand or the eye. The horses wheeled, screaming, their hooves plunging as the men tried to get them under control.

"Leave them," Rawl said, his face set. "They're no help at all. We've got who we've got."

"Right," Ben said. The mission was failing, but he would still get vengeance on the landowner. The Earl of Cork would have to take other action against Churnet and Trent when he could. He shouted to the men who remained in the courtyard. "If we can't obtain the mill for his lordship, no one shall have it! Down to the barn! Burn it! Smash everything and go!"

"There are women and children inside," Martin told the Scottish captain. "Help us!"

"Aye, we're ready for it," the man said, showing white teeth in a fierce grin. "To me, men of Douglas!"

"Aye! Douglas to the rescue!" the Scotsmen bellowed. They charged the mercenaries, whose ranks parted before them like curtains opening. The kilted men scarcely got a half dozen blows in before the way was open to them. They bounded up the steps and into the house. Martin immediately heard men screaming for mercy.

"Are ye with us, man?" the leader asked him. He looked like a good fellow, young and bright eyed, with a neat red beard and large hazel eyes.

"I've got a score to settle first," Martin said. He looked around for Ben, but didn't see him. He did spot a couple of the invaders heading downslope toward the lane that led to the weavers' shed. He broke the twelve-gauge in half, tipped out the empty shells, and reloaded from his pocket, then strode after them. If Aaron was in the shed, he was going to get him out safely.

Margaret paused before dropping an alabaster Florentine bust on the milling fighters below, and looked out across the lawn at the sound of horse tack jingling. What now? What more disaster could possibly befall them?

Horsemen streamed toward the house. The second man held a banner aloft with a snake or some other twisty beast on it. She didn't recognize them, but saw that they were clad in woolen plaids and kilts. Scotsmen? Had the king sent for allies from the north to help take over their estate?

The men leaped off their horses and ran toward the door, pistols and swords at the ready. Margaret took aim at the leader, who was nearly underneath her. Then, he lifted his head, jaunty plume of his bonnet bobbing beside his face, and winked at her! She was so astonished that she let the bust slip out of her fingers.

It smashed down upon a couple of the invaders' heads, knocking them flat on the steps. She realized with a start that they were trying to run away from the Scotsmen. But did the de Beauchamps have two enemies, or only one?

"We should help the men," she called to her mother. "We do not know how they are faring."

"We are helping them, my dear. We are staying out of the way," Delfine said, coming up with a hefty, plain, dark wooden box that Margaret recognized as one in which Nat kept small treasures from his childhood. She threw it out of the window and was rewarded with a wild cry from below. "We can't fight soldiers hand-to-hand."

"We must be able to do something!"

The room was nearly bare now of ornaments and all Nat's possessions but one. Margaret couldn't bring herself to throw his precious guitar out, but everything else including the chamber pot underneath his bed had gone. She looked around for more missiles. There was nothing, unless they dismembered the bed frame. The heavy wooden trunk at the foot of it was too wide to go out of the casement.

They had barred the door, hammering a chair back underneath the handle, and tied torn bedclothes into ropes to secure the chair in place. Now they could do no more but huddle together with Petronella in the middle of the ring. Margaret's younger sister had seen this all as a great adventure at first, but now her nose was pink, and tears dripped down her cheeks. Delfine gathered her young daughter to her heart. She held out her hand to her elder, but Margaret shook her head. She had never felt so helpless. She was no coward, but the ongoing sound of gunfire and yelling had shredded her nerves. The frustration made her impatient. She must have more ammunition to use!

She tugged her brother's mattress onto the floor and pulled the slats out of the bedframe. Holding one of the dry boards to the fire in the grate, she waited until it was ablaze, then dropped it out of the window onto the fighters. She went back for another one. She would not stop until the nightmare ended.

Fewer and fewer men were below to receive the brunt of her attacks. Margaret felt satisfaction as more and more of the invaders ran away toward their horses and fled. She soon ran out of wood to burn. There was nothing else to be done until and unless they heard someone trying to break into their room. The curtain poles and the kitchen knives were ready for them to make their last stand, which she would with all the strength in her body.

Until...

"Margaret de Beauchamp, come forth!"

# Chapter 43

Martin dashed down the hill after Ben and the ragtag soldiers. He brought up his gun to fill them with buckshot, but they dodged back and forth, throwing off his aim. The ground underneath his feet was slippery. He only had four or five shells left. One of them had Ben's name on it.

The soldiers shouted as they dashed toward the barn. The door swung open, and two men peered out, looking puzzled. The rest came hurtling toward them and streamed inside.

"Burn it!" Ben shouted, at their heels. "Smash everything!"

Martin made it to the bottom of the grassy slope. If he'd thought about it, he never would have charged into a room alone with fourteen armed men, but Aaron could still be in there. He ratcheted back his shotgun and kicked the door wide.

The men inside were piling up a heap of cloth bales and smashing stools and pieces of looms on top of them. One knelt beside the pile with flint and steel, striking furiously to make a spark.

Martin was on top of them before the man could get the fire going, and kicked the steel out of his hand. The man turned terrified eyes up at him, and dashed out the doorway without a word.

"Come back here, you coward!" Ben snarled. The man vanished out of the door.

The rest of the men pulled shelves and tools off the wall and added them to the heap. Another knelt down with tinder and steel. He struck a light and tipped a ledger page into the small flame.

"Leave those alone!" Martin bellowed. He brought up his shotgun. Ben ducked behind the shelves of folded cloth. The up-timer hesitated. He didn't want to destroy the weavers' hard work, but he had the man cornered.

Then, to his horror, Ben reached down with a cry of triumph.

"Looking for him?" the pockmarked man asked. He hauled Aaron out of the heap of fabric bolts by his neck. Aaron struggled, but Ben had a tight grip on him. He pulled the boy in front of him.

"Are you all right, son?" Martin asked, keeping his voice as calm as he could.

Aaron couldn't choke out a reply, but he nodded.

Martin had the gun leveled at Ben's head. Martin could tell that he'd take a couple of buckshot pellets to the face. Blood had dribbled down his neck.

"Let him go or I will kill you."

"You speak English," Ben said. "So, it's true. You're not from the Germanies. You're an American!" He wore a fierce grin. A sharp knife suddenly appeared in his hand. He held it to Aaron's throat. Martin's son struggled until he felt the blade touch his skin, and froze. "Is that an American gun? I'll take that. Hand it over to me."

"Let my boy go."

"Not until I have that gun." Ben gestured with the knife. He kept Aaron in front of him.

The mercenaries started pulling the looms over. When they yanked the first aqualators away from the wall, water came spurting out of the valves.

The sudden jets of water distracted Ben for one vital second. The knife hand went wide.

"Drop, boy!" Martin shouted.

Aaron went limp and fell to the floor, away from the blade. Ben lost his grip on the boy. He bent over to grab him, but missed.

Martin, seeing his chance, waited for Ben to straighten up, and pulled the trigger. Ben threw up an arm to shield his face.

Most of the buckshot hit Ben in the chest and arm. They ricocheted off his breastplate and greaves, and knocked his helmet flying. Martin saw blood spurt from his wrist. He'd have to hit him lower. Stray pellets hit several of the ruffians pulling the shop apart. He racked the gun again.

But Ben was on the move. He was a skilled rogue. The mercenary ducked around his fellows, using them for cover. Martin tracked him with the shotgun's barrel, looking for the best shot.

Ben tore loose a piece of old Fred's loom and threw it at him. Martin sidestepped it and aimed again.

Then, he fell sprawling on the floor. Two of the men tackled him from behind and began punching him in the kidneys. One sat down on his back and began hammering his head against the floor.

Martin struggled to get up. He tried to turn his head. Had Aaron made it outside? The place was full of old, dried wood. It was going to go up in flames. He fought to hold onto his gun, but it seemed like ten people were trying to pull it out of his hands. Feet connected with his ribs, but he was not going to let go.

Aaron crawled underneath the leg of the nearest loom, then looked around. Dad! Dad was in trouble! Aaron crawled close to the wall of the weavers' shed, making for the door. It seemed a mile away. He had to get more help. No time to save the record player. His mom would much rather get Martin back in one piece than *Johnny Cash's Greatest Hits.*

The soldiers were creating chaos, flinging lengths of cloth out like they were making beds, and yanking the equipment away from the walls. One hefted a huge cone of dark blue yarn, Fred Wilkinson's pride and joy for his serge weaving, and heaved it at him. It hit Aaron in the side, knocking him over. The man laughed like crazy, and went on tossing around the neat spools and shuttles. Aaron rolled back onto his hands and knees and moved as fast as he could, ignoring his bruised ribs.

At last, he made it to the door. He climbed to his feet and scrambled outside. The manor house! There were soldiers fighting all around the side. Some looked like the men in the weavers' shed, but a lot more had on plaid skirts and broad caps like French berets. One of them spotted him, pointed and let out a loud whistle.

Aaron didn't wait to find out what the whistle meant. He didn't dare go that way. He hobbled as fast as he could toward the low bridge over the stream. He'd find help at one of the farms.

To his relief, he heard people shouting to him. A host of horses and wagons was riding toward him on the other side of the bridge. The weavers were back! Ivy stood up in the back of a cart and waved to him.

Aaron waved back frantically.

"Dad's in there! They're tearing up the barn!"

"The hell they are!" Fred Wilkinson bellowed, brandishing a pitchfork. He and his sons led a force of men armed with farm implements, shears, and all kinds of weird ironwork straight into the tall shed. Master Blackford spurred his horse over the span.

Smoke had begun to billow out of the building.

"Here you go!" Daniel Taylor tossed Aaron an ancient pickaxe fixed to a long handle. "Come on, we'll get your dad out! Some of you, get water! Hurry!"

Aaron charged after his friends.

Inside, the chaos had gotten far worse. One of the looms was on fire, and the invaders had pulled the aqualators down. Despite the water spraying them in the face, they were smashing the clay tiles on the floor. Their captain directed them from one loom to another, ensuring that none of the water computers survived intact.

"Now, you stop that!" Fred shouted. He rushed at them, ready to spear the captain with his fork. The man tried to dodge him, and tripped. Fred started beating him with the heavy metal tines.

"Let me go!" the man shouted in a German accent. "I surrender! Leave off!"

Two of the weavers hauled him to his feet and tied him up, using some of the ropes of yarn that had been strewn across the floor.

The other invaders tried to rush toward the door, but the weavers had no intention of letting them go. The rage at seeing their workshop in pieces sent them into a frenzy. The usually calm Daniel Taylor went after the men attacking Martin, smacking them with the billhook. They ducked, covering their bleeding heads. Daniel's apprentices gathered around, beating the attackers with their makeshift weapons. Martin rolled out from underneath the melee and came to his feet with the shotgun still in his hands. His teeth were clenched.

He spotted Aaron. "Get the record player and get out of here. Now!"

"Yes, sir!"

"I'll help you," Ivy said.

She and Aaron dashed to the end of the room and dove into the shadows where he had left the boxes. To his horror, Ben crouched there. He grabbed Ivy's wrist.

"Dad!" Aaron shouted.

This time, they weren't alone. At his cry, half a dozen apprentices and journeymen came rushing up behind him. Ben rose, holding his knife to Aaron's belly. He sheathed it and seized the pickaxe from Aaron's hand. The blade had been honed sharp. He put it underneath Ivy's neck.

"Now, you will let us out of here," the pockmarked man said. He coughed, as the smoke was getting thick. "Drop the gun and move back. Go!"

The crowd of defenders fell still. They moved backward, their eyes fixed on the man, the blade, and the girl. Martin dropped the shotgun. It clattered on the floor.

Ben pushed Ivy toward the door. He stooped to pick up the long gun, but Martin shoved it under the nearest loom with his foot. Ben snarled, but kept moving, backing away, never letting his eyes move from his opponents. The rest of the mercenaries moved with their leader. Aaron kept pace with Ben, staying far enough away not to endanger Ivy. He knew the subterfuge of distraction wouldn't work a second time. He shot his father a helpless look.

Martin let his eyes go over Ben's shoulder. Aaron wondered what he was seeing. They were nearly all the way out. Then—

Splash!

Alder and Samuel Wilkinson shot the buckets of water they were carrying straight into Ben's face. That was long enough for Ivy to kick Ben in the knee. He staggered. She twisted out of his grip and ran to her father. Aaron rushed at the man and wrestled for the axe. In moments, half a dozen men had pounced on Ben, kicking and punching him, forcing him to the ground. Martin slowly approached, the shotgun under his arm.

Ben looked up at him. He showed his teeth in a mouth filled with blood. "Yer going to shoot me now, aren't you?"

Martin swung the gun out and turned it barrel side up. "You're not worth the ammunition." He brought the stock down on Ben's head like a hammer. Aaron cringed at the THUD. Then, Martin turned and walked away.

None of those wrecking the equipment escaped, either. They

were tied up and marched outside, very much the worse for wear. Then everyone joined in a line to fill buckets from the stream and throw the water onto the blaze.

"It's a mercy that woolens won't burn easily," Master Matthew said, when the last smoldering ember had been stamped out. "We didn't lose much of them. They'll all have to be cleaned and treaded again to get the smell of smoke out of it. But, by the Lord, the aqualators! Every one of them is ruined!" He looked around in dismay.

"We'll send for replacements," Aaron assured them. "It'll cost for the rush order, but we could get them in a few months.

"Months! We've got orders to fill," Master Walter said, glumly. "These wretches have a lot to answer for."

"These men will face justice at once," Master Blackford said, his face set. "Is Sir Timothy all right?"

"Trapped in the house, sir," Aaron said.

He looked up the hill. The scene had gone quiet, too quiet. All of the fighting seemed to have stopped.

The weavers gathered themselves together and crept up the hill toward the house.

The line of men forcing themselves into the front hallway seemed never ending. Sir Timothy came around the corner again and discharged the ancient hunting rifle into the mass of invaders. Nat braced the historic pike at an angle. Two men ducked around the breach in the pile of furniture, swinging swords and long knives. When he saw the first appear, a burly man in a faded gray tunic, he jabbed the point into the man's side. The ruffian turned, snarling. Nat hadn't hit him hard enough to do any harm.

"Ah, that's no' the way to do it, master!" Will, one of the grooms, said. He swung a shovel at the man in gray and knocked him backwards. The man staggered and came back again, sword raised. Tim, another groom, met the blow with an iron rod from the stable. The two of them grappled, trying to disarm the other. The man pushed Tim away and slashed with his sword. Tim cried out. Blood welled up from his sleeve. Will smashed down on the intruder's head with the shovel. The man fell. Will kept raining down blows until the man stopped moving.

The second man raised a pair of pistols and fired. Nat ducked as soon as he saw them. The explosive discharge made his ears ring. He felt the rush of one ball pass overhead, but there was a burning sensation along his scalp. Hot liquid poured down into his eyes. Blinded by his own blood, he jabbed the point again and again, retreating past the door of the sitting room. Percy and two footmen pushed between him and the invaders. The man who had shot his guns drew a knife. Percy brought the metal rod down on his shoulder. The blade fell, but the ruffian went for him with outstretched hands. Nat jumped on the man's back and was swung around as if he weighed nothing, while the footmen wrestled with the other fighter. His blood spattered them both.

Behind him, his father and the groundskeepers were fighting with a seemingly endless line of men coming in from outside. Martin had never returned. He had gone out after one of the leaders. Things continued falling on the incomers from the window above, including burning brands. Bravo, Margaret, even if they barely slowed down the intruders.

"Keep them from going upstairs!" Sir Timothy cried. He tried to withdraw to load his rifle again, but it was impossible. Instead, he turned it to use the stock as a bludgeon.

Piers the reeve fought like a demon. The family knew that he had served the king in battle, hearing stories from him around the fire during the winter. They'd never seen his prowess in person. Now Nat understood why he had been given a commendation. He wielded a sword in one hand and a cook's knife in the other. A big man in a red coat went for Sir Timothy. The master of the house swung his blunderbuss and connected with the side of the man's head. He didn't even flinch. Piers lunged with his long blade and stabbed him in the back of the left knee. The man let out a gasp of pain, but kept moving. Piers closed the distance and brought the knife up, plunging it into the attacker's side. Blood welled, darkening the coat in a deeper shade of red. As the invader toppled, Piers turned, looking for other opponents.

Seeing their giant felled by the manor's swordsman, no invader wanted to face him alone. Three men circled Piers. The reeve made feints with his now bloody sword, keeping them out of arm's reach. He made a lightning-fast sally against the enemy on the left. Then, Nat heard a crack. Piers looked down at his chest, and deflated toward the floor. Thick, dark redness colored his normally neat waistcoat.

"Piers!" Nat cried. He couldn't tell if the man was alive or dead.

Sir Timothy, kept at bay beside the groundskeepers, took a hasty glance toward his fallen friend.

"Keep fighting, Nat," he said. "I pray he will survive. I pray we all will."

Nat stood with his back to the main staircase. He swung the pike at one face after another. He stopped seeing individual features or uniforms, only hitting out at people he didn't know. He dashed blood away from his face. The wound in his scalp stung. His arms felt heavier and heavier.

The attackers seemed endless in number. The servants were doing far more than he could. He was grateful for them. Soon, they were stepping on bodies. Some groaned, but others lay still. At least one had been speared by the pike in his hands. He had to keep fighting, to save his family. His mother and sisters were above stairs. They must be protected. He was a de Beauchamp. If only James was there. If only Julian had lived! He was the weakest of the brothers, and he knew it. But he would make his father proud.

Two men clambered over the fallen bookcase, heading straight for the stairs. They trod right on top of poor Piers. Nat swung the pike and hit their sword blades. They had more skills than some of his previous opponents. They parried and slashed at him. Nat's pike went flying. He fell on his seat on the lowest steps. The men rushed at him. Nat felt on the floor for a weapon, any weapon, and came up with Piers' sword in his hands. He gripped the hilt in both hands, and thrust it upward. To his amazement, it struck one of the onrushing thugs in the belly. The man gasped and his own sword fell. The other man brought his weapon down. Nat ducked, unable to forestall the blow, but the first man fell on top of him. He lay with his back on the stairs, pinned.

Then, a horn sounded from outside. All of them stopped still, looking out of the ruined front door. Horsemen, a whole company, came barreling toward the house. Around the dead man lying over him, Nat could just see them leaping off their steeds and rushing inside.

"Who are they?" Sir Timothy shouted.

Nat didn't know, but they must be allies.

They came in, swords flashing, and disposed of one of the ruffians after another with the precision of a well-trained troop. The attackers realized that they were now the quarry. A few fled at once, but the most of them surrendered. Nat looked up with huge eyes as a tall man with a neatly trimmed beard came in and pulled the body of the attacker off him. He helped Nat up with a steady, gloved hand. His fellows disposed of the assailants harrowing his father, tied up those who surrendered, and tossed the bodies of the dead out of the door onto the stairs. Of the fallen defenders, they knelt to offer aid. To Nat's relief, Piers was still breathing. A Scotsman with a pouch slung across his shoulder took lint and bandages out and pressed down upon the wound in the reeve's chest.

The leader came to doff his hat. The rest of the new arrivals arrayed themselves behind their leader.

"Sir Timothy de Beauchamp?" the tall man asked, offering his hand to Nat's father.

Sir Timothy gathered his wits and his dignity. His fine clothes were torn and splattered with blood. He straightened his lapels and clasped the outstretched hand.

"I am, sir. May I ask the name of our rescuer?"

"My name is James Douglas," the tall man said. "Son of William Douglas, Marquess of Douglas and Earl of Angus. I'm . . . a friend of a friend."

Sir Timothy frowned. "Who?"

"I'd rather say to the person for whom I was sent," James said. "Your daughter, Margaret."

"She . . . she is upstairs, sir," Sir Timothy said. He turned to Percy, whose arm was being bandaged by one of the newcomers. "Pray fetch Mistress Margaret."

"Nay," James said, with a broad grin. "Will you let me call her?"

"If you wish, sir. I owe you more than a mere shout at my daughter."

The tall Scotsman stood at the bottom of the stairs and let out a bellow that all but shook the house.

"Margaret de Beauchamp, come forth!"

Margaret heard the call. She looked out of the window. There did not seem to be a single living person outside. Amid the debris that she, her mother, and the servants had flung out, and the remains of the front door, lay a dozen or more dead bodies. A few of the picketed horses remained, but several had been taken in haste by the fleeing invaders. Instead, nearby the house was a couple dozen very fine steeds with polished tack and saddles. The newcomers had put an end to the fighting, but to *what* end? Did her father and brother survive? Where were the Craigs?

She looked at her mother. Delfine had stopped like a statue at the cry from below. Petronella still clung to her skirts.

"Who is that?" Margaret asked. "What do you think he wants? Where is Father?"

Lady de Beauchamp shook her head.

"If your father is not summoning you, then there are three possibilities, my child. One is that your father cannot call you, for one reason or another. Either he is wounded, or . . ." She swallowed. Margaret didn't need her to finish the sentence. "Or this is our conqueror, and he requires us to submit to him."

Margaret's blood froze in her body. She picked up one of the curtain rods and brandished it like a sword.

"Or?" She hoped the second alternative wasn't worse.

Delfine managed a tiny smile. "Or your father is allowing him to. Whichever it is, we cannot remain in here forever." She spread a hand toward the ruined bed and the lack of all other furnishings. "There is nowhere left to sit."

"Don't go, mistress," Hettie said, setting her chin in a defiant grimace. "I'll go and see what he wants."

Margaret pulled her spine as straight as the curtain rod. "I'll go myself. He wants me."

"Then I go with you, mistress," Hettie said. Margaret smiled at her. She took her friend's hand.

"Unbar the door."

The kitchen maids made way for her. Margaret held herself upright, her chin high. She was all too aware that her hair was all over the place, her lace collar was askew, and her dress had splashes of soup all over it. But she manifested the dignity of a queen, and walked down the stairs with Hettie at her side.

Below, her father and brother stood amidst a force of men in green, black, and gray. Despite the horrendous mess and blood everywhere in the anteroom, the newcomers were relatively clean and tidy. Sir Timothy met her eyes. She looked for reassurance in his gaze, but he kept his face solemn. Nat's face and shirt were covered with blood, and he had a white bandage covering the top of his head. Margaret was horrified, but she didn't dare show any concern or fear.

At the bottom of the stairs, a tall man with red hair and beard awaited her. As she came to the last step, he drew back a pace and removed his hat.

"Mistress Margaret de Beauchamp?" he asked.

"I am," she said, forcing her voice not to tremble.

He grinned broadly, showing teeth that were almost American in their whiteness. He felt in his belt pouch and brought out a small black box with a glass lens on the end. Margaret recognized it, and her eyes went wide.

"I am to tell you that Harry Lefferts sent me."

# Chapter 44

***September 1635***

Margaret sat in the family pew of the Church of St. John the Baptist, feeling exhausted. It was taking weeks for the ruin of the house and the weaving barn to be cleaned up. The repairs to the roof of the weaving shed and to the front door would take far longer. James, as he begged the family to call him, no title, had mustered his men to help Sir Timothy. They drove the surviving invaders toward the town gaol like sheep. Margaret didn't want to ask about their fate.

So many of the defenders had been injured, and four killed, including Jacob Damson's son-in-law, Andrew. Sir Timothy arranged with Mr. Olney to pay for the funerals. He included enough for a mass of thanksgiving, with gratitude offered for the timely intervention of the Scotsmen on Saturday, the eighth of September, the feast of the Birth of the Blessed Virgin. That day had come at last, and Margaret accepted it as a time to rest and reflect.

The church resounded with music from the huge pipe organ, operated by Mistress Tamsin with many flourishes and grace notes. The air was filled with scent from the enormous clusters of lilies, roses, and all the flowers of late summer that had been donated from the manor's gardens. Margaret breathed in the odor, trying to dismiss the feelings of loss. So much had changed in a single afternoon!

Several rows behind her, Martin Craig sat on the aisle, ignoring his son and Ivy Wilkinson. The two young people sat huddled together, Aaron's arm over her shoulders. Sometimes, the girl shed tears that the lad wiped away with the hem of his sleeve. It might be years before they saw one another again, if ever.

From Martin and Aaron, Margaret heard the account of the attack on the weavers' shed and the fire. While she and her father were grateful that the weavers had stepped in and no one had been grievously injured, the knowledge that their livelihood had been destroyed, or nearly so, weighed heavily on them. It had been hard to go visit the ruined building. The room stank of ash. Part of the roof was gone. The empty sky mocked her as she had surveyed the wreckage left by the raiders. All the looms had been damaged somewhat, and every single one of the aqualator trays was smashed to fragments. The pipes had been pulled from the walls, which now bulged from the water running into the wattle-and-daub between the ancient oak beams. Bolts of fabric were scattered like cards, and the invaders had somehow unwound hundreds or thousands of yards of thread all over the room like a mad spider's web. Fred Wilkinson moped around like a lost soul. The loom that had been passed down to him from several previous generations had been pulled apart and used for kindling by the mercenaries. He was on the verge of quitting the trade, until Margaret and the other weavers had talked him out of it.

Margaret felt deep affection for the men and women who worked for her and her father. They'd seen her through the worst thing that could have befallen them and were willing to work to bring all back to normal. She worried that the future dream was gone forever. With no aqualators, the brocade could not be produced, or not as quickly as it had been all that summer. They would have to write to numerous clients to tell them that their orders would be delayed, if not cancelled outright.

Her insistence that it was time for the Craigs to go home was now a vital requirement. With nothing to repair or teach anyone else to tend, there was no real need for them to remain in England. Though the people of Barlaston had entirely embraced them and kept their secret safe from anyone outside the community, their presence presented a danger to the de Beauchamps and to themselves.

With heavy hearts, Aaron and Martin had agreed to take ship as soon as possible. When the service of thanksgiving and the feast to be provided by Sir Timothy and Lady de Beauchamp ended, Ranulf Bracey stood ready to convey them all the way to Liverpool. The *Meadowlark* was scheduled to arrive on Monday, the tides being with them, and would convey them safely to Hamburg. Margaret could not thank them enough for all that they had done. Aaron had promised fervently to goad the factory at St. Malo to make new aqualators ahead of the de Beauchamps' competitors so the weavers could fulfill those remaining orders. He and Margaret had reluctantly agreed that Master Matthew and Daniel Taylor, soon to receive his mastership, could teach anyone the basics of maintenance. At least, she could rely upon the orders still outstanding from Admiral Simpson and the new Prime Minister, William Wettig, for standard, ordinary woolen fabric.

She gave a sigh for the loss of the brocade looms. What fabric they had completed was largely still intact, but for the overwhelming odor of smoke imbuing the wool. Master Blackford assured her that cleansing and fulling it all over again would take out the smell. The fabric would still command premium prices, and its scarcity might cause yet another bidding war. Her father's eyes, dulled from the disaster of the invasion and its aftermath, brightened at that. Margaret had argued fervently that of the remaining fabric, at least one bolt, probably two, must be sent with the Craigs back to Magdeburg to be given to Rita Simpson and her goodmother. They had waited long enough, in their kindness, and who knew how long it would be until more could be made? Very reluctantly, Sir Timothy had agreed. Margaret knew he saw gold slipping through his fingers with every yard he could not sell.

There were also moments that were both happy and sad. Hettie had taken her aside a few days ago to tell her, privately, but with shining eyes, that Oliver Mason had finally made his feelings known. If Margaret would allow her, she wanted to say yes to his proposal of marriage. Margaret felt a wrench, knowing that things would never quite be the same between her and her friend—yes, her friend—but she couldn't say no. She wanted Hettie to be happy. Hettie and Oliver were to have the banns read for the first time during that day's service. Hettie wore a crown of flowers and looked like she was already a bride. Margaret was glad for Oliver. He would never be cared for so well as when Hettie moved into his cottage and took over his life. She hoped one day that she could be as happy as her friend.

With a shy glance, she peered at the man seated next to her. Since his arrival, Lord James Douglas had never been far away from her. Her mother, on James's other side, engaged him in quiet conversation, awaiting the beginning of the service. He seemed fascinated by her, following the butterfly movements of her hands as she spoke. Lady Pierce, her dear friend and neighbor, sat between her and Sir Timothy, who occupied the aisle seat. The elegant old lady beamed upon them, as though she had arranged for the arrival of the noble Scotsman and his warriors. Through careful questioning of their new guest, Lady Pierce had elicited that the Douglases were kin and friends to the powerful Duke of Argyll, who had befriended some of the strange visitors from overseas. They had prevailed upon that gentleman to send aid and assistance to the woman to whom the Americans wished to protect. Master Blackford, with his wife, children, and beadle in the pew behind, added a few compliments to Lord James, mentioning what he had seen of his skillful leadership during the raid on the house and barn. Next to the Scot, Nat nodded as the guild master spoke.

Margaret smiled to herself. Alex's timely arrival was yet another debt that she owed to Rita Simpson and the ineffable Harry Lefferts. Who knew when she would be able to pay back any of it at all? She was so far away from the Americans, yet kept them close in her heart.

And James? Well, James was all too easy to get used to. He was handsome, charming, self-deprecating, and had a warm burr in his voice that felt like a cat's purr. It took very little time for Margaret to become accustomed to having him there, eager to be of service, happy to learn all about her and her family's fortunes and misfortunes. He took interest in everything she did. The best that she could tell, it was genuine. He told her all about his own life, how his elder brother had assumed their father's responsibilities and office, and how little room there was for a second son underfoot. Nat sympathized with that sentiment. James and Margaret's brother had swiftly become fast friends. She looked forward also to introducing him to her brother James the next time he returned from sea.

Ah, but James Douglas was an unlikely match for her. The ruin of the aqualators brought the baronetcy of Churnet and Trent right back down to the uncertain vagaries of income that they had enjoyed for the two years preceding their arrival, with the same possible inability to satisfy their tax obligations to the crown. She absolutely refused to be sold into marriage for the sake of financial security. It was unfair to James to only consider him for his purse, when he was such a marvelous man in his own right. If the day came when the looms were restored and they could fight their way back to supremacy in English weaving once again, perhaps she could hope for him to approach her father for her hand. She sighed. In any other way, he seemed so compatible with her.

Nat kept leaning across her to chat with James. He could hardly contain his excitement. For the last many days, he'd spent all his free time with Mistress Tamsin, teaching her the notes he had taken down from Aaron's collection of music from the future. At first, she'd been skeptical, but was at last won over by Mr. Olney's enthusiasm and the beauty of the music itself. During the service for the Blessed Mother, Mistress Tamsin would perform some of Nat's notations. Nat was to play a solo on his guitar. James, who played guitar as well as fife, had taken to the modern music like a duck to water.

Mr. Olney took his place and began reading the preparation before the service, and called down God's blessings on the congregation. Margaret settled herself and tried not to allow herself to be distracted. The banns were read. Hettie and Oliver beamed as their names were given. A few cheers came from the back of the church, and Mr. Olney sent an indulgent shake of his head their way.

His sermon stirred Margaret's heart. Mr. Olney referred to those who had come to the aid of the community in months past, and those who had arrived more recently. Both were appreciated deeply in the hearts of the people of Barlaston. Margaret could not agree more. She sent a grateful glance back toward Aaron and Martin. Aaron's father offered her a smile. Margaret turned to James and looked into his eyes.

"Thank you," she whispered.

He took her hand and squeezed it. Margaret felt her heart leap in her chest. Propriety demanded that she not maintain contact with a gentleman with whom she was not related, but she couldn't have moved her hand again if a winch had been attached to her wrist. Nor, she admitted, did she want to. His skin was warm, and smoother than she would have thought for so active a man. Her attention was torn thereafter between James and God.

"... And though the devices upon which we have come to rely are no more, the fortunes of the community will be rebuilt because the Lord will provide," Mr. Olney said, raising his hands. "Let us pray and prepare to accept the Lord into our hearts."

During the Liturgy of the Sacrament, Nat slid quietly off to the side and retrieved his guitar. He reappeared in the organ loft. Mistress Tamsin applied her fingers to the keys, and Margaret recognized the opening chords of her favorite Beatles song. The soloist, Mistress Priscilla Stanley, opened her mouth, and the lyrics emerged in her deep, warm voice. Nat's guitar joined in, adding a beautiful counterpoint to the song. Margaret was delighted. It was the perfect tribute to the gentle Mother of Heaven.

At first, there was definitely uncomfortable stirring in the congregation at the unfamiliar hymn, but within a few lines, everyone had relaxed and was absorbing the beautiful music. Margaret sent up a thought—not a prayer, for that would be blasphemy, but a blessing to the young men of the future who had given her family and her people that gift of comfort. She wondered if they would like the rendition of their song. She hoped so.

"So, what will ye do now?" James asked in an undertone, as the song ended, and Mistress Tamsin swept into a familiar hymn.

She knew exactly what he meant. She shook her head. "We'll rebuild, as Mr. Olney said. The delay will cost us, not only in time, but in exclusivity, now that it's no secret that the aqualators were involved in our success. The chances are that everyone will have them soon, even if we get more a little before them." She let out a rueful chuckle. "It's a shame that we could not make them here. Oliver Mason certainly tried."

"So, the materials are at hand?" James asked.

"Yes," Margaret said. "Aaron said that the clay is as smooth as that in use on the continent. If we knew what we were doing, we would have had substitutes for the faulty pieces weeks ago."

The thought struck her like a bolt of lightning. Why not make the aqualators right there in Barlaston? The clay was here. The potters were here. The only thing missing was the knowledge to make them correctly. Surely Aaron's counterpart, in equipment manufacture rather than programming, existed in the USE. She would ask Aaron to find her just such a person and send him—or her—to England to help.

Aaron had shown her that aqualators had more applications than just telling a loom what to do. The Treasury in Magdeburg ran on them. What if... what if they could make trays with numerous functions? They could supply the local weavers as well as their own. And supply them with calculating machines as well. And what about going further afield? Never mind the duchy; they could branch out across the entirety of Great Britain! She had long known that the wool trade in the nation was failing. Why should the computer trade not rise in its place? There were weavers in plenty, but there was absolutely nothing like aqualators being made anywhere closer than the continent. They would be unique, and soon be in demand *everywhere.*

She knew she could persuade her father to back her notion, as he had trusted her with the brocades. The de Beauchamp fortunes would rise again, and nothing could stop them. She sat up straighter, seeing her idea as if it already existed.

James grinned. "I see an idea blooming in your mind, my girl," he said. "Nothing will dampen your spirit for long, will it?"

Boldly, she squeezed his hand back.

"Never," she said.

She let the grand music lift her heart, and her dreams filled her mind with possibilities.